ADAM COLEMAN

THE NECROMANCER

First published by Busybird Publishing 2024

ISBN:
Paperback: 978-1-923216-16-7
Ebook: 978-1-923216-17-4

Cover image: Busybird Publishing

Cover design: Busybird Publishing

Layout and typesetting: Busybird Publishing

Busybird Publishing
2/118 Para Road
Montmorency, Victoria
Australia 3094
www.busybird.com.au

*For Vernon, without whom this novel
would almost certainly never have been finished*

1

The Interview

Ten years ago

Nervous as he was, Alex Hicks couldn't help but wonder at quite how *ordinary* everything was.

He had walked in through the ordinary main entrance, down an ordinary hall, past ordinary doors, and into an ordinary—drab, even— office. He now sat across a desk, also ordinary, opposite a middle-aged woman. Her hair was pulled back into a severe bun. Glasses with chunky, horn-rimmed frames were perched halfway down her nose. She was wearing a frilly, pale green blouse. She wielded a plastic biro pen above a notepad and her attention flitted between an open manila folder and a new-looking tablet. A very *ordinary* scene, altogether.

What did you expect, Alex? he thought to himself. *A levitating parchment, enchanted quill and talking cat?*

The woman, Nerida, had said nothing since greeting him with some rote pleasantries at the main entrance, paired with a suitably firm handshake and what felt like a grudging smile. As he sat opposite her, he was trying hard to keep smiling, and even harder not to fidget. His hands remained resolutely clasped over his left knee.

"So," Nerida finally said, as her eyes left the folder and the tablet to meet his. At least her smile, begrudging as it was, had returned. "You don't have any *gifted* in the family at all?"

He knew this question was coming, but he had not expected it right off the bat.

"No," he said, trying to affect an air of nonchalance. "I mean, there is the family legend about a great uncle who was and, you know, went a bit crazy. But that's quite common, isn't it, and not what you …"

"Yes, no," she replied, with a slight smile that felt like it carried at least a bit of warmth. "I mean, no parents or grandparents or anything?"

"Nope, not at all. Definitely not."

"How did you find out that you were gifted? And when?"

"Well, I sort of explain that in my application. I was about thirteen. We were visiting a family friend with a pool."

Alex realised that he was undoing and doing up the buttons on the new dark-blue blazer he had bought for this interview. He had agonised at length about what to wear the night before, which wasn't something he usually did. It was clearly more a response to the nerves than anything. After all, it wasn't as if the woman sitting before him would be interested in his fashion choices. But then, everything helps, doesn't it?

Alex continued talking, hands newly crossed in his lap. "My sister and brother—both older—were holding their heads underwater, seeing who could do it the longest."

"I see," Nerida said, nodding.

"Yes, so I realised after a while, and so did everyone else, that I could basically stay underwater indefinitely. I didn't need to breathe at all. It was an extraordinary feeling—I remember that."

"I imagine it was."

Alex was now getting into a rhythm. He had told this story many times before. Without realising it, he had started gesticulating with his hands. He did this when nerves gave way to enthusiasm. His grandmother would say he was 'talking like an Eye-talian'.

"Then, I suppose, I got excited. I was thirteen. After I knew I had an audience—as the adults realised how long I had been under water—I sort of launched myself out of the pool on a big wave and landed upright at the side. It was quite a scene. Lots of people definitely got wet."

"Of course." Nerida was writing sporadic notes as she nodded again, matter-of-fact. It occurred to Alex that she would have heard hundreds of similar tales. Perhaps it was unreasonable for him to expect much of a reaction.

"Anyway, it definitely made coming out three years later easier. I mean, after something like that, nothing was a shock!"

Nerida smiled. No laugh, but at least Alex's attempt at levity had not fallen completely flat. Then, she frowned slightly, as if in contemplation. Alex thought he understood why.

"Are you wondering why there had been nothing before that big reveal?" he asked. Then, before waiting for a reaction: "I've wondered that too. I think it may be because my *affinities* are very strong around water. And I think I didn't have much to do with water as a kid, ironically enough. My parents were not beach people, and—"

Nerida, who was still frowning in contemplation, nodded with a sense of conclusion. "It's actually not unusual for those in your situation, from ungifted families I mean, to manifest like that at a much later age than those from a gifted family. There is a lot we still do not understand about it."

To break the following moment of silence, which seemed preferable to fidgeting, Alex offered, "What was it Mark Twain said? It wouldn't exactly be magic if we could explain it all scientifically."

"Well," replied Nerida, "That is by no means the settled position among either practitioners or scholars. In fact, that whole question, is one of the things you could expect to debate as part of your studies, if you are accepted."

If, thought Alex. As if—*if*—both he and this seemingly ordinary, emotionally unresponsive woman, with her big, old-fashioned glasses and equally old-fashioned shirt, needed reminding that the whole purpose and premise of this exchange revolved around that very question of his acceptance: *IF you are accepted …*

The awkward silence had returned. Alex realised that his floppy fringe had become askew, and that his hand had deputised itself, without his permission, to put it back into place. *Stop fidgeting!*

Killing the awkward silence, Nerida asked: "Cutting to the chase, the million-dollar question …"

"Yes?"

"You haven't studied or done much in the whole magical space up to now, have you?"

Alex said nothing. That was a rhetorical question. He knew, and she knew from his application, that his interest in mystical matters was a recent one. At least in terms of anything you could put in a CV.

"So why have you decided to apply for the full residential degree course, rather than just the diploma?"

The million-dollar question, indeed. Alex had been expecting this. Clearly, Nerida wasn't someone to beat around the bush. And it was true. Alex wasn't from a magical family. His father was a police officer, his mother a prosecutor. And he hadn't made any great attempt to explore his gift before. Even though he was only 18, there were classes he could have taken, clubs and societies he could have joined—even magic camps he could have attended. Why hadn't he? Why the sudden interest in something he could have pursued years ago as a child? It was, on balance, a fair question.

"It's true that I didn't pursue magic when I was at school," he conceded, "but that doesn't mean I never planned to study it when I finished school. Which is why I applied here. As you can see from my school results and activities …" Alex had been deputy head prefect, captained the debating team and even managed to make the first hockey team, to everyone's surprise—including his. "… I clearly do not do things by halves. If this is a part of me, and it is, I want to explore it properly. Doing a diploma is the equivalent of doing a short cookery course—I want to train as a chef!"

Nerida's notetaking had gone from sporadic to constant. Alex's analogy prompted both the warmish smile and the nodding to reappear. It seemed as if she liked his answer. Alex became more animated.

"And, to me, you need to remember that magic really is magic. I obviously didn't grow up around it. I'm really excited to learn more about it, both as a practitioner and academically. The full course will allow me to do that." He paused briefly and, for the first time, noticed there was a half-full glass of water in front of Nerida. This gave him an idea. "I also have what I understand is a high level of natural aptitude."

Nerida paused her notetaking and looked at him.

Alex pointed at the water glass. "Let me show you." Not waiting for a response, Alex gestured at the glass. His dark blue eyes glowed with blue light, a striking effect even through the office's bright, fluorescent lighting.

The water in the glass gathered itself into a ball and floated into the air, as if in zero gravity, up until it was at Nerida's eye level. For a moment, it simply sat in the air. Then it froze into a ball of ice, remaining suspended above the desk.

Nerida scribbled down more notes.

Alex gestured again, and the water immediately turned to vapour, spreading out through the room. Then he clicked his fingers, and the water was back in the glass, liquid again. He ran his finger up the side of the half-empty glass and it filled with water, up to the top, until he moved his finger away. Then he tapped the glass, and condensation started to form on it as the water immediately chilled.

"So, you can draw water from the atmosphere, I see," nodded Nerida, again with a smile. It wasn't clear to Alex whether it was the grudging one or the warmer one.

"I could do ice, too, though it's probably cold enough."

"That will not be necessary," she replied, picking up the glass and taking a sip of the water.

Alex smiled. While Nerida didn't seem impressed by his demonstration, she hadn't been clearly underwhelmed, either. Which meant, as the interview concluded and he exited the ordinary office, walked past the ordinary doors and out of the ordinary main entrance into the Melbourne sun, he allowed himself to think he may have done *just* enough to be accepted.

For a little while, he gazed back at the equally ordinary-looking exterior of the building, its understated sign proclaiming it *Melbourne Magic School*. It felt more likely than ever that this place was where he would spend the next three years of his life. Where he would become a fully-fledged, fully qualified magician.

With that thought, he finally let his hands have free reign over his hair and resolved to enjoy the rest of his afternoon.

☼

Alex may have been relieved to know that the home of Nerida Stein, Admissions Officer and Associate Professor of Transformation Magic, was far less ordinary than her office. Her compact but cosy living room was dominated by a feature wall painted in deep burgundy, and the room abounded with fabric-covered furniture, rugs, knitted cushions and plush throws in a melange of warm colours. A riot of assorted porcelain figurines, colourful glassware and quirky ceramic pieces meant her many manila folders struggled for purchase, often finding themselves stacked on the largely rug-covered floor.

There were even distinctly magical touches. Sketches and vivid paintings of birds flitted, swooped and soared across the many canvasses adorning the walls. Elaborate dream catchers of various sizes swirled with magical energy, while chunky crystals glowed intermittently. Dominating her burgundy wall was an ornate mirror. A fashionable magical novelty in the mid-twentieth century, it was a mirror in which the viewer's reflection would frequently take on a mind of its own.

The two concessions to modernity in the room were both Apple products. A new MacBook Air lay closed on a chunky old wooden desk in a study nook to the side, and an iPad sat on her cluttered, 1950s-style coffee table with its swirly, rounded wooden frame and glass top. The tablet competed for space on the table with more piles of manila folders.

Nerida was presently moving many of these folders, but not with her hands. Rather, the pile of documents moved themselves from the coffee table to an increasingly precarious looking pile on the floor.

She was smiling, the warm one, only bigger and warmer than anything she had ever shown to Alex. This was one of her favourite tasks, which she was doing with one of her best friends.

That friend was standing in front of the magical novelty mirror. He was John Bishop, Melbourne Magic School's Professor of Manipulation and Telekinesis—and one of the most powerful practitioners and scholars of that affinity in the world. A few years older than Nerida, he was a tall, slim man, with close-cropped, balding grey hair and a long, thin, kindly face offset with a cheeky smile. His reflection was affecting an opposite expression, with its arms crossed and sporting an exaggeratedly grumpy pout.

A glass, filled almost to the top with pinot noir, drifted towards him. Its trajectory was a little wobbly: Nerida had enjoyed a few glasses of wine already. "Neri, we don't want to be drinking too much and forgetting our choices."

"I'm fine," Nerida declared from her big, pink couch. "You know manipulation has never been my strong suit."

"Indeed, my dear," John mused. "It looks like we are done with the definites."

"We are," agreed Nerida, as she gathered up the last of the manila folders.

John strolled away from the mirror. His fitted slacks and jumper made him look like an artist (*sans* beret) as he planted himself on the couch. He gestured at the folders, which conveyed themselves to him, and started looking through them.

"You know, Neri, I think it is a magic power in itself to decipher your handwriting."

"Har, har!" she responded. "Where shall we start with the maybes?"

"How about this one?" John said, gesturing at a file. "This Hicks gentleman."

"Oh," said Nerida, placing her tablet in front of her face. "That's a difficult one. I actually liked him," she admitted, sipping her wine. "He was very, well, cute, I suppose. Handsome. He had this floppy hair." Nerida touched her own, still pulled back into a bun. "He kept trying to stop touching it. It was quite adorable, really. And he was wearing a blazer, a nice blazer. Dark blue."

"Hmmm …" noted John. "Is there anything more relevant for us to consider, dear?"

Nerida thought for a moment. "Well, I'm not sure about him. He wants to do the full course but hasn't really done any magic study before. We could be setting him up to fail. It would be like letting someone into an MBA program when they don't even know what a stock exchange is."

"*Neri*," said John, with a sense of fond resignation. "We have this conversation *every year*. The uni expects us to bring in a quota of kids from non-magical families. And, each year, you argue against *every single one*. Meanwhile, we're practically vying with the School of Philosophy to be the least popular, least commercial faculty there is!"

"But, Johnny, we also see these types *every year*. You know it."

"Sure, but there *are* diversity quotas we need to meet, too."

"Seriously?" spat Nerida. "If we're still talking about that nonsense in ten years …"

"What, you'll turn yourself into a fish and go live in the sea?" Then, as the bottle of pinot noir floated past him again, remaining a little wobbly, he added, "Or maybe you'll just drink like one?"

"Maybe I will," Nerida replied, as she took another big sip of wine. "What is your view on Hicks?"

She noted that John was examining Alex's application more seriously than normal. "Hicks … Hicks," he said, very slowly.

"Yeah, what about the name?"

"Nothing," insisted John, through some more sips of wine. His teeth were starting to turn pink, his lips black. "His demonstration was impressive too."

"It was," Nerida conceded. "But still in party trick territory, really. Except—"

"—Except, taking water out from the atmosphere. That is pretty advanced."

"I suppose it is."

"That's it," declared John, putting Alex's file on the floor—by hand this time. "I think he's in. I'm making a captain's pick!"

"You know that those aren't a thing," Nerida insisted. "You just made them up at some point."

Picking up the next folder, he asserted with some glee: "It is either Hicks, or this amateur illusionist dilettante who wants to be bigger than David Copperfield."

"OK, Hicks it is, then."

2

The Distillery Case

Present Day

Detective Alex Hicks strode north along Spencer Street towards the Victoria Police Headquarters. Its glass-and-steel structure glittered in the morning sun as it dominated the western edge of Melbourne's central business district.

Alex was wearing a sharply tailored, expensive-looking blue suit, the jacket slung over his shoulder, coupled with a lighter blue shirt and a very dark blue tie. ("The blue ensemble," his boyfriend called it.) His hair was closely cropped, but he still instinctively brushed at it with his hand as he approached the entrance to the building.

Standing just before it was his partner, Senior Detective Isabella Greco. She was a flamboyant and boisterous woman, from an equally boisterous Italian family (which she talked about, *a lot*). She was in her late thirties and had two children with her husband, who ran a landscaping business. "He knows how to use his hands!" she would say, to Alex's obvious discomfort.

Despite their differences, Alex and Isabella, who had been working together since Alex made detective a couple of years ago, enjoyed a fun and supportive professional relationship. He smiled as he approached, her masses of curly hair and big brown eyes shining, like the Police Headquarters, in the sun.

In turn, she greeted him with a smile and a "Happy Friday!" She held two takeaway coffee cups: a big one for her, and a smaller one that she proffered to him. "Your macchiato's a bit cold," she said. "But I'm sure you could heat it right up if you just stuck your pinkie finger in it."

Alex scoffed with distaste. "Why would I need to put my finger in my coffee to warm it up?" He frowned. "Besides, you know I don't do that here."

"There's nobody around to see."

"No," insisted Alex. "That is the last time I confide in you about anything!"

"Don't say things you don't mean," she chuckled, as they walked into the huge office building. The pair sipped their coffees as they cleared security and entered the lift, ultimately discharging themselves into a large, open plan space.

Once there, they made their way towards a big whiteboard around which two of their close colleagues were standing. The first was Frank Pavlovic ('Pav') who was what Alex thought of as a classic, throwback police officer from the seventies. Short and stocky, with a belly that almost conquered the billowing shirts he preferred, with sleeves always rolled up to the elbows, Pav had sported a bushy, greying moustache for decades and teamed his billowy shirts with almost equally billowy slacks. And fat ties.

He also enjoyed teasing Alex. Never anything too bad, nothing reportable. Always stuff that could be passed off as "just a joke." Nonetheless, Alex was convinced that Pav disliked him for his sexuality and his being made detective unusually young. Alex suspected that Pav believed this was due to the influence of Alex's father, who retired recently as an assistant commissioner in the force. Alex sometimes wondered whether Pav might suspect that he had magical abilities, mainly because he said things like "that's magic" or "you're a magician" whenever Alex had a halfway good idea about a case. He ultimately put that one down to his own paranoia, though.

Next to Pav stood his partner, Cecile Nguyen. Just a couple of years older than Alex, Cecile was also young for a detective. But Pav adopted an avuncular, mentor-like relationship with her, as if she was his daughter.

With her hair in a sensible ponytail, and her lips painted fire-engine red, Cecile greeted Alex and Isabella with a smile.

They had a case to discuss. A frustrating and difficult one.

"OK," declared Cecile, in a formal tone. She gestured at the whiteboard, which was adorned with photos and notes inked in marker pen. (There were newer, more modern alternatives to the whiteboard available in these high-tech police premises but, as Pav would say: "If it ain't broke, mate …"). "The Daylesford Distillery case. Now, I know it feels like we have been over this again and again, but the feds and the higher ups are insisting we dot all the 'i's before we close the case. So, have we missed anything? Have we exhausted every possible lead?"

Cecile pointed at a portrait on the whiteboard of a fifty-something man with an ugly, square face, shaved and balding grey hair, and a bushy beard. "This is Rodney 'Hot Rod' Church, a bikie bigwig with many aliases. Alleged drug trafficker, possible people trafficker, contract killer procurer and all-around bad dude. But a bad dude who has, since he was very young and stupid, managed to evade conviction for anything beyond a parking ticket. Not even a speeding fine!"

Pav made to say something, but Cecile pre-empted him. "He even managed to dodge Operation Ironside." The 'Ironside' reference was to an extraordinary police project in which hundreds of criminals had been convinced to use a supposedly super-encrypted messaging app that was actually operated and surveilled by law enforcement agencies.

Not to be silenced, Pav declared, "Hence why the important people are so bloody obsessed with him and want us to find something; any bloody fucking thing, to pin on him."

"Indeed," agreed Cecile, as if she had heard this gripe many times before. "But this is our chance to finally stop chasing the wild goose. Let's go through it all in sequence." She pointed at the portrait again. "Fact one: Hot Rod and some of his associates have large investments, $10 million all up, in the Daylesford Distillery. And they've supposedly been taking a more active interest in the facility. They've recently been seen near the distillery, and we have intel about loud phone calls with the owner. The question is, why?"

"We can rule out money laundering," noted Isabella, "given this is a legit investment. Hot Rod and the gang had already cleansed the money."

"Yep," agreed Cecile. She pointed at another image on the board, which depicted a fairly ordinary-looking industrial building, set in verdant surrounds. "This is the place. The local cops have it under surveillance but have found nothing out of the ordinary."

She gestured towards another portrait on the wall, showing a handsome, if slightly weathered, clean-shaven, middle-aged male face. "The distillery is operated by Ian Kirk, who parlayed a brief international cricket career in the 90s into selling whisky investments. He's 48, divorced, no kids. No criminal convictions at all, or even any known connections. No obvious financial problems, no overly lavish spending. He has some overseas-sourced income, maybe something to do with cricket. The Tax Office do not seem to have any concerns about it."

"To be fair, they are generally more concerned about income that is *not* declared," said Isabella.

"Hmmm …" Pav looked at a picture of a nondescript white van, photographed in the distillery carpark. "It says here that the van comes and goes quite often, especially after hours—and almost always driven by Kirk. Could he be coming back at night to cook the books?"

Isabella shook her head. "The whole thing is a registered managed investment scheme. There is something like $250 million worth of whisky sitting in individually owned barrels at the site. It's all audited; the auditors haven't raised any concerns."

"Maybe the auditors are just shit?" offered Pav.

"Maybe they are," conceded Isabella. "But, if the powers that be are leaning on us to find something, they would have done the same to ASIC, which would be much better placed to find shortcomings there."

"I agree, that is not our bag. Let's leave the financial services regulation to the financial services regulator," Pav conceded. "But remind me. The way this works, yeah, is that an investor buys their own barrel—or barrels—of whisky for some silly amount. Then they pay this Daylesford Distillery outfit to store their barrel for 12 years, hoping to then sell the whisky to some sucker for lots more than they paid for it?"

"That's right," replied Cecile. "The business started eight years ago, so even the earliest investors have four years to wait to find out if they bought a lemon."

"And also relying on the company to somehow market and distribute this stuff so well that you make a decent return after all these fees and costs." Pav was starting to sound almost passionate. He looked across to Alex, who had perched himself on a desk, his legs dangling towards the floor. He was touching his hair more often than usual; for Pav, that indicated Alex was being thoughtful, rather than nervous. "What do you think your boyfriend would make of this as an investment, PB?"

'PB' was intended to stand for 'Pretty Boy'. Pav had never explained it, but the 'PB' naming had emerged after Pav, on discovering Alex had a boyfriend, had inquired whether his boyfriend was a "pretty boy," as Alex apparently was.

Alex, clearly distracted by the question, said curtly: "He would probably say it was shit. But then, as we have agreed, policing shit investments is not our job."

"Fair enough," replied Pav.

"Anyway," said Cecile, "there is no obvious evidence of fraud and no clear reason why Hot Rod would be shaking down a business he's legitimately invested in, even if we think the business model makes no sense."

"Agreed," said Isabella, taking Cecile's metaphorical baton. "Person three." She pointed to a portrait of a youngish man, maybe in his mid-thirties. Unlike the first two photos, this was a professional shot, presumably taken from a LinkedIn profile. But, even with fancy lighting and filters, the subject had a strange face, gaunt in places, flabby in others, with large, round eyes. He looked 'froggy', thought Alex, and— unreasonably—untrustworthy. "This is Mike Hart. He sold the distillery site to Kirk when he moved his family distillery business to a bigger site up the road."

Cecile looked at her tablet. "That business being Hart Liquor. They make cheap rocket fuel, basically—think bottom shelf at the Lion." The Melbourne Lion was a team haunt, just down the road from the police complex. Far from a gastropub, and boasting sticky floors, beer-brand bar mats and poker machines, it wasn't the place to take your date, but appealed to many cops' down-to-earth sensibilities. Pav loved it. "This is a *proper sort* of pub, PB," he would insist.

"Since taking over the business from his parents," continued Cecile, "he's tried to grow it with some ideas like cross-selling other things to pubs: snacks, even furniture. That didn't work, but records show the business is going pretty well, anyway. Certainly, there are no obvious financial problems."

"But what is the connection, then?" inquired Pav, smiling briefly at the mention of the Lion, before reverting to an air of mild frustration. "There isn't even a commercial rivalry here, is there? Kirk's stuff is above the top shelf, while I may well be having two-for-one Harts at happy hour tonight!"

Cecile smiled. "Real connoisseur, eh Pav?"

"It all tastes the same when it comes back up, Cec."

Pav scored a laugh from his mentee and Isabella. Alex continued to stare at the whiteboard, seemingly lost in thought.

"No business rivalry, Pav," said Isabella. "But there was some kind of dispute over the sale of the distillery site."

"That's right," agreed Cecile. "There were disagreements over the state of the equipment, or something, so there was haggling over price. Legal papers were filed, but then they settled. Seems the terms were confidential."

Pav perked up: "Aha, yes, and Hot Rod fancies himself as a bit of a *mediator*, doesn't he? Maybe he helped Kirk resolve things to his advantage and now is calling in a favour?"

Cecile shook her head, again consulting the tablet. "That is the most recent update we have. Basically, we couldn't find any evidence that Kirk was ever a client of Church."

"*Client?*" wondered Pav, aloud, as if he found the concept of an outlaw bikie gangster having 'clients' bizarre.

"Oh yeah," said Cecile, grinning a little. "Hot Rod's apparently legit, at least with this business. Rodney Gareth Church is the sole director of Premier Dispute Resolution Pty Ltd." Cecile read from the company website: "Our business offers confidential, expert dispute resolution assistance to discerning clients who wish to avoid the cost and risk of legal action."

"You're kidding!" snorted Isabella, sharing Pav's disdain. "Remember when crims didn't try to appear respectable?"

"These two wouldn't," declared Pav, looking towards Cecile and Alex. "Registered companies, silly websites. Pah! Proper crims back in the day would have laughed at that bullshit."

"Well, if the oldies are done reminiscing about the good old days," retorted Cecile, "the point is, based on the limited, discreet inquiries we were able to make, Hot Rod's business had neither Kirk nor Hart as a client. Which is not to say it's not possible that—"

"—But, even then," declared Isabella, "the timing does not work. Why would Hot Rod be coming to cash in a favour now, what, eight or so years on? And what sort of favour? It's all just speculation."

"Agreed," Pav seconded.

After a pause, Cecile pointed to the final photo on the board. This was another professional shot of an attractive, middle-aged woman, with her hair in a neat bob and wearing deep red lipstick. "This is Jennifer 'Jenny' Hooper. She also played cricket for Australia in the '90s, back when the women's game was less of a thing than now."

"Even less of a thing, you mean?" countered Isabella, with a tone suggesting she remained dissatisfied with the level of recognition women's sports received. If Pav had wanted to contest that notion, he chose (wisely) not to verbalise it.

"But," continued Cecile, "she has made her living as an accountant. And this is the thing: she used to work at Hart's as the financial controller but took a promotion to become CFO at Daylesford Distillery."

"But no links with Hot Rod?" asked Pav.

"None," Cecile replied. "Though word around town is that she and Kirk may have had a fling."

"Was she married?" Isabella inquired.

"Does it matter?" Pav shot back, somewhat irritably. He thought about making the obvious point that they were not the adultery police and, in fact, taking a prurient interest in women's sexual choices—whether they were married or otherwise—is not a very feminist thing to do. But, again, as he tended to, he thought better of it. In truth, Pav found Isabella a little intimidating. Not that he would ever admit that, either.

In the end, he remained silent, and Isabella conceded. "No, it doesn't, I guess."

"So, to summarise," declared Pav, making sweeps of the pictures and comments on the whiteboard with his hands. "We have a bikie who has invested a big chunk of cash in a whisky investment scheme that we all agree is shit, but also seems legit."

Both the women nodded in agreement.

"And the whisky scheme director—who has no criminal record, convictions, nor connections—has been getting calls and visits from the bikie and his cronies for reasons unknown. Then we have an idiot son who sold his old family distillery to the director, got into a dispute with him, settled it, then tried to expand his business, failed, but nonetheless still has plenty of cash and, again, no connections to the bikie—or any other criminals—that we can find."

"All fair," agreed Isabella.

"Oh, and we also have a woman who used to work for the idiot son, but then went and got a job with the director—who she may or may not have been shagging at the time, when she may or may not have been married, meaning she may or may not be a scarlet woman."

"I never said anything about scarlet women!" exclaimed, Isabella. "It's all very interesting, but there's nothing here."

"Agreed," nodded Cecile. "Let's close this bloody case. I've spent way too long on it already."

"So, we are all agreed, then," declared Pav, sounding satisfied. Then he looked at Alex, who was still perched on the desk, legs dangling. He had remained silent the whole time, rubbing his chin and touching his hair. "PB, do you agree?" Pav demanded.

Alex stared at Pav for a moment, then looked back to the whiteboard. "The names are a weird coincidence, aren't they?"

"What?" Pav responded, in disbelief.

"Yeah," said Alex, deliberately ignoring Pav's reaction. "Kirk is Scottish for 'church'."

"I didn't know that, actually," said Isabella. "You learn something new every day!"

"That's it?" Pav thundered. "You've been sitting there this whole time, silent as a fucking sphinx, with your little grey cells marinading in their own fucking magnificence like Hercule fucking Poirot. And *that* is what you come up with—some lame observation about the meaning of names?"

Alex smiled at Pav. "I do have a theory," he said. "I mean, it's crazy. Ridiculous, even. But, still, I think it just might be right."

"Well, go on then," urged Cecile, sounding excited. After all, given her work on it, closing the case without a result would have been an unwelcome anticlimax. "Tell us what it is!"

He did.

"Well, that sure is crazy," said Pav in response, but his tone wasn't as dismissive as his words.

"But," said Isabella.

"Yeah, but," agreed Cecile.

"Is it worth checking out, though?" asked, Alex, rhetorically. "I think it is. It wouldn't be too hard to do, if we could get some help from Daylesford."

"I agree," said Isabella. "Pav, you must know someone at the station there."

Pav responded as if Isabella's question had broken his train of thought. "Yeah, I do, but we don't have much to give them, do we? Just an idea. A hunch."

"So? Call in a favour or something," Cecile insisted. "You must know someone up there who would do you a solid."

"Yeah," said, Alex, smiling, sure that Pav would ultimately concede. "It's one evening's work that could pay off big-time."

"Or make me look like an idiot," countered Pav.

"Don't be a jerk and make the call," chided Isabella.

"OK, OK." Pav looked back to Alex. "How could I say no to that face?"

Alex slouched back in his chair in the smoking area in the beer garden at the Melbourne Lion Hotel. He was feeling relaxed. The group had been there for some hours now. He had taken off his tie long ago and undone the top buttons on his shirt. He'd also had several drinks. More than four, he thought, but less than six. Certainly not seven, he was sure. Fairly sure, anyway.

Cecile sat opposite him. Isabella had disappeared to talk to some other police officers whom she'd spied standing around. And it was mainly standing room on this Friday night in the smoking area at the Lion. Alex reflected that lots of cops clearly liked to smoke, at least when out. Cecile was one of them. As the group knocked back drinks, she smoked one cigarette after the other. She had declared herself one of those "I only smoke when I drink" people. Alex envied them. If he had a cigarette, he would never stop. He had found that out the hard way, more than once.

It had been a convivial evening, in the twilight of a warm, sunny Melbourne day in early autumn. Familiarity, booze and a sense of anticipation about the Daylesford Distillery case had reduced inhibitions.

Conversation had ranged, broadly in sequence, across: 'The good old days' ("Things were different back then, but not necessarily better," Pav had declared); Isabella's upcoming 20-year high school reunion, Cecile's 10-year one a couple of years ago, and Pav's most recent however-many-decades one ("Fuck, what a bunch of grumpy old geezers and batty bloody sheilas"); the state of Isabella's husband's business and the often outlandish demands of his clients ("I'll tell you about batty bloody sheilas, Pav"); the ongoing Russian invasion of Ukraine ("How is the Pav–Putin bromance going, a year in?" "Fuck off, Alex!"); and, finally, Alex's boyfriend, whom Isabella had met but Cecile and Pav had not ("He's very handsome, but I wouldn't say he's a pretty boy. More, you know, masculine." "Does that mean he's, like, the man in the relationship?" "Fuck off, Pav!").

Alex leaned in and drained the dregs of his scotch and soda. Pav was getting another round, seemingly taking his time.

"You know, Pav must have qualified for one of those lifetime, rolled-gold baby-boomer pensions a decade ago. Why doesn't he just retire?"

Cecile chuckled. "What would he do with himself, besides drive his wife up the wall? And I don't want him to retire. I like him. And he likes you."

Alex scoffed. "He likes making fun of me, you mean? I think he's homophobic, and probably racist, too."

"He's not racist, Alex. Look at what he's done for me over the years."

"Racists are like that, though. They don't say anything racist because they know they're racists and are hiding it." This explanation made more sense to Alex than it appeared to make to Cecile, who looked amused.

"So, to clarify," said Cecile, holding a glass of sour white wine (the Lion wasn't the sort of place to employ a sommelier), "Pav is homophobic because he makes fun of you and your boyfriend, and he's also racist because he's always super-supportive and nice to me?"

"Well, when you put it like that," replied Alex, sourly.

Cecile looked even more amused.

"What?" demanded Alex.

"It's funny, because you're mates and you don't even realise it."

"No, we aren't!"

Alex's phone pinged. It was a text from Josh, his boyfriend: *You still in the city?*

Yeah, he replied. *At the Lion.*

Fine establishment. Can I come pick you up?

Sure. But Pav's here.

I finally get to meet him! See you soon.

As Alex put his phone down, he saw Pav emerge from inside, carrying several drinks. "You can stop with that *mates* crap," he whispered to Cecile as Pav approached.

"Mates!" Cecile whispered back.

"Here you go, kids," said Pav, as he put the drinks on the table. "And, I've got word—"

"And?" Cecile demanded, leaning forward. Isabella suddenly reappeared.

"Yep, I confirmed it. They do stock Harts spirits here." Pav laughed as the others glared at him. "I also heard from Daylesford. You were right, PB."

☼

A little later that evening, Alex sat in the back of an Uber with Josh, the two of them leaning towards each other so their heads touched, as they often did.

Alex and Josh had been a couple for three years and had lived together for two. They had literally bumped into each other at a wine-shop-cum-bar, called Magasin de Vin, in Armadale, an affluent Melbourne neighbourhood almost always described as 'leafy'.

Alex had been there with a (straight, female) roommate nursing a broken heart. Josh was there with a friend and colleague, Simmo, whom Alex had since come to know well, not always to his delight. After introducing himself as "Just a nice Jewish boy," Josh summarily convinced Alex that their two small parties should be combined into a foursome. "After all," he declared with confidence, "what better way to heal a broken heart than meeting new people?"

While the heartbroken roommate did not take to Simmo's non-existent charms, Alex was besotted with Josh from the start. When the group left the wine bar, Alex and Josh kissed for what seemed like ages; there was no doubt that they would be seeing each other again. And again. From then, they were just together, Alex and Josh.

It didn't hurt that Josh *was* incredibly handsome. Big eyes, megawatt smile, 'movie star looks' as people say. He was also tall and athletic, the sort of guy who was always popular in high school. Which was, Alex would admit if pressed, his 'type'.

Of course, Pav had given Josh his seal of approval after Josh had shared a drink with the group at the Lion. Alex had expected nothing less.

As their Uber turned down St Kilda Road, a tree-lined boulevard flanked by upscale apartment buildings, offices and grand private schools, the car radio commenced a news bulletin. *As Russia's invasion of Ukraine enters its second year, analysts warn that Russian President, Vladimir Putin, may resort to banned chemical or magical weapons to salvage the campaign …*

"That came up at drinks," Alex said to Josh, wondering momentarily whether the latter might have fallen asleep. "Hopefully, Simmo won't mention it tomorrow."

Josh yawned but sat back upright in his seat. "Why would he do that?"

"Same as Pav," Alex replied. "They're both closet Putinistas who have had to re-evaluate."

"So why would he mention it, then?" wondered Josh, disinterestedly.

"I dunno," insisted Alex, sitting up very straight now. "The people we put up with for duty and career, huh?"

Josh remained languid in his seat. "It's not just duty, though, babe. Sure, Simmo helps me out, but I also like him. A bit like you and Pav."

Alex guffawed, a bit too loudly. "Pav and I are not friends!"

"Aren't you, though?" replied Josh casually. "You seem to be. You meet for drinks. You have this banter thing going."

"No, we don't!" replied Alex. "I drink with Pav because we're cops and that is what you're expected to do." Responding to a disbelieving look from Josh, he stressed: "Yes, *even today*. That, and just about every cop in Victoria—probably Australia—owes him some kind of favour. We couldn't have tested my theory and cracked the case today without him."

"So, babe," declared Josh, "it sounds the same as me and Simmo. We help each other. He's a bit different; it requires a bit of tolerance on both sides, but we're mates."

"Until you make partner at the firm, at least," said Alex. "Then you can stop letting him invite himself to dinner at our house to show off his new squeeze."

"Are you saying you don't want to meet Charlotte?" asked Josh.

"No, that is not what I'm saying," replied Alex. "I'm saying that we can both dispense with them at some point."

"Nah," said Josh. "Simmo and I are mates. You and Pav are mates."

"No, we aren't! You're worse than Cecile."

By this point, the Uber had pulled over outside The Victorian, the luxury building in which Alex and Josh lived. Alex pressed his entry key on the glass door as it opened into the cavernous lobby with its marble floors, 24/7 concierge and inoffensive modernist artworks.

Moments later, both boys exited the lift and entered their sub-penthouse apartment. Set across two levels, the home had dark wooden floors, white walls covered with artworks, marble table and kitchen tops, myriad lamps and low-hung light fittings, and sleek brown leather furniture.

Josh went upstairs to their huge bedroom and shut the door. Meanwhile, Alex slumped onto their plush brown leather sofa.

A bottle of whisky and glass travelled through the air towards him, a little wobbly, until both bottle and glass sat on the coffee table in front of the sofa. Alex poured himself a shot of the whisky, clicking his fingers to create some ice from thin air. In the background, he heard a soft buzzing noise. Josh was brushing his teeth.

Alex gazed across the expanse of the main living area of their home. It was a huge dwelling in one of the most expensive apartment buildings in the city. This was because Josh Goldman was rich—*very* rich. Partially, that was because Josh was a successful banker at a private equity firm. (In the office, he was affectionately known, to his mild chagrin, as 'Sachs'.)

The original Goldmans, Josh's great-grandparents, had migrated to Melbourne in the early 20th century. They set up a haberdashery, which became a chain, which then became a series of department stores. It was a well-known story locally, and the Goldmans became a prominent Melbourne business dynasty.

Josh had asked Alex to move in with him just over two years earlier. He had done so on a Saturday morning, in bed, with a laptop resting on his stomach. The laptop contained a spreadsheet setting out all the steps in what was to become their moving-in 'project'. Alex had realised, even by then, that Josh had a spreadsheet for *everything*.

After that morning, Josh was relentless in identifying, obtaining, customising and decorating a home for the couple. It started out with the house search. Josh had initially wanted somewhere detached, with character, maybe a period home. Alex, who had grown up in backyard-and-double-garage suburbia, liked the idea of something high-up, low-maintenance, "with a view". He got what he wanted.

Ultimately, Alex resolved that the only sensible course was to let his hot, rich, adoring boyfriend get him whatever he wanted. After all, what else could he do?

Alex padded out onto the main balcony. (There were three in total.) The evening was warm, but the cold never bothered him anyway, unless he let it. Looking to the left, he observed the Melbourne skyline, with skyscrapers lit up, emblazoned with the names of corporate tenants. As with most cities, downtown Melbourne was prettiest when its bright lights shone against the dark.

He took another sip of whisky. From the corner of his eye, he saw Josh walking down the stairs from their bedroom, through the living room, towards him. As Josh always did for bed, he was wearing pyjama bottoms—in this case, ones that ended just above the knee, and featured clouds on a baby blue background. The rest of Josh was like a classical statue: broad-shouldered, lean and muscular.

"Come to bed, babe. You've had enough."

Alex came into their main bedroom, with its polished wood floors, abundant rugs and myriad sketches of birds. He liked this room most of all, with its own balcony and floor-to-ceiling windows overlooking the Botanic Gardens.

On the bed sat some pyjama bottoms, full-length and covered with images of eggs and bacon. Josh had worn these the night before. Alex liked wearing pyjamas that Josh had already worn. Alex would smell them, as he did now, before putting them on. Being Josh's, they were slightly larger in the waist than would suit Alex, and quite a bit longer in the leg.

At least twice a week, Josh would tell Alex to take the pyjama bottoms off right away. Tonight, though, Alex simply snuggled with his boyfriend after brushing his own teeth. Both of them were too tired and drunk for sex, and too mindful of the day to come.

"Don't forget," said Josh, yawning. "We'll need to go to the market early tomorrow morning."

"I know, babe."

3

Orientation Party

10 years ago

"What did you expect? Like, Hogwarts with hormones?"

Alex smiled as he cradled a bottle of beer. He was now well into the orientation party for the new class at Melbourne Magic School, which was being held in the school's cafeteria. A huge *Welcome!* sign glowed with many shifting colours; strobe lights pulsed and refracted across a series of disco balls that hovered in the air. It definitely felt like a magical party. There was also a recruitment stand for the magic athletics team, though the pair of volunteers manning it seemed more interested in downing drinks than attracting sign-ups. Alex had been mulling over a try-out himself, but that wasn't for today.

Instead, Alex was having a good time, meeting lots of new people and, hopefully, coming across as a cool, interesting individual. He was wearing the blazer again. After being accepted into MMS, Alex had decided that this was certainly his 'lucky blazer'. He had paired it with a colourful silk scarf, tied loosely around his neck.

He had changed his hair, too. The old floppy look had felt a bit 'private schoolboy'—which was fine when he was one, Alex reasoned, but not anymore. So, he had let his hair grow out at the front and back, creating what he saw as a short, neat mane. Like a lion. He liked that idea.

He was going for an edgy, hopefully sexy, preppy-type vibe. He was pretty sure the look suited him. A new style for a new man. He would make new friends. He would fit in on his own terms, or not at all. He would stop worrying about what other people thought.

And, also, a boyfriend would be nice. He had tended, intentionally or otherwise, to go for guys—older guys, straight guys, generally unavailable guys, straight-up dickhead guys—who were just not boyfriend material. Well, no more. He was going to find someone who wanted to hold hands, go on dates, cuddle, swap clothes, read the same books together, have matching pyjamas, and all the things he associated with proper romantic relationships.

But Project Boyfriend would have to wait. Tonight, he was making friends. And doing a pretty damn good job of it, he thought. He'd successfully made small talk with a whole range of people. Magical 'affinities' were a popular icebreaker. Some of the more prospective new friends he had met were Emma (affinity: mentalism; redhead; funny); Julius (affinity: illusion; "Yes, my ancestors were genuine witch-doctors in Kenya. It's *true*!"); and Jack (affinity: body and healing; fellow nice private schoolboy with *very* floppy hair; also filed under Boyfriend Project: he was definitely looking at Alex a certain way).

And now, before him were Yolanda (affinity: "Earth, in the whitefella model, but I'm also here to study indigenous traditions which are different, all tied to country. MMS has the best program for that") and Nikki (affinity: body and healing), Yolanda's senior 'buddy'—someone apparently appointed by the school to informally help new students from 'ungifted' families learn the (enchanted) ropes. Or, in Yolanda's case, who came from a magic family, because she had moved down from Sydney to attend MMS. Alex wondered where his own 'buddy' was.

It was Yolanda who had asked the Hogwarts question. And, thought Alex, he had best answer it. "Has everyone at this school read Harry Potter?" he asked, in genuine bewilderment. After affinities, Harry Potter was the most popular icebreaker among newly-minted MMS students.

"You mean you haven't?" smiled Nikki in reply. "You might want to get on Amazon!"

"I mean, I've seen the films …" Alex trailed off. Both Yolanda's and Nikki's faces betrayed a view that watching the films alone was an insufficient commitment to the Potter cause. But Alex was going to fit in on his own terms or not at all—he doubled down: "And isn't the whole thing completely, like, *unrealistic?*"

Thankfully, neither Yolanda nor Nikki seemed offended. But they weren't conceding the point. "Sure, it is," laughed Yolanda. "But when is the last time someone wrote like that about magic?"

"Yes," Nikki agreed enthusiastically. "So maybe it's ridiculous that there is this secret magic world that muggles, mystifyingly, have no idea about."

"Like, how would that even work?" Alex challenged. "There is even a whole 'Ministry of Magic!"

"Sure," replied Nikki. "But you could say the same about cop shows, or medical shows, couldn't you?"

"And books," added Yolanda. "I mean, I doubt Hercule Poirot or Miss Marple accurately reflect the lives of real investigators."

That was true; Alex's police officer father's work was nothing like an Agatha Christie novel—as much as he was a big fan of them.

"Then there's Twilight," continued Yolanda, almost triumphantly now: "With all those sparkly vampires. But vampires have been extinct for over 100 years!"

"Yes," declared Nikki. "And even when they did exist, they didn't fucking *sparkle!*"

Alex grinned back at them: "Totally agree. Twilight was shit. Unity ticket there."

Instead of responding—Alex had hoped, with laughter—Nikki was instead looking off to Alex's side. "Do you know Robbie?" she asked.

Nikki was looking at a tall Eurasian man. Robbie, no doubt. Alex had the impression that Robbie had been looking at him for a while, in that *certain way.*

Robbie smiled and walked—glided, sailed?—towards Alex, all long limbs and effortlessness. He was wearing skinny blue jeans and trainers, and a slightly looser dark shirt with the sleeves rolled up and sort of half tucked-in to his jeans. He had what looked like intentionally messy, slightly wavy hair, and wore a big watch and bracelets.

The Boyfriend Project may have to be brought forward, Alex thought.

"Sorry, sorry, *sorry,*" said Robbie, as he approached Alex. "Alex, hi. I'm your senior buddy. I had meant to call. I'm Robbie." Robbie proffered his hand, then said: "Actually, let's hug!"

The two young men embraced. Robbie's body felt hard and warm, and his arms boasted obvious muscles. Robbie held Alex tight for what seemed like a long time.

Finally letting him go, Robbie looked at Yolanda and Nikki. "Hey, Nik, how are you?" he asked, pleasantly.

"I'm good, Robbie," Nikki replied, in exactly the same tone. "This is Yolanda. She's doing the First Nations program."

"Oh, that's cool," Robbie enthused. "Have you taken her to the Billabong yet, Nik?"

"Not yet," replied Nikki. "But I will."

Robbie looked to Alex. "The Billabong is the coolest place here—*by far!*"

Alex thought he should say something. But he found himself in the unfamiliar, uncomfortable situation of being lost for words. Sadly, gushing "You are so good looking!" at someone you had just met remained socially unacceptable, even in the otherwise enlightened 2010s.

Nikki attempted a rescue, of sorts. "Don't worry, Robbie, Alex here was doing very well before you arrived."

"Was he?" said Robbie, with a Cheshire Cat grin.

"Yes," agreed Nikki, sounding sincere. "Your buddy is quite the conversationalist. We even talked about Harry Potter. Didn't we, Alex?"

Alex hesitated. What if Robbie was one of these bizarre real-life-wizard-cum Harry Potter superfans? Fitting in on your own terms, or not at all, was one thing, but applying that principle to a mega-hot potential Boyfriend Project candidate seemed like taking a good idea a step too far. Especially when Robbie was, Alex was now sure, *most definitely* looking at him in that *certain way.*

Fucking say something, Alex!

"Yeah, um, so I'm one of the Harry Potter refuseniks ..." Alex managed, trying to sound confident (and failing).

"You are?" exclaimed Robbie. "Me too! I'm practically in love with you already." (The latter, Alex told himself, was a joke, but maybe not quite *just a joke*.) "I could barely even make it through the movies. It's all so unbelievable."

"I know!" Alex practically cried out.

Nikki looked quietly satisfied with herself.

"Hey, I have an idea," Robbie announced. "To make up for being a tardy buddy, how about I give you a private orientation tour of the campus? Now. Just the two of us?"

Nikki and Yolanda's expressions suggested this was a good idea. "Hey, you have three years to get to know me," noted Yolanda, by way of encouragement.

Alex wondered momentarily whether he might collapse at the knees with excitement. But he managed a firm "Yes, great!" instead.

"Excellent!" declared Robbie. "Night, ladies!" he said, grabbing Alex by the hand and pulling him away. Alex managed a quick "Bye" as Robbie pulled him towards the bar. "OK, drink first, then we can 'port."

"'Port?" wondered Alex, aloud.

"Yeah, teleport. That is my affinity, manipulation and telekinesis. It includes teleporting. That is actually the most fun part. Can I get two whiskies, Kenny?"

Robbie seemed to know the bartender. (*He probably knows everyone*, thought Alex.) Kenny poured two oversized measures of neat whisky into plastic cups and handed them to Robbie. In turn, Robbie handed one to Alex.

"Drink up!" It felt a little like an order. Neat whisky wasn't really Alex's drink of choice. At his high school, beer was the standard beverage at parties. His school theatre friends would feel sophisticated by drinking rosé or (worse) Moscato. But, of course, those tastes belonged to his former self. Grown-up Alex, by contrast, could definitely be the sort of person to knock back a stiff nip of straight spirits.

Alex's throat seemed to disagree with this new resolution as the whisky burnt its way past it, but he nonetheless downed the measure and kept it down. Robbie did the same.

"OK," he said, grabbing Alex's arms again. "Put your right arm around my waist and hold my hand—like we're doing a waltz."

Alex complied. Being close to Robbie again felt electric.

"Ready?" asked Robbie.

"Yes," Alex replied, trying to sound certain.

"Here we go then."

And just like that, the boys vanished.

"Where are we?" asked Alex.

"Sorry," replied Robbie, with a cheeky grin. "We're outside. I wanted to do a test run. Some people have a reaction to teleporting."

"We're ten metres from the party!" Alex said, motioning back towards the music and chatter of the MMS building.

"I know, I know," Robbie pulled a packet of Peter Stuyvesant cigarettes from his pocket. "Want one?"

"You mean you teleported me out here so you could have a cigarette?"

"Yeah, sorry. I was getting a bit desperate. I meant what I said about test runs, though. Some people would be vomiting now." He offered the cigarette packet to Alex.

Alex took one, knowing he shouldn't. He didn't smoke, and smoking was bad for you. And addictive. Alex's dad, who smoked himself, had said so.

Robbie lit his cigarette just by tapping it with a finger. He did the same for Alex. "You'll learn about this in prac," he said. "Basic flame, then first aid, light and telekinesis."

"I know," replied Alex, having dutifully read the course handbook cover-to-cover.

Robbie looked Alex up and down. "So, Alex, tell me your story. Why are you here?"

Alex gave Robbie a potted history. He mentioned his parents, his siblings, school, and the manifestation of his powers.

"And so why study magic?" Robbie asked.

"I guess because I didn't know what I wanted to do with my life, unlike my parents and siblings—they *always* know what they want—and, you know, magic is something I really want to explore. Coming from a m—"

"You were going to say *muggle*, weren't you?"

"One day," Alex declared, "JK Rowling will get her comeuppance!"

"Boyfriend?"

Wow, that was direct. "No," admitted Alex. "Never really. Not a proper one, anyway."

"I see," replied Robbie, conveying essentially no meaning. Cigarette now smoked, he said: "Time to waltz again, properly this time!"

"Wow!" Alex enthused, very much in wonder.

The pair had materialised in a huge space. It was rectangular, maybe the size of a cricket pitch. But it was *inside*, with a ceiling many storeys high.

In one corner stood a huge stack of large, shiny metal balls, the size of beanbags. There must have been more than thirty of them. Above the boys' heads was a series of platforms, at various heights, that hovered in the air and shifted of their own accord.

About a quarter of the space was taken up with a series of discrete areas, each larger than a full-size domestic swimming pool, representing the elements. One was a massive pile of earth, studded with rocks and with a range of different trees and bushes clinging to it. Another was a barely smouldering fire. Then there was one, the most remarkable, that was essentially a self-contained storm of pulsing wind, rain and lightning forming a sphere. Lastly, there was a simple, straightforward pool of water.

Alex scampered away from Robbie to just soak in the whole area. He looked back to Robbie, who was smiling proudly. "Where even is this?" Alex inquired.

"In the school," replied Robbie, as he cantered—like a thoroughbred horse—towards Alex. He was so *elementally* sexy, Alex thought. "It's a form of spatial magic," continued Robbie. "Like the TARDIS in *Doctor Who*, the school is much bigger inside than out. It's a subset of manipulation, which is my affinity, like I said."

Alex nodded. "I see." He was less interested in an explanation than in just admiring the scale and magical nature of the space. He was reminded of Yolanda's comment about Hogwarts with hormones. Things were certainly not so *ordinary* anymore.

"This is the games room," said Robbie. "It's where we practice our affinities and have competitions." Alex knew about this. Magic competitions had been held as far back as Ancient Greece. Robbie gestured to Alex to follow him as walked towards the pool. "This is your affinity, yes, water?"

"Yep, it is," agreed Alex. "With some wind and stuff."

"OK, then," Robbie challenged, pointing at the large pool of water. "Let's see what you can do. Could you freeze it?"

Alex scoffed a little, with confidence. "Yeah, I can freeze it." Which he did.

Robbie knelt and touched what was now a massive ice cube. "Impressive. That took you, what, 20 seconds?" he said.

"Wait, is this like a test or something?"

"No, dummy," Robbie smiled. *That smile!* "Just a chance to show off. Here," he continued, taking Alex's hand again and walking him towards the self-contained magic storm sphere. "Let's see what you can do with this."

"Wait, shouldn't I melt the ice, first?" asked Alex, wondering—for the first time—whether this nocturnal, unauthorised jaunt through the more exciting parts of the university might be something that could get him into trouble. After all, he had spent his whole high school career trying not to get into trouble. But, of course, this was the new Alex, an Alex who perhaps enjoyed being a bit naughty, once in a while. And there was also the Boyfriend Project to consider.

"Nah, it'll be fine," insisted Robbie. "Come on."

Alex stood before the remarkable, self-contained storm. "If I calm it too much, will it, like, break?"

Robbie put his hands on Alex's shoulders. Alex almost jumped. "No. Just relax. Do it."

Alex looked at the storm sphere. His eyes glowed blue. He started gesticulating, like a conductor with an orchestra. The storm in the sphere became more intense, the clouds darker, the lightning brighter, the wind louder—although contained in the sphere, the wind and thunder were still very much audible.

He settled the storm down, slowly and gently, until the storm sphere was so quiet and peaceful it had become almost non-existent. Then he let it come back, slowly, to its original level of intensity.

That was fun!

"Impressive," cooed Robbie, in Alex's ear. "You have to try out for the elements competition team. Seriously." Robbie had managed to hold onto Alex's shoulders as he 'conducted' the storm and his stomach was pressed against Alex's back. Alex wondered how long he could bear this sort of arousal.

He broke away and turned back to Robbie. "OK," he challenged. "If we're showing off, it's your turn."

Robbie affected an expression that seemed to say, "I thought you would never ask!" He vanished momentarily, then appeared in the corner of this cavernous space, near the pile of metal balls. He stretched out his arms and eight of the balls raised themselves into the air. Alex scurried towards Robbie, to get a better view.

Waving his arms like a juggler who never touched the balls, Robbie sent them around and around; up-down, forwards-and-backwards, seemingly across the breadth and height of the practice room. Some whizzed past Alex where he stood, as he clapped at the performance.

"I'm not done yet," Robbie asserted. The eight balls disappeared. Robbie pointed upwards. The balls were hovering at various heights around the room, moving in step with the shifting platforms.

"Shit!" said Alex in admiration.

"I was school champion last year in manipulation and telekinesis." Robbie looked rather self-satisfied. Did he do this with all the boys? But Alex had little time to reflect on this as he started to levitate into the air.

"I thought you could help collect my balls," called out Robbie—was that a double entendre?

But as Alex, against his will, rose higher and higher from the floor, he started to feel panicked. "Let me down, Robbie!" he cried. "I'm not great with heights!"

"Sorry, sorry, I didn't know!" Robbie replied. He teleported so he was standing below Alex. "Here, I'll let you down slowly and catch you!"

He did.

As the pair embraced, Alex felt a huge urge to kiss Robbie. But even the new Alex proved too shy for that. Why couldn't Robbie, with his long limbs, muscles and evident self-assurance, make the move?

"Time to waltz again," said Robbie.

The next place they found themselves was also large, but more typical than the 'games room'; something more like a museum.

This end of the museum-room was dominated by portraits, which hung from floor to ceiling. There were some recognisable ones: Queen Victoria and Prince Albert; Napoleon and even the founder of Melbourne Magic School, Reginald Barker. All the portraits were animated, looking this way and that with changing expressions. Paintings like these had been a popular magical novelty in the Georgian and Victorian eras. There were some similarly mobile busts as well, one of which—Alex was quite certain—was of Julius Caesar.

Caesar's marble eyes followed them as Robbie took Alex by the hand again and led him past the animated artworks. The displays in the next room were much more martial in character, dominated by enchanted weapons and armour. Many of the swords, halberds, guns and cuirasses glowed with faint magical energy.

There were some remarkable pieces within the collection. There was an ancient-looking Viking sword whose elaborate runic inscriptions glowed red; a katana of more recent vintage was adorned with Japanese characters that shone a pale green. Then there were suits of plate armour that also shimmered with obvious enchantment.

Robbie didn't let go of Alex's hand as they perused the exhibits. "Sadly, we cannot have a sword fight with these." (Another double entendre?)

The third room in the museum had a more varied collection than the first two. But many of them were also Victorian magical novelties, especially stuffed animals—including everything from owls and falcons to tigers and crocodiles—which moved and made noises like they were alive. But there were also other artefacts, like more floating disco balls ("circa 1970, L.A." said the card) some of which had, presumably, been on loan to the party.

But Robbie led Alex to a more ordinary looking item: a delicate, dark-wood desk-type thing that was old, ornate and oriental. It was displayed with many of its myriad drawers and containers opened, which were filled with various pouches of powders and vials.

"This was my great-great-aunt's," asserted Robbie.

"Oh," said Alex properly interested: "What was it for?"

"My ancestors had a magic show. They travelled all across China," explained Robbie. "This chest held my great-great-aunt's makeup—she was the star of the show, very famous at the time—and also powders and potions to do little tricks to make the effects look more striking."

"You mean like little explosions and stuff?" asked Alex, leaning towards the desk.

"Yeah. Then there was the revolution. Mao did not like magic, it was *counter-revolutionary.* Worse than the bourgeois elements, if anything."

"Worse than the Great Persecution?" offered Alex, referring to the historical persecution of magicians.

"Yeah, even worse than that," confirmed Robbie. "But, here, look at these." Two large, dark balls, seemingly made from crystal or glass, hung in front of him. They looked like oversized marbles. "Recognise these?"

"I think so," offered Alex. "Are they communication orbs?"

"Exactly!" Robbie was smiling again. "They were a popular magic item before the telegraph and telephone, and they even showed up in *Lord of the Rings* with Sauron or Saruman or whatever."

Alex concluded that Robbie had almost certainly not read the *Lord of the Rings.* Alex plucked one of the orbs away from Robbie, looking into it. The darkness cleared.

Holding the other one, which also became clear in his hands, Robbie said, "Let me show you."

Then, he vanished.

"Lex? Lexi?" The sound came from the orb, or maybe even directly into his mind. But in the clear orb, he could see Robbie, surrounded by trees and a body of water.

"I'm here," replied Alex, chuffed that Robbie seemed to be trying to come up with a pet name for him. *That was something else boyfriends do*, he surmised. "Where are you?"

"At the Billabong," said Robbie, moving the orb around to showcase the area. "Why don't I come back and bring you here."

Robbie reappeared in the library, holding the orb. He took the one from Alex and placed both back on the stand where they had originally stood.

"Another waltz, Lexi?" he said, before they both vanished again.

"This is the coolest place so far!" Alex enthused as he looked around the Billabong.

Unlike the games room, but on a similarly massive scale, the Billabong had the sense of being outside. Alex could see the night sky and stars. They looked magic, too—but he concluded that might actually be the effect of the company.

Ranged with native trees ("Mangroves?" wondered Alex silently, in general ignorance of native flora), sand and dirt, the area was dominated by a big, largely still pool of water, with a sandy island towards the middle.

"There is a bunyip here too, and yowies," said Robbie. "But don't worry, they're all friendly."

Robbie released Alex from the waltz position, and Alex continued to survey the area. There were some glowing lights in the water—he even thought that he saw a platypus, and some fish. "I love it," said Alex. "It's amazing."

"Yeah." Robbie started unbuttoning his shirt and kicking off his shoes. Pulling off his socks, he decreed, "I think we need to go skinny dipping."

Alex didn't know how to react. He wanted to go in the water, but skinny-dipping seemed like something Alex—even the *new Alex*—would hesitate to do. Robbie seemed to find Alex's hesitation amusing. He pulled down his pants with magic, then his underpants with his hands, and stood naked on the dirt-sand. He was mesmerically hot; he was also hard. Alex felt paralysed with lust and indecision.

"Don't worry," said Robbie. "Here, let me help." Robbie walked, *glided, sailed* up to Alex with his characteristic elegance, despite his nudity. He pulled the lucky blazer off Alex's shoulders. He started unbuttoning Alex's shirt. Alex, now committed and with a view to helping out, pulled off his shoes, pulled down his pants and took off his socks.

"I thought so," said Robbie, as Alex stood newly naked before him. "You were embarrassed because you're hard." That was true. Alex had been hard since the games room. And now, with Robbie totally undressed—with his broad shoulders, his muscular arms, his chest, his big nipples, his six-pack abs, standing there—Alex was harder than ever.

"I'm hard, too," said Robbie, stating the obvious. "Shall we go in?" he asked, as both boys stood naked on the side of the Billabong.

"Yes, let's."

As they walked towards the edge of the water, Alex touched Robbie's nose. "So you can breathe like me," he said.

Robbie nodded: "You're *very* good at this, aren't you?"

"Yeah," replied Alex, cockily. "I am."

The two boys held hands under water. Alex was as comfortable there as on land. Robbie was less so, but Alex's spell meant that he could breathe with ease, never needing to stick his head above water.

As they had seen from the surface, there were fish and platypuses. There were also glowing aquatic spirits, or faeries, which could have been local or introduced magical fauna—and which danced and glowed around them as they explored the Billabong.

Sometime later, they emerged onto the island in the centre of the lake. A big rock that Alex had spotted earlier turned out to be no such thing. Rather, it was the bunyip, a huge man-seal magical beast.

"Climb aboard," Robbie ordered.

"What?" sputtered Alex.

"I told you, it's *friendly.*"

Robbie was right. As the creature entered the water, it let the boys cling to its huge ears as it swam around the Billabong with extraordinary grace.

Eventually, the bunyip left the young men where they had begun and where their clothes sat in a neat pile. The pair kissed again. Alex moaned. He also, with a wave of his hand, dried both him and Robbie off instantly.

"Have they assigned you your room?" Robbie asked Alex.

"Yes."

"Last waltz, then."

It was fair to say that the accommodations that Alex had been allocated were spartan and basic. They were especially so this evening, since what earthly possessions and personal effects Alex had brought with him remained either in a pair of small suitcases in the corner, or were stuffed between his and Robbie's waltz-positioned bodies.

Robbie extricated himself from the waltz position, and the shoes and clothes fell to the floor. (Alex's favourite blazer was unfortunately crumpled by the teleportation exercise; but this did not bother him in the slightest, at the time.) While Robbie made no attempt to pick the clothes up, or put them on, or leave, Alex was still somewhat confused by Robbie's next move, which was to sit on the small bed resplendent in his nakedness.

"Is everything all right?" asked Alex. It was all he could think to say, while trying to hide his disappointment.

"Um, yeah," replied Robbie, unhelpfully.

Alex was annoyed. And the new Alex let people know when he was annoyed: "It's just that, given preceding events, I was expecting that you would have thrown me on the bed—"

"—And been inside of you by now?" offered Robbie, sadly no less sexy for being sexually frustrating.

"Yes," agreed Alex, still standing next to the bed. Still hard, still frustrated.

He thought of a conversation he'd had with his father, after Alex had announced that he was going to go to magic school. Weirdly, his dad had decided at that time, very belatedly, to share with him the typical information about the birds and the bees.

"Ali," he had said: "There are going to be boys—men—when you go to uni."

And his dad has presented him with items, lube and condoms, that were familiar. He wondered whether he should have told his dad—his beloved dad—that there had already been 'boys' and 'men'. Unavailable *boys*, straight *men*, older *men*, and straight-up dickhead *men*. None of whom had been too particular when it came to safe sex, nor remotely consistent when it came to calling him, loving him, even liking him. (Was Robbie just another one of them?) But he had said nothing. He had taken the big packet of condoms, the large bottle of lube, and kissed his dad on the cheek.

"Or is this the time," Alex started to pace, and point, and on some level realise he might be getting a bit melodramatic, "when you tell me that, like, you don't *do* the *boyfriend thing*. Because, you know, you aren't one of those guys who fucks guys like me and just never calls. At least you're *upfront*!"

Robbie looked like someone who realised they had made a *faux pas* and cared that he had. (Alex found this gratifying.) Robbie put his hands in the air and said: "OK, let's start again." He patted the bed. "Sit."

Alex complied. Robbie put an arm around Alex's shoulders, drawing him in so the two boy's heads touched. Alex liked this.

"So here is the thing. Someone from the uni asked if I could be your buddy."

"You mean, you didn't volunteer?"

"No. They asked if I could mentor you, and my mother said I should. And you do not disobey *my mother*."

Alex nodded absently, enjoying smelling Robbie, but also still keen to stop talking and start having sex.

"Anyway, so I was busy, and lazy, and didn't call you …"

"You're forgiven, depending on what comes next."

"OK. So, I saw you at the party, cracking jokes, making people laugh. I wasn't sure whether you were hotter than hell, or an angel."

"Wait," said Alex, pulling away, but liking Robbie's description. Maybe he could be both? "I'm not understanding the problem here."

Robbie laid back on the bed, looking into Alex's quizzical eyes. "There was this stuff the uni gave me about this buddy system and sex and consent. Like, maybe there's been an issue with it in the past. I dunno; I just wanted to make sure you were really into it."

Alex laughed. "Wait, you were seriously worried that I didn't want to have sex with you?"

"In my defence," declared Robbie, getting up and pushing Alex onto the bed, "I didn't think you'd respond so badly to a pause in proceedings."

That was probably fair, reasoned Alex. He squirmed and moaned under Robbie's weight, as the latter kissed his neck and chest. He did, however, take the chance to ask: "What about the boyfriend thing?"

Robbie smiled *that* smile again. "I'm definitely not against being boyfriends, *Lexi*." The pet name!

Alex was in heaven. And, indeed, the next day, Alex decided that he had just enjoyed the closest thing possible to, officially, the best sex ever. He also thought that he and Robbie would look very fetching in matching pyjamas.

4

A Dinner Party

Present day

Alex woke to Josh gently shaking his bare shoulder.

As he opened his eyes, he saw his boyfriend, wearing off-white linen shorts and a pale blue shirt. Josh looked terrific in shorts, with his long, lean, olive-skinned legs. Taking his own to be too skinny, pale and hairy, Alex owned just one pair of shorts, worn grudgingly to the gym.

Alex yawned and raised himself up, resting against the bedhead. He saw that, along with the shorts and shirt, Josh was wearing a pair of fancy trainers with anklet socks.

"Get up, babe, we need to go to the market."

Culturally, police tended to start and finish work early. This did not accord with Alex's own circadian rhythms, which tended towards being a night-owl and getting up late. But Josh always worked back from a deadline and a spreadsheet—even a dinner party one—allowing for plenty of time to achieve perfection. Which meant it was time for Alex to rise.

"OK, OK." Alex pulled himself out of bed and walked into the couple's palatial ensuite bathroom. He shucked off his oversized pyjama bottoms and pulled the tap of their his-and-his dual-outlet shower. (Though they only generally used one of them.) Having washed his body, his hair and his face, Alex stood at the mirror, wondering whether he should shave. Always carrying a very light beard, and having shaved yesterday, he determined not to bother. (Pav would not be around to make a remark about 'kids today' and 'scruffiness'.)

This left him to brush his teeth, dry his hair and apply some fancy face creams. Then he marched back into their bedroom, clad in his towel, to determine what to wear. Ultimately, he landed on a polo shirt and chino trousers. Josh emerged with a grocery trolley (or 'granny trolley', as they both called it) and declared they would walk the twenty-or-so minutes to the market.

There, they were methodical. First, because they needed to eat something, they ordered bocadillas from the Spanish grocer—rolls, in this case with Manchego and chorizo, rubbed with salt and tomato— some of the best sandwiches in Melbourne. After that, they went to the organic butcher for a piece of eye fillet; one of the seafood places for scallops; the best deli for puff pastry, bacon, Parma ham, cheeses, lavosh and assorted nibbles; and the Iranian-run fruit-and-vegetable shop for mushrooms, spinach, shallots, garlic and raspberries.

Ultimately, with their purchases in the granny trolley, Josh had declared their shop complete. And, with that, and his shapely calves and ankles, he walked back towards the house with Alex in tow.

The evening's menu was 'traditional'. It comprised scallops with lardons and celeriac purée, beef Wellington with sautéed spinach, and chocolate soufflé with raspberry coulis.

Once the pair arrived home, attention turned to food preparation. Alex peeled and sliced the celeriac into pieces and put them in the oven. He also ensured the soufflé mix was ready, and the coulis was on the induction burner, with the berries stewing slowly with sugar. As Josh looked on, doing little but offering mild encouragement—and possibly looking at the spreadsheet—he declared, "Babe, maybe you could have a nap now, if you want? I can take things from here."

Josh was congenitally unable to nap once he was awake, but Alex was quite able to. He took the opportunity and retired upstairs. Josh placed wireless headphones in his ears and started listening to the audio version of the *Economist* app.

As he listened, Josh prepared the main course, which was his speciality. He fried off a 'duxelles' of blended mushrooms, shallots and garlic in a dry pan and let it cool. He seared the eye fillet at high heat, waving away the smoke from the cooktop until the beef was browned and let it cool. He laid out the Parma ham, spread out the duxelles and wrapped it in cling film with the beef. He left it in the fridge, before completing essentially the same process with the pastry. Lastly, he took the pastry offcuts and, as the celebrity chefs would advise, cut designs of flowers and leaves to adorn the dish.

"Hey, babe, they must be coming soon," announced Alex, as he descended the stairs from the bedroom.

"Can you look after the stuff?" Josh called out to Alex, as he passed him walking up to the bedroom.

"Of course, babe."

"No drinking until the guests arrive!" Josh ordered in return, as Alex prepared the nibbles and checked that the apartment itself was presentable, which it was. (Josh had insisted that the cleaners come twice a week. Alex wasn't sure that was necessary but, being messy and unwilling to clean things himself, he had relented.)

Ding! went the bell. Alex buzzed their guests up.

"Ah, hi mate. Hi Alex!"

Simmo was some years older than Josh. Physically, they could scarcely have been more different. Simmo was a shade shorter than Alex, but much wider. With his hair and dress sense, he reminded Alex of Tucker Carlson: the conservative American cable TV pundit, of whom Alex was quite sure Simmo was a fan.

Simmo and Josh's differences were not just physical. Simmo had grown up in Melbourne's north-western suburbs, in very modest circumstances—which he wasn't at all reticent about mentioning in conversation. After finishing as the Dux at his high school, Simmo had excelled at university. "I was first in my family to go—ever!" he would remind anyone who would listen, and some who wouldn't, and ultimately found himself a rising star in Melbourne's small financial élite.

He revelled in his 'working class boy made good' background. He navigated social circles on his own terms—which Alex admired, given his own history—and was a master of knowing when to charm, and when to shock other people's posh and entitled sensibilities. He did, as Alex would grudgingly acknowledge, have a sort of rugged charisma about him, which probably helped.

"This is Charlotte," Simmo announced, with a disarming air of pride and tenderness.

"Hi!" she said, pleasantly. Alex embraced the slim, red-headed woman, who wore an extremely elegant green dress with matching jacket and had almost mesmeric (matching) green eyes.

"My boyfriend will be here momentarily," declared Alex. "Would you like a drink?"

"Oh," Simmo replied, "we brought some Dom. Shall we have that to start?"

Simmo produced the bottle, which Alex opened—cautiously, since he wasn't a believer in letting the cork fire itself across a room. He then gathered up some champagne glasses from a kitchen cupboard, by hand (not magically, in light of the company).

As Alex handed Simmo and Charlotte their drinks, Simmo started to notice his surrounds. Since he had never before been to Josh and Alex's place, he took a wander around the ground floor of the apartment. "Oooh," he enthused, seemingly in awe. "This place is amazing!"

Alex was almost certain that Simmo was struck by the scale and opulence of the apartment. But his words hewed to more tasteful observations, perhaps due to the presence of Charlotte. "I love how you've decorated it. It's like something in a magazine—in a good way, I mean. Lovely."

"It certainly is. I adore all the different patterns on the rugs and with the marble surfaces." That was Charlotte. And she was right. Alex had not originally intended it, but much of their design approach was based on contrasting patterns: in the marble tables and benchtops in the kitchen; the selection of rugs that strew the living area; and even a feature wall, adorned with a large artwork of multiple wood panels that swirled with charred patterns of various intensities from the finest to the darkest. That piece was an obvious artefact of magic.

As they spoke, Josh descended the stairs from their room. He was still wearing the same shirt and trainers but had swapped the shorts for tailored trousers and added a dark blue box jacket. The others naturally turned to look at the stairs as he approached them.

"Thanks," Josh said, as he kissed Alex on the cheek. "It was all mainly his doing. The decorating, I mean."

"Well, I chose things, you bought them," replied Alex.

Alex went to pour Josh some champagne while giving himself and Simmo a top-up. Josh embraced Charlotte like a long-lost relative. "It's so great to finally meet you!" he gushed. "I'm so glad you made it."

"Well, of course I did," she replied. "I've been so looking forward to meeting you two as well." She looked to Alex as she said that, presumably so Alex did not mistake her 'two' for a 'too'.

"Here, sit down and have some nibbles," Josh said, wrapping his arm around Charlotte's shoulders and leading her towards the sofa and coffee table.

This left Alex and Simmo hovering near the entrance to the apartment. Alex thought of suggesting that the pair move to the coffee-table-nibbles region, but Simmo was busy inspecting a variety of framed photos on the sideboard by the doorway. The sideboard was festooned with images of Josh and Alex: underneath the Eiffel Tower; at Times Square at Christmas, in the snow; shirtless with face paint and glitter on a party boat on Sydney Harbour; and pictures of them with family.

Simmo seemed to be looking, in particular, at a snap of Alex with his siblings and parents, taken during a family holiday when he had been at MMS, in front of a wooded backdrop. "Such a good-looking family," mused Simmo.

"Thanks," replied, Alex. "Those are my siblings, Ivan and Catherine."

Simmo pointed his finger at Alex, and his dad: the two had posed next to each other in the picture. "You're so much like him," said Simmo. Then, pointing to Alex's brother and sister, "While they're just like your mother."

It was true. Alex and his father looked very similar. He was slightly shorter than his wife, with soft features and light brown hair. His wife's greater height and sharper, more angular features—and blonde hair— were magnified in Ivan and Catherine. Alex decided not to mention that both had also inherited his mother's—and his father's, to be fair— propensity for success, be it social, career or, just, in life.

"Wait," declared Simmo. "Waaaaiiit! Ivan, Catherine, Alexander. Those names, they're all Russian. They're all tsars!"

"Si!" Charlotte's voice could be heard across the room.

"Don't worry, hun," he said back. "I promise I'm not mentioning the war!"

"You're right," acknowledged Alex. "My mum studied Russian history at university; Mum and Dad even visited Russia before I was born. Hence the names."

"A Russophile?" suggested Simmo.

"A Russia scholar," insisted Alex.

"Well, there you are," said Simmo. "I guess I could be a detective too!"

"Enjoy the ninety percent pay cut," said Alex. Then, taking Simmo by the arm: "Come on, let's join the others."

Charlotte and Josh were laughing and chatting, though not really touching the nibbles, as Alex and Simmo sat themselves opposite. While Simmo put some soft cheese on a piece of lavosh, Josh asked: "Hey, what's with the champagne? What are we celebrating?"

"Ah," replied Simmo, downing his cheese and cracker and taking a big sip. "I forgot to say—maybe I got distracted by the property—but I'm pretty sure the partnership is happening."

"Really?" replied Josh, leaning forward, looking like an excited cocker spaniel.

"Yeah, mate," insisted Simmo. "If the deal goes ahead, it's a dead cert. I've made a point of it." to Alex and Charlotte, Simmo noted apologetically: "Sorry, shop talk. All a bit on the QT."

Josh allowed for the merest moment of silence before deflecting the conversation towards Charlotte. They talked about her job ("I'm basically a baby barrister, corporate and commercial stuff, mainly." "She's great, though," gushed Simmo, in response. "She'll be a King's Counsel before you know it."); where she lived ("Armadale. My whole family lives there, pretty much." "Josh and I met in Armadale!" Alex exclaimed. "He basically just picked me up there and then at *Magasin de Vin*."); and Simmo's recent efforts to buy Charlotte a car: ("I think I'm suffering a choice overload" "Petrol or electric?" asked Josh. Simmo rolled his eyes. "Josh drives a Tesla, hun. Practically put the whole firm onto the bloody things. Lucky he can just about make it down to Portsea for the polo on a full charge!" "Shut up, Simmo!")

Then, by some unplanned and unexpected twist of conversational logic, talk turned to crypto-assets. "OK," said Alex, getting up. "I'll prep the starter and leave the money people to debate the blockchain or whatever."

As he walked to the kitchen, he heard Josh remark: "He's being silly. He knows about this stuff. He even reads *The Economist*. I mean, he *actually* reads it."

The starter, intentionally and by design, did not take long to cook. As the scallops sizzled briefly in the pan, Alex put the beef Wellington main course (which looked impressive, even uncooked) into the oven. As he plated up his starter dish, the others came to the table and sat down, having barely made an impact on the nibbles. Alex would see this as wasteful, but Josh would insist that a good host would never take the risk of under-catering on the snacks.

"These look fabulous," said Charlotte, as she sat down. The table, of which less than half was being used for their small party of four, had been meticulously set by Josh with their (well, Josh's, really) best china and one of many extant sets of Goldman family silver. At the centre of the table stood a magnificent bunch of orchids. These were flanked on either side, lengthways, by large candles in big silver candlesticks. Then, next to each of those was a dark glass orb, together forming a pair on the table, resting on elaborate silver bases.

The group started eating as Josh passed around a bottle of pinot grigio. In the minutes since he'd gone to the kitchen, the conversation had moved from crypto to the (only slightly less dreary) topic of inflation, streaming services (something to do with choice overload, again) and tech 'unicorn' firms. ("I reckon there will be more actual unicorns than tech ones again, soon enough," Simmo declared with confidence.)

As the scallops were swallowed and plates cleaned of celeriac puree, Alex noticed Simmo's eyes gazing at the dark orbs in front of him. These, of course, were magical communication devices. Josh had seemed even more committed to acquiring them than he had been with all the other items in their home, after Alex had noticed them in one of the many auction catalogues they had perused.

Charlotte seemed to notice her boyfriend's quiet curiosity. "They're communication orbs, Si," she declared, to Alex's shock. "Like magic walkie talkies. May I?" she asked, gesturing at the orb closest to her.

"Um, sure," replied Alex, lost for words.

The orb rose from its base and sailed through the air into Charlotte's hands. The darkness faded from the orb, and it became transparent.

"Sorry, I forgot to mention," said Simmo, beaming, almost beside himself. "Charlotte is a magician too."

Charlotte stood at the edge of the balcony, smoking a cigarette that she had just lit, as all magicians do, by tapping the end of it with her finger.

Following her unexpected magical demonstration with the communications orbs, Charlotte had declared that there had been enough showing off and asked if it would be alright if she had a smoke on the balcony.

"Of course," Alex had agreed, using his magic to open a cupboard and summon an ashtray to float into his hands.

"Would you like to join me?" Charlotte had asked. Alex answered in the affirmative, while giving Josh a reassuring look. "Don't worry, babe, I won't have a cigarette."

Now, turning her head away from the view of Melbourne's city skyline to look Alex in the eye, she said, apologetically, "I hope my little party trick wasn't too much of a shock."

"Not at all," replied Alex, genuinely. "I mean, it was a surprise. A pleasant one, if anything."

"Good," said Charlotte. She paused, as if weighing up a possible answer to a question. Then she said: "You don't do much with magic, do you—or spend any time in magic circles?"

"No."

"And you're not in the Magic Squad, at work?"

"No, just a regular detective," Alex replied, without elaboration.

"I see." Charlotte smiled. "Well, I'm glad I got a chance to meet you. That is why I insisted on Si basically inviting ourselves over to your place."

"Oh, so you could meet me?" said Alex, surprised. "I figured Simmo just wanted to show Josh off to you."

Charlotte chuckled a little. "Well, he *did*, of course. But I could've met Josh any old where. Coming over here meant you would definitely be here as well. Also," she continued, "Si did want to see your house. He has a thing about people's houses. He must have watched every episode of *Grand Designs* and *Location, Location, Location*."

Alex guffawed. "Wow, really? You think you know a person."

"Yeah," agreed Charlotte, butting out her cigarette in the ashtray. "Shall we re-join the lads?"

"Yep," said Alex, moving towards the door. Suddenly, he paused. "Wait, you didn't ask me about my affinity."

"Oh my God!" cried Charlotte, in jest. "What sort of a magician am I?"

"Anyway, it's water, ice, wind," said Alex.

"Mine's transformation. Transformation of the self, especially," said Charlotte. "I could turn myself into an elephant right now."

"Impressive."

"Or," she grinned, slyly, "I could do my impression of Si. It's pretty uncanny."

Alex and Josh lay together in bed, Josh stroking Alex's hair. Alex was wearing Josh's baby blue pyjama bottoms from the night before. Josh was wearing full-length ones with pink-and-white checks. Josh quite liked the colour pink.

"That went really well," said Josh. "I know it was a lot of effort for you, babe."

"That's OK. I really enjoyed it," replied Alex.

"Charlotte was great, too, wasn't she?" asked Josh, rhetorically.

"Yeah, yeah, she was," agreed Alex, sincerely. "Weird coincidence that she was a magician, though, wasn't it? When we were outside, I think she wanted to ask why I stopped doing magic but was too polite to actually push it."

"Nothing wrong with being polite," Josh replied. "You know what Simmo told *me* when you were out—that he's going to pop the question."

"Really?" Alex sat up in bed. "That is a big deal."

"It is," agreed Josh, also sitting up. "He insists he's never felt anything like this about a woman before." Josh affected a slightly deeper voice. "'When you're my age, *Sachs*, you don't muck about.' He's even gone ring shopping with one of her friends this week."

"Well, I'm happy for him," said Alex. "He always seemed like the sort of guy who talked shit about his conquests or whatever, but actually wanted to settle down and have kids and get secretly bossed around by his wife."

Josh laughed. "That's exactly it! And even you would have to admit Charlotte does seem to reduce Simmo's occasional dickhead tendencies."

"Occasional?"

"Come on, babe. He was pretty good company tonight."

"OK," conceded Alex. "At least he didn't mention the war."

Josh looked at Alex, in *that way*. "How about you take off those pyjama bottoms?"

Alex complied, with some enthusiasm. Josh looked at him again, not in *that way*. "What?" asked Alex.

"Oh," said Josh, grinning. "The mention of dickhead tendencies made me think we could have another dinner party and invite Pav."

"Do you want to sleep in the spare room?" countered Alex.

He didn't.

5

Road trip to Daylesford

"So, it was the van that made you make the connection?"

Isabella was in the driver's seat as she and Alex drove to Daylesford in an unmarked squad car. They had exited the city and its traffic, entered the Western Freeway and passed the cookie-cutter housing estates of Rockbank and Sunbury on Melbourne's outer north-western fringe. They were now halfway to Daylesford, a charming tourist town 115 km northwest of Melbourne.

Daylesford was known for its mineral springs and associated spas, its central lake and its vibrant LGBTQIA+ community. (It was often described as the 'gay capital of regional Victoria'.) However, until the Daylesford Distillery had started selling barrels of whisky to possibly over-credulous and under-critical investors, the town had not been known for distilling, or for boutique spirit investment schemes. The marketing and legal disclosures of Ian Kirk's company had, nonetheless, made a point of the town's fresh and natural sources of water.

"Yes," agreed Alex, "it was. Coming and going after hours, it made me think—and I cannot believe it's true—that, maybe, Kirk was selling his investors' whisky under the table to Hart, then coming back and refilling the barrels with Hart's cheap plonk. All at night, after the workers at the distillery had gone home, and probably in plastic drums in the van."

"And Hart is just sitting on this stock?" asked Isabella.

"Yeah," said Alex. "Then, I guess, at some point, Hart plans to announce a new line of premium whisky, sold direct to the public."

"Ostensibly acquired from overseas," added Isabella.

"Yep, hence the overseas income for Kirk." Alex shifted in his seat and adjusted his hair. "But the whole scheme is just stupid. Someone is going to find out at some point: actually tasting the whisky, for example."

"He did fool the auditors," offered Isabella.

"Sure, he did. They may have checked the barrels were there, but they would hardly be tasting the contents. So, it was all good, for now. But what is the exit strategy on such a dumb scam, especially if you're divorced and have no kids?"

"Flee the country with the cash?"

"Correct," said Alex. "And what do you need if you want to do that and disappear?"

Isabella thought for a moment. "A fake identity!"

"Correct again. And where, if you're a former cricketer turned investment spruiker with no criminal connections, might you look for a fake identity?"

"Your big investor who happens to be a notorious bikie gangster with multiple aliases?" said Isabella, nodding in understanding

"Indeed. And Hot Rod—being nobody's fool, by all accounts— realises that, if the guy whose scheme he's invested in is looking for phoney papers, something dodgy must be going on."

"But he has no way of knowing what," Isabella mused. "So, just like us, all he can do is put Kirk and the distillery under surveillance and try to figure out what he's up to."

"Elementary, my dear Isabella!"

"Wait," said Isabella, "what about that Jenny woman? How does she fit in?"

"No idea," replied Alex. "She may have nothing to do with it, or she could be the brains behind the whole thing. Not that brains are especially in evidence."

"Anyway, it looks like we're here," said Isabella, as they pulled into the carpark.

✿

"This is ridiculous—what are you looking for?" harrumphed Ian Kirk. He glared at the uniformed police hunting around the site for evidence, whom had preceded Alex and Isabella's arrival with search warrants in hand.

"Samples of the whisky in your barrels, for starters," replied Alex. "And the plastic drums in the van that you used to drive the whisky to Mike Hart's distillery up the road and bring back his rocket fuel to replace it with. Also, maybe the fake identity documents you got from Hot Rod, assuming he ever actually gave them to you."

"What the hell are you on about? That is preposterous." Ian Kirk was affecting an air of bravado, but he had the look—Alex thought of it, illogically, as a look 'behind the eyes'—of a suspect who had suddenly realised that they have been found out. Alex imagined that Kirk was now undertaking a tortuous mental calculus: *How much do they know? What can they prove? Should I confess or brazen it out?*

"It's preposterous," replied Isabella. "But you did it."

Kirk stared at Isabella, no doubt assuming (correctly) she was the senior partner in their pairing. Alex reflected on his insufficient personal gravitas. Often people reacted to discovering his occupation with a startled, "You don't look like a cop!"

Eventually, Kirk seemed to settle on an approach. "Not that I'm suggesting there is anything to prove but, hypothetically, how would you show in court that I swapped the whiskies, if I did?"

"Firstly, we have our lab guys working on what tests we can run to identify the whiskies," said Isabella, sounding more confident than Alex would have. (It was true that the crime lab was working on what tests to run, but their technicians would not necessarily be successful and had offered no guarantees.) "Then we can get expert whisky judges to testify," Isabelle continued. "Or maybe we could get the jury to do a taste test!" She was smiling now. Isabella had quite a line on playing the TV-style wisecracking copper. Which meant maybe it was best that Kirk had looked to her as the leader. "We will find a way. Trust me. And, of course, our colleagues will be arriving at your mate Mike Hart's place as we speak. Maybe you want to talk to us before he does, at the station?"

Ian Kirk hesitated, finalising the mental calculus. "OK," he said, in quiet defeat.

The trio walked out of the distillery building and towards Alex and Isabella's unmarked police car. As Alex went to open the door, he heard a shout. "Hey, Kirk, you fucker—I want my fucking money!"

Alex had to blink to make sure he wasn't imagining things. He wasn't. Racing towards him, Isabella and Ian Kirk, was Rodney 'Hot Rod' Church, apoplectic with rage and accompanied by a henchman who was trying, unsuccessfully, to calm him down.

"I'll kill you, you motherfucker!" screamed Hot Rod, face crimson. "You two, get away from him, or I'll ..."

"We're police!" shouted Isabella, in disbelief as much as alarm. (Had Hot Rod not seen the marked police cars in the carpark? Was he simply too furious to notice, or care?)

Hot Rod reached into his big leather bikie jacket. Alex saw it at once: a pistol.

Time froze, as did the air in front of the three people by the car, forming a thick shield between them and the furious, armed bikie. A shot rang out, the bullet uselessly burying itself in the sheet of ice.

Then the ice shattered into tiny fragments and whirled, in a cyclonic wave of wind and frost, towards the two gangsters. It sent Hot Rod's pistol flying and swept the two men into the air, leaving them suspended above ground, shaking their legs, waving their fists and swearing with impotent rage.

Alex's eyes glowed bright blue.

"Wow!" marvelled Isabella.

Alex sat in a nondescript room in the still-fairly-new Daylesford Police Station. A local officer had included him in a coffee run; he was cradling an almost empty cup of takeaway coffee, which had been surprisingly good. He looked, and felt, miserable.

Events had been a blur after he had used his magic to stop Hot Rod from shooting Ian Kirk. Everything had happened so fast. He'd never been shot at before, and had certainly never used magic on the job before. He was also shaking slightly, no doubt the after-effects of the shock. (Perhaps the coffee had not been the best idea, but a stiff drink wasn't an option for an on-duty police officer.)

Alex's gloominess wasn't helped by the fact that Pav had just entered the room in high spirits. "You've got us an amazing result today, PB," he enthused. "Really extraordinary. Kirk and Hart are both cooperating. I guess having a big-time organised criminal wanting to kill you does that to a person."

Alex said nothing.

"Which means that we're going to be able to identify and return the stolen whisky to the …" Pav sneered slightly, "… *Investors*. It'll be a great news story; the Corporate Affairs guys will be chuffed."

Who gives a fuck about the Corporate Affairs guys?

"Oh, and Hot Rod seems to have calmed down and realised he made a big fucking mistake. We reckon he will do a deal. Imagine that—a Teflon felon for two decades and he goes and shoots at the cop with the magic fucking powers!" As he said the M-word, the penny dropped. "Oh, that is what you're so miserable about, is it? Your secret identity is out?"

Alex tried not to completely lose it. "Yes, Pav, that is exactly what I am *so miserable about!* That, and getting shot at wasn't so much fun either." He laughed bitterly. "But I guess that doesn't matter to you, does it, Pav— because now you have a whole new thing about me to make fun of!"

"Hold on, Alex," Pav said, attempting to sound conciliatory.

"Yippee!" sneered Alex, waving his arms and adopting an exaggerated, deep voice. "Now I can add cheap cracks about *PB's* magical ability to the ones about his appearance, his sexuality, his competence, his father's success, his boyfriend—"

"Alex!" shouted Pav. This was enough to stop Alex talking, but not enough to stop him glaring. Pav's expression was different now. Alex wasn't sure whether Pav was going to cry, slap him in the face, or storm out of the room. (On reflection, Alex accepted that all three would have been quite understandable.) "You're dead-set the only person I know who could turn what is objectively the most successful day of your professional career into an exercise in amateur dramatics."

Alex wanted to say something but didn't.

"But you're going to need to calm down. You're needed back in Melbourne."

Alex's heart sank even lower. "Why, by who?" But, he thought, did he really have to ask? Surely, it would be Professional Standards. Using ice and wind magic to apprehend suspects wasn't exactly endorsed in the police manual.

"Do you think they give me that sort of information?" replied Pav. "Here, I'll drive."

The ninety-minute trip back to Melbourne was dominated by Pav's occasional attempts at one-sided banter, his terrible 1980s Spotify playlist, and his best reassuring noises. "I wouldn't worry about any investigation of the, you know, *incident*," he'd said. "I mean, you're basically a hero. And Hot Rod and his henchman weren't even injured, barely a scratch. And, you know, if there is one, an investigation, I'm one of the union peer support people." The thought of having Pav as his support person in any Professional Standards interrogation made Alex feel even more down about, well, everything.

Alex found himself wondering whether it was possible— mathematically, scientifically—for his day to get any worse. But as they arrived back at the glittering Victoria Police headquarters and found themselves sitting in another nondescript room, Alex discovered that it was, indeed, possible for thing to get worse. Because he had been summoned, not by Professional Standards, but by the formidable head of the Magic and Supernatural Squad, Chief Superintendent Karen Park.

And, furthermore, standing by her side, as handsome as ever, was Senior Detective Robert Chang. He looked almost exactly the same as ten years before. Alex could pick three differences: one, he was wearing a quite sharp dark grey suit and white shirt—which he filled out very well; two, he had grown his hair out and was wearing it in a neat man-bun, which did not suit him *at all*; three, and maybe this was Alex's imagination—or wishful thinking—his eyes and general demeanour had lost the sort of cocky confidence that Alex remembered. Maybe Robbie had been worn down a little by work and life. *Join the club,* he thought.

"We need your help with something. A case," declared Chief Superintendent Park. "A magic case."

Robbie? Magic case? You have got to be kidding me, universe!

6

A Promising Start to the Semester

10 years ago

Room 12A at MMS was less like the games room, museum or Billabong, and more like a high school science lab. The area was divided into a series of individual high benches, each with a small working space, a basic basin and a tap. (Alex had no idea what these were for.) The walls of the room were covered with posters urging students to "Be Careful", "Know First Aid" and "Call for Help Immediately in Case of Fire"

Alex stood behind one of these high benches. He was joined by about eighteen new MMS students in the class. Standing closest around him were the new friends he met at the night of the orientation party: Emma, Julius, Jack and Yolanda. Despite having abandoned them at the party for Robbie (no regrets!) they had quickly coalesced into a social group. Now, several weeks into the semester, they were routinely meeting up for lunch, study, coffee, drinks, and parties.

Emma and Alex had hit it off especially well. They had bonded over the cheap Monday night tickets at a local arthouse cinema, which had become a standing event. They had seen a Bulgarian melodrama, an Australian horror, and an obscure period film since the start of the semester. However, while Emma was a confirmed film snob, Alex had broader tastes. The Fast and the Furious films were a guilty pleasure, for example.

"So, as you all know by now, we call them affinities because they are how you instinctively manifest your power." This was John Bishop, the Admissions Officer and Professor of Manipulation and Telekinesis. "And," he continued, "You do it almost automatically, often without needing, or having had, any training at all in the discipline."

In front of each student sat a small pile of metal balls, like those Robbie had manipulated in the games room, but much, much smaller. This was the second Telekinesis prac. In the first few weeks of the semester, they had studied basic flame—though working with a candle, rather than a cigarette.

"But, as many of you would have discovered with your work on flame recently—or, indeed, in our first class here on telekinesis—developing even a basic proficiency in other forms of magic can take lots of time, effort and practice."

As Professor Bishop's eyes scanned the faces in the room, many of the students felt that he might be referring to them, in particular, with his reference to the previous session. The classroom had certainly become strewn with small metal tripping hazards rather quickly.

"However, it's quite possible to master a discipline quite different to your original affinity, with enough hard work and determination. So, let's start practising!"

The students turned their attention to the metal balls in front of them, willing them to levitate, spin or roll at their command—with varying levels of success. Almost immediately, Alex heard the first set of tripping hazards clatter to the ground.

Julius, on the other hand, was doing well. His little metal globes stood still in the air, rising slowly to his eye level.

"Very good, Julius," said Professor Bishop, as he paced the floor. "Focus first on keeping them stable, then you can start to explore movement." Julius beamed with satisfaction.

Emma's orbs were also staying in the air, but were less stable than Julius's, wobbling a little unsteadily.

"Good start, Emma," said the professor. Then he addressed the group at large. "The manifestation of magical power is at the intersection of will and imagination. Some of you will find it useful to visualise what you're trying to effect magically. Others may prefer a more physical approach. Think about how you breathe, how you raise your arm, how you run."

Alex looked over at Jack, who was looking particularly 'nice' today. He was wearing a fitted white polo shirt and blue box jacket, and his hair was flopping right over his eyes. His attempts at Manipulation and Telekinesis, however, were not a success. As Alex, and others, looked on, Jack cringed with embarrassment as the metal balls in front of him dropped chaotically across his bench, then onto the ground.

The professor continued to talk, as Jack, red-faced, scurried to pick them up. "And once you've created an effect on the physics and chemistry of our universe, you then need to maintain and control it. Which will mean, especially as you learn a new discipline, that you need to really concentrate and maintain your focus." He paused as he passed Yolanda's bench. She was maintaining her spheres steadily in the air. "Yolanda, good, good—make sure you keep *concentrating*."

Alex wondered how the professor had managed to memorise everyone's names so quickly, not knowing that John Bishop was also Head of Admissions and had personally reviewed all the students' applications.

"Ah, Alex," he said. Alex had the metal balls spinning above his head in a circular pattern. "Excellent! I think we have a natural on our hands!"

Alex also became red-faced but, unlike Jack, with gratification rather than embarrassment.

Show-off!

That was Emma, talking silently into his mind. She had started doing this recently. On the one hand, this showed how close they were becoming. On the other hand, Alex was utterly unable to respond to her without actually talking out loud. He was also sufficiently new to the sensation of psychic communication that he almost lost the necessary *concentration* and *focus* to keep his balls in the air. However, he did recover after a moment of wobbling.

Sorry, sorry. I wasn't trying to trip you up!

Alex didn't hold it against her.

Hey, why don't I teach you how to do this, so you can answer back? Given how quickly you picked up telekinesis, and the flame stuff, too, I suspect it won't be too difficult for you. And it's not like I can read your mind.

Actually, she *could* read his mind, if she had wanted to. But mentalism was possibly the most heavily restricted and regulated of the magical disciplines and, other than completely forbidden fields like necromancy, was one of the most feared and mistrusted. However, it also had many psychological and psychiatric applications.

Let's talk before lunch.

Which they did, as their friends headed off ahead of them to the MMS café once class was over. "Yeah, so I'm in," said Alex.

"Cool."

"Speaking of peer tutoring," said Alex, "I was wondering whether maybe I should ask Robbie to help Jack with this telekinesis stuff."

Alex didn't need to be able to read minds to tell that Emma was sceptical, at best, about that idea. "Are you sure? Given how Jack feels about you."

"Oh," replied Alex airily, "I'm sure he has moved on from that."

"You know full well he hasn't!" insisted Emma. "At least ask him first, before you say anything to Robbie."

"I will," Alex agreed. "Now let's get lunch."

As they approached their friends at the cafeteria table, the conversation seemed to be about the upcoming afternoon of theory classes, following their morning of prac.

"The thing about the theory classes," Jack said, holding a forkful of pasta, "is that, like, if you're studying magical history or whatever in just a regular lecture theatre, you may as well be studying actual *world* history."

"Yeah," agreed Yolanda. "Or law, accounting, agriculture, whatever."

"Which most of us are going to need to do after this to make a living, anyway," added Julius. "That or become an illusionist on a cruise ship or some shit."

"Hey, Jack," Alex said as the pair arrived at the table. Jack perked up immediately.

Not in front of everyone, Alex!

"Can I talk to you for a sec?"

"Sure!" Jack practically leapt from his seat, swallowing his mouthful of pasta in a gulp.

Once the two were alone and Alex had shared his bright idea with Jack, rarely would a nice young man have looked as crestfallen as Jack in that moment. "Yeah, sure, thanks. That would be great." he mumbled, without a shred of sincerity or enthusiasm.

Smooth move, Alex. Smooth fucking move! That was another 'psychic' message, from Alex to himself.

✿

"Wait, is Jack the one that looks at you like Narcissus looking into his own reflection in the pool?" Robbie had quite an interest in the classics.

Alex was unimpressed. "Don't be nasty, Robbie."

"Can't I be nasty? I mean, he's a *love rival.*"

Alex laughed. "No, he isn't. He's just a friend who has a little crush on me and could use some help with basic telekinesis."

The couple, as they now definitely were, were sitting outside at a tapas restaurant in the university neighbourhood of Carlton. They were, to Alex's great satisfaction, on a date. (They had been on many since their first night of passion.) Robbie was presently attacking some patatas bravas in tomato sauce.

"Some crush," he countered. "Besides, you just said he wasn't even keen."

Alex sighed, then popped a prawn, bathed in very garlicky oil, into his mouth. After pausing to chew and swallow, he explained: "It's like I said. I asked him if he wanted me to ask you to help him with telekinesis practice. He clearly didn't want to, but didn't want to say no."

"Didn't want to reject a kind offer of help from a friend?"

"Exactly," agreed Alex.

"Which leaves us in a situation where both Jack and I have to participate in an activity that neither of us want to do, because my boyfriend failed to read the room," declared Robbie.

"What do you want me to say?" Alex asked. "Can't you just do it, *for me?*"

"OK, OK," agreed Robbie, sitting back in his chair. "Geez, these potatoes are good!"

"You're the best!"

"Besides," said Robbie, sounding more than a little thoughtful. "I was actually going to ask you a favour, too."

"What is it?" Alex inquired, before swallowing a black olive.

"I was wondering if, maybe—" Robbie swallowed a spoonful of beans, "—I could talk to your dad about being a cop."

Alex was surprised, but also intrigued. "Why?"

"Because I need to work out what I'm going to do after this year, Lexi. If I want to work in magic, there aren't many choices—unless I want to become the opening act for some shitty illusionist on a cruise ship."

Alex quietly chuckled, thinking of Robbie and Julius as a double-act entertaining wealthy retirees in the Caribbean. "Sure, of course. But you know my dad has nothing to do with the Magic Squad?"

"I know," said Robbie. "But he has been in the force for decades, yeah, and has been super successful. He must be able to give me some insights into the whole thing."

"True," agreed Alex, eating more olives. "Wait, does this mean you want to meet my parents?" he asked, grinning with satisfaction. (The Boyfriend Project continued to be a resounding success!)

"I guess it does, Lexi," Robbie smiled, also with satisfaction.

"OK, I'll set it up!"

7

Swotting with Alex and Robbie: Summoning

R obbie was lying on his bed, arms folded behind his head, wearing just a pair of tracksuit pants and his black-framed reading glasses. He often wore the pants to bed, disdaining Alex's suggestion of matching pyjamas as "a bit weird, Lexi". Resting on his stomach, open pages down, was his third edition copy of *Introduction to Magic Theory and History*, by JL Loftus and GK Modigliani, published by Melbourne University Press. It was one of those heavy hardback textbooks.

Robbie had decided he had done enough reading for one day.

Alex, who was sitting at Robbie's small metal-and-glass desk, had not. He was reading the fourth edition of the very same textbook. Alex spent a lot of time in Robbie's room. This was, partially, because Project Boyfriend was—Robbie's rejection of matching pyjamas aside—going incredibly well. It was also because Alex's room had become a mess. Robbie, on the other hand, was a tidy person. Indeed, the last time Robbie had visited Alex's room, he'd found himself, to Alex's mortification, picking clothes up off the floor. Since then, it had been back to Robbie's every time.

As well as being much neater, Robbie's room also felt homier. It had a nice, wooden bedside table and matching sideboard, topped with framed family photos, and a couple of recently added pictures of Robbie and Alex. (Alex had noticed these immediately, with delight.) On its walls were three reproductions of belle epoque posters advertising cabaret magic shows in Paris. These were gifts from Robbie's mother, who had hunted them down at various antique shops to celebrate Robbie's acceptance into magic school.

Taking pride of place, though, on the wall above the desk, was a large, antique wooden cross of Lorraine. It was one of his mother's most prized possessions and, she insisted, it would watch over Robbie and guide his studies while he was at MMS. Robbie's mother had not, unlike Alex's father, complemented her gifts of decorative and religious objects with quantities of condoms and lube. It's not that she was naïve enough to imagine that the clean cut, handsome, unfailingly polite ("Hello, Mrs Chang") young men Robbie brought home while he was in high school were just 'study-buddies'. Nor—despite her intense Catholic faith—did she disapprove.

"Aren't you done with reading, Lexi?" Robbie asked, still lying back in bed.

Alex turned to look at his half-naked boyfriend, whose big bare feet slightly overshot the length of the small bed "No, Robbie, I'm not done with summoning."

Robbie smiled, put his textbook on the bedside table and ran a hand down his body. "You're saying no to this so you can read about *summoning?*" The cockiness was almost sexier than the reading glasses, if that was even possible.

"Yes," said Alex, turning back to his book.

Summoning and Necromancy

Summoning is an affinity among magicians and a unique discipline that involves effecting the entry of entities and energies that reside within what is usually referred to as the spiritual plane into the material one, then controlling their behaviour. Little is known about the spirit dimension of existence, as no human being has ever entered it and returned.

Because the entities and energies of the spiritual plane are extremely varied in type, power and size, the summoner can often use them to have a similar effect on the physical universe as that of most of the other schools of magic. For example, if a summoner wants to light a fire, she can summon a fire sprite; if she wants to fly, she can summon a flying spirit, such as a phoenix, to carry her. The breadth and variety of abilities this gives the summoner has led summoning to be seen by many as the most powerful form of magic.

Summoning is also the magical discipline that makes the greatest use of rituals, involving spoken incantations, imagery and iconography, and reagents (particular plants. chemical substances or objects that are consumed in the process). These rituals magnify the power of the caster, in light of the extreme amount of magical energy needed to physically manifest and control powerful spiritual entities. The use of rituals associates summoning in the public imagination with what is often termed the 'occult'.

This, and summoning's association with the spirit world itself, has made it especially subject to suspicion and prohibition throughout history. This is due, in part, to spiritual entities being likened, erroneously, to evil supernatural entities found in religion, such as demons. While spiritual entit es are not inherently evil in a religious sense, they can be dangerous if the summoner loses control over them and fatal attacks on humans by summoned creatures have happened, if rarely. As such, popular concerns about summoning are not totally unfounded.

The other reason summoning has inspired particular fear among the ungifted is its sub-discipline of necromancy. This is a branch of magic that involves using spirits to reanimate the remains of the dead, often creating immensely powerful and dangerous beings that are highly resistant to both magical and physical damage and injury.

Little is known about the mechanics of necromancy, much like other elements of the spirit world. In particular, while popular

> folklore assumes that the spirits animating necromantic beings (or the 'undead') are the spirits or 'souls' of the dead bodies that have been reanimated, that is actually unknown—but is regarded as highly unlikely. (This is similar to the popular belief that naturally occurring manifestations of spiritual energies in our physical universe are 'ghosts' of the dead.)
>
> While popular misconceptions about necromancy, including that it involves essentially enslaving the souls of the dead, may magnify popular horror at the practice, necromancy is nonetheless universally banned among magicians, including in war, where it was prohibited in the original Geneva Conventions.
>
> Indeed, the most powerful necromantic entities are created from the desecrated remains of recently deceased magic users. While these entities do not retain the magical abilities of the deceased magicians hosting them, they display heightened superhuman strength and enhanced supernatural powers associated with the undead. These may include the ability to disappear into darkness, become incorporeal, grow in size, teleport, disrupt some forms of magic such as transformation, exercise charm and mind control …

"*Lexi,*" crooned Robbie, as he raised himself off the bed.

"Nearly done," replied Alex.

Robbie put his hands on Alex's shoulders and started to massage him through his t-shirt. Then he looked at the open page of Alex's textbook, which showed an image of a medieval woodcut depicting a horrific, horned, skeletal abomination that was created though necromancy and was said to have murdered several people in France.

"Ugh, necromancy," spat Robbie. "That stuff is nasty."

"Looks that way," agreed Alex.

"They have some stuff about necromancy in the museum, actually. Even the skeleton of something like that," Robbie said, pointing at the image on the page.

"Really? I've never seen it," replied Alex, sounding altogether too curious to Robbie.

"You don't want to, Lexi. That shit gives me the creeps. Have you ever seen me cross myself?"

"No. I don't think I even knew you were Catholic."

"Well, I'm not Catholic. Not really. My mother is Catholic, though; hence the Lorraine cross you obviously haven't noticed."

"I guess I didn't make the connection. Sorry, babe," said Alex, not sounding especially sorry.

"Anyway, I *did* cross myself when I saw that bloody thing in the museum. It was horrible."

8

Two Dead Bodies

Present day

After he took mere moments to process the shock at their initial meeting, Robbie had to conclude that Alex—given the day he was having—looked remarkably calm and put-together. And to be fair, still looked remarkably *good*, in general.

After all, it's not every day that you crack a major fraud case, almost accidentally bust the Teflon gangster, get shot at *and* get dragged back into a world you had tried to leave behind. *And then there is you, Robbie. Don't forget you*, he thought to himself.

But nothing could prepare anyone for *this*.

Even more so than Alex, Robbie had seen a lot in his policing career. Before today, he might have boasted that he had 'seen it all' and that he had the psychological scars to show for it. There had been dead bodies, of course; and both bodies and lives ruined by hostile magic. There had even been that gang of sex traffickers who had put mind control charms on women and made them … "No!" Robbie insisted to himself. No well-meaning colleague, no conscientious counsellor, *nobody* was going to make him think about *that* case any more often than his own stupid brain forced him to.

But this was definitely up there. Robbie touched the small cross that he wore under his shirt.

"You crossed yourself," said Alex, very quietly, almost like he was afraid he was going to cry.

Robbie was surprised by how the thought of Alex in tears made him feel. "Yeah, I found God recently," he replied. (He didn't add: "At the bottom of a magic mind-control sex-trafficking ring," as much as that would have been accurate.)

"You said it before," said Alex, sounding even closer to tears. "About the necromancy."

Robbie remembered, though he had previously forgotten that conversation ten years before. He did not say anything.

Instead, Robbie forced himself to look around the room again. The walls were covered with spattered blood. The paintings of birds, those that had not been torn to pieces at least, continued to teem with magical avian motion. Amid the ruins of wrecked dreamcatchers, smashed crystals and shredded furnishings was a body. Its stomach and abdomen had been ripped open; its innards were scattered messily across the floor and walls. Its deathly head and face were largely intact, if almost entirely separated from the ruins of the rest of the body. Robbie had recognised the face immediately: Nerida Stein.

Almost right next to Nerida Stein's awfully disfigured and dismembered corpse was an even uglier and more disturbing set of remains. They looked male, which was about all Robbie could tell. They were bloated, with bloody foam oozing from the nose and mouth. The skin was green and, in some places, red. The corpse's hands were twisted into talons with sharp nails. Its teeth had been sharpened into fangs. Small horns grew from its bloodied, bald head. Its eyes, even now, glowed red. But, most disturbing of all was that this thing had, so obviously, once been a human being.

And it stank, horribly.

"It's a *revenant*, Robbie, isn't it?" asked Alex, sounding less like he was about to weep.

"Well, it's a necromantic entity, sure," Robbie replied.

"No, but definitely a revenant," insisted Alex. "That is the term, I think, for a re-animated corpse, between three and six days dead, or maybe a bit over a week with embalming?"

"Yeah," replied Robbie. It was true, but Robbie had also not remembered this until Alex raised it. Who remembered *that* part of their magic study?

"If you look at the state of the revenant's corpse," intoned Alex, sagely, "that's about right with the timing. And this one," continued Alex, in his increasingly businesslike way, "probably came in through the window. Incorporeal." Alex pointed at the largest window in the room.

"There was no forced entry," offered Robbie, by way of effective confirmation.

"And this was a professor of transformation. Someone who would've been able to defend herself."

"Yes. Her name was Nerida Stein. She was from MMS," said Robbie. (Alex did not say that, yes, he knew exactly who she was.)

"And, if you're trying to kill a powerful magic user with a summoned revenant, you'll need the most powerful sort of entity."

"Agreed."

"Which means reanimating a powerful magic user fairly shortly after death," stated Alex, with a sense of conclusion. "We need to investigate the murder weapon here," he said, pointing to the ghastly remains of the revenant. "Which powerful magicians died in the last week or so?"

"We're looking into it," said Robbie.

"You would think someone would have called it in, by now," said Alex. "I imagine this *thing* would have left quite a mess at the original grave site."

Robbie just nodded, and the two left the crime scene in silence. Once outside, Alex gulped for breath. Then, he vomited.

Robbie lit a cigarette. He wanted to say something comforting. He wanted—or, at least part of him did—to offer physical comfort. But he didn't know what to say and he certainly doubted Alex would welcome a hug from *him*.

Then, his phone rang. He took the call. "Alex, if you're feeling OK, we need to get a move on. Someone *has* called in from the cemetery. A while ago, apparently, but nobody made the connection until now."

"You drive," said Alex, simply, walking towards the car.

☼

"Someone definitely *did* drop the ball on that report," declared Alex.

Robbie and Alex were standing at the secondary crime scene, in an otherwise pristine cemetery of lovingly tended grass and largely new gravestones. The disturbance at the gravesite was nothing that could have been achieved with a shovel—or even an earthmover. It looked more like a volcanic eruption, with a deep crevasse where the grave once was, lined with ripped grass, scattered piles of dirt and pieces of what remained of the casket.

Around the site of the crevasse, which was sealed off with police tape and being carefully searched by forensic officers, also stood the remnants of a complicated ritual of necromantic summoning. There was a large, ruined shape that looked like a pentagram enclosed in a pair of concentric circles, linked with triangles. What substance this eerie shape had been etched in would no doubt be confirmed by the forensic officers. Around the pentagram and circle were the charred remains of what might have been reagents, used in the spell to summon the revenant.

"I guess," said Alex, "nobody would really have seen this if the perp did it at night."

"No," agreed Robbie, looking across the green expanse. "He would have been fine until this morning." Robbie used 'he' deliberately: 90% of homicides globally were committed by men, which corresponded with his own experience.

"This will be big news, won't it?" said Alex, touching his hair. Robbie knew that meant he was thinking, but presumably not just about the inevitable media coverage.

"Yeah," he agreed. "And I suspect that there will be a taskforce set up."

Alex nodded. "At least there's no revenant actually on the loose. The killer shut it down immediately, didn't he?" Again, *he*, playing the percentages.

"Indeed, he did," agreed Robbie. "Like a purpose-built device."

"Yes," mused Alex. "We're, what, almost 15 kilometres from Nerida's house. The killer had to somehow maintain control of this thing, then dispel it immediately. They must've been close by the whole time."

"Agreed," said Robbie.

"Yeah. And how?" Alex wondered. "Were they driving? Could you drive and hold control of something like *that* at the same time?"

"Or were they travelling some other way?" wondered Robbie.

Alex looked over to a forensics officer, who had just picked something white off the ground, on the fringe of the crime scene. Alex motioned her to come and show her what she had found, which she did.

"Gatekeeper," he said, looking at a small white business card.

"What?"

"That's what the card says: *gatekeeper*," insisted Alex, as the forensics officer bagged the card and walked away. "Whoever did this must have known we would find this scene, and that card. Why?"

"Misdirection, I assume," insisted Robbie absently. "Why else?"

"Probably," agreed Alex. "I take it we have an ID on the corpse?"

"Yep," Robbie confirmed. "Mewan Dissanayake. Originally from Sri Lanka, long-time magic professor in the UK, then became dean of MMS a few years after you—we left."

Alex nodded, touching his hair again. "After my time then," he said. "But it looks like we will be crawling all over MMS."

9

Robbie and Alex at Home (Not Together)

Robbie exited the train at Glen Waverley railway station: the end of the line. Robbie had grown up in the area, gone to school locally, and now found himself back here. There were, of course, many worse places to live than this comfortable pocket of Melbourne suburbia. But there was something about coming back 'home', to a place you thought you had left—especially when that return was forced by unplanned, unwanted circumstances—that made one feel they were 'back to square one' or had simply failed at life.

Robbie lit a cigarette once he was out of the station. His place—his mother's place, actually—wasn't far. The house was, like many newer homes in the area, one of three detached units that had been built on a large block after the original post-war dwelling on the site had been demolished. One of his neighbours, out gardening, waved and said hello. Robbie did the same, but he was still thinking about conjured abominations, slashing talons and that *smell*.

Robbie opened the door. He didn't need a key; the door unlocked and opened at his gesture and closed behind him. Once inside, he called out to his mother—"You home, Mum?"—then walked through the simple but tastefully appointed living room, beckoning a bottle of whisky and a glass into his hands from the kitchen as he did so.

He opened the sliding door to the outside courtyard, took a seat and poured himself a nip by hand. It was not yet dark and the evening was warm. He lit another cigarette, looking at his mother's tidy collection of both potted and planted flowers. Not that they were much of a distraction from his thoughts of horrified screams and desperate, futile struggles. They were very pretty, though. He downed the glass of whisky and immediately poured himself another one.

"Robbie," his mother said as she came outside. "I didn't hear you come in." She had an expression on her face that Robbie could easily translate. You could call it the 'you look terrible, darling, and are you really having whisky on a Monday?' look.

Michelle Chang was a slim, elegant woman. Her ancestry was European, including French—hence the Lorraine cross—and she had always dressed and carried herself with a quiet strength and dignity.

"Your father called," she said.

"Did he?" replied Robbie. Robbie had tried to forgive his father for walking out on them five years ago in a ridiculous, quasi-elderly-life crisis, as he had put it at the time. And walking out with a younger woman, who happened to be an accountant at the local tax agency franchise his parents had run successfully together for decades. "Was the fucking secretary not available, Dad?" he'd shouted at him at the time, in an outburst he refused to regret.

The sale of their business and the family home had left enough cash for Michelle to buy this place, not far from Robbie's childhood house. Two years after his parents' sudden split, the end of Robbie's own relationship—of course, he couldn't blame his lousy father for *that*—had sent Robbie back to Glen Waverley, and back to his mother.

"He wanted to know whether you were involved with that horrible murder on the news." As she said that, his mother looked like she might be eyeing the whisky for herself.

"Of course he did," smirked Robbie. As someone who had given up magic, or the professional practice of it at least, for accountancy ("When you were an immigrant from my generation, you didn't pursue magic, or join a band," he had explained) Robbie's dad had maintained a jealous interest in Robbie's work. Personally, Robbie often thought that doing tax returns might make for an easier, less traumatic life than investigating cases where magic had been placed in the service of humankind's worst depravities.

"Yes, I am. And yes, it was awful." And he felt like adding, but didn't: "I'm only telling you this because I know you want to know too, Mum."

"Have you eaten? I made a chicken casserole."

Robbie wondered whether his mother might have made this dish specifically because she thought he was working this horrific case and might need cheering up. His mother's signature chicken casserole—with shallots, mushrooms, white wine and a bit of cream—was a very comforting dish, indeed.

Robbie ate, and Michelle told him about her day. This ranged across a Church welfare committee meeting (her involvement with the Church having become even more intense since her retirement); a tricky tax return she was working on (she still did some freelance work, mainly for friends); and a dinner she was organising for some of her former employees from 'the old days'. It was all so wholesome and normal that it almost made Robbie stop thinking about vital organs being shredded by undead talons. Almost.

"My ex from uni, Alex, you remember him?" asked Robbie, mopping up the last of the sauce with a piece of bread. "He's working the case with me."

"Alex," mused Michelle. "Yes, Alex, the one before Jack."

"Yes," replied Robbie. "The one before Jack."

With dinner done, and after a final shot of whisky, Robbie suddenly felt very tired. It had been a long day. He walked up the stairs to his room, with its familiar cabaret posters and Lorraine cross. One of the few benefits of the divorce was that at least Robbie had not found himself back in his actual childhood bedroom. That would have been too dark altogether. As he now did every night, he prayed. Tonight, he prayed for the souls of a woman horribly murdered, and of a man whose remains had been desecrated to enable it.

Then, his phone pinged. It was from a gay hook-up app.

Wanna cum over tonight? (Pun intended ☺)

Robbie recognised the handle. Its owner and Robbie had 'messed around' a few times. He also recognised the distinct sense of malaise that messages like this made him feel. Until the end of his relationship, hook-up apps had been a mystery to him. He hadn't needed them. Before, there had always been 'nice boys', met through school, sport, and underage events put on by local gay charities. Then there had been uni guys, then Alex, then Jack.

By contrast, there were few nice boys on the apps he would consider bringing home to his mother. Instead, there seemed to be heaps of closet cases, weirdos and fetishists. He'd received a message once: "You're super-hot for an Asian! Are you a halfie?" (*Fuck off!*). He'd viewed a profile proclaiming that its owner was "not into tatts or Asians. Sorry!" Given how few Caucasian men did *not* have tattoos, Robbie wondered how that particular dickhead ever got any action at all.

All of this meant that his sexual experiences in the last few years had been a sequence of casual, broadly unsatisfying and emotionally neutered affairs in other people's often-squalid homes or even more squalid motels. Then there was what they wanted him to do. (Given his professional experiences, the apparent craze for choking, whether as choker or choked, was utterly out of the question for him.) Robbie, despite being—alongside his mother and most of their congregation—highly liberal and sex-positive, at least for Roman Catholics, was pretty sure God would prefer he found a boyfriend, a normal one. A nice one.

Not tonight, sorry, he replied to the message.

Then he undressed, put on the tracksuit pants he still preferred as sleepwear and went to bed. Staring at the Lorraine cross in the darkness, he found himself pondering what would drive someone to use the body of a university professor to kill another university professor. What on earth could be the motive?

At least he'd stopped thinking about the moment of the murder itself. And, all things considered, he slept surprisingly well.

As Robbie sat chatting with his mother over chicken casserole, Alex sat, largely in darkness, in a big, brown leather seat. On the marble coffee table next to him was a bottle of whisky, a glass, and a plate with sliced cheddar cheese, pickles and plain potato crisps. (Yes, this was 'dinner'. He and Josh were not great at keeping food in the house.)

His phone had pinged earlier, with a message from Josh: *Will be working late. Having dinner. About the Deal.* Alex had not replied. After all, why ruin his partner's day just because his own had been such an appalling shocker?

And the darkness worked. In it, Alex could hear and see the gunshot from that ridiculous bikie. He could see how he had sent the wave of ice, wind and water to trap him. He could see the shape of the abomination that had killed the woman who had interviewed him so many years ago. He could almost see what could have been, had he not outed himself as a magic user and gotten pulled into this case. He could see the burglary cases, the fraud cases, the car theft cases—even the occasional assault and sexual offence cases. The things he had known before, before he ruined everything and had to investigate a sorcerous atrocity.

He poured yet more whisky.

"Hey, babe, why are the lights off?" Josh had arrived home.

"Bad day."

"OK," said Josh, switching the lights on. He sat down opposite Alex, moving a chair. "Tell me about it."

Alex did. The high of solving the distillery case, then the sequence of ever more subterranean lows: the new case, the revenant, and even the involvement of his ex.

"Wait, can they make you do this case?" asked Josh, bemused and concerned.

"Well, I don't know if they can *make* me," replied Alex. "But, if you got asked to do a project at work that you were not keen on, would you say no?"

"I guess I wouldn't," conceded Josh. "But then, you know, it's not like you really need to work, babe."

"What?"

"It's true," insisted Josh, realising he had hit a nerve. "Most of the partners' wives at the firm don't work, or they do something like charity events and stuff."

"I'm not your wife, Josh! I'm not even your husband!"

"Alright, babe," Josh said, sitting himself on the arm of the seat that Alex was on. "I was just saying."

"I don't want to quit my job, babe," said Alex. "And this isn't one of those situations where I want you to solve the problem, like, practically. I just want you to listen and give me a hug or something."

"I can do that," said Josh, smiling reassuringly. And he leaned over the seat and embraced Alex, who planted his face into Josh's shoulder.

And he cried. Everything came together and he wept. Josh did nothing but continue to embrace him, until he said, "I reckon you need to go to bed, babe."

Josh almost, but not quite, carried Alex up the stairs into the bedroom. He sat him on the bed and undressed him, like a small child, even helping him into the pyjama bottoms Josh had worn the night before. (These were inscribed with snakes and ladders, like the board game.) He pulled the doona over Alex and went to undress himself. Alex began to cry a bit less, beginning to sniffle and clear his throat.

Soon enough, Josh climbed into bed and pulled Alex towards him. Alex again found Josh's shoulder and cried onto it: this time, now, more gentle sobs. In Josh's warm embrace, Alex had never felt so safe and comfortable.

"I love you, babe," Alex said.

"I love you, too," replied Josh.

"Sorry, I didn't even ask about the deal." Alex had now stopped sobbing completely.

"That can wait until tomorrow, babe."

10

Alex Tries Out for
the Magic Sports Team

10 years ago

"That's great, Lexi!"

Robbie looked on with satisfaction as Alex raised himself several metres into the air and hovered steadily with a churning wind at his feet, and the games room pool beneath him.

"I might need to think of a way to jazz it up for the trials," said Alex as he descended. "Maybe something with ice?" Looking at the contained storm, he added, "Also, don't the really good ones do something with both the water *and* the storm apparatus? I'll need to work on synchronising something—doing two things at once."

Robbie nodded. "OK, Lexi. You're right. But you're doing amazing already."

Alex walked up to Robbie and kissed him. "Well, I have a very good coach."

"And you seem to have conquered your fear of heights," said Robbie.

"What?" said Alex, confused.

"Remember our first night together?" said Robbie. "I lifted you up and you kind of freaked out. But you seem fine in the air now."

"Oh, that," replied Alex, shamefacedly. "That was a bit different, though. I mean, we had just met and—"

"So, it was more about trust than actual heights?"

"Yeah, I guess," admitted Alex. "But it's not like I could just say that, could I? 'Please let me down because I'm not sure I trust you. But can you please be my boyfriend too?'"

"Fair enough," agreed Robbie. "So can I do it now?"

"Robbie!"

"OK, OK, next time," he said, smiling wickedly. "Anyway, training session is over. I need to apply my coaching skills to your friend Jack's hopeless telekinesis."

"Thanks for doing that for me, Robbie," said Alex. The pair walked towards the games room exit, hand in hand. "And I've organised a dinner with you and my family, like you asked."

Robbie stopped walking. "Lexi, I said your dad, not both of your parents. I was thinking a one-on-one with whisky and cigars, talking about the police and, I dunno, my honourable intentions." Then, he stated to look genuinely horrified. "Wait, you said your *family*. Does that mean …?"

"Yes," Alex confirmed. "Catherine and Ivan too. *Please*, Robbie. I tried to contain things, but they all insisted, particularly Catherine." Alex adopted a haughty tone, in imitation of his elder sister. "Wow, Alex's first *proper* boyfriend! We just *have* to meet him!"

"But all of them at once?" complained Robbie. "What if they don't like me?"

"They will," insisted Alex. "I promise!"

"The things I do for you, Lexi," replied Robbie, as he started walking again towards the exit.

"You're the best!" cried Alex.

"I don't get why my uniform for the tryouts consists of these shorts and literally nothing else," whined Alex. "Half of the events aren't even *in* the water, and it's not as if I can't dry myself immediately if I get wet."

Alex and Robbie were in the changeroom next to the MMS games room, where trials for the MMS magic athletics team were about to commence. The changeroom was about the most ordinary part of MMS, with lockers, benches, linoleum floors and that distinct, not entirely pleasant changeroom smell that seemed to be the same everywhere. There were many young men in various stages of undress or skimpy uniforms, with a slight hubbub created from multiple quiet conversations.

Alex was slouched on a bench as Robbie pulled on his fitted bottoms and singlet, in black and MMS maroon. Alex was wearing a pair of blue—signifying the joint elements of water, wind and ice—shorts, with the MMS crest and name in gold, and staring distastefully at his bare legs.

"That is how it's been since, like, the 1950s," said Robbie. "And it's the same for all the elements: water, fire, earth."

"Well, that is fascinating history, Professor Chang, but it's not really an explanation, is it?" replied Alex. "Just because someone decided something in the 1950s, when we didn't allow Asian immigration, or let married women into the public service!"

Robbie chuckled. "Babe, seriously? It's probably a legacy of when this stuff was more entertainment than sport. Someone standing in ice, or walking through fire, in just some shorts makes it look real. Like they aren't just doing some non-magic illusion in a special suit or are fakes like Harry Houdini. Also," he added, "the earth guys do often get pretty dirty."

"Still," said Alex, sourly, "you would think they could update things."

Robbie looked at Alex with a sense of indulgence. "Lexi, your body is amazing. I don't understand why you're so funny about it. Especially your legs. I really like your legs."

"You only ever see my legs when they're over your shoulders, and you're fucking me," insisted Alex. "Usually in the dark. Can't you just admit that I'm right?"

"OK," said Robbie, smiling. "First, that is a much dirtier response than I would have expected from you." Alex blushed a little; he had been surprised by his own comment. "And second, I'm looking at your legs now, and they are fine."

"You would say that, though," argued Alex.

"Third," declared Robbie, "you only have to wear the official uniform for these tryouts and in competitions. In training, you can wear long pants, leather shoes, a trench coat, whatever you want."

Alex was poised to react, but a voice broke into their conversation. "Hey, R, great to see you!"

That voice, with a distinct American accent, belonged to a tall, muscular, very handsome man. He sported very short, almost shaved black hair, very dark skin, and a pair of red MMS shorts, suggesting a fire affinity. Alex suspected he also sported no hang-ups about his body in general, or legs in particular.

"Hey, Assane!" cried Robbie. "Great to see you!" The pair embraced. Assane, who was smiling widely, was as tall as Robbie but broader, and even lifted him a little off the ground as they hugged.

Assane looked Alex up and down, in a way Alex wasn't sure how to take. It certainly didn't seem that he was looking at Alex *that way*. Was he looking disapprovingly at Alex's legs?

"Alex, yeah?" said Assane, disarmingly. "Robbie has told me about you. Said you're very good with the water, wind and ice. Especially for a first generation."

"Like, you mean, for someone from a *muggle* family?" posed Alex.

"Well, yeah, I guess," said Assane. "Most of the people that sign up for magic sports are multi-generational. I didn't ..." he looked to Robbie for support. "It wasn't meant as a diss."

"He's just nervous," Robbie replied. "And he has a thing about showing his legs."

"What's wrong with your legs?" asked Assane.

Alex wasn't to be deterred. "Well, I guess we will have to see how this horrible muggle who doesn't really belong here goes, won't we?"

"Dude, I didn't say that!" Assane said, exasperated. Then he planted his huge arms either side of the bench, leaning forward and making Alex lean back. "And, if we're playing victim Olympics, can I mention that my enslaved ancestors were trafficked to America to clear land for the plantations with their magic?" Assane leaned even further in, as Alex cowered. "And that they were seen as *so* dangerous, they were kept in special cages?"

"What is it with you established magic people and knowing what your relatives did in the nineteenth century?" said Alex, precarious, but clearly not willing to concede the point.

"A," announced Robbie. "I think you've made your point. My boyfriend is practically falling off the bench—and you really cannot blame every pretty white boy for slavery."

"He started it," said Assane, pulling back and putting his arms across his chest.

"No, I didn't!" whined Alex. "You did!"

"OK, time out," declared Robbie. "Let's reset, shall we? A, why don't you tell Lexi about your art project. He's pretty into art."

"Is he?" asked Assane, grinning.

"Yeah, I guess I am," conceded Alex, aware of Robbie's eyes, entreating him to be nice. "What sort of art do you do?"

"I used to do fire art," Assane said, clearly enthusiastic. "But my work now is based around telekinesis. Robbie taught it to me." He spread his arms in a circular pattern. "It lets me paint the whole space."

"A is a postgrad, doing a residency in magical art. It's a pretty big deal," added Robbie. "He's from America, obviously."

"Sounds cool," said Alex, as he sat back up on the bench, crossing his legs. His words did not match his unenthusiastic tone.

"Oh, come on, Alex," said Assane. "Let me show you how I work one time, OK? I'm not actually trying to get off on the wrong foot with a potential teammate."

"Alright," said Alex, still sounding somewhat unhappy—and unwilling. "What? I said yes!" he cried as he looked at Assane, then Robbie. "I would love to see the *artiste* in action."

"Excellent!" said Assane, as if Alex's affirmative answers had been much more sincere than they clearly were. "Good luck out there," he continued, turning to leave. "And, oh, I know the *uniform* is a thing. Like, the shorts and nothing else. But, once you get into the magic games, you'll forget all about it. I did. And your legs aren't even *that* skinny. See you out there in a moment!"

"Your friend is a jerk, Robbie," said Alex.

Robbie smiled. "A bit, yeah. But, Lexi, your 'I am a middle-Melbourne, middle-class muggle' victim thing is not always going to get the best response, is it? Particularly when you, like, misread the room." Robbie trailed off as Alex scowled at him.

Alex grinned. "Are you worried about pissing me off by telling me to pull my head in?"

"Yes," said Robbie, simply.

The pair looked at each other, then kissed. "I know you're going to nail this," said Robbie.

Then, they joined the general exodus from the changeroom.

Alex and Robbie walked into the cavernous games room space, alongside a gaggle of other magic athletics students, all giggling and chatting to one another. Standing in the centre of the room was a severe, large woman with a whistle. She looked like a coach from an American high school movie. And, just as Alex was thinking this—yes, she *blew the whistle*.

"Manipulation and telekinesis trials are first," declared the coach, whose booming voice projected with ease across the huge room. "Elements participants should go to the grandstand."

Alex looked across to the side of the room. There, he only now noticed, was a stand (not so grand, to be fair). The elements athletes, notable by their semi-nakedness, were drifting towards the seats. There was a larger stand, too. This, he was sure, must be of recent construction, where interested non-athletes could watch the trials. This larger stand was maybe half-full, likely with friends and family of those trying out. Alex wondered why it hadn't occurred to him to ask any of his own friends, let alone family, to attend. Nerves?

"Wish me luck, Lexi," said Robbie.

"Good luck, Robbie," replied Alex, kissing Robbie on the cheek. As Alex padded over towards the 'grandstand', he saw Yolanda going in the same direction. "Hey, Yol," he said. "You didn't say you would be trying out for this."

"Hi, Alex," she said, smiling. "I kept it quiet. A lot of the others aren't so keen, or their affinity isn't part of the games."

This was true, many students didn't bother to try out—they wanted to focus on the academic or social sides of studying magic. Affinities like healing or mentalism weren't part of the games at all. Illusion and summoning were in a separate try-out, with separate rules. The latter disciplines reminded Alex of figure skating and ice dancing: treated as much like an art as a sport. Transformation contenders, however, were third on the bill today.

"But I've been training," she said. "And I reckon I'm in with a shot, at least." Yolanda, who was wearing the earth affinity female uniform—green shorts but with a fitted, matching green singlet top (admittedly, a midriff-baring one)—grabbed Alex's hand as they walked towards the seats. "Who is the big black guy in the red shorts?" asked Yolanda. "He seems to be looking at you."

He was. He was also tapping the seats next to him, as if he was saving them for Alex and, presumably, Yolanda. "That's Assane," groaned Alex. "He's friends with Robbie. He was giving me a lecture about his ancestors and slavery before."

"You didn't do your whole muggle victim routine with him, did you?" asked Yolanda.

"Yeah, I guess I did," conceded Alex. "But he started it!"

"Geez, Alex," replied Yolanda. "Maybe I should give a lecture on the invasion of Australia too, then, whitefella," said Yolanda, grinning.

"Maybe we could sit somewhere else?" asked Alex, hopefully.

"Nah, mate!" declared Yolanda, pulling Alex over to the seats next to Assane.

"Hey Alex," said Assane. "Your boyfriend will be up soon. Who is this?"

"Yolanda," said Yolanda. "I'm a first year, with Alex."

"Cool. I'm Assane. There is some tough competition in the elements category for the team this year."

"I'm used to being underestimated. Bring it on!" replied Yolanda.

"I like your style," said Assane. "This one," he said, pointing to Alex, "seemed more concerned about his legs being too skinny than he was about competing."

"That's not …" Alex started to protest.

"I don't get it," said Yolanda, confused, ignoring Alex's attempted interjection. "Your legs are fine."

"Now we are starting the telekinesis and teleportation trials," declared the coach, voice booming again. "As always, if you're not part of this particular event, please stay on the grandstand and well away from any action. This is for safety reasons."

"Thank God, it's starting," Alex whispered to himself.

There were six manipulation and telekinesis practitioners vying for two spots: one for the individual event, and an additional one to partner with the individual winner for the team event. Much like gymnastics, magical competitions were based on 'routines', generally scored by judges, but sometimes also timed. A panel of three (Alex recognised John Bishop, but none of the others) sat at a booth, also previously unnoticed by him, at the other end of the giant room.

"Your boyfriend is a shoo-in for this, I reckon," declared Assane, placing a hand on Alex's shoulder in an altogether too familiar gesture. Alex did not reply.

The manipulation and telekinesis routine involved 'juggling' large metal balls, as Robbie had shown Alex the night they met. It also involved a combination of self-propulsion and teleportation through an obstacle course made up of the floating platforms. At the end of the routine, the athlete would teleport some or all of the balls to the end of the course, however many they could, and arrange them how they wished.

Robbie stood at the far left of the six contestants. He would be the last to try out. There was polite clapping as the first contender came forward. She levitated six of the balls, sending them flying around herself in a constrained, yet steady circle. She sent them up into the air. They danced to her telekinetic tune, steadily but unremarkably. Her face, even from Alex's vantage point, was strained with concentration.

Then she sent the balls back to the ordered pile in the corner of the games room, much as she had left them. She propelled herself up to the first floating platform of the obstacle course. In a series of telekinetic lunges and teleportations, she navigated the course, finally teleporting down at the other side of the games room. There, she teleported six of the balls, holding them in front of her in a three-by-two rectangular wall.

Again, there was polite applause. The next contestant completed the course. Then the next, and the next. As the subsequent hopefuls finished their trials, there were differences at the margins. Some juggled the metal balls across a greater area than others, or did so more quickly. Others were faster on the obstacle course. But the overall performance and scoring were similar.

That was until the penultimate competitor, Nora, a second-year student according to Assane. She juggled more balls than the others—eight, rather than six. She also did so across greater distances, both sideways and upwards, and faster. She was also quicker to complete the platform course. She appeared at the end of the course, and conjured eight of the metal balls, rotating them in a diamond pattern. The applause was louder than for the others. The judges' note-taking and discussions were more intense. Their weighted scores—including a mix of time, speed, distance and more qualitative judgements—were notably higher. Robbie didn't look especially concerned.

Then, it was his turn. Grinning widely, betraying no sense of stress or doubt, he sent twelve of the metal balls swinging around frenetically, though with a clear pattern, up and down to the floor and ceiling of the games room. They flew as close to the four walls as was allowed for safety. Sending the balls back to the corner of the space, he completed the obstacle course. To the naked eye, it was hard to tell which parts involved telekinesis and which parts teleportation: he was essentially a blur. Almost immediately, he stood at the end of the obstacle course, with twelve balls floating around, twisting and swirling in a circular pattern in front of him.

The magic athletes and spectators erupted with cheers and claps. The judges gave much higher scores, then announced that Robbie was the individual telekinesis representative for MMS, with Nora as his partner for team events. Robbie looked over to Alex, grinning.

Assane put both his hands on Alex's shoulders. "I told you he was a shoo-in. Now it's your turn."

"So, Alex, are you still thinking about your skinny legs?"

"No," replied Alex. "Or I wasn't until *you* mentioned it."

"Told you so," said Assane, triumphantly.

Alex and Assane, along with Yolanda and eight others, were lined up for the elements trials. The elements competition wasn't as structured as the telekinesis one. There were no set slots for each element—rather, the combination depended on which four practitioners were the most compelling, irrespective of what element they represented. Likewise, there was more discretion for the athlete on how he or she performed their routine. Judging, however, was similar, being based on the scale of the exercise, its precision, a lack of errors and general flair.

Aside from Alex, Assane and Yolanda, there were three competitors in green shorts (earth); two in blue (water, wind and ice); two in red (fire and smoke) and one in white (the rare sub-affinity of electricity). The electricity contestant had long, dirty-blonde hair and blue eyes. He looked more like a surfer than a magician.

"Do you know who that is?" Alex asked Assane.

"The electricity guy? No idea," said Assane.

Assane, Yolanda and Alex were first up to compete, in that order. Assane looked at Alex and said, "Just go nuts. Don't worry about anything. You'll do great!"

"OK," said Alex, uninterestedly.

Assane looked at him for a moment, then sauntered over to the marked starting position in front of the pool-sized zone of slightly smouldering ashes. To say he looked confident and assured would have been an understatement. He knelt, assuming a position akin to a sprinter waiting for the starting gun.

Then, he burst into flames.

He surged through the air in an arc of flame, landing on the smouldering ashes. These burst into flame at the same time, reaching metres into the air.

Assane rose again, atop a huge plume of fire, like a phoenix rising from the ashes. As he lifted himself higher and higher, he waved his hands—as if conducting an orchestra—and great arcs of fire swirled around him, like wings.

Assane clapped his hands, and the flames died down, replaced with a far duller fire and lots of black smoke, which circled around him in something that looked a bit like a controlled whirlwind.

Alex, the watching magic athletes and the other observers looked agog. This was impressive.

In his final act, Assane clasped his hands together, pulling the smoke towards them until it formed into a sold ball in his hands. He then descended slowly on a tower of bright flames until he landed on the now inert ash, put his ball of solidified smoke on the ground, and took a small bow.

Everyone erupted with applause.

"That is a hard act to follow," complained Yolanda.

Alex just nodded, speechless.

Yolanda was up next. Despite her comment, she seemed calm and composed as she walked to her marked starting position in front of the large mound of dirt, rock and vegetation.

She stood tall and raised her arms. A huge 'tentacle' of gnarled branches, leaves, pebbles and dirt shot out of the pile of earth and arced up, then down, consuming Yolanda. It then pulled back into the pile of earth.

The earth then convulsed in regular, rhythmic patterns, throwing rocks, dirt and plant matter into the air. Then the earth 'tentacle' again shot up into the air, with Yolanda at its head. It stayed suspended in the air as Yolanda extended her arms, like a cross, and bushy branches materialised and spread metres out from them. Another branch shot up from her head.

Green leaves quickly formed around Yolanda and the branches, ultimately creating an image of a tree much like that in a child's picture book, with a huge trunk and a massive circular top of green leaves. Yolanda was entirely obscured by her creation.

All at once, the leaves fell away, revealing Yolanda wrapped in branches. These now receded, quickly and elegantly, back past her arms and down past her head. Her tree lowered itself back into the pile of earth, bringing Yolanda back to the ground.

Yolanda bowed. Everyone clapped. Assane whooped.

"Talk about a fucking hard act to follow!" whispered Alex to himself.

Still, there was nothing for it. Alex felt his legs shake as walked to his starting position. It would occur to him only after the fact, and despite Assane's dig, that he hadn't thought about his skinny legs once as he waited to compete. Assane was right, annoyingly. The starting position was in front of the pool of water that Alex had frozen the night he met Robbie.

"You can do it, Lexi!" shouted Robbie.

Not sure that's helpful, Robbie, thought Alex.

"Go kill it, Alex!" Assane cried out.

That's definitely not fucking helpful!

Alex bent his legs, a bit like a diver, and leapt into the air. Beneath his feet a pillar of ice formed and surged upwards. Much like Yolanda's earth tentacle, but in reverse, the ice stream arced upwards, then downwards, dropping Alex into the pool of water, which immediately froze.

Alex waited, just for a moment, in the frozen pool. *So far, so good.*

He shattered the ice, and it started to melt. He sent the ice and water—and himself—surging into the air. There, he stood atop a roiling plume of water and ice. He held this position for a few moments, counting down: "Three, two, one."

As he hovered in the air, the contained storm apparatus started to churn and darken in a consistent rhythmic pattern.

The ice was now fully melted and the water became vapour; Alex disappeared into a cloud of steam, held in the air by an invisible eddy of wind. He let the steam disperse, just widely enough to not frizz everyone's hair, then pulled it back towards him. It was at this point that he admitted to himself that, yes, he was really nailing it!

The contained storm apparatus flashed with lightning, then went completely dark, before resuming its previous pattern.

Meanwhile, the water now circled him as a smooth, huge sphere of liquid. He let the water slowly sink back into the pool. The water was still, aside from the agitation caused by the wind keeping him aloft, and a small frozen platform on the side of the pool. He gently descended to that platform, stepped out of the pool, and gave a little Assane-style bow.

Thanks to both receding adrenalin and his general sense of elation, Alex didn't really hear the applause as he walked over to the small athletes' stand.

Robbie was consumed with excitement, running up to Alex as he approached and sweeping him into his arms. "That was amazing, Lexi. I knew you could do it!"

"Thanks, Robbie," he replied.

The pair finished the journey to the stand, holding hands. There, Yolanda was picking twigs and leaves from her hair and wiping soil off her arms with a towel. She got up to embrace him as he approached. As, unfortunately, did Assane.

"You dark horse," she told him as they hugged. "That was great."

"I knew you would nail it!" declared Assane. Then, without warning— let alone permission—he pulled Alex into a bear-hug, lifting him clean off the ground. Alex wondered whether he should be affronted by this level of uninvited physical affection. But he was more concerned, given the amount of naked flesh contact—with Assane's hot skin and hard, bulging muscles—that he might have another physical reaction that could prove a little embarrassing.

"OK, thanks, Assane. You can put me down now."

Assane did as he was told, and the little group sat in the small stand. The judges announced Alex's scores. They were good, even slightly higher than Yolanda's and just a fraction of a point lower than Assane's. Alex started to think that he might actually win a spot in the team.

"I should've brought some clothes," said Alex, looking back down at his legs.

"I brought some tracksuit pants," announced Robbie, pulling a pair out of his bag and handing them to Alex, who put them on.

"No shirt, I take it?" he asked.

"I didn't realise that would be an issue. Sorry, Lexi," said Robbie. "But I guess you could wear mine." Before Alex could say it wasn't necessary, Robbie had pulled off his singlet and handed it over.

"Any excuse to show off the bod, huh?" said Assane, grinning at Robbie.

"I don't see you putting any clothes on yourself, A."

"Hey, I'm just staying in uniform!"

Alex ignored them. He'd never worn Robbie's clothes before. Robbie's shirt smelled so much like him. It made him think about what Robbie might want to do to him later, by way of celebration.

The next contestant was up, another earth practitioner. Their routine was competent enough, but not nearly as spectacular as Yolanda's. The same applied to the next set of contenders.

The fourth and final earth athlete stepped forward. He had orange-red hair, a classic carrot-top, and freckles covered his face and shoulders. He had some of the self-confident look of Assane as he stepped, smiling and nonchalant, to the starting position.

"That's Ryan. He's good," said Assane. "He made the team last year."

And he was. His routine centred more on manipulating rocks, but its scale and ambition were similar. He sent flurries of rock, along with himself, into the air, and had the stones circle around him, bobbing rhythmically. He made the pile of earth pulse and heave, even more than Yolanda had done. This felt like the first performance that could challenge the leading three, all of whom were silent.

In the end, the redhead's routine scored just lower than Yolanda's. She was visibly relieved.

"That means the three of us are in!" declared Assane, triumphantly. "Now we just need to see whether Ryan will be in the team with us, or the electricity guy."

Said electricity guy now walked towards a marked starting position. This position wasn't in front of any of the four obvious element spaces. It was only when Alex looked up, noticing a long metal pole had descended from the ceiling, that the starting point made sense.

A moment later, the pole, the contestant and—seemingly—much of the whole cavernous space flashed and crackled with electricity. It took Alex a moment longer to realise that one of the walls of the games room was criss-crossed with wires, as the electric surfer raced along these as a ball of blinding white energy. It wasn't even clear whether the surfer was surrounded by electricity or had *become* electricity.

Then the lightning arced from the wall onto the earth apparatus, with the small trees crackling with electricity. He then 'bounced' himself off the earth apparatus, again carried by what looked like solid, pulsing energy. Setting foot back on the ground, he did a bigger bow than any other competitor.

The applause was somewhat muted. Alex suspected that this was because people were stunned. Electricity practitioners were rarely part of these events, so a display of such skill and power would be a novelty for many attendees. It certainly was for Alex.

"I'm pretty sure he will be joining us on the team," said Alex, to nobody in particular.

He was right.

"Yeah, James, but Jamie to my friends." This was the electric surfer, talking to Assane, who had gone up to him and shaken his hand. (He had not, in his overly familiar way, given him a big hug and swept him off his feet, as he had done to Alex.)

"Hi Jamie," said Alex.

"Yes, hi," said Yolanda.

"Hi," replied Jamie. "Are you two first-years as well?" he asked, looking at Alex and Yolanda.

"Yeah, we are," replied Yolanda, grinning. "We swept aside the old guard, didn't we?"

"Yeah, we did," agreed Jamie.

"Except for Assane," Alex clarified. "He's like postgrad or something. I'm not even sure he's still technically a student here."

"I am," insisted Assane. "Alex is just being mean because I called him out for pretending to be a victim."

Jamie looked slightly confused.

"Anyway," declared Yolanda, "we should go out and celebrate."

"OK, but maybe give us an hour or two to freshen up?" said Alex.

"You and Robbie want to *celebrate* together first?" said Assane.

"Alex and Robbie—the telekinesis guy—they're a couple," Yolanda explained to Jamie. "I probably should have a shower anyway," she continued.

"Let's meet out the front in an hour-and-a-half," stated Assane, conclusively. "I'm sure that's long enough for you and Robbie, Alex."

Just as the group was dispersing, an earnest-looking young man with curly dark hair and glasses sitting at the end of his nose bounded up to them. "Hi, my name's Nathan, I'm from the *Cockatrice*—the school paper," he explained, a little breathless. "You guys were amazing. I think is the first time we've had three first-years in the elements team since, like, before we were all born."

"Yeah, we are pretty damn good," declared Yolanda, grinning.

"So, you wouldn't mind if I did a little story about it, maybe with some quotes, like that one?"

"Well, maybe not that one," replied Yolanda. "But yeah, sure, why not?"

The others nodded.

"And you,' said Nathan, looking at Jamie. "You were something else. We haven't had an electric in the elements team since the nineties. I actually checked that one."

"Yeah, we aren't super common," agreed Jamie.

"I will need your full names," said Nathan. "Let's start with you, then, Jamie."

"James," said Jamie. "James Archer."

11

Taskforce Revenant

Present day

Robbie sat on the Glen Waverley line train into the city, as it trundled through every one of its too many stops. (The line suffered from a shocking lack of express services.) His long hair, pulled back into the bun he had worn for the last several years, was still damp, almost wet. He hadn't had time this morning to properly dry it; drops of water occasionally coalesced around the strands and dropped onto his forehead, which itself was scrunched up in thought.

The news websites had, of course, caught hold of the necromancy case. Some were sensationalising it and, despite Alex's earlier observation, not even reporting that the revenant summoned to kill the victim had been summarily banished and wasn't still at large.

This wasn't unusual in terms of coverage of magic in the popular press. While the emancipation of magicians had started far earlier than other rights movements—before slavery had been abolished in the British empire, let alone America; earlier than women's suffrage and long before feminism, gay rights, or anything to do with gender—progress had been far more gradual and grudging.

Robbie's phone pinged. It was a property listing for a place in Prahran, a trendy Melbourne neighbourhood. The sender was one of Robbie's oldest friends, Evan Ellis, back from his time going to underage gay events as a teenager.

"An unapologetically hot 'pad' in one of Melbourne's premier café, dining, shopping and nightlife precincts," the listing gushed. "This modern home will appeal to the discerning first home buyer—or the savvy investor. Boasting polished floorboards throughout, coupled with European appliances, this compelling dwelling is minutes' walk from everything Prahran has to offer."

This friend, who worked in real estate and bought his first property at about 21—an 'investment' one, of course—was, in fairness, trying to help. After all, at 31, Robbie should really have his own place. He earned a decent income, in the scheme of things. And there had even been offers of financial assistance, both from his mother and his ridiculous father.

If he were being honest with himself—which he wasn't inclined to do today—Robbie's current housing situation was less to do with a lack of financial resources or options, and more due to his abiding fear of being completely alone. Obviously, his mother couldn't sleep in the same bed with him, comfort him when he woke in fright, or listen as he shared awful memories in the middle of the night. But at least she was *there*, making coffee in the morning, dinner in the evening—and available to chat with him at other times when he needed company.

Meanwhile, the idea of returning, at the end of each day, to a dark, empty home; then waking up in one each morning—with only his whisky bottles, empty cigarette packets, cabaret posters and Lorraine cross for company—filled him with something like dread.

Missed you last night. The alternative was pretty shit, but I had to make do. Want to see some photos?

That was the guy from the app, again. "How romantic!" Robbie muttered out loud. Unfettered access to hook-ups certainly didn't seem like fair compensation for his loneliness. But the train had pulled into the downtown Southern Cross station, also the end of the line. And Robbie knew it would be another big day.

No, I don't. But let's chat later, he texted in response.

Police headquarters was buzzing with movement when Alex arrived, late. Given the day he had yesterday, he did not feel at all guilty about it. It was clear that a taskforce to investigate the 'necromancer murder' had been established. It was also clear that Alex had just missed the assignment of duties for the day.

Amid the hubbub and chatter of police officers agreeing plans of attack for their tasks, and making for the lifts to hit the road, Alex searched for a familiar face. To his surprise, he saw three: Robbie, Isabella and—of course, *of course*—Pav. In the circumstances, he was pretty happy to see even the latter, though his heart sank when he saw Pav talking to Robbie.

"Hey, PB," Pav called out as he noticed Alex. "Looks like we're all going to be working on your witchy murder! And I just found out that you and this gorgeous gentleman," Pav patted Robbie on the shoulder, as the latter looked at his shoes, "used to date! You really do bag the lookers, PB, and I speak from an entirely disinterested sexual persuasion."

"Excuse Pav," smiled Isabella. "He's just a dickhead. It's a condition. Besides," she continued, "we have work to do, don't we, Pav?"

"Alright, yes," said Pav. Then, he said to Alex: "Izzy and I have been tasked with going down a list of known—what do you call them?—summoners in Melbourne and interviewing them about their whereabouts the night of the murder. Needle and haystack duty, basically. The superhero squad, though—" Pav gestured at Alex and Robbie "—you two are off to interview the head of the magic school."

"Are we?" asked Alex, looking at Robbie.

"Yep, we are," he replied. "Crawling all over MMS, like you said."

In the car on the way to MMS, a short drive, Alex found himself wondering about his ex, and why they had been paired together. There had been no time for explanation yesterday. The whole thing had seemed to Alex like an absurd state of affairs. However, looking at Robbie, who was watching the road, lost in thought with his silly man-bun and inscrutable expression, Alex was reluctant to broach the subject. Would Robbie even know why they had been brought together? Did he have anything to do with it?

As they approached MMS, Robbie started talking about the case. "Tammy Mazur is the new dean ... a summoner, as it happens. Word is that there were a few issues with the staff and morale before she was promoted to the top job."

"And maybe after?" wondered Alex.

Their car pulled into one of the few visitors spots available.

"I have to go, Laurence. I think the police are here." Tammy Mazur put down her phone.

She was clearly agitated. Her bob haircut framed her wide head in much the same way that her cardigan framed her wide body. She had a face that might have normally seemed kindly, but now looked harried and stressed. Alex assumed the 'Corporate Affairs guys' at Victoria police—and its commissioners—might be looking similar to Tammy Mazur right now, though, in her case, the anxiety would be magnified, given dealing with a murder wasn't exactly part of the job description for a university head.

"Sorry, I was just talking with our chair—our outgoing chair," she said, failing to appear calm while surveying the many manila folders on her desk for no apparent reason. When she finally looked up from her desk and its pile of files, she asked, "Are you the detectives?"

Alex supressed a smile at this, being familiar with the sentiment. And, to be fair, both he and Robbie were still quite young, and possibly looked even younger than they were. But Robbie hardly lacked gravitas, with his height, broad shoulders and commanding voice. The man-bun, which must surely skirt the perimeter of Victoria Police grooming requirements, couldn't help, though. (Alex dismissed any thought about why he seemed so obsessed with Robbie's hair, or why he struggled not to look at Robbie in general.)

Meanwhile, Robbie did not skip a beat. "Yes, we are. I'm Robert Chang, from the Magic Squad," he said, flashing his badge. "This is Alexander Hicks, from Melbourne CID. We're both magic users and are part of the Revenant murder taskforce. And," he said with emphasis, "we need to know whatever you can tell us about Nerida Stein and Mewan Dissanayake."

Robbie's firm introduction, delivered in a reassuring, school principal tone, seemed to settle the nerves of the new dean of Melbourne Magic School. (Why couldn't Alex do that?) She stopped darting her eyes around the folder-covered surface of her desk and sat, looking Robbie in the eyes. She motioned for the two detectives to sit too, and there were three plastic chairs to choose from opposite her. Alex sat, pulling out a notepad and pen, and largely let Robbie take control of the situation.

"Where should I start?" asked Tammy.

"With Nerida," replied Robbie. "How did she get along with her colleagues? Were there any rivalries, jealousies, anything out of the ordinary?"

"Not really," said Tammy, sounding unsure. "But, before I started and, you know, even now, there were some problems of—of morale, I suppose."

"What sort of problems?" inquired Robbie. "And was Nerida particularly affected?"

Tammy seemed to think for a moment. "Yes, I think Nerida was," she conceded. "You see, her great friend, John Bishop, applied for the dean job that Mewan got. A lot of the staff wanted John to get it. But he and Nerida were especially close."

Tammy picked up a cup of coffee, which Alex hadn't noticed before, given the clutter on her desk, and took a gulp. Robbie just watched, retaining eye contact with Tammy.

"They did the undergraduate admissions together, you see," she continued, eventually. "John was nominally in charge of it, but she made most of the decisions, really. Working with John was a real highlight for Nerida. When John was passed over for this job, Nerida was upset." Tammy suddenly exclaimed, "Wait, I know you! You studied here—

what, 10 years ago? I took you for first year Theory and History of Magic, and you won the telekinesis games one time."

"Twice, actually," said Robbie, completely deadpan.

Tammy looked embarrassed. "Yes, sorry, I mean I know it's not relevant to this. But you still look exactly the same, except your hair's different. That is why I didn't recognise you."

Robbie was impassive. Alex, again, supressed a smile. That hair!

"Anyway, so Nerida," Tammy said, "she was a bit discombobulated at the whole situation. But, you know, she did hang around. She didn't leave."

Robbie said, again deadpan, "And nobody, you think, would want to do her harm? On the MMS staff?"

"No," Tammy cried. "Nothing like that. This is so horrible!"

Robbie seemed to be deep in thought, so Alex touched his hair and asked, "What about Nerida's research? What was she working on?"

Tammy looked at Alex quizzically, clearly not thinking about Nerida's research. "You," she said. "You're familiar as well."

"I was in your class too," replied Alex. "But I dropped out after first year."

"I see," said Tammy. Then: "Wait, weren't you two—"

"Could you please answer my colleague's question?" directed Robbie, exemplifying charismatic authority.

"Sorry, of course," she replied. "In recent years, Nerida's research had focused on gender, in terms of differences in affinities; why women are more likely to study—but less likely to actually work in—magic; and how magic is potentially hostile to gender-diverse people."

"So, she was a feminist?" suggested Robbie.

Tammy scoffed slightly. "Not really. I mean she *was* a feminist, on some level, but that was mainly about playing the grant system. I mean, we're not a business or law school. We need to get money from the government to survive, and Nerida knew how to get grant funding."

"Did she develop your indigenous program for that reason?" asked Alex, taking some notes.

"Yes, yes she did," replied Tammy cautiously. "Though, you know, she actually believed in that. Certainly more so than the other stuff."

"I see," said Robbie. "Is there anything else we should know about Nerida?"

"No, I really don't think so," insisted Tammy, earnestly. "It was just, you know, workplace stuff. Nothing so unusual, nothing to explain …"

"OK," said Robbie, calmly. "What about in her personal life? Did you know anything about that?"

"Just a little," said Tammy, looking sightly flustered again. "But, you know, there was nothing unusual. Nothing *sordid*. She was usually single, sometimes there was a man, but nothing out of the ordinary."

"The same man, on and off?" asked Robbie.

"No, definitely not," insisted Tammy. "And none recently, anyway."

"Thanks," said Alex, pleasantly. "We will need a list of other summoners on the faculty—sorry if someone has already asked for it."

"No problems at all," replied Tammy, looking uselessly at the surface of her desk again. "First off, there is our Professor of Summoning, Harry Archer," Tammy said, with a tone that was hard to place.

"That name sounds familiar," said Alex.

"Yes, you might recognise the name," her voice now more clearly disapproving. "Harry is a bit of a talking head on the radio and TV on magic-related matters. The Archer family is also a very prominent magic family, which you probably know."

"Yes, I do know," said Robbie. "And how did Harry Archer get along with the victims?"

"Well," Tammy started, cautiously, "I'm sure this has nothing to do with the *murder*, but, ah, Nerida and Harry did not get along."

"Any particular reason why not?" pressed Robbie.

"Harry and Mewan were very chummy," she said. "Mewan really promoted him, I mean, literally. Made him an associate professor at 30. Many of the faculty thought his rise was too meteoric, too quick. Underserved. Some thought he had undue influence over Mewan, that he used it to get ahead and flaunted it. They called him Prince Harry."

"Then there was the TV stuff and his family connections?" Alex asked, a leading question.

"Yes. That too," she said. "It's a thing in academia. If people think you've not really paid your dues, it makes people upset. Resentful." Alex reflected that the police force wasn't so different, in that respect. Just ask Pav. "And, yes," she continued, "being so … telegenic, becoming almost a media celebrity. None of that helped."

"We'll need to talk to him," said Robbie simply.

"Of course," replied Tammy, pulling a piece of paper from a pocket. "I figured you'd ask. He's at this address currently, examining a haunting. He does that quite often."

"Thanks," said Robbie. "We will meet him there. One last question, where were you on the night of the murder?"

Tammy bristled, then checked herself—the question couldn't have been a surprise. "I was with my husband at home. We were belatedly discovering *Squid Game*."

"I see. Thanks," said Robbie. "We'll need to check that. Could we get contact information for him?"

"Of course," replied Tammy. She seemed to like the expression 'of course'. "But he's on the staff too. He's the head librarian."

"We'll talk with him, too," said Robbie. "But I think we need to talk to Harry Archer first."

On the longer drive to meet 'Prince Harry', Alex and Robbie initially remained silent. This started to bother Alex. He had always enjoyed chatting with his partners, notably Isabella, and wondered how their partnership could possibly work if they refused to talk to each other about anything but the case. They couldn't stay personal mysteries to each other forever.

However, it was Robbie who spoke first. "How are your parents, Alex?"

"Fine, fine," he replied, as if talking about the weather. His parents had liked Robbie, the smoking aside—which was a bit hypocritical in the case of his dad. "Yours?"

Robbie remained silent for a moment that seemed like ages. "OK, I guess. But they're no longer together."

"Oh," said Alex. "I'm sorry about that."

"And Jack and I broke up too, a few years ago," declared Robbie.

After that, an awkward silence seemed entirely acceptable. And the silence maintained itself until they arrived at their destination.

With his boyish smile, facial fuzz that sat somewhere between 'designer stubble' and an actual beard—and a penchant for wearing chinos and blazers—Harry Archer looked more like a speaker at a technology conference than a professor of magic. He also looked absolutely nothing like the sort of self-styled 'paranormal investigator' that one could still find on TV, despite their practices and theories having been scientifically debunked.

Yet that was essentially what he was doing, if in a more sensible and rigorous way, at a typical suburban home. "So, you've seen the apparition—um, the ghost—here," said Harry, pointing to a staircase. "And in your room?"

The young boy nodded. "Yes, my father. His ghost."

"Would you like to see his room?" That question was from a woman. One who wasn't yet old, but whose face was pale, lined and weathered with worry—even through the make-up that, Harry suspected, she now rarely wore. She was in elegant clothes, but ones that looked like they would have been fashionable several years ago. She was holding her son's hand as he stood behind her, almost as if she was shielding him from a hazard.

"Yes, let's do that," said Harry, trying to sound cheery.

The small party made its way slowly up the stairs and onto a landing, from which a hall led to several bedrooms. As they walked, Harry Archer paused, breathing deeply and seemingly testing for a breeze with his hands.

"You don't have any, um, equipment," the boy said quietly. "The others had, like, stuff."

Harry looked at the woman. "Did you get other *investigators* in?" Contempt for any such 'investigators' was clear in his voice. The woman didn't immediately respond. "You didn't pay them, did you?"

The woman just shrugged in response. "I didn't know what else to do."

Harry knelt down and gently put his hand on the boy's shoulder. "Ben, those people, the people with the equipment. They were phonies. Do you understand? They didn't know what they were doing."

The boy, Ben, just looked scared and confused.

Getting up, Harry suggested, "Now, let's go into your room."

The group entered the bedroom. It looked like any ordinary young boy's room, if a little bare of decoration. This could be said about the rest of the home, too. Harry wondered how long their family had been in there before bereavement took over and precluded further interior decoration. He made a show of walking around the bedroom, touching the bed, opening the cupboard, looking out the window. "Ben," he asked the boy, "When you saw your dad, his ghost, had you been asleep?"

The boy hesitated. His mother squeezed his hand. "Benny, you can tell him," she said, reassuringly.

Ben nodded. "Yes. Sometimes, I see him over the bed. Sometimes, I get up at night and see him on the stairs."

Harry tried to look sympathetic. "And were you scared, Ben?" he asked, as gently as he could.

Ben looked as if he might be about to burst into tears but rallied. "He, he looked like he had been in the accident. There was blood. It was scary, but—"

"—But you also wanted to see your dad?" Harry finished.

Ben just nodded and sniffled slightly.

"You stay in here, Ben," instructed Harry. "I need to talk to your mother. We will be right outside. Is that OK?"

Ben just nodded again, as his mother peeled away her hand.

Standing outside, in the hall, Harry declared, "Look, there is nothing here. Your son needs a psychiatrist—or a better one—not an exorcist or something."

The woman, prematurely aged and consumed with grief herself, seemed to accept this, but only very grudgingly. "You don't understand how difficult it is. Ben, he won't sleep, he's obsessed."

"I understand," replied Harry. "Or, really, I don't. I never lost my father to a car accident when I was a young kid. I never had to deal with that. And it's like I said over the phone: these sorts of cases, it's never really a haunting, anyway. Not like many of us think of that sort of thing. In many ways, our minds are a greater mystery than anything the spirit world has to offer."

The woman was breathing deeply. She seemed like she might be about to cry.

"Even if there was a spirit here—which there isn't, I could tell if there was—it wouldn't actually be your husband. These energies, they observe, they mimic. That is why people sometimes see them taking the form of so-called 'ghosts' of the dead. The spirits show themselves as people they have seen, even decades before. Hence all this guff about ghosts hanging around, 'haunting' places. But what your son has seen—how could a spiritual energy in this house have seen your husband in a car crash several kilometres away? Do you understand?"

The woman nodded. "Yes, I think I do." Her demeanour suggested that, while she might 'understand' cognitively, she was upset that Harry wasn't able to do anything. But what could he do? Bring her husband, the father of her son, back from the dead?

"Trust me," Harry said, a bit more lightly. "I'm the summoning professor at Melbourne Magic School. And don't give any money to those ridiculous charlatan ghost hunters. Or let them anywhere near your house—or your child!"

The doorbell rang.

"Are you expecting someone?" asked Harry.

"No," the woman replied.

"I am," said Harry, breezily. "Police, actually. I should go talk to them."

Harry did not wait for a reply. He bounded down the stairs, checked his appearance in a mirror near the front door, then opened it. He looked at the two detectives before him. "You're too young and handsome to be detectives, surely?" he quipped.

"Nonetheless, we are," replied Robbie, coldly.

Harry stepped out of the house and onto the front yard driveway. "I reckon I've done all I can in there," he declared. Then, pulling a packet of cigarettes from his blazer pocket, asked, "I can have a ciggie while we talk, yeah?"

"Sure," Robbie said. He resisted the urge to have one himself.

Alex asked, "What were you doing in there?" It was a common technique he used. Easing in: get the witness—or suspect—to talk about themselves first; build rapport.

Harry smiled. "I was looking into a haunting," he said easily. "I do it a bit; banishment of spiritual energies at large in our world is one of the more *practical* applications of summoning."

"Successful day at the office, then?" inquired Alex, also trying to sound airy.

"Well, not really," replied Harry, as if talking to a friend about the weather. "There was nothing there. There rarely is, especially in cases like this."

"Indeed," said Alex. "And what brought you here today. Research? Altruism?"

Harry cackled. "No, not quite *altruism*. But research, yes. I'm actually writing a book, on hauntings, *ghosts*, all that nonsense—and offering people the *facts*."

Robbie and Alex remained silent, expecting that Harry would continue.

"I mean, it's the 2020s," he exclaimed, with feeling. "And we still have fucking conmen fleecing people with stories about evil spirits, dead people whose souls—souls!—stalk their relatives, literal ghosts haunting houses, cemeteries. It's all a load of bullshit. I know people won't stop believing in nonsense. We still have people who read horoscopes, for fuck's sake. Numerology, homeopathy, Scientology! People who refuse to vaccinate their kids, deny climate change. But, you know—"

"—You could at least get a book deal out of it?" ventured Alex.

"Even a TV show," added Robbie, naturally taking over in the expectation that the discussion would be becoming rapidly less friendly. "We know you like seeing your face on TV already."

Harry smiled, sardonically. "How long have you two been doing this together? Quite the double act, aren't you?"

Robbie and Alex remained silent, again. Harry threw away his finished cigarette. "Don't think I don't remember. I was a tutor when you," Harry pointed to Robbie. "Won the telekinesis championship twice. And you," he pointed to Alex, "You were there for about five minutes, following him around like a puppy dog. He was obviously fucking you. Told you he loved you. Is that right?"

"This isn't an MMS reunion, Harry," said Robbie, sounding just close enough to losing his temper. "It's a *murder investigation*. Just answer the questions, OK?"

"And what question is that?" bristled Harry. "The one where I admit that, yes, the research for the book, the TV and radio stuff, are kind of a Plan B for the academic career that is likely to be fucking derailed by the new dean, her buddies and the whole *baby boomer cabal* that never liked me to start with? Is that the question?"

Harry lit another cigarette. Robbie again resisted the urge to do the same.

"Can you tell us about this *cabal*?" asked Robbie, sounding over-pleasant.

"For starters, this—this!" He pointed back at the house. "This was *supposed* to be a proper scientific study, with a *team*, a *budget*. But, thanks to Nerida Stein, it's just me going around, talking to grieving families and fucking *kids*, hoping to find genuine spiritual manifestations. It's taking me ages."

"Why Nerida Stein?" asked Alex. "Wouldn't it be Tammy Mazur who made the decision on whether to fund your research?"

"Yes, it would. And Tammy is reasonable. She's at least *professional*. But we would have needed to apply for a government grant. And, as far as Tammy was concerned, Nerida was the grant *guru*. Everything needed Nerida's stamp of approval."

"And she refused to give it?" This was Robbie.

"I tried to talk sense into her. I practically *begged* her," said Harry, bitterly. "I even tried to get Leon Mazur to help, but he didn't. And I thought at least he and I were friends—I spent enough fucking time listening to his waffle in the library."

"Why do you think she said no?"

Harry spat in response. "Because she didn't—they didn't—don't—*like me*. They thought I had some weird, sort of mesmeric hold on Mewan—which I fucking didn't. They were put out to pasture for a while, where they belonged. Then Mewan retired, Tammy got the top job, and, since then, I've been basically a pariah at MMS. It didn't help that Nerida had them all wrapped around her little finger. I even thought …" Harry suddenly trailed off. He seemed to realise he'd been ferociously attacking the character of a murder victim—giving himself a very clear motive.

"Thought what?" asked Robbie. "We need to know everything, Harry."

"But that's just it, I don't *know*."

"Know what, Harry?"

"That Nerida and Leon were having an affair!"

"But you suspected it?"

"Yes. A few months ago, Leon started talking about Nerida more than he used to. And in more affectionate terms than before. I picked up on it because, well, it's no secret John bloody Bishop has been holding a candle for her for a decade."

"And that amused you because you didn't like John Bishop?" Robbie asked.

Harry smiled. "Yes, it did. Bishop was just as much a part of the *cabal* as the others. He's a bitter old dickhead. He practically *laughed* at me when I asked him to talk to Nerida about my application. So, yes, it did *amuse* me."

"Is there anything else, Harry?"

"Just that she was a phoney, too. She would apply for all these grants about women and magic, indigenous magic, but she was just playing the system. That is why Tammy thought she was so great—she could get the money in. But that was not the real Nerida. The *real* Nerida was super-exclusive with the admissions. She was against people from non-magic families."

"Was she?"

"Yes, she was!" insisted Harry, as if this was a very important matter. "She was just an unpleasant individual, frankly." Harry paused. "But *my* reaction to that—as I have explained—was to look for a career Plan B, not, you know, summon something to kill her."

"But you could have done that, couldn't you?"

"You mean as a summoner, with an occasional interest in necromancy?"

Harry replied. "Yes, I could have. But *I didn't!*" Harry looked at the two detectives. "I take it there was a pentagram, ritual stuff, reagents? I wouldn't have needed any of that."

"I guess we will need to take your word for that."

"I guess you will," agreed Harry. "And the entity—the revenant—was it just the standard?"

"What do you mean by 'standard'?" asked Robbie. He was starting to wonder whether Harry might be obliquely probing him and Alex for material for his TV and radio appearances.

"I mean the old, typical horns and talons routine," said Harry, far too casually. "Was there any, say, insect or rodent element to the revenant?"

"What?" sputtered Robbie. Alex said nothing, but had a sense he knew where Harry was going.

"That's just it," declared Harry. "I'm sure Tammy or one of the others told you this. I used to do research about necromancy when I was younger. Just about every summoner does. In Europe in the Middle Ages and Renaissance, it was quite common for necromancers to summon beasts with other *characteristics*. Insects and rodents were common. Not just nasty looking human skeletons. Which suggests you're looking for an amateur."

"Or a professional who wants to look like an amateur," said Robbie. "Where were you on the night?"

Harry grinned sardonically, again. "I was by myself, Detective. There is no alibi here."

"I see," said Robbie, looking Harry up and down with evident distaste. "I think that's all for now. But we might need to talk to you again. Maybe more formally."

Harry affected an offensively phoney friendliness. "Whatever I can do to help!"

"In that case," asked Alex. "Does the term *Gatekeeper* mean anything, in particular, to you?"

Harry's expression was inscrutable. "No. No more than it would to anyone else, I don't think." He crossed his arms. "Unless, of course, there is some specific context about this case?"

"You know I cannot tell you that," replied Alex, smiling sweetly.

"Then, like I said, no. Nothing special that springs to mind. I will let you know if anything occurs to me. Goodbye, *Detectives*."

With that, Harry Archer—summoner, professor, occasional media commentator, and aspiring author and broadcaster—turned around theatrically and stomped towards his car.

"That dude was an insufferable fucking jerk," Robbie grumbled on the ride home.

"He definitely acted like one," replied Alex. "But didn't you get the impression that he was treating the discussion like a performance? A bit of a show."

"How do you mean?" said Robbie.

"Well, mainly how fervently he seemed to dislike the—what was it?— *baby-boomer cabal*, and believe so strongly they were out to get him. It was all too … passionate, I guess. Almost rehearsed, even. I mean, who uses terms like *cabal* in real life?"

"Sometimes people seem passionate because they actually *do* believe something, Alex."

"Of course, of course," Alex conceded. "But it raises a question, doesn't it? If you believed he was sincere, and I thought he was at least exaggerating, that means his performance was 50% success and 50% failure."

Robbie looked at Alex, for a moment. "Wait, was that a question?"

"No, no, sorry; the question is, which reaction did Prince Harry *want* *us* to have? Yours or mine?"

Robbie just looked bemused.

"The other interesting thing," continued Alex, "Is that, while he was quite happy to detail his own very clear motive to murder Nerida Stein— he also managed to tease motives for both John Bishop *and* Leon Mazur."

"I noticed that too, Alex."

12

Theory and Philosophy of Magic Class

10 years ago

"I leave you guys by yourselves for five minutes, and you go and join the magic jocks." That was Emma, all artfully layered clothes—including a great, quirky cardigan—red hair and oddly unjustified indignation.

The trio sat in a tutorial room for a discussion of *Has Magic Failed?*, a best-selling non-fiction book by Professor Julia Chen of Harvard Magic School, which explored whether magic had a positive, or even at all significant, impact on society.

There were about ten other students in the classroom, including Jamie Archer. With his hair pulled back into a man-bun, he looked a little bit less like a surfer. But also, Alex thought, that style did not look great on him—or anyone. At the head of the tutorial room stood their young tutor, Harriet Atkins, who seemed content to wait for the final stragglers to arrive.

"I wouldn't say I'm a magic jock, Em," insisted Alex.

"I am, though," declared Yolanda. "And I'm not *against* it, either. Alex is more of a magic twink, I guess."

"How do you even know what that word means?" countered Alex.

"I'm a woman of the world," replied Yolanda. "And one with access to the Urban Dictionary website."

"Wait, what does it mean?" asked Emma.

"Basically, a cute young gay man. Boyish, vain, generally a bottom. Likes taller, older, cooler guys—like Robbie—to fuck him."

"Yolanda!" cried Alex.

"OK, then, that does make sense," replied Emma, matter-of-fact. "So, let me rephrase. I leave you guys alone for five minutes, and one of you becomes a magic jock and the other becomes a magic twink. I mean, I definitely figured you as a bottom, Alex."

"Em, can we talk about something other than my sex life?" pleaded Alex.

"No," replied Yolanda. "You should have seen it when Robbie met Alex, Em. This one practically lay on the ground and put his legs in the air."

"This is so unfair," he complained. "I hardly interrogate you two on your intimate partners."

"That's because we don't have any," replied Emma.

"Yeah," agreed Yolanda. "Us talking about your boyfriend fucking you is a good problem to have. At least you *have* a boyfriend. So, did he do you at the Billabong on that first night? Robbie seemed really into the idea of the Billabong."

"No!" Alex insisted. "We went back to my room. And can we *please* talk about something else?"

"Then there's Assane," said Yolanda, clearly ignoring Alex's plea to change the subject. "What is the deal with him?"

"Wait, who is Assane?" asked Emma.

"He's *definitely* a magic jock," replied Yolanda. "And, weirdly, an artist. And he does not have any of Alex's unwarranted body image issues. His body is *amazing*."

"Wait, when did you see his body?" asked Emma.

"At the tryouts. The uniform for the elements boys is a pair of coloured shorts and nothing else."

"Really?" replied Emma. "Oh, actually, I did see that when I watched the magic games. How weird."

"*I know*," replied Alex. "It's weird, and stupid."

"Well, you will just need to get used to it, now you're on the team, magic twink," declared Yolanda.

"Are you really going to keep calling me that?" groused Alex.

"Yes!"

"But wait," said Emma. "Back to this Assane dude. Is he into Alex as well? Are we looking at some kind of love triangle here? How exciting!"

"No, Em," said Alex, decisively. "Assane is straight. He's just really … dominant. And he pushes the boundaries with me, because he knows I won't make a fuss and lack, I dunno, authority and gravitas. He's like my siblings—and, given this conversation, you two as well!"

"Yeah, sure, Assane is *obviously* straight, Alex," replied Yolanda, ignoring Alex's other comments. "He sure wasn't sweeping me into his arms after I scored high for the trials."

"You would've slapped him, or buried him in rubble or something," replied Alex. "Anyway, can we *please* stop talking about this?"

"OK, class is about to start anyway," said Emma. "But, just to clarify, I wouldn't say you lack authority or gravitas. It's just, I don't know, quiet authority and gravitas."

"Quiet?" sputtered Yolanda. "Sorry, Alex, I love you, but you talk all the time."

"OK, everyone—time to get to it," announced Harriet Atkins, in her own surprisingly loud, authoritative voice. The small class fell silent immediately. Yolanda and Emma had remarked before on Harriet's commanding presence and obvious intelligence, and declared they were lucky to be in her tutorial group. The term 'girl-crush' had been used, Alex was sure. It didn't hurt that Harriet was also a mentalist, Emma's affinity.

"I hope you've all read the book," continued Harriet. "I'm going to expect active participation from all of you. But first, some context. Chen argues that, after the great emancipation of magicians, there was great optimism that magic could, along with science and technology, solve a lot of society's problems. However, while science and technology have advanced remarkably and become the heart of the whole economy, less than half of magic-users—and those are just the ones we know about— actually work in magic-related fields. And almost half of those work in entertainment, the military or emergency services.

"While there are a lot of other facts, figures and arguments in the book, Chen argues that magic has disappointed in terms of its positive impacts on the human race. So, my question to the class is, do we agree with that conclusion—and why or why not?"

The class stood silent.

"Come on," Harriet coaxed the group. "Someone has to get us started."

Aren't you going to say anything, Alex? You know you want to. (Emma.)

Em, be quiet, you know she can 'hear' you as loud as if you were talking! (Alex)

Indeed, I can. (Harriet) *And I see you've picked up a new skill, Mr Hicks.* "Emma, would you like to start us off?"

"Um, sure," replied Emma. "I guess what struck me in the book is that anything to do with magic doesn't really lend itself to mass production. Now, in theory, you could do mining with earth magicians and make steel with fire ones, but there were just never enough of them to scale things up." Despite being put on the spot, she seemed assured in her response.

Good answer, Emma. (Harriet)

Now who's the show-off? (Alex)

Quiet, Alex. (Harriet)

"The same applies to more modern technologies, doesn't it?" Emma continued. "You could do similar things to, say, air travel and communications with magic, but nothing like on the same scale as we can with planes and phones. On that level, I think magic has been disappointing, but I'm not sure that is the way we should be thinking about it."

"How should we be thinking about it, then?" asked Harriet. *Great answer, by the way!*

Emma beamed and blushed, the girl-crush clearly in full-swing. "I guess I was thinking about things like the arts, and sport—and philosophy and theology. People generally think these things advance society in their own ways, but nobody suggests they should be keeping your lights on or powering your car or whatever."

"Yes, yes, great point," gushed Harriet. "Does anyone have a response to that?"

"I hadn't thought about that before, but I really agree." This was Lizzie, a student Alex hadn't had much to do with. "But I think there is a difference in that magic was used in a lot of practical ways initially, but then technology took over and replaced it."

"Go on," encouraged Harriet.

"Well, I was really struck by the material about sailing ships. At one point, half the British, French and Dutch naval officer class were wind and water mages. It helped them take over from the Spanish and Portuguese as the major maritime powers, because they were slower with the emancipation. Then, of course, steam power came along."

"Where would Captain Cook have been without Joseph Banks to help put wind in his sails?" agreed Harriet. "Yolanda?"

Yolanda had put her hand up, politely. "I wanted to say something," she said. "But it may be from a slightly different angle. Is that OK?"

"Of course, of course," replied Harriet, encouragingly.

"Well, the first thing—more on topic—is that there *are* practical applications for magic. A lot of them add value to the more mass-market, mass production approach. Take my family's landscaping business. We can do things like mature trees instantly on site and do much more delicate and elaborate arrangements than you can do just with a digger and shovels. But the thing is, like Emma said, there aren't many of us, so it's expensive. But it's not like we are—what did you say, Em—elevating the human condition or whatever."

"I said 'advancing society', I think, Yol. But I like your line more!"

"So," said Harriet, "less of magic as art and philosophy and more of magic as a luxury good. A sort of pricey option on the general family sedan of society."

"I guess," replied Yolanda, smiling. "And that may be related to the other thing I wanted to say."

"Go on," urged Harriet, nodding.

"Well, like it says in the book, magic users—everywhere they have gathered data on it—earn more, live longer, and have fewer health and social problems than the general population, even controlling for other factors. I guess my point is, if magicians as a group are quite privileged, then isn't that worth considering too? At least magic seems to be doing something for the magic users. I mean, you mentioned Captain Cook, so I couldn't help but compare magicians to my people … you know, my other people …" Yolanda paused, as she had the distinct impression that Jamie was rolling his eyes at her comments.

"Keep going," said Harriet.

"Sorry, I just thought Jamie might have something to add, given his expression."

Jamie looked flustered. (Even ten years ago, a university tutorial wasn't the place to be accused of cultural insensitivity!) "What? Oh, no, it was nothing to do with your point about indigenous people or anything, Yolanda."

"What were you thinking about then, Jamie?" said Harriet, gently, presumably hoping to forestall a more pointed inquiry from Yolanda.

"Well, it's just," Jamie said, slowly, "so far, we're comparing ourselves to artists, philosophers, sportspeople, theologians, luxury goods. Aren't we a bit more special than that? I know some of the history is contested, but we used to be heroes, demigods, advisers to emperors before the Church and the state decided to supress us. Exterminate us, even."

"And what are the implications of that?" queried Harriet.

"The implication is that I think the whole premise of the book is wrong," declared Jamie. "Why does it even matter that magic is a less efficient than lightbulbs or the internal combustion engine? Why do we need to justify our value—our existence—to people who persecuted us for centuries and often remain suspicious or jealous of us, or both?"

Jamie's remarks hung in the air as the tutorial participants grew silent. It was clear to everyone that someone had expressed a sentiment that was controversial, even *politically incorrect.*

"Alex," said Harriet brightly. "Do you have anything to add? You've been unusually quiet."

Wow, that was backhanded. (Alex) *Wait, did I think that, like, out loud?*

Yes. (Emma and Harriet in unison)

"It's hard for me," Alex replied. "I'm still so new to this. So, while I could engage with the arguments in the book, intellectually, they are so overshadowed for me by the wonder of being able to move objects with my mind, talk without talking, even heal a scratch with my hands—let alone compete in magical competitions. So, I don't know if magic users are special, but I really do think magic is, irrespective of its material contribution to society."

It seemed like the whole tutorial group was smiling with relief. "Interesting perspective, Alex," said Harriet, smiling, matter-of-fact. *Thanks for the save.*

Anytime. (Alex)

13

Charlotte Gets a New Brief

Present day

Charlotte sat in her office in chambers, a bulky brief sitting unopened on her desk. She'd been reading emails instead of looking at it.

She wasn't sure which of her two most negative qualities she disliked the most: her tendency to procrastinate and delay things, or her tendency to become obsessed with things when she finally took the plunge. Obviously, the two were interlinked. The very reason she was finding excuses not to open her new brief was that, once she did, she knew she wouldn't be able to do anything else until she'd read through it in detail, reread it, taken copious notes, and made sure she was absolutely, fully, one hundred percent across it. It was the same with work, uni (both the magic and legal ones), choosing what to watch on Netflix or buying a car.

At least, she thought, she had *finally* done the latter. She'd spent weeks agonising over the various merits of what seemed like the endless array of small SUVs available to Australian consumers. Before this, even elementary concepts like fuel economy were unexamined mysteries to her.

Simon must have been surprised by her zealous thoroughness. But he had, she reflected, been amazing. He followed her along to every test drive: he offered opinions and counsel ("Yeah, this one's economical, but there is such a thing as *performance*, hun. And do you really want to rule out the RAV-4?"), indulged her indecisiveness ("There's no rush, I like looking for cars with you") and listened patiently as she shared her new-found knowledge ("I think I even understand what torque means now!").

Then, yesterday, when a final decision had finally been made, she simply handed over to Simon to do all the haggling. His performance, as expected, was magisterial: "We're cash buyers and are not going to get any of your low-value insurance or add-ons, so just put all that away."

Mind you, there had been some disagreements. Simon had wanted her to look at luxury models: "I'm not letting you buy me an Audi, Si!" She had wanted to look at electric vehicles. Simon—unsurprisingly, given his attitudes to Josh's Tesla—dissented. "You don't have a garage, where will you charge it?" This was an entirely fair point to make, but Charlotte suspected it wasn't the real reason Simon did not want her to get an EV. Still, compromise is important in relationships, isn't it? And Simon did promise that, next time, he would get her an EV.

That comment, and a suspiciously quiet side conversation Simon had with Charlotte's father at dinner last night, made her think a marriage proposal may, indeed, be imminent. (Simon was the sort of man who would ask permission to take a woman's 'hand in marriage'.) The thought of a proposal made Charlotte excited, and not at all nervous. She had no doubt she would say yes. After all, she was in love with Simon, more so than she had felt with anyone else. And they both wanted children. With her being thirty-three, and him turning forty this year ("I wouldn't really call it an age *difference*," she had insisted to friends) neither were in the mood to wait around.

Open the brief, Charlotte! Do your job!

Which she did. And she got obsessed, as expected. She read through the whole day, with a kindly colleague reminding her she should really eat something. (She bought some sushi.) She kept reading, making notes—and preparing a cheese toasty for dinner—until well into the evening. It wasn't until late the next day that Charlotte felt like she had quite mastered the brief. And, when she had, she noted some magic names. Names that had not been especially familiar before. But, having read the coverage of the revenant case, with its summoned horror and associated murder, she decided she must make the call.

"Hey, Alex, sorry, it's Charlotte. Remember me? Sorry to call out of the blue. Are you free for a drink this week? I have something I need to tell you. About your case."

14

Swotting with Alex and Robbie: Enchantment and Ritual; Robbie Meets the Family

10 years ago

"How do I look?" asked Robbie.

"Fine," said Alex, his nose in his copy of *Introduction to Magic Theory and History*.

"Lexi, you didn't even turn around."

"I don't need to. You always look good."

"Lexi, I'm serious."

"OK, OK." Alex turned to look at Robbie. Of course, he looked good. He was wearing a nice shirt, fitted slacks, pointy-toed brown shoes, and his typical chunky watch and bracelets. "You look amazing, Robbie," he declared, sincerely. "But we're not even leaving soon. Go find something to do."

Alex and Robbie were in Robbie's room again. In a couple of hours, they would be making the journey to the Hicks' suburban family home to meet Alex's parents and two siblings. Alex was trying to study. Robbie was pacing, unusually nervous.

"Easy for you to say," replied Robbie. "You aren't meeting your boyfriend's family for the first time, together, *all at once.*"

"Robbie, I've told you. The conversation will go like this: lots of polite questions about you and your family, and lots more super-embarrassing anecdotes about me."

"How can you be so sure," replied Robbie, "if you haven't taken a boyfriend to meet your family before?"

"I know my own family dynamic, Robbie."

"OK then," Robbie conceded. "But why aren't you nervous, then?"

"I *am* nervous. But I'm *trying* to study to take my mind off it. You, on the other hand, want to pace around the room thinking of worst-case scenarios."

"Fine. Maybe I'll change again and go for a run. Or go to the gym."

"Good idea," agreed Alex. "What is it the coach said? Magic comes from the mind, which lives in your brain, which is part of your body. So, keep that body in shape and your magic will improve. Also, we make you wear swimming trunks to compete, which is yet another reason to keep in shape!"

"Shit, Lexi, you really aren't letting that one go."

"OK, here's a deal. I'll let the unnecessarily skimpy uniform issue go if you do some exercise for an hour and leave me to study. OK?"

"Deal," agreed Robbie. With that, he disrobed and put on some athletic gear, using a combination of hands and magic. He kissed Alex on the cheek and teleported away. Alex was already reading his book.

Enchantment, Magnification and Ritual:
How they enhance a magic-user's power

Since people first started using magic, understood to be in the Neolithic era, the primary source of magical power has been the magic user. However, starting in prehistory, there is archaeological evidence to support the use of mechanisms to improve the basic power of the magic user through enchantment and ritual. The following sections explain each of these means of power improvement and how they interact.

Enchantment

Enchantment is the storage of magical energy in an object. It's the most common and, in many ways, most powerful form of magical enhancement. In a manner opposite to the storage of physical energy, such as in batteries, storage of magical energy actually increases the volume of total energy over time, rather than decaying it.

The magical energy stored in an enchanted object can then be drawn out by a magic user to make the magic user's 'spells' more powerful. If the magical energy in an enchanted object is used sparingly—or even occasionally replenished—the enchanted object may remain 'charged' indefinitely.

The enchanted objects most often used by magicians, both in history and in fiction, have been either wands and staffs, or forms of jewellery such as amulets, rings and crowns.

However, not all enchanted objects are designed to be used by magicians themselves. Indeed, many enchanted objects, including weapons and armour, have been designed to be used by non-magic users.

While these are commonly enchanted items, any object can be enchanted. For example, rocks have been found at Neolithic cave-painting sites which retain some degree of magical enchantment. Furthermore, the 'quality' of the object used in an enchantment has no bearing on the effectiveness of the enchantment. (Though, in the case of weapons, this may well affect its overall utility.)

A further use of enchantment in respect of non-magic users is to enchant an object with a spell so it can be cast (intentionally or otherwise) by a non-magic user. The most frequent use has been in magical *traps*. The ability of magicians to create hazards through enchanting objects has often been cited by those who are suspicious or distrustful of magic.

Finally, while enchantment makes use of powers from the schools of magic and is not itself a separate discipline—it is a particular skill. Especially earlier in the period of emancipation, it was not unusual for magicians to seek to specialise in enchantment as a vocation, rather than work as a magic practitioner.

Rituals

Ritual refers to the process of enhancing a magic-user's power through actions, movements and words. Simple rituals may involve reciting a brief incantation, or tracing patterns in the air. More elaborate and carefully sequenced rituals may use chants, written symbols on surfaces and the use of either enchanted objects or reagents.

Compared to enchantment, the process of how rituals increase a magic user's powers are not well understood. One theory is that, just as claims that a prayer makes a religious believer feel closer to their chosen deity and enhances their devotion, rituals simply bring the magician closer to his or her inherent magical ability. Another is that rituals may draw additional energy from the spirit world to augment the caster's own power, whether or not the magic user is themselves a summoner.

Magnification

Magnification is the use of multiple magic users to create a particular magical effect or cast a particular spell. It is often used as part of a ritual. There is evidence that even magic users of differing affinities, or lacking expertise in the relevant school, can nonetheless help amplify the power of the magnification, at least to some extent. For example, a manipulation and telekinesis practitioner may help magnify a spell to create a storm, alongside water, wind or electricity practitioners.

Interaction between enhancements

The use of enchanted objects, rituals and magnification in casting is not mutually exclusive, but cumulative. That is, a combination of enchanted objects, rituals and magnification can work in aggregate to enhance the power of the magic user or users. Furthermore, the incremental enhancements of using multiple, improvement techniques are greater than linear.

For example, two spellcasters casting the same spell will enjoy a power slightly greater than double their intrinsic ability. Should they further increase their power through enchanted objects and rituals, the incremental enhancements in their power will again be greater than the sum of the components' parts.

Robbie and Alex finished their cigarettes a short walk from the late 1980s-era, double-storey suburban Hicks family home. Robbie rang the doorbell by hand.

Alex's sister Catherine opened the door, to Alex's mild surprise. "Hi, Ali!" she practically squealed, placing kisses all over his face. "And you must be Robbie!" she cried, with even more enthusiasm, hugging him and kissing his cheek. "Come in!"

"Are you already drunk?" Alex whispered to her once Robbie had entered the hallway.

"No. And don't be like that, Ali," Catherine whispered back.

"This way," announced Alex, as he led Robbie hand-in-hand through the hallway to an open kitchen-dining room where his brother, Ivan, along with parents Yvonne and Max, had placed themselves around a counter. On the counter stood a neatly arranged tray, with as-yet-unopened wine bottles and glasses that looked polished to a sparkle. All three immediately leapt to their feet as Robbie entered the room, offering hugs and compliments.

"How about a Tom Collins, Robbie? I made them," said Catherine, proffering a tall glass to Robbie with a smile.

"Of course, thanks," he replied, trying to remain super-polite.

"And you, Ali?" asked Catherine.

"Yes, thanks," said Alex, as his sister handed him a frosted glass of gin, soda and sugar syrup. (The drink was delightful, he would have to concede.)

The group was ushered by Yvonne into the spacious living room, cluttered with homey trinkets, ornaments and artworks, clearly collected over many years. "Just sit wherever you want, Robbie," Yvonne insisted.

"I made some smoked salmon nibbly-things," declared Max, getting up to pass around a tray.

Everyone except Ivan took one of the little brioche discs topped with fish and dill cream cheese. "Smoked salmon isn't really my thing," Ivan said to Robbie. "The rest of them love it, though."

"Very nice," said Robbie, who wondered whether he should address Alex's father as Max or Mr Hicks, and decided not to directly address him at all.

"I hear you got Robbie to join the—what do you call it?—magic sports team," said Ivan. "You must be very convincing. I was sure Ali was completely done with anything resembling sports when he finished school. I was surprised he didn't burn his hockey sticks."

"To be honest, he didn't seem to need much convincing," replied Robbie. "And he's really good. He made the main squad, which is unusual for first years."

"It's true I prefer magic to hockey," agreed Alex.

"You like doing things you're good at," said Yvonne. "We all do."

"And, I mean, magic has to be more fun than hockey," declared Catherine, who had been a star netballer at school—still played for the alumni team—and never thought much of hockey, either to play or watch.

"Did you play sport in high school, Robbie?" inquired Ivan. "You look like a footy player to me."

"Yeah," replied Robbie. "In the midfield. I was fast."

"I knew it!" said Ivan. "I was a forward. Well, I still am, I play for a local team."

"I gave it up after school," said Robbie. "When you can magically manipulate and teleport objects, having to use your feet and hands alone feels like … I guess like wearing shoes that are a size too small. Does that make sense?"

"Yes, it does!" replied Ivan, with surprising earnestness.

"Just like me and hockey," said Alex.

"What, you wanted to freeze the puck or something?" grinned Catherine.

"Field hockey doesn't even use a puck, Kat!"

"On that note, the adults will go and finish off the starter," declared Max. "Coming, Yvie?"

Alex's parents disappeared into the kitchen. Catherine finished off her Tom Collins. "Maybe I should get us some wine?" she suggested.

"I can do that, if you like," offered Robbie. "It'll at least get the party trick phase of the evening out of the way."

"Cool, we were too polite to ask for a demo," replied Catherine.

With that, Robbie waved his hand and the tray of wine bottles and glasses appeared on the coffee table.

"Wow!" said Catherine.

"Impressive," agreed Ivan.

Robbie set about offering wine around, pouring it and 'handing' glasses to the Hicks siblings using his magic.

"Were you popular at high school with the magic and footy?" asked Ivan in a way that made Alex feel unreasonably embarrassed.

"Well, I guess, like, popular enough," replied Robbie. "But people are a little, I dunno, suspicious about magic, party tricks aside. That and sexuality kind of put a bit of a ceiling on things."

"That surprises me," said Ivan, sounding too flattering, almost flirtatious. "But high school kids are pretty stupid, aren't they?"

"You never said that when you claimed to be the coolest kid in school," retorted Alex.

"Ivan *was* the coolest kid in school, though," said Catherine, smiling.

"After I graduated, obviously. And having your cool older brother and even cooler older sister around during those peak sexuality-related bullying years was probably a good thing for you, Ali."

"I'll be forever grateful, sis," Alex deadpanned back.

Robbie chuckled. The Hicks siblings looked at him, possibly a bit confused. "Sorry," he said, unnecessarily. "It's just this sibling dynamic. It's cool to watch. I'm an only child, so never really experienced it."

"Where did the wine go?" That was Yvonne, from the kitchen, who had presumably finished her Tom Collins too.

"Robbie teleported the wine in here," replied Ivan. "It's his magic party trick."

"Oh, I see," replied Yvonne. "Well, bring it to the table. The starter is ready."

The group stood up. Robbie took magical hold of the wine and tray. Catherine declared: "We will have to seat Robbie and Ivan at separate ends of the table to contain the bromance. Anyone would think these two were the boyfriends."

"Well, I'm irresistible," joked Ivan.

"Or, like, very close half-brothers," continued Catherine. "You kind of look alike."

"No, they don't!" said Alex, sounding alarmed.

"I dunno, we kinda do, a bit," said Ivan. "What can I say, my little bro has good taste in men. Well, this time, at least."

"I'm not going to say anything," said Robbie, walking towards the kitchen with the levitating drinks tray.

"He's smart, too," said Catherine, grinning.

The starter was a potato and leek soup, which Robbie enjoyed. Conversation remained focused on sibling-related matters.

"Being the eldest, Robbie," declared Catherine, "I always had the strictest rules. Curfews, interrogations about where I was going, who with, all that stuff."

"I don't think we were stricter with you than the boys," replied Max.

"Oh, yes, that as well," said Catherine. "When you're a daughter, parents take a keener interest in your, shall we say, chastity."

Yvonne guffawed. "Kat, I hardly think we did anything to stop you having sex."

"You did, though, at least sort of," countered Ivan. "By the time Alex was old enough to vanish for hook ups …"

Ivan stopped talking as he noticed the combined glares of his parents and siblings, not least his younger brother's.

Desperate to end the pause, Max asked Robbie, "What is it like living on campus—at a magic school, no less?"

"He really is nice, and this is going well," said Yvonne. "I mean, it is, isn't it?"

The group was down Robbie and Max. Robbie had (a bit shamefacedly) asked if he might be able to go out for a cigarette. He brightened when told that Max, to his wife's disapproval, also smoked ("Just a few a day," he insisted) and that there was a 'smoking lounge' on a deck out the back. Max declared to Robbie, "we've got half-an-hour 'til the main's ready, so let's bring one of the bottles out and talk about the cop stuff".

This provided an obvious opportunity for a mid-event Hicks family debrief.

"Yeah, I agree," conceded Alex. "No disasters so far."

"Oh please!" declared Catherine. "As if we would have said anything stupid with your first ever proper boyfriend."

"And who isn't an absolute jerk, too," continued Ivan.

"He's nice, isn't he?" added Yvonne. "So nice and *normal*."

"I didn't realise that would be so much of a *shock*," retorted Alex. "OMG, Alex has a boyfriend who isn't a total *jerk*. The world's gone nuts!"

"Don't be like that, Ali," said Ivan. "It's good. We like him. You like him. He likes you. It's all good. But sorry about the mention of the, er, jerks you used to hang out with."

"To be fair, you did stop yourself," conceded Alex.

"And, Ali," noted Catherine, "I doubt Robbie thought he was taking your virginity or something the first night he had sex with you. It's not like your arse hadn't been around at least some of the block before."

"Wait, now you're bottom-shaming me?" sputtered Alex.

"Is that even a real thing?" questioned Catherine. "Besides, my point here is that you are, like, an unreliable narrator. You should be in the Psychiatric Journal. AHPS: Alex Hicks Persecution Syndrome."

"That's enough, you two," declared Yvonne. "Be nice. I'm going to plate up the casserole."

Which she did. And it was a chicken casserole. Robbie decided it wasn't quite as good as his mother's, but pretty good nonetheless. The conversation roved across magic competition ("Is it, like, American college sport?" asked Ivan. "Yeah, I guess it is," said Alex.); food likes and dislikes ("Normally, the recipe would call for mushrooms, but Kat really isn't a fan," said Yvonne.); and police work ("Dad, do you think Robbie would be good in the police?" asked Alex, clearly hoping for a particular answer. "Of course, Ali, we need more like him.")

And the evening carried on, with make-your-own sundaes for dessert, free-flowing wine and equally free-flowing conversation. Indeed, the evening had been so convivial, and long, that its attendees found themselves overly drunk and tired at an overly late hour.

"I should probably order a cab," said Catherine. "It's been so great to meet you, Robbie!" Both were slumped in armchairs in the living room.

"Just stay here tonight, Kat," replied Max. "It's late, and you can always get a cab home tomorrow."

"See?" said Catherine. "More strict boundaries."

"Even though the chastity issue has obviously resolved itself in the negative," needled Ivan.

"Don't be an idiot, Ivan," countered Yvonne.

"I guess we should go, too," said Alex, also in an armchair. He was less affected by booze than the rest of his family through a heroic effort in abstemiousness, in spite of the stresses. Robbie was the same.

"Why don't you two stay as well?" suggested Max. "Ali's bedroom is still here. And I think it's a queen, bigger than what you guys have been sleeping in on campus." (Robbie had mentioned the small bed issue when Max had raised the issue of on-campus living arrangements.)

"Sure, thanks, if that would be OK, Mrs—" said Robbie.

"Yvonne!" insisted Yvonne. "You're far too polite. And I *insist* you stay."

"What about you, Ivan?" asked Robbie. "Are you staying?"

"I live here," he replied. "As much as you and Alex have to put up with a smaller bed, my girlfriend and I need to deal with—"

"—A big bed and parents to make you breakfast," cut in Yvonne. "Go to sleep, Ivan. Go to sleep, all of you."

"Yes, Mrs Hicks," said Robbie, intentionally cheekily. Yvonne looked the exact opposite of upset, though, as all of the Hicks siblings, plus Robbie, went upstairs.

"So, this is your teenage bedroom, Lexi?" said Robbie, by way of a rhetorical question. "With posters of One Direction and X-Men?"

"Yeah," said Alex, sounding bashful. "The One Direction thing was a bit of a secret. Well, to the kids at school, at least. But I guess I identified with the X-Men in a big way. You know, people with powers, who are different."

As if ignoring him, Robbie continued. "And your family was amazing tonight. I mean, you were right that they were very polite talking to me, but there were literally no super-embarrassing anecdotes about you."

"True," agreed Alex. "When you were away talking to Dad, they argued that they would never have done anything to sabotage my first *proper* boyfriend, who isn't a *jerk*."

"Oh yeah," said Robbie. "That was about as close as they got to an embarrassing anecdote: Ivan's abandoned attempt to tell me all about your shitty high school hook-ups with losers."

"Robbie!"

"What, you've told me all about them already. And he *did* shut up pretty quick, didn't he? How many of them were in here?"

"What do you mean?" asked Alex, genuinely confused.

"The shitty hook-ups. How many of them were in here with the posters and—wait, are they Warhammer figurines?"

"It was a brief flirtation—with the figurines, I mean," insisted Alex. "And, no, none of the hook-ups were in here. Like Ivan said, I vanished when I did the hook-ups. Do you really want to know about this?"

"Maybe a little," said Robbie, grinning. "But it sounds like this was more a place for homework and masturbating, while thinking about what these dudes would do to you? Which is actually pretty hot."

"Wait, Robbie," said Alex, waving his arms in front of him. "I know what you're getting at. We cannot have sex here tonight. Literally, all my family are here. They will hear everything."

"I promise to be quiet, Lexi," said Robbie, as he started undressing Alex, mainly with his magic. He also started kissing him on the neck.

"You're not the one I'm worried about!" cried Alex. "You know how I make ... noises when you're doing me."

"Well, I would be happy for you to tone those down too," replied Robbie.

"What do you mean, tone them down?" grumbled Alex, who was now completely naked. "Do you think I, what, fake it or something?"

"Don't be like that, Lexi," said Robbie. "I thought you knew how much I love it when you moan, whimper and beg me to go harder. And that you, I dunno, play it up a bit because you want to make me happy. Not a bad thing."

"I don't," insisted Alex. "I can't help it!" Robbie pulled Alex in and kissed him, deeply. He then unbuttoned his pants and let them drop to the floor. Putting his hands on Alex's shoulders, he pushed the smaller, younger man down onto his knees, and towards his crotch.

"That makes things even hotter, then," declared Robbie. "And think about it like this, Lexi: if we *don't* have sex, your family might think they did something wrong and conclude that the evening was a disaster."

Alex didn't have time to form a response to this proposition before Robbie arranged Alex on the bed—just as he liked him—and proceeded to do to Alex what nobody had yet done to him in this room. And Alex, true to form—and as much as he tried to supress himself—moaned, whimpered and begged throughout.

Once they were done, and as Alex panted into Robbie's chest, the latter said, "You know, Lexi, I think I might be falling in love with you."

Alex was ecstatic to the point of speechlessness.

"Lexi, did you hear me?"

Alex finally responded. "Yes, sorry." Then, he added, "I think I might be doing the same, Robbie."

15

Checking in on the Taskforce

Present day

"The problem with these taskforces is they collect so much fucking *information*," declared Pav. "Most of which is not fucking *information* at all."

Pav was sitting around a table with Alex, Robbie and Isabella in Victoria Police headquarters, debriefing as part of an ad-hoc subcommittee of detectives on the Revenant case—established just hours ago, via text, by Karen Park.

He continued. "I mean all the bloody psychics, psychos—pretty much the same bloody thing anyway—weirdos, busybodies who know fuck all about anything, let alone the case, plus the total cranks," he fumed, seemingly to nobody in particular.

"Taskforces are always like that, Pav," said Alex, soothingly. "And, unlike me, you must have been involved in them before."

Pav ignored him. (What a surprise.) "Listen to this one," he said, reading from a sheet of paper taken from one of many files on the table. "'These magic people are dangerous. We should put them all on Kangaroo Island.' I mean, who calls up a police hotline just to say something dumb and bigoted like that?"

"Awww, are you expressing sympathy for us, Pav?" teased Alex. "That's not like you."

Pav at least noticed him this time. "Maybe I am, PB. Take what Izzy and I were doing today, the needle-in the-haystack stuff with the"—he made quotation marks with his fingers—"'known summoners'. I mean, I get it. Say a kid goes missing, which is always a high-profile case. One of the first things the cops do is work out what pedos there are in the area, then try to find out if they have alibis."

"Wait, I'm not following this, Pav," said Isabella.

"Don't you get it?" he said, gesticulating intensely. "In that situation, the people getting targeted by the cops are *pedos*—they have already done something wrong. Those summoners we were hassling today haven't. They just have a particular magical affinity. It's not fair!"

"Ah," Isabella nodded, smiling. "I get it now. But I've never seen you get so passionate about something, Pav!"

"Other than football, especially Collingwood," added Alex, unhelpfully.

Pav ignored him again. "And, it makes no sense anyway, because it's not like you guys are like the X-Men with specific powers. Affinities, yeah, but you can learn others, right?"

"Yes," Alex confirmed. "We also aren't mutants, thankfully."

"See, so why target any one group—or anyone at all, just for being a magic user?"

"You've made your point, Pav," said Isabella. "I'm just glad there weren't nearly as many of them as I had expected. We're almost done."

"There aren't nearly as many of us as people think, overall," said Robbie, speaking for the first time. "Magic users, I mean. I read there are more people in the census who claim to be Jedi Knights than real-life magicians."

"That's a fun fact, Robbie," said Pav, smiling.

"Stop sucking up, Pav."

"Nothing wrong with being friendly, Alex. And it *was* a fun fact!"

"So, just to put this discussion back on track," said Alex, "did the needle-in-haystacks exercise yield anything like a lead?"

"If it had, Alex, don't you think Pav would have been bragging about *that*, rather than going on his little woke rant?" That was Isabella.

"Woke is extra pronouns and oat milk," declared Pav indignantly. "It's not *woke* to treat people fairly, Izzy."

Isabella pretended to recoil in horror. "Oh my God, that's not Pav—it's a magical doppelganger come to kill us all!"

That prompted some laughter from Alex and Robbie, and even a chuckle from Pav. Then Alex said, "We spoke to some of the faculty today."

"Did *you guys* find any leads?" probed Isabella.

"We definitely picked up a suspect," Robbie said. "Harry Archer. A real central-casting douchebag. He was very open about his motive, while denying he did it, obviously. "

"The one from TV?" asked Pav. "He was even talking about this case last night on one of the news shows."

"The very same," said Alex. "He claimed Nerida—apparently MMS's grant guru—refused to support his grant application. He really went at her."

"Why did she say no?" asked Isabella.

"Because she didn't like him. MMS is now run by a baby boomer *cabal* and they all—but *especially* Nerida—had it in for self-appointed millennial victim, Harry Archer."

"Millennials vs boomers," scoffed Pav.

Alex looked thoughtful. "He was an odd one. He was just too passionate, too dramatic. I thought he was trying to put on a show—"

"I thought he was being sincere," said Robbie, finishing Alex's sentence for him. "And that he was a total dick."

"He did use the word *cabal* in real life," said Isabella. "Who does that?"

"That's what I said," agreed Alex.

"He also managed, with some prompting, to provide possible motives for two other faculty members: John Bishop and Leon Mazur—both affairs of the heart," added Robbie.

"He didn't need *that* much prompting, Robbie," Alex sought to clarify.

"No, he didn't," Robbie agreed.

"It all sounds interesting," said Isabella, "but it still feels like early days."

"Early days are the best ones to crack cases. You should know that." That was Karen Park, who had just swept into the meeting room like a stern, elegantly attired force of nature. "But, from the looks on your faces, it seems we haven't quite done that today."

Isabella tried not to sound defensive. "Have any of the other teams got any firm leads?"

"No," she replied simply. "I would have thought that was obvious from the look on *my* face. I've been told that I smile when I'm in an especially good mood." And, indeed, she did smile, quickly, a little. She put a piece of paper on the table and looked at Robbie and Alex. "Boys, I need you to go to the MMS library tomorrow. There is a book there that some of our researchers think includes instructions for the summoning ritual used by our killer."

With that, she swept out of the meeting room, without waiting for any sort of confirmation that her orders were understood and accepted.

"Is she always like that?" asked Isabella, when she was sure Karen would not be able to hear.

"Pretty much," replied Robbie. "She's right about smiling though. I'm pretty sure I've seen her smile. At least once!"

"I think I might be developing a bit of a girl crush," said Isabella, ignoring the others' comments.

"On that note," said Alex, getting up from the table. "I need to go meet a girl." He turned and exited the room.

16

Discussing the Magic Routine;
Alex Sees the Artist at Work

10 years ago

"He sounded a bit like a magic supremacist, that's all I'm saying," declared Yolanda.

"Is magic supremacism even a real thing?" replied Alex.

Alex, Assane and Yolanda were in the games room for training. Alex was wearing a t-shirt, athletic trousers and trainers. Yolanda and Assane, to Alex's consternation, were wearing the same revealing uniform they had at the trials.

"Don't they think the Hittites were a mageocracy?" wondered Assane. "The Byzantines certainly were. Besides, Lexi, aren't you a bit over-dressed?"

"Only Robbie calls me Lexi," countered Alex. "If you want an unnecessary pet name, my family calls me Ali. Also, I'm not over-dressed. You're under-dressed!"

"OK, *Ali*," replied Assane. "Does anyone have any ideas for the joint routine, while we wait for Jamie?"

"The electricity angle is definitely an opportunity," said Yolanda. "But we need to think how it'll all work in sequence."

"Hi, sorry!" Jamie appeared, wearing only the white shorts he had at the trials.

"Overdressed!" whispered Assane to Alex.

"Fuck off," replied Alex.

"We were talking about how your contribution is going to be key," Yolanda said, coolly, to Jamie.

"I was thinking that, too," replied Jamie. He didn't notice Yolanda's tone, or at least pretended not to. Then, he smiled. "Not wanting to blow my own trumpet but, I guess, I *really am* special."

Assane's studio and exhibition space in a large warehouse-type building near MMS was so large, Alex wondered if it might, like the MMS games room, be magically larger inside than out—the TARDIS effect.

"People always think this place is magic, like the games room, because you can't see how big it is from the street," said Assane, as if reading Alex's mind.

"Do they?" replied Alex casually, as if he had been thinking no such thing.

"It isn't though," said Assane, with what Alex was thinking of as his *Assane grin*: a big, beaming, irritating smile that Assane put on when he was feeling happy with himself. And, given Assane was almost constantly happy with himself, he was almost always *Assane grinning*. "It's just fucking *big*."

"It is big. And you get this whole space?" asked Alex.

"Yeah, which is lucky, given what I'm doing now."

The walls of the huge room were layered with large wooden panels, which bore intricate patterns and images created by precise charring of all different levels of intensity. They were, thought Alex, certainly impressive.

"My fire period," said Assane. "I'm doing something different now."

"Is that what those are for?" Alex was looking at what he could only describe as two 'rooms within a room', their exteriors painted in the same white as the walls of the studio-cum-gallery. The 'room' on the right was lined with large tubs of paint and had a doorway with no door, revealing an entirely black interior. The one on the left had its door closed.

"Yep," replied Assane. "Did you bring the change of underwear?"

"The one you told me to bring, but refused to explain why? Yes, I did," said Alex. "And yes, I'm also wearing underwear that, what was it you said, I don't mind throwing away after."

"Oh good," said Assane. "I'm glad you did."

"And that did not strike you as an odd request to make, without any kind of explanation?" said Alex, exasperated. Why do I need to bring underwear to a fucking gallery?"

"Because, Ali," said Assane, "You're probably going to get paint on yourself."

"What?"

"Here, I'll show you," said Assane, motioning Alex towards the room with the closed door. "It will make sense when you see what I'm doing now." He opened the door.

"Wow!"

The room, lit magically by an orb hovering near the ceiling, was like standing in the centre of a bouquet of flowers. Colourful petals, stems, leaves and pistils were painted across the entirety of the room: the floor, walls, ceiling, even the door, which Assane had closed behind him. The 'brushstrokes' of the 'painting' were quick, vivid and ever-so-imprecise, giving an illusion of movement to the images of the flowers.

"This is why I needed to learn telekinesis from Robbie. So I could float in the air to paint everything, the whole room."

"And you used telekinesis to actually paint it too, didn't you?" asked Alex. "I mean, no paintbrushes."

"Yeah, I did," said Assane, sounding impressed. "You have a good eye. Not much gets past you, does it?"

"I'm not sure what that's supposed to mean," replied Alex, rather resenting Assane's backhanded compliments and almost constant mind-games. "I do have to admit, though, that this is amazing. Is there anything you *aren't* good at?"

"You couldn't just leave it with the nice compliment, could you, Ali?" replied Assane, (grinning, of course).

"Hey, I'm just trying to keep up with you!"

"That's fair," replied Assane. "And you aren't even doing too badly at it. In fact, I could really ask you the same question."

"What question?"

"Is there anything *you* aren't good at?"

"Well, I couldn't do this," replied Alex, stepping out of the room, followed by Assane.

"No, you couldn't," declared Assane (possibly too definitively, thought Alex). "But then, I wasn't the star of the magic team in first year. Nor, as Robbie tells me, was I acing both the practical and theory classes."

"Do you have a point, or are you just altruistically trying to bolster my self-esteem?"

Assane laughed. "You have Robbie to boost your self-esteem," he replied. "But I do have a point."

"Go on," urged Alex, unenthusiastically.

"I was going to say, you and I are pretty much the same. Except you do this whole self-deprecating thing, and I don't."

Ouch. "Well, you certainly don't *do* modesty," countered Alex. "I've actually thought, if women were as into self-confident, alpha male show-offs as people on the internet seem to think they are, you would have a harem, or at least a girlfriend."

"Ouch," Assane actually said it out loud. Then he *grinned* again, and made his comeback. "Though you're right, not every woman has the same type as you."

It occurred to Alex, alarmingly, that, were he in a romantic comedy film or young adult novel, this would be the point at which he and Assane would kiss passionately and—depending on the particular genre and audience—either have wild sex on the floor of the gallery, cut to a post-coital scene of them in bed together; or perhaps just have them walking hand in hand in a park.

Thankfully, though, this was nether a romantic comedy film, nor a young adult novel. Alex already had a boyfriend—an *awesome* one—

and Assane was *obviously* straight. He was just far too into ribbing and banter; he needed to be dominant and in charge *all the time*. Alex resolved, therefore, to give Assane what he wanted.

"OK, you got me. You win this round," said Alex. "But, I have to say, this is the weirdest friendship dynamic I've ever experienced, and that includes high school, which is *saying* something."

Assane smiled with what seemed like real warmth and happiness. (How un-Assane like!)

"What?" asked Alex, warily.

"Ali," said Assane, "that is the first time you've accepted that we are friends."

Alex felt touched by this and did not even want to fire back with a witty rejoinder, even though Assane had left this option wide open. (After all, how can you expect a cocky show-off like Assane to drop the tough-guy act and show some emotional vulnerability when, if they do, you go for the jugular?) Unfortunately, barbs aside, he couldn't really think of an appropriate response.

But he didn't have to. "Now," declared Assane, sounding serious. "I need you to take off your clothes."

Alex stood, in just his underwear, at the open doorway to the room on the right, with its walls painted black and lit, like the other room, by a floating orb of light. Assane had disappeared into a side room to "change and get a couple of things".

Alex turned around as he heard Assane re-enter the main space. Assane had changed into an old-looking windcheater and shorts. He was wearing goggles and carried another pair of them along with what looked like a smock.

Assane looked at Alex. "They're really not that bad, you know, Ali," he said. "Your legs."

Alex raised his voice. "Fuck, Assane, I wasn't even thinking about that before you mentioned it—*again*. The friendship-brokered ceasefire has lasted all of five fucking *minutes!*"

"OK, sorry. I'm *sorry*. It's not like I try to be an asshole intentionally. Or not all the time. Anyway, put these on." He handed Alex the goggles. "Like I said, you're likely to get some paint on yourself."

"Which is why, *unlike you*, I'm half-naked," complained Alex. "I could have brought some shitty old clothes to wear too, Assane."

"Ah, well that is the thing," replied Assane, sounding apologetic. "Here, I brought you a smock. You can wear that."

"Wait, so making me wear my underpants to watch the great artist at work was, like, a prank or something?" sputtered Alex. "You are such a tosser!"

"Hey, I thought better of it in the end." insisted Assane, as Alex put on the smock.

"True but—wait, why couldn't I just put the smock on *over* my clothes?" asked Alex, as the 'reason' began to dawn on him.

Assane did his biggest, most annoying grin ever. "Sorry, I just couldn't abandon the plan altogether, Ali."

"Is it too late to, like, revoke the friendship thing altogether?" greased Alex in reply.

"Don't be like that, Ali. Like you said, at least you get a chance to see the great artist at work. When my stuff is in the most prestigious galleries and selling for millions, you will be able to say that you saw the artist create one of his seminal works, in your underwear!"

"Glad to hear you have such realistic expectations, Assane," Alex deadpanned back. "Now, how about some actual painting?"

Assane hovered in the air, with bubbles of paint he had pulled from the containers outside the room. These ranged in colour from white to blue to pink and yellow. Summoning these about him, he sent them splashing, but in very controlled ways, around the black walls of the room-within-a-room. He did this once, then again, then again. Alex got splashed with some paint, as Assane and the zero-gravity paint bubbles whizzed and swung around the room. But nothing, Alex thought, that would justify the underwear thing.

Assane was barely touched with errant paint himself; his performance showed remarkable control and deliberation. As he delicately sprayed paint across his room-as-canvas, Alex started to see the work come together. While the first room put the audience in the centre of a bunch of flowers, the second put them in the centre of the universe.

Galaxies of various types took shape as Assane twisted and turned in the air, sending paint splattering in very intentional directions. Alex wasn't sure quite how long the process took—it certainly seemed less than an hour—but it left the images across the walls with the same slightly blurred, moving quality as the flower room, as if the viewer were an astronaut in a spaceship at the heart of the cosmos. It was impressive; but, thought Alex, less so than the flower room. There were unfortunate planetarium vibes.

"How did you do this so quickly?"

"I'd planned it out all out before, Ali," said Assane. "This bit was like the tip of the iceberg. I could show you my sketches."

"That's fine," replied Alex. "I'm surprised you didn't claim this was all in your head from the start."

"That wouldn't be credible, even for me," replied Assane, with the typical grin.

"I guess not," said Alex, nonetheless enjoying Assane's planetarium painting. "It's a shame I can't go in."

"No, you can't," insisted Assane. "You need to let the paint dry. Now, aren't we supposed to be meeting Robbie and getting drunk?"

"We are," said Alex.

17

Alex and Charlotte Have a Drink, at the Lion

Present day

By some odd confluence of events, Alex and Charlotte found themselves having their drink, not merely at the Lion Hotel, but at the same table in the outdoor smoking area where Pav had declared that Alex's Daylesford Distillery theory had been confirmed.

Midweek, the pub was quieter, but still doing reasonable trade. Alex and Charlotte were sharing a bottle of rosé, which rested in a cooler by the table, and some ham croquettes. (Alex wondered whether the Lion might actually, in words Pav might use, 'be starting to go posh'.)

Charlotte had been keen to offer Alex information about his case but, so far, she had focused more on the limited wine list, small-talk and smoking cigarettes. Like a true performer, she seemed to be delaying the main event. Alex thought they should really start talking about her case information, but he was too taken by the new, big ring sitting on her wedding finger. So, he started with that.

"Simmo popped the question, I see."

"Yeah," replied Charlotte, beaming. "Just last night. You're probably the first person to see the ring other than him, me and my friend Laura. Do you like it?"

Obviously, there was nothing else to say to this question than some variation of "Yes, I love it!" But the ring was actually an elegant design, with a large white diamond (Alex had no idea what sort of cut) in a white gold setting. So, he said, "Yes, it's really lovely. I'm surprised Simmo has such good taste!"

Charlotte smiled, indulgently, like one might to a pet. "I know you and Si have an interesting relationship. But he really likes you, and he practically *loves* Josh. I suspect he will be the best man, so we may need to find you a role at the wedding too."

"Don't try too hard," replied Alex. Charlotte laughed, even though Alex wasn't really joking.

"Anyway," she said, looking at her new engagement ring. "We'll let you know when there's a date and venue and everything. I'm worried it will all be a lot of work."

"Sure, looking forward to it." At least that was sincere. Alex liked weddings and, honestly, he quite liked the couple who were getting married. So long as they didn't expect him to be MC or something.

"Of course, we haven't really even been *discussing* that stuff yet. It's all so, well, not exactly sudden—I've seen it coming for a while—but new, you know."

"I understand," said Alex. "Should we get onto the case?"

"Yes, yes," agreed Charlotte, enthusiastically. "It's so weird. When I was going through this brief I got a couple of days ago, so many names came up. Names connected to your case."

"Connected to MMS?" asked Alex, taking a sip of wine.

"Yes, but let me explain the situation first." Charlotte pulled out the brief from her bag, which landed on the table with a thud.

"That looks like a quarter of our case file," joked Alex.

"That's it, though," said, Charlotte, getting excited. "I know there's a taskforce for your case, the—" she lowered her voice, "—Revenant case. Which means you're getting all sorts of information being triaged all over the place."

"Yeah, it's a bit of a new experience for me," conceded Alex. "Being just part of a machine, not always having all the information."

"Yes, well, that's why I wanted to tell you about this Sourcery matter. That is, like regular sorcery, but with a 'u'."

"Sourcery?" replied Alex, as if trying to remember something. "You mean that app you can use to hire a magician to do stuff?"

"Yes, that one," replied Charlotte.

"They've had some trouble, haven't, they?" continued Alex. "Some deal that went wrong, maybe?"

Charlotte looked at him quite surprised. "So, you know about that?"

"Well, I know a little bit," he confirmed. "Josh always gets the *Financial Review*. But, anyway, give me the full story—the financially illiterate cop version."

Charlotte smiled. "OK. Years ago, some tech guys from magic families in Melbourne had this idea—inspired by Uber and the rest—to create an app to allow people to hire a magician to do a show, train your horses, or even just clean up a big mess. It actually took off. They expanded overseas."

"So far, so good," observed Alex, sipping some wine.

"Yeah," agreed Charlotte. "But then, the business teamed up with another start-up, PayNow—a fintech, they call them—to offer some regular Sourcery users advances on their expected income."

"Kind of like one of those salary advance apps, or even buy now, pay later, I guess," replied Alex. "But riskier, I would imagine."

Charlotte looked at him.

"What?" said Alex. "I told you, Josh gets the *Financial Review* and I read it."

"Alex, this whole self-deprecating, *I'm just a financially illiterate* cop routine of yours—which you've now done *twice*, once at dinner and now here—is starting to get frustrating!"

"Sorry, sorry," said Alex. "It's just the way I am. Also, it can help with witnesses, you know, being underestimated."

Charlotte smiled at him. "I think they probably get disabused of that pretty fast. Anyway, Sourcery and PayNow teamed up to offer these advances—which is also a competitive advantage for Sourcery, because it makes it harder for a competitor to come in."

"No Lyft to their Uber, you mean?" offered Alex.

"Exactly," said Charlotte. "But—and this will become important later—there was this unusual arrangement, called a cross-shareholding, between the companies."

"Like Anglo American and De Beers, or those Japanese *keiretsu* companies?"

Charlotte frowned at Alex, now amused. "Yes, exactly like that. And I'm not going to say anything, except that you would not get away with this sort of false modesty if you weren't a white man from a middle-class background!"

Alex blinked. "I'm not sure I do get away with it, though," he replied. "I'm a detective. I remember things. It's one of the myriad ways that I'm fucking abnormal. Is that OK?"

Charlotte appeared momentarily speechless. "Well, I wouldn't have said you were *abnormal.*"

"It's OK," replied Alex. "It's true. I actually tried to be normal—well, MMS normal at least—when I went to uni and it was an absolute fucking disaster. Abnormal is better for me. At least I get to show off my bizarre knowledge of South African and Japanese corporate structures."

Charlotte smiled at him. "That got rather deep and meaningful fast, didn't it?"

Alex smiled back. "Yeah, sorry, like I said—"

Charlotte cut him off. "Don't say abnormal again. You know, I think I like you, Alex Hicks."

"And I like you too, Charlotte Bonnet. Though, if you really wanted to get on my good side, you would have also accused me of having pretty privilege. A colleague of mine, Pav, does it all the time. It's his only redeeming quality."

"Don't get ahead of yourself, dear."

"Fair enough," conceded Alex. "And it would appear that we are out of wine."

Charlotte returned soon enough with another bottle. She sat down and topped up their glasses.

"So, as I was saying, *about the matter*," she continued. "So Sourcery and PayNow team up, including taking stakes in each other, and start offering these advances to the magicians. And it takes off. As in really *takes off*."

"You mean, it expanded way beyond just the magicians on Sourcery?"

"Yes, that's right," confirmed Charlotte, with an expression that suggested she was wondering how much of this story Alex already knew. "But it also expanded differently to how you might expect. Initially, PayNow approached big employers, offering to provide a service where their staff could claim their wages in advance. But the employers— including government agencies—were lukewarm, at best."

"It all looked too much like payday lending, I guess?"

"Exactly. So, they started looking for other customers and basically landed on trade finance." She paused for a moment. "I'm assuming you know what that is."

"I think so," said Alex modestly. "You mean they advanced cash to companies secured against their sales to customers, then collected the cash from the customers when the bills became due."

"That is exactly what I mean. And, like I said, it *really* took off. Soon enough, they were funding everything from coal mines in Europe, agribusinesses in South America, to forestry companies in Appalachia."

"Appalachia, you say?" said Alex.

"Yes," replied Charlotte. "You know, in the USA. Very rural, lots of mines and stuff."

"Oh, I know where Appalachia is," said Alex. "It's just a weird coincidence. Isn't that essentially your fiancé's spiritual home? Simmo must have read *Hillbilly Elegy*."

"Don't be a dickhead, Alex."

"OK, fair. Go on. How did it all come crashing down?"

Charlotte looked at him again, with that 'how much of this do you already know?' expression. "Overall, by then, PayNow was doing billions in business in the trade financing space. There were major banks in Europe and big investors in America involved. The company issued massive amounts of bonds to finance everything. They bought insurance to support the creditworthiness of the bonds."

"But they said yes to clients that other players said no to," said Alex, "And maybe the receivables they were financing did not always—at least *technically*—exist, but they dressed that up with their alleged status as a tech company—"

"Alex!" cried Charlotte, accusingly. "Have I told you anything you don't already know?"

"Not a huge amount, to be fair," conceded Alex. "But you're a great storyteller, so at least finish. Then I have questions."

"Fine," replied Charlotte. "Yes, there were questions about the veracity of some of the invoices PayNow was monetising. Some of the big investors in the bonds ran for the exit. Then the insurance company balked at renewing coverage. Talks about going public became fears of a bankruptcy."

"It's an old story," observed Alex neutrally, sipping wine. "That much, I know. But I assume you're going to tell me why I should care, for my case, and the something—or, I assume, someone—that the companies had in common, leading to that cross-shareholding."

"Yes," said Charlotte. "I will. First, the *someone* they had in common was Laurence Archer, the all-around bigwig in both business *and* magic." She continued: "His son went to MMS, actually, and is about your age. Jamie, I think."

"I see," said Alex, sounding interested now, but ignoring the reference to Jamie. "He's *also* the outgoing chair of MMS."

"Yes, he is. And, at least in the case of Sourcery," continued Charlotte, "the financing was a bit different to a typical start-up. Instead of going to venture capital firms or Silicon Valley or whatever, they focused their initial fundraising on the Melbourne magic community."

"Including at MMS, I assume."

"Yes!" declared Charlotte, now a bit excited herself. "Do the names Mazur and Bishop mean anything to you? What about Dissanayake?"

"Well, you know I can't tell you that," replied Alex. "But, obviously, yes. Was Archer involved until the bitter end?"

"No," replied Charlotte. "He wasn't. He bailed as a director of PayNow fairly early. He even managed to cash out some of his investment in a funding round—PayNow definitely went to venture capital and Silicon Valley for funding."

"But the Sourcery business?"

"The thing is, that is actually profitable," replied Charlotte. "There's a group of original magic investors—like the Mazurs and Bishops—who have engaged me to contest the original cross-shareholding arrangement, and try to pull the original app out of the whole shitshow."

"And it's worth something?" asked Alex, now on the edge of his seat, sipping wine.

"Oh yeah," said Charlotte. "There is even an offer to buy it, for over a billion dollars, but that's a secret."

"There is?" wondered Alex, many permutations of means and motives circling in his head.

"Yes, from Bailey and Badenoch," Charlotte declared. "Si and Josh's firm."

"Shit!" exclaimed Alex. "No wonder you wanted to tell me!"

18

Alex Learns About Magic Supremacy

10 years ago

Alex and Emma sat at a table, drinking coffee at the MMS café.

Hey, Em, is magic supremacy really a thing? I mean, there's a Wikipedia page about it, but that doesn't mean much, does it?

Of course it's a thing, Alex. It has been for decades, centuries.

But like, not here? Not on campus?

Yes, here on campus! Obviously! You really are so naïve about magic.

Gee thanks, Em.

Sorry. But why are you even asking?

Yolanda thinks Jamie, the blonde, surfie-looking guy, might be one. Remember that thing he said in class?

"Yolanda, Julius. Hi!" That was Emma.

Yolanda and Julius were smiling, holdings hands and definitely looking at each other in *that* way. "You two weren't doing that annoying thing where you talk to each other in your own heads, were you?" accused Yolanda.

"No," replied Alex.

"Shit, you're a terrible liar, Alex," replied Yolanda, smiling.

"Yes, we were," conceded Emma, unapologetically. "You know, I could teach you to join in, if you feel left out."

"I'll think about it," said Yolanda, taking a seat at the table.

"I need to get going, babe," said Julius to Yolanda. (He seemed to barely notice anyone but Yolanda.)

"Sure, babe," she replied. He kissed her on the cheek and left.

Alex twirled his finger in the air. "So, Julius and you?"

"We can get to that later," replied Yolanda, dismissively. "Tell me what you were talking about."

"Oh, nothing. I was telling Em how well the routine is coming along."

"No, you weren't. Which makes zero for two, Alex."

"We were talking about magic supremacy," explained Emma, smiling.

"Oh really?" replied Yolanda. "You looking to join the club, Alex?"

"Wait, there's a *club*?" sputtered Alex, in disbelief.

"Of course there isn't actually a club, silly," scoffed Yolanda. "Magic supremacy is socially toxic. Why do you think everyone went silent when Jamie just *vaguely hinted* that he might be one? For that matter, how can you be *so* naïve, Alex, about everything?"

"I was saying the same thing, at least about magic," added Emma.

Why am I always subject to these fucking pile-ons, huh, Emma? "OK, fine, I'm naïve. I admit it. I must have led a sheltered life, aside from the borderline sexual predators, of course."

"I suppose borderline sexual predators are probably quite attracted to naiveté," said Yolanda, as if she was discussing something academic and esoteric—rather than men who had basically *taken advantage* of him. "I mean, it stands to reason."

"Fuck off," Alex grumbled in response.

"OK, I'm sorry, Alex," said Yolanda, realising she might have pushed things a bit too far. "I mean, it's like this. Magic supremacists cannot have their own club, so they set up, like, a front. Something respectable, but which allows them to meet up and be evil together."

"I'm pretty sure it's the Magic History Club here," declared Emma. "I mean, they just *look* like magic supremacists. And what do you need a Magic History Club for in a university that has a *whole department* dedicated to magical history?"

"I reckon you're right, Em," said Yolanda. "Magic supremacists do sometimes even call themselves *historians*. Alex, maybe you should ask Jamie if he's a member? I bet they're always looking for new recruits!"

"Yes," agreed Emma, smiling. "Maybe you could infiltrate the club and tell us about all the nefarious goings on?"

"Or maybe you two could just give it a rest?" suggested Alex, lightly.

"Hey, you were the one who seemed so interested in it!" insisted Emma.

"Maybe I was, but I'm *much more* interested in you and Julius, Yol."

"Yeah, so, me and Julius. We got together. It happens." Yolanda was beaming, almost glowing, despite her casual choice of words.

"That's great news, Yol!" declared Emma enthusiastically.

"For me," said Alex, "The big issue is, following our earlier conversation—now that you have a boyfriend—does that mean you have to stop talking about my sex life, or that I can start talking about yours?"

"Alex, you're far too well brought-up to quiz a lady about her sex life," replied Yolanda. Then she beamed again. "But it's pretty awesome!"

"Don't you two have training now?" asked Emma. "You know, for that routine that was coming along *so well.*"

They did.

19

Alex and Robbie Go to the Library

Present day

The library at Melbourne Magic School represented the school in microcosm. Part of it was much like any other university library. It had basic metal shelves stacked with ordinary books, journals and periodicals. There were computer terminals and photocopiers, and small study rooms with tables and audio-visual connections for students to work on group assignments. It even had 'chill-out zones' with beanbags and couches, where students could relax and read quietly. All very ordinary, as Alex had observed as a student.

Then, there was the 'Grimoire Room', which was next to the museum and housed the school's collection of spell books and scrolls. It wasn't an especially large collection—most of the more profound magical writings were created in the old world, centuries ago, and were rare—nor a large room. But it was a dramatic one. The often-ancient tomes were stacked across tall, ornate shelves, accessed by enchanted ladders that moved around of their own volition. The books themselves were often infused with magical energies. Some hummed, others glowed, while some were almost incorporeal, like ghost books. Some vanished altogether and reappeared, apparently at their own whim. Others physically moved: jiggling, opening and shutting, shooting out from their shelf, then coming back.

Unlike the main library, with its fluorescent lights, this room was lit by floating orbs of magical light.

In front of the moving, manic collection of books sat a huge, also ancient, wooden desk, oddly teamed with a computer, printer and plastic in-and-out-trays. Behind that desk sat Leon Mazur, Tammy's husband. He was a tall, very slim man, with grey hair and a neat salt-and-pepper beard. He had ushered Alex and Robbie into this part of the library to speak because, as he had put it: "The students cannot come in here without permission, so it will be private."

Alex and Robbie sat on the other side of the desk, on matching old and uncomfortable wooden chairs. "So, let's get it out of the way," said Robbie. "You were with your wife on the night of the murder?"

"Yes," replied Leon. "We had dinner—I made carbonara—then watched TV. Just a regular night, really."

"What show were you watching?" asked Robbie, casually.

"*Squid Game*. That Korean Netflix show. I hated it. Nasty and violent. Nihilistic. But Tammy loves it."

"But you watched it together?" probed Robbie, by way of confirmation.

"Oh yes," confirmed Leon. "We watched it together. I mean, she didn't like *Mad Men*, but I really enjoyed it and she watched that with me. That's married life, isn't it?"

"How did you get along with the victim, Nerida?" asked Robbie.

"Well. Very well," insisted Leon. "We were friends. My wife and I had her over for dinner, and John—John Bishop—we were all pretty close. But Nerida and John were best friends. It's all so sad."

"How did you all get on with Harry Archer?" asked Robbie.

"Harry?" said Leon, nervously. "Um, I guess Harry and my wife, and Nerida and John, they didn't quite see eye-to-eye."

"Is that right?" said Robbie, coolly. "How so? And why?"

"Ah," said Leon. "Harry and Mewan—the former dean—were very chummy. It was like he was Mewan's surrogate son or something. And I think some of us, to be fair, took John not getting the dean's job out on Harry."

"It sounds like you were more sympathetic to Harry than some of the other faculty."

"The older faculty, you mean?" said Leon, smiling gently. "I guess I *was* a bit more sympathetic. Academia can be very political. I always hated that stuff, which is probably why I ended up running the library. Less politics here."

"But your wife, John and Nerida, they were not fans?" Robbie probed.

"No," conceded Leon. "But it's not like they were *antagonists* or anything, either. After Mewan left, Harry got this idea that my wife and the others were out to get him. Which they weren't. He called them a cabal, a *baby-boomer cabal.*" Leon chuckled quietly. "I don't think we're all even baby-boomers! We're not *that* old."

Robbie went to ask something, but Alex got in first. "It sounds like you two spoke about this? Maybe even in here?"

"Yeah, we did," admitted Leon. "Harry was a voracious reader. He loved the old stuff here. We would talk sometimes, as he read. You cannot take these books out of the room—they're too precious, some are even dangerous—so we would chat sometimes."

"So, you two got along, at least?" asked Robbie.

"I suppose we did. I mean, I tried to help, even calm him down a bit. Harry, he … well, he's very good at some things, but not always so good with people."

"What do you mean?" inquired Robbie.

Leon sighed. "Harry is very talented with magic, but also just very smart. And handsome, and witty too. His big problem is that he cannot stop *selling* himself. It rubs some people up the wrong way, understandably. Sometimes, he would be here, reading," Leon gestured at the big, old wooden desk, "and he couldn't resist telling me about how he had been on TV the night before, talking about some weird magic cult in America, or that illusionist who became invisible to rob jewellery stores in Sydney. It often seemed like he was performing a role."

"He didn't do a great job selling his grant application," observed Robbie. "He said you refused to talk to Nerida about it."

"I did talk to Nerida about it! Harry just refused to believe me. He was very angry with me about that. As if he thought I had magical powers of persuasion over her."

"Why might he have thought that?" asked Robbie, trying to sound innocent.

That didn't work. Leon Mazur smiled condescendingly and said: "We were not having an affair, Detective. I doubt I'm anyone's idea of a sexy librarian."

Alex and Robbie did not look entirely convinced.

"The answer is no," said Leon, firmly.

Robbie changed tack. "What about the books, then? Necromancy ones. Do you keep records of who accesses them?"

"Like I said, you cannot 'check out' any of these books—so there is no system like that—but we do need to keep records about everything to do with necromancy. It's the law. I will print off a copy."

"How many necromancy books do you have?" asked Robbie, scanning the shelves.

"Heaps. But mainly in the main library. There's lots about necromancy that has been published, put online. It's a popular subject. So many young magic users go through a necromancy phase. It's a power thing, maybe. *You* did."

Leon was looking at Alex, who started to blush. "Wait, you remember me?" he asked, awkwardly.

"Oh, yes," replied Leon. "I actually remember both of you. You were together, at least for a while. You came here to the library together, and studied and giggled with each other."

"Mr Mazur," intoned Robbie, his voice an octave deeper than usual. "We're looking at someone who conjured a revenant to commit a murder. Not a script kid." (The latter term had been borrowed by magicians from information technology. As it happened, IT was among the most common non-magic career choices for magic users.) "There is one particular book we're interested in. Can you tell us who has read it recently?"

"You mean the *Treatise on Magick Relating to the Dead?*" said Leon, as his printer whirred. "We have two. One, in the original French. The other is a rare translation. We have one of three extant copies of it, the others are in the British Museum and the Boston Magic School Library. That translation is much more popular. It will show up in the printout."

"You do still have the book, though? It's not possible that someone took it away without registering?" asked Robbie.

"Of course, it is *possible* someone could have taken it," said Leon. "The faculty have access to this part of the library, for example. But I think the book is still here. Let me check."

Leon looked back to the rows of rowdy books, shuffling magical ladders and floating lights. "Give me the *Treatise on Magick Relating to the Dead*, published 1784," he said, loudly.

After he did so, a large, aged grimoire—bound in black leather—pulled itself off the shelf and carried itself slowly to the big, wooden desk that the group were seated around. As it landed, Alex, Robbie and Leon stood up. The book sat still on the desk, wrapped in its own miasma of dark energy, as if it was sucking away the light around it.

"Here it is," declared Leon, looking admiringly at the heavy tome. At one page, maybe two-thirds from the bottom of the book, the edge of a white card stuck out. "It looks like the latest reader has even left a bookmark," he stated.

"Let me," ordered Robbie, pulling the book towards his side of the desk. He put on some latex gloves, while he peered at the edge of the white card. "Does that look familiar?" he asked Alex.

"Yes," Alex agreed, thinking of the pure white business card saying only 'gatekeeper' at the scene of the summoning of the revenant.

Robbie opened the book to the page saved with the card. A plume of smoke and flame erupted from the page. Robbie fell back, managing to avoid any burns. From the fire emerged the torso of a beast, humanoid with bat wings, horns and reptilian features. Its long, skinny arms and taloned hands scrabbled at the detectives. Its massive nostrils and fanged mouth gushed smoke and flame towards them.

It was an *ifrit*, a malignant fire spirit assassin, and it burst into full form from the grimoire. It stood on the big oak desk, growling, grasping a flaming whip, snorting smoke and swinging its demonic tail. Then, it lunged towards Robbie. But he, unlike Alex or Leon—the latter of which cowered on the other side of the table—reacted immediately. With a gesture, he sent the apparition flying into the far wall, next to the shelves holding MMS's trove of spell books. The evil spirit landed with a loud thud and struggled against Robbie's telekinetic magic.

Alex rallied, his eyes glowing blue. The corona of flame around the summoned beast started to wane, burning off as steam. The creature howled, presumably in agony.

"This is a very climate-controlled environment, for the old books," Leon called out from wherever he was now hiding. "There's only so much water you can pull from the atmosphere in this room."

Alex didn't dignify that observation with a response. Instead, he tried to bind the summoned creature with ice, as Robbie continued to force it into the wall. But his ice was, indeed, brittle and ineffective, as the monster pulled off and broke any bonds that Alex sought to apply. Then, it arced its flaming whip in his direction. Alex raised his arms and winced in pain as the whip burned his skin.

Freed from Alex's magical attacks, the *ifrit* now stalked in the corner of the old library, its body aflame and its reptilian tail whipping across its cloven-hooved legs. As it crouched, preparing to charge the detectives again, Robbie stood, legs planted firmly on the ground and his enchanted Magic Squad issued pistol pointed squarely at the monster.

He fired. *Bang, bang!* His gun pulsed with magical runes and sigils. The barrel flashed with blue light as he fired. The flaming monster quivered and howled as the shots hit its body, spilling whatever it had instead of blood and leading it to vanish, leaving nothing but smoke and ash in its wake.

Leon stared at the two detectives in shock. Alex grimaced, clutching his arm. Robbie calmly holstered his pistol and looked with concern at Alex. "We need to get you to the healers."

"Wait, I can do that," Leon said, breaking through his apparent shock. He took hold of Alex's arm, gently. "This isn't too bad, really." His eyes glowed with white light. The red burn mark on Alex's arm rapidly disappeared, until his arm was entirely as before. "See," said Leon, now smiling proudly. "Magic healing works an absolute treat on burn injuries, if we can get to them right away. Healers have been doing this since the Crimean War."

"Thanks," said Alex. The pain in his arm was now completely gone, but he was still very rattled and shaky. Indeed, he was disappointed in himself that he hadn't reacted as quickly as Robbie had, nor even as quickly as he had when Hot Rod had fired at him. "Sorry, I was a bit slow off the mark," he said, not even quite sure to whom. "I'm new to these magic cases."

"That's alright, Alex," said Robbie, with a warm chuckle. "We all have to go through our first magical booby-trap. It's basically a rite of passage."

The two smiled at each other, then suddenly realised they were still in the presence of a member of the public, a witness, possibly even a suspect.

"This is now a crime scene," said Robbie, looking severely at Leon. "We will need to call this in, and nobody is allowed into this room. Do you understand?"

Robbie was using what Alex called his 'authority voice'. It was even deeper than his regular voice and was always accompanied by a look of extreme seriousness that brooked no argument.

"Yes, of course," said Leon.

"But before we go," said Alex, "could we see who the last faculty members were to sign out the book?"

"Sure," replied Leon. "That horrible fire thing managed to miss the printout." He pulled the sheet of paper from the printer. "Hmmm …" he said.

"What is it?" asked Robbie, in the authority voice.

"The last faculty members to read the book were Harry Archer, then Nerida Stein and, before that, Mewan Dissanayake—but Mewan was former faculty when he read it. Does that count?"

"Yes, it counts," said Robbie.

"My suit and shirt are ruined," said Alex, sourly, as he and Robbie stood outside MMS. Crime scene officers had swarmed into the university after they called in the ifrit incident. Groups of students, who had previously ignored the unfamiliar pair of young men in suits, now openly gawked at them. Robbie lit a cigarette—he had been smoking a lot, thought Alex—and eyed Alex's burnt sleeve.

"If you're going to stay in the Magic Squad," he said, grinning a little meanly, "You might need to invest in some cheaper suits and shirts. They look expensive."

"They are!" Alex whined back at him. "My boyfriend …" He trailed off. He was, of course, going to say that his boyfriend bought his suits for him. (Well, paid for them, anyway.) Which was true, but why tell Robbie that? It wasn't as if he was super comfortable having a rich banker boyfriend with family money who paid for everything—and had basically offered to turn him into a house husband. And how would mentioning his rich boyfriend come across—like he was bragging, rubbing Robbie's nose in it, especially given Robbie was single? *Or was he?* wondered Alex. He didn't exactly say he was single, just that he and Jack had broken up.

Robbie seemed to ignore Alex's reference to his boyfriend. "There was a card, wasn't there, in the grimoire?" he asked, by way of changing the subject.

"Yeah. I was tempted to read it, but I figured we needed to leave the book alone for the crime scene guys. We'll have to make sure we find out what it says, and whether it's the same type as the one at the other summoning site."

"Surely it is?" said Robbie, sounding incredulous, as if it went without saying that it would be the same and, by implication, that it was left by the same person who reanimated Mewan Dissanayake's corpse into a monster to murder Nerida Stein.

Alex, though, wasn't so sure. "It probably is. *Probably.*" He grinned at Robbie. "But I'm learning, with these magic cases, never to make *any* assumptions."

"Fair. You're a quick study, Alex. You always were."

Alex ignored his comment, especially the second part. "Of course, the bigger question on my mind is, why did whoever placed that summoning enchantment in the necromancy book do it? What was their motivation, and who was the intended target?"

"This *bigger question* shtick is a bit of a thing with you, isn't it?"

"Yes, that, and touching my hair. They're basically my signature moves."

"But you've *always* touched your hair."

Alex ignored Robbie's comment, again. "I think there are two main possibilities. First, that the perp assumed Leon would, on hearing about a necromantic murder, open up the treatise—out of curiosity, maybe, or because he wanted to do some amateur sleuthing himself—and get fried by the ifrit. Which would mean Leon Mazur was the target and someone—some magic user—is trying to kill him."

"That makes sense," said Robbie, nodding and blowing out some smoke.

"It does, sort of," agreed Alex. "But the problem is that (a) Leon actually didn't open the book until we were around and (b) why leave a card with the book, therefore explicitly linking this attempted murder to the successful murder of Nerida Stein? Unless they actually aren't related, but this second perp wants us to think they are, *and* he somehow found out about the card at the other summoning site."

"Which sounds unlikely," said Robbie.

"Yes, which leaves the second possibility, which is that the killer, the original killer, had no intention of killing Leon Mazur, and this was just a further bit of dramatic misdirection to make this case seem more complicated than it is and send us down some rabbit hole of red-herring leads."

Robbie thought for a moment. "That is possible. But it's pretty dramatic, isn't it? Elaborate."

"Prince Harry dramatic and elaborate?" pondered Alex. "But the problem is, if *our* Prince Harry is involved with this, why sign out the book? It's not like he would've needed to do any revision to be able to summon an ifrit. And he could have probably accessed the book to booby-trap it with a summoning spell without needing to sign it out. He's faculty, after all; nobody would question him looking at any book, assuming Leon wasn't around. Harry would be putting himself in the frame when he didn't have to."

"Yes, that's true," agreed Robbie. "It doesn't make sense." He continued: "But aren't you missing the third possibility?"

"What's that?" asked Alex.

"That someone was actually trying to kill *us*," said Robbie, as if he was stating the bleeding obvious.

"Oh, come on, Robbie," scoffed Alex. "I dismissed that out of hand."

"Why?"

"Because it's ridiculous. We're part of a police taskforce. It's not like we would, what, be scared off the case because there's a little bit of danger. This isn't a trashy thriller novel! And what if that thing *had* killed us—police would be crawling all over the case *even more*. Besides, you don't kill two magic users with offensive affinities with something like an ifrit. A body and healing mage like Leon Mazur, maybe, but not us. I mean, if I wasn't such a rookie magic cop, the thing wouldn't have lasted 20 seconds."

Robbie looked at Alex with a bemused, but affectionate smile. "Do people ever tell you that your mind works in rather strange ways?"

"All the time. I should really add that as my third signature move."

"We should get back to the station and debrief," declared Robbie, looking at Alex with an inscrutable expression.

As the pair walked to their car, Robbie's phone pinged. It was Evan Ellis, his old friend: *Come out on Saturday. You need a break!*

"Something important?"

"No, nothing," said Robbie. "Just a social thing."

20

Melbourne Magic School
Takes on its Arch-rival

10 years ago

"Are we going to smash it?" shouted Assane, as he, Alex, Yolanda and Jamie joined in a huddle.

"Yes!" cried Alex, Yolanda and Jamie in unison.

"Are we going to the nationals in Canberra?" shouted Assane, even louder.

"Yes!"

"Are we going to lose to—" Assane adopted an exaggerated sneer— "*Monash?*"

"No!" they all shouted, louder than ever.

This was the big one, the 'derby' between old arch-rivals.

There were three magic schools in Victoria: Melbourne Magic School, founded in 1855 as a specialist part of the University of Melbourne, itself created just two years earlier; Monash Magic School, created in 1958 as an original faculty of Monash University; and Hopetoun University, a magical technical college still focused on diploma-type courses.

Hopetoun students were less likely to be from established magic families and, therefore, less likely to compete in magic contests. As a result, aside from a couple of very rare upsets, the Victorian championships

165

were generally seen as a head-to-head battle between MMS and Monash. Because of this broader rivalry (though University of Melbourne students might claim any such 'rivalry' existed only in the minds of Monash students) these magic games attracted audiences, even outside the parochial magic schools themselves.

On top of that, this year, the competition was being held at MMS. Which meant the crowd was big, loud and very much rooting for the home team. The atmosphere and expectation left all four teammates buzzing with nerves and excitement. The fact Robbie and Nora had already trounced their opponents piled on the pressure even further.

"Quiet, please; the elements competition is about to commence." The crowd dutifully went silent. Hopetoun would go first, followed by Monash. MMS would be third.

"Saving the best for last," whispered Assane to Alex.

"Let's hope so."

Hopetoun—which fielded two fire practitioners, one earth, and one water—put on a competent routine, but not one that would have warranted qualification for the MMS team. They didn't use the contained storm apparatus at all, and the team's displays lacked coordination between the different elements.

Once the Hopetoun team had finished, there was respectable clapping—aside from a small, diehard group of Hopetounians, who whooped and cheered, waving banners in the school's purple colours.

"No big upset on the cards this year," whispered Yolanda.

"Don't be mean," admonished Alex.

"I'm not mean. I'm just competitive. Like you."

Monash was up, with two earth practitioners, and one each of fire and water. At the start of the routine, the earth mages radically expanded the area of the earth apparatus, sprouting it with tall, dense, eucalyptus forest. Then the fire mage created a large spherical ball of flame above the forest, no doubt representing the sun. Quickly, the forest began to dry out, becoming more yellow, less green, with dry underbrush forming.

"It's a cute idea," said Alex, quietly, but loud enough for all of the huddled group to hear.

"Yes, it's sort of artistic, isn't it?" said Assane, neutrally. "A comment on the Australian landscape."

"While we invested more in spectacle and, like, wow-factor," replied Yolanda. "Despite having a bona-fide artist on the team'"

Suddenly, the forest was aflame. The fire burnt bright for many seconds. Then, the water mage rose into the air, shaping a large sphere of water—much like Alex had done in his qualifying routine. The sphere dispersed into clouds and the mage sent a violent rainstorm over the forest, crackling with thunder and dumping enough water on the forest both to put out the fire and send rivulets of water running onto the games room floor.

"Flooding rains. Cool," said Yolanda, approvingly. "Clever."

"But not very technically ambitious," declared Jamie. "And they didn't use the storm apparatus, either. Maybe they couldn't figure out how to work it in?"

"Or their water guy is just not as good as ours," suggested Assane, smiling at Alex.

"Jamie is doing our storm routine, Assane, not me," said Alex. Then, he looked to Jamie. "Are you OK to do the *showstopper*?" he asked. "It looks like we could probably get away without it."

"I am," he replied, sounding steely. "We do the routine as planned. The A-game one."

"Agreed," said Yolanda. Assane also nodded.

As the Monash team concluded its performance, islands of blue-clad Monash attendees cheered and clapped uproariously among the sea of MMS maroon. In the crowd, Alex thought he saw a familiar, reassuring head of red hair.

Here to support the magic jocks, Emma?

Just go and nail, it, dummy.

Alex smiled. Then they were up.

First, Yolanda expanded the earth apparatus to a similar scale to the Monash mages. But, instead of a forest, she created a massive single tree, whose dense, leafless branches reached high into the air. Next, Alex, Assane and Jamie levitated themselves on pillars of wind, fire and electricity, respectively. They each carried huge, spherical concentrations of their affinity element: Alex had water, Assane had fire, and Jamie raised the contained storm apparatus, which crackled and flashed intensely with lightning.

The three spheres hovered above the tree, looking like a crown: fire on the left, water in the middle and what now looked like solid lightning on the right. Then, the spheres came together. The fire and water spheres formed a dense cloud of steam around the top of the tree, almost like a dense leaf canopy made of water vapour. Alex remained in the air. Assane dropped to the ground and created a moat of licking flames around the base of the tree.

Jamie launched himself towards the system of wires, creating a dazzling mosaic of electricity on the wall. Then, it was time for the 'showstopper'. Jamie, again at the head of a huge arc of electricity, flew right into the centre of the massive cloud atop the tree. It glowed with white light and crackled with noise as lightning swirled inside. The flames around the tress leaped higher.

Then the routine was over. The crowd erupted—even the blue and purple fans seemed enthusiastic.

As the group hugged, Yolanda declared: "We're going to Canberra!"

"I think Nathan wants to talk to us," said Jamie, as the journalist for the *Cockatrice* waved at the group. They walked towards him as the crowd kept clapping.

Alex pulled Jamie aside. "Jamie, after we talk to Nathan, there was something I wanted to ask you."

"Sure, no problem," replied Jamie, altogether nonchalant.

21

Robbie and Alex Interview
John Bishop

Present day

"So, I see you two got the band back together." That was John Bishop, still looking like an artist *sans* beret and seated in a bleak interview room at Victoria Police headquarters. Robbie and Alex sat opposite. Robbie had just started the tape and given the time, date and attendees to the recording device.

Alex thought he detected a certain puffiness around John Bishop's eyes, hinting at a lack of sleep. This could be suggestive of grief—or guilt. Alex generally tried to avoid reaching conclusions about witnesses and suspects based on mannerisms and body language, simply because they could be so deceptive. (The moment *behind the eyes*, when a suspect realises the police might be onto them, was the exception that proved the rule.)

"Though, Robbie, I'm not sure about the man-bun. What do you think, Alex?"

"Tell us about your relationship to the victim, Nerida Stein," ordered Robbie, in full *authority Robbie* mode.

John Bishop hesitated for a moment. "Nerida was my friend. My best friend. We knew each other, and worked together, for decades."

"Were there any conflicts, at work or in her personal life?" asked Robbie.

"Do you mean Harry Archer?" suggested John Bishop, smiling nastily.

"What about Harry Archer?"

"Well, I *assume* you've spoken to him. And he told you about the *baby-boomer cabal* and all the rest of his paranoid, persecution complex drivel."

"And what would be your view on that *drivel*?" inquired Robbie.

"Well, I suppose that it was just that, drivel. Harry had this meteoric rise when Mewan was dean. Then Mewan wasn't dean, and the meteorite crashed to earth a bit. No surprise, but Harry was embittered about it."

"I see," said Robbie, with dispassion. "Did he ever say or do anything to make you think he wished Nerida harm?"

"To me?" John guffawed. "Of course, he never said anything to *me*. Why would he? Like I said, I was Nerida's best friend. And, if you mean 'did he make threats', there was nothing I heard about."

"So why raise him immediately?" asked Robbie, now sounding steely.

"Because you asked me whether I knew about any interpersonal conflicts with Nerida, and I answered your question, Detective," replied John, sounding equally steely.

"And the source of this conflict was, what, purely generational and related to career advancement?" inquired Robbie.

John appeared to think for a moment. "It really went into overdrive when Nerida refused to endorse his proposed grant application. Something about chasing spooks, I recall. He even asked *me* to talk to her about it. I mean me, of all people!"

"I take it you didn't?"

"Of course not," snorted John Bishop. "If Neri thought a grant application wasn't a goer, it wasn't a goer. That was my view, and Tammy's. Even Mewan rated Nerida on *that*. Of course, he would have supported it anyway, for his little *Prince* Harry."

It looked like John Bishop wanted to say more, so the detective let him.

"I was actually surprised he was so upset. I always got the impression that his academic career was basically a side hustle—I think that is the term they use now—for his TV and online presence."

"Did Nerida disapprove of that?"

"Yes, she probably did. She was a stickler for *everything*. But I don't believe she would have refused to support his application because of that. Or the fact Harry is an insufferable little shit. But *Harry* thought that."

Robbie decided it was time to move on. "What about her admissions role? You did that with her for two decades or more?"

"Is that a question?"

"Yes."

"Are you asking me whether that might have been a, what, motive for her killer?"

"Couldn't it have been?"

John laughed. "MMS is not Harvard or Oxford, Robbie. Nobody is killing anyone to get in." He looked at Alex, eyes like daggers. "Look at this one," he said. "I basically ordered Nerida to let him in, and he was gone within a year."

"We aren't talking about Detective Hicks."

"No," countered John. "But it rather proves my point, doesn't it?"

"It doesn't," Alex interjected.

"Wow, it speaks," smarmed John. "Do you have a question for me?"

"Yes," replied Alex, without any of Robbie's gravitas or aura of authority. "Why is it that you remember us, and me specifically? You would have had hundreds, even thousands of students over the years."

"I don't know," insisted John. "You were a good-looking couple. I overruled Nerida to let you in and you were doing fine until, for whatever stupid reason, you vanished. So, yes, I remember you—and Robbie."

"OK," replied Alex. "I think that answers my question."

"Oh, and there was that time I caught you and—who was it, that artist guy—in the museum looking at the revenant skeleton. Isn't it weird what you remember and what you don't?"

"And I seem to recall your comment: no matter what one's affinity, with enough practice, any magic user can master any discipline," Robbie shot back.

"Sounds like me," countered John. "Is that an indirect way of asking whether I have taught myself summoning and necromancy?"

"Yes," replied Robbie.

"No, I haven't."

"And," Robbie persevered, "do you have an alibi for the night in question?"

"No. I'm a confirmed bachelor. I was alone."

"OK," said Robbie. In a slightly warmer tone, he said, "Mr Bishop, we're trying to find out who killed your best friend. So, we need you to tell us everything—anything and everything—that might help us do that. Was Nerida acting strangely? Had she changed any of her habits? Anything?"

"There was something."

"Go on," urged Robbie, leaning forward.

"So, for quite a while—less than a year, but definitely more than six months—Nerida seemed to have something going on. She was less available socially, and I had to organise more of our catch-ups. She used to initiate them more, but I found myself being the sherpa."

Robbie asked, "As if she had picked up a new obligation or interest?"

"Yes, like that," agreed John Bishop. "It *could* have been a gentleman friend, but she would normally have told me about that. She usually did, when she met a man."

"So, she dated quite a bit?" prompted Robbie.

"Oh yes," agreed John, almost sounding wistful. "Neri frequently had boyfriends. She was great company, funny, and attractive. But she was obsessed with the early part of relationships, when everything is new and exciting—and very passionate. That we-cannot-keep-our-hands-off-each-other phase."

"Which, of course, does not last," said Robbie.

"No, it doesn't. Then she would get bored, I guess. Move onto the next one. The thing is, she realised she was like that in relationships, but only when she wasn't in one. Then there would be a new beau and she would be declaring him the love of her life after a few weeks. Then," John made a flicking motion, presumably to say, "Then she gave them the flick."

"But you don't think there was a new man before her death?" prompted Robbie.

"No, I don't," replied John. "But I'm not sure what else it could be. Or maybe she was just keen to spend more time by herself. It's not as if I actually *asked* her. It really didn't seem like a big deal, until—"

"Until her death," finished Robbie.

"Death by a *fucking summoned revenant*! That suggests some serious motive, doesn't it? I mean, not something random."

"That's what we're trying to find out," replied Alex gently.

"I hope you do," replied John.

"Is there anything else you want to tell us?" asked Robbie, not cold, but certainly calm and professional.

"No," replied John. "There isn't."

"Last question, then," said Alex. "Why didn't you go for the dean's job after Mewan left? Or did you?"

"No, I didn't. I guess I just thought my time had passed. And I found going for it the first time and not getting it a bit … traumatic, I suppose."

"Thank you for your time," said Robbie, neutrally. "Interview terminated at—"

Robbie was in the smoking area of the Lion with Alex. "So, give me the hot take on it, Lex, um, Alex?" Robbie asked, cradling a scotch and soda. "Was John Bishop being entirely truthful?"

"It's hard to say. There are so many things going on in this case. So many moving pieces, and magic just complicates the picture. I have to say, though, you're really good at the interviews."

"Not your strong suit?" inquired Robbie.

"I guess I just don't have your gravitas and sense of authority," Alex replied. "I never have. Even—"

"Even when we were together?" Robbie finished.

"I was wondering, though," said Alex, changing the subject. "While nobody might kill to get into MMS, maybe people might bribe the admissions officer? Remember those rich people and celebrities a couple of years ago, who went to bizarre lengths to pay off people to get their kids into the University of *Southern California* or whatever?"

"Not exactly Stanford or Yale," agreed Robbie.

"No. And some of these magic families here, could they have greased the wheels with Nerida? Could that have become a motive for murder?"

"Motives, though," replied Robbie. "Motives are for TV shows and novels. Most killers kill, their reasons make little sense. Or they're just abusers, or psychos."

"Yes, I know," conceded Alex. "But still."

"Someone from this huge taskforce must be looking at the admission files anyway," reasoned Robbie. "So, we'll probably find out if there were some marginal applicants who made it in."

"Like me, you mean?" mused Alex.

"For God's sake, Alex!"

"And then there were Bishop's comments about Nerida and some new hobby, or interest, or man," Alex continued, ignoring Robbie's rebuke. "It could be anything, couldn't it?"

"Yes. Or it could all be totally irrelevant," replied Robbie. "Let's talk to the guys going through her emails." Robbie's expression changed. "Why did you never mention looking at that revenant thing at the time? It was with Assane, wasn't it?"

"Robbie, it was ten years ago!"

"I know, Alex. But you started it!"

"OK. It was because I knew you wouldn't have approved."

22

Alex and Assane Get
a Fright in the Museum

10 years ago

"That really is *nasty*," declared Assane.

"Yeah," agreed Alex. "And, despite what Robbie said, it's not just a *skeleton*, which makes it even worse."

Indeed, standing in the poorly-lit semi-darkness of the closed museum, before Alex and Assane, was a massive glass tank—with macabre Victorian brass embellishments—containing the fully preserved corpse of an abomination. It looked a little like a human body, but one that had been chaotically twisted and mutated. One arm was short and muscular, the other was long and thin, as if it would have dragged on the ground when this thing was, what, *alive*? Both arms ended with similarly vicious claws.

Even more striking was that the horror had a number of bizarre bat-like features. Its stubby legs ended in thin, bat claws, as if it would hang from a tree. It had a set of small, misshapen wings. Even its head and face were an ugly amalgam of human and bat. Its mouth was filled with prominent, almost snake-like fangs—or, perhaps, like those of a vampire bat.

"The worst thing is that it was once human," said Assane.

"Yeah. I don't think I've ever seen anything so creepy."

"Me neither. Why did you make me come here with you, at night?" asked Assane.

"If you come during the day, you have to sign a form. Something to do with legal requirements around necromancy. Besides, if you're going to look at something like this, you may as well do it at night for the full terrifying nightmare experience."

"But why bring me along for the ride?"

"Because Robbie wouldn't have approved. And he's apparently still tutoring Jack on the manipulation and telekinesis stuff."

"Still?" asked Assane. "Has Jack still not got it?"

"He has, I think," insisted Alex. "Now they're doing a masterclass, Robbie says. At least that means they're getting along better. Besides, I figured you would've seen this thing already."

"I haven't. Not all of us think necromancy is cool."

"I didn't say it was cool! Anyway, you could hardly have let me come here by myself. What if the thing came alive and attacked me?"

"Don't be stupid, Ali."

Thud! Ouch! Shit!

Had this been a cartoon, Alex would have jumped into Assane's arms in surprise. Instead, he simply jumped, as did Assane. And they wound up sort of in each-others' arms anyway. They also both yelped.

The pair were suddenly bathed in magic light, as a figure—a slightly limping one who had clearly banged his knee on something—approached them.

"Bloody hell, Assane. You should know better!" This was John Bishop. "Sneaking into the museum at night to look at that *thing*! You're not a first year!"

"Sorry," said Assane, meekly.

"I put him up to it," declared Alex, also meekly.

"Did you just, Mr Hicks," replied John. "I thought you would be too sensible to be into necromancy."

"Sorry," replied Alex, even meeker, like a scolded child.

John Bishop softened, somewhat. "Don't worry. It happens all the time. Here's the deal: you can look at that awful thing for as long as you want, but don't expect sympathy from me for your nightmares. Also, you need to sign the form tomorrow. It's the law."

"We will," the two young men said, in unison.

Then, like that, John Bishop was gone.

"I think I need to sit down," said Alex, almost dizzy with post-shock adrenalin. Instead, he fell further into Assane's arms, breathing heavily. Assane was also struggling. "Sorry I got you into trouble," Alex practically whispered in Assane's ear.

"That's OK, Ali," said Assane, soothingly. "I did agree to it and, like John said, I'm a big boy now."

The pair paused in silence for a moment, as they started to regain their composure. They weren't even looking at the revenant corpse anymore. They were looking—really *looking*—at each other.

"Thanks for coming with me," said Alex.

Assane kissed him.

On reflection, Alex was certain that he did not kiss back. Almost certain, anyway. At the very least, he did not kiss back much, not much *at all.*

"What the absolute *fuck*, Assane!" he shouted, pushing the taller man away immediately. (Well, almost immediately. Very quickly, at the absolute minimum.)

"Sorry, sorry. I'm sorry," stammered Assane. "I didn't mean, I mean, we both just got a shock."

"Yes, yes we did," agreed Alex. "But where on earth did that come from?"

"Oh, come on, Ali. You cannot be that clueless, we've been flirting with each other for months."

"No, we haven't!" cried Alex in response.

"Yes, we have," snapped Assane. "Do you think I normally start playing dominance games with everyone I meet? And do you always do that freakishly sexy self-deprecating, humblebragging, cocky-yet-submissive routine? A blind person could see what was going on!"

"What do you mean, routine? I was just responding to you and your fucking dickhead moves! If I knew anything about routines, or being freakishly sexy, don't you think I would've had more than one boyfriend in my life who actually likes me, and cuddles, and answers my calls, and lets me cum?"

"Ali, you're literally doing the routine right now," retorted Assane, actually smiling a little.

"No, I'm not!" said Alex, sounding more whiny than passionate. "And, besides, you're basically blaming me for leading you on. Like a rapist!"

Assane clearly did not wish to dignify this comment with a response.

"OK, I didn't mean that. But what did you think was going to happen? That I would be, like, 'Oh, Assane, you are so magnificent. I will leave Robbie and be with you'?"

"Ali, I just like you. That's all. And, if you mean what happened just now, I think it's safe to say I wasn't *thinking* at all."

"Well, *obviously*. So how about this? We forget this ever happened. We never speak of it again. We go back to our rooms. We sign that stupid form for John Bishop. We agree that we will behave like normal people around each other. You will not play those dominance games, which—according to you—make me respond in ways you find sexually irresistible. So, are we agreed?"

"Yes, Ali, we're agreed. Now let's get out of here."

"Where did you find this old geezer pub, Ali?" asked Yolanda, as she looked distastefully around the outdoor smoking area of the Melbourne Lion Hotel.

"It's a cop pub," replied Alex. "Has been for years. Not sure why, but there's some talk of building a brand-new Victoria Police headquarters just down the road."

"How fascinating," replied Yolanda, in a tone that suggested it was anything but. "I take it you didn't bring me here to introduce me to your father or something?"

"No," said Alex, sipping a scotch and soda and sucking on his second cigarette. "I wanted to talk to you about a couple of things away from campus where we wouldn't bump into anyone."

"Ooo, I see," said Yolanda, leaning in conspiratorially, putting her sour white wine to the side. "How ... *clandestine*! Are you wanting to tell me a secret?"

Nice to see you're enjoying yourself, Yol! "Yes, two secrets, actually. But you have to promise, *promise* me you won't tell *anyone*. OK?"

"OK, I won't. Unless you've committed a crime or something, which seems unlikely, given who your parents are." She paused, looking suddenly even more excited. "Wait, is it about Assane?"

"Yolanda!"

"What? I said yes. I promise not to tell anyone. Now spill!"

"Alright," said Alex, pausing for effect and prompting Yolanda to lean towards him even more. "So, the first secret *is* about Assane—"

"What did you do?" demanded Yolanda, who seemed excessively, irritatingly excited.

"*I* didn't do anything, Yolanda. *He* did. He kissed me."

Alex wasn't sure he had ever seen someone look so triumphant, and for such unjustified reasons. Affecting an air of fake innocence, Yolanda said, "But I thought Assane wasn't into you. That he was just a dominant guy with dickhead tendencies."

"OK, Yolanda," said Alex. "You can do the whole 'I told you so' thing. You can tell me how naïve and hopeless I am, or you can be quiet and let me give you all the gory details."

Yolanda sat back in her chair and sipped her wine. "Alright," she said. "You win. I hate it when you win."

"Must be a novel experience for you, Yol."

Yolanda laughed. "True. Now get on with the story."

Alex did. Yolanda was entranced, interrupting his account to ask clarifying questions, making sure she got every detail. "So, you didn't kiss back, at all?"

"No, of course not! I pushed him off immediately!"

"Immediately?"

"Yes, immediately."

"Then what happened?"

"Well, he said sorry," replied Alex, speaking quite carefully. "But he also said—and this will be familiar to you—that we had this, sort of, dynamic going. He asked me if I thought he 'played dominance games with everyone he meets' or something. It felt like he was accusing me of asking for it, which—to be fair—he probably didn't mean to do."

"No, he probably didn't. And, in his defence, everyone except for you could see what was going on from the Moon, let alone orbit."

"Apparently so," groused Alex. "But in *my* defence, he accused me of putting on a routine where I'm simultaneously cocky, self-deprecating and submissive. Which is apparently irresistible to him."

"Well, it's at least endearing," said Yolanda. "And, like you say—in your defence—you basically do that with everyone."

"I know!" agreed Alex. "Well, everyone who is more, what, dominant or assertive than me, which is *practically* everyone."

"Mind you," said Yolanda, "it has worked for you, this incident aside."

"What do you mean?" replied Alex.

"Shit, Ali. You're doing the routine now! Do I need to spell it out? You have two gorgeous men throwing themselves at you. You have heaps of friends—you're one of the most popular students on campus. Not to mention star of the magic team. Need I go on?"

"Well, you *could*."

"Just to be clear, Ali, comments like that are part of the cocky element of the routine. My least favourite part of it."

"Yeah but, without that, wouldn't I just be some kind of doormat?"

"Maybe," conceded Yolanda. "But what are you going to do?"

"Nothing," said Alex, definitively. "Forget it happened. Stay civil. Try to act normal around each other. I couldn't think of anything else to do. And it's not like there weren't extenuating circumstances."

"True," said Yolanda. "I think I would do the same thing. Or—" she grinned. "Maybe suggest a threesome."

"Yolanda!"

"You do make it so easy, my darling, when you're so easily scandalised."

"Fine," said Alex. "That's Assane taken care of. My second one is even juicier."

"Really?" replied Yolanda. "The first one was juicy enough, I had forgotten there *is* a second one." She looked at her empty wine glass.

"Should we get another drink first? Alex?" Concern flashed across her face as she saw Alex look suddenly alarmed. "Is everything all right?"

"Yes, fine," said Alex, calming down. "We need to find another place. I just saw my father here and if he catches me smoking, I will be in big trouble!"

As they scurried hurriedly from the Lion, Yolanda said, "At least give me a sense of what it's about while we're walking."

"Sure," agreed Alex. "You know how we were talking about secretive magic supremacists with front clubs, and you and Em suggested I should infiltrate one?"

"Sure," replied Yolanda blankly. "As a joke, obviously. What about it?"

"Well, I did. I infiltrated the club."

"You WHAT?"

23

Robbie Hits the Town

Present day

Robbie sat up in bed, crossing his legs—which were clad in a pair of grey tracksuit pants—and scratching his bare chest. His hair, freed of the man-bun Alex disdained, hung across his shoulders. It was early (at least weekend early, for a childless single man) but years of early-rising police hours had meant Robbie's sleeping-in capacity had maxed out at 8 am. He was also a bit 'dusty'—not quite hungover—and was starting to feel hungry, including for some nicotine.

However, doing more than sitting in bed, propped up with pillows, seemed like too much for now. He picked up his phone from the bedside table and started reading the news. The necromancer case was still getting a run, if not quite as much as before, especially given that all the outlets had finally realised that there was no necrotic horror on the loose. But interest had been bolstered by Alex and Robbie's encounter with the ifrit. Some publications were doing whole stories on the nature of ifrits, their powers and their relationship with Middle Eastern folklore and religion.

Robbie's phone rang. It was his old friend, Evan Ellis. "Wow, E," Robbie said down the line, "an actual phone call. This must be the most exciting property opportunity *ever!*"

"Don't be a dick, Robbie. I'm calling to make sure you actually come out with us tonight."

"I didn't agree to come out, though," said Robbie. He was smiling. He had planned to join his old mate and his friends in the evening, but there seemed no urgent need to telegraph this to Evan, yet.

"Yes, I *know*," said Evan. "That is why I'm calling. Unless you make a solid commitment to come, you will bail—you always do—and you *need* to unwind and have some fucking fun!"

"Do I?"

"Yes, you *do*!" Evan insisted, passionately. "I've been reading all about this case of yours. What a fucking shitshow. Horrible. And were you one of the cops attacked by that fire spirit thing?"

"You know I can't tell you that," replied Robbie, breezily. Given Evan had already thoroughly woken him up, he rose out of bed and walked down the stairs to the living room and kitchen.

"That is basically a yes," countered Evan. "Which is why I'm taking time out of my glamorous wheeler-dealing day to call you—"

"Does wheeler-dealing mean putting out those auction signs on the side of the road?"

"We discussed you being a dick already," Evan shot back. "You need to see some people. You need to have fun. You really need to *get laid*."

"Thanks for your concern, E," said Robbie, who was now downstairs, opening the pantry to get some cereal. "Who is coming and what is the plan?"

"Well, you know, the usual," replied Evan. "Derek is coming, so is Mark and Lucas."

Robbie and Evan knew Derek from the underage events they had met at as teenagers. Meanwhile, Mark was one of Evan's colleagues at the real estate agency. Lucas, an artist—at least, an aspiring one (whose work Robbie did not quite 'get')—was Mark's on-off, open-relationship boyfriend. (Robbie found the idea of that utterly exhausting.) "And the plan?" he inquired.

"The usual, again," replied Evan. "We're going to Supermarket. First, drag trivia—you're good at trivia—then dancing, hooking up, fun. Remember fun?"

Robbie poured some milk into his cereal. He hadn't received a call exhorting him simply to catch up with Evan and 'the lads' before. Something was up. "That's it?" he asked. "Going out with the lads—that is all you're calling me about?"

There was a moment of silence on the line. "OK, OK, *Detective* Chang. You've caught me out. There is something."

"What?"

"A new boy, Robbie. A 'nice' boy—I know you like 'nice' boys. His name is Winston. He joined the firm a year-and-a-bit ago."

"Winston?" mused Robbie. With a name like that, Robbie deduced that the boy would be ethnic Chinese. (Caucasians did not name their children 'Winston'.) But that was fine, wasn't it? It wasn't like Robbie peppered his hook-up app profiles with offensively exclusive, ethnic expectations. Of course, he didn't. And he had been with Asian guys, he was sure. At least a few times. He must have.

"Yeah, Winston," said Evan. "Oh, I get it, you're realising he's Chinese. I mean, like, ethnic Chinese. He was born here, in Melbourne. Wait, should I be talking about this? Is this a problem?"

"Relax, Evan," said Robbie. "I'm not trying to cancel you. I'm just, I mean, is this, like, a set-up? You know I'm not really in the market for a boyfriend."

Evan paused again. "You do realise, Robbie, that it has been years since you had a boyfriend. When does this market of yours actually open? Once a decade?"

"No comment," Robbie said. "And you told *me* not to be a dick."

"OK, sorry. But you'll like Winston, I guarantee it. He's super-cute, he's even good at trivia, and he is so, *so* gagging for someone to fuck him."

"Evan!"

"It's true, though. He's twenty-two, lives with his parents. He has had, like, one boyfriend *ever*, that his parents let sleep over. He hates the apps—I mean, who doesn't? I reckon he hasn't been fucked in over a year. Maybe more. He's practically re-virginating. It's sad. He needs your cock."

"Alright," said Robbie. "I'll come along, I promise, if you stop talking like that. As in, right now."

"Great!" cried Evan on the other end of the line. "Winston will be thrilled. I owe him a favour. I basically outed him at the office. Accidentally, of course."

"You what?"

"I'll explain later. Anyway, tell your mother you might be bringing home a *very* nice young man tonight."

"OK, bye," said Robbie, and hung up. He ate some of his cereal, which was already starting to get soggy.

His mother appeared. "Who was that, darling?" she asked.

"Just Evan. He's convinced me to go out tonight. You know, with the gang."

"Not a bad idea, I think," said Michelle. "You've been doing too much work lately. Do you want coffee?"

"Yes thanks, Mum," replied Robbie, eating more cereal. "Oh, and Evan says I should tell you in advance that I might be bringing a boy home tonight. A nice one."

"It's been a while," Michelle retorted, pouring coffee.

Robbie and Evan stood at the bar of Supermarket, waiting for the espresso martinis that Evan had insisted the group all have, to celebrate being just one point behind the 'sad old queens' (Evan's words) at the next table, who were in the lead after the first round of drag trivia. Robbie suspected Evan's celebratory mood might have more to do with the fact that all four homes his agency had put to auction this Saturday had sold well. "Don't bet against Melbourne property, bitches," he'd declared just after Robbie had arrived.

"So, Mark and Lucas," asked Robbie, casually. "They're off again?"

"I reckon they're over for good, *finally*."

Robbie looked over at their group's table, where all four boys seemed to be chatting amiably and noted, "They seem to still be getting along just fine."

"Of course they are," replied Evan. "They must be *relieved*. All that *'is Mark coming home tonight? Where did Lucas sleep yesterday?'* must be fucking *horrible*. I know they're both addicted—*addicted*—to drama, but we all have our limits. I mean, Robbie, you *know* my views on monogamy."

"E, I think I know your views on literally everything."

"Exactly. You're into it, monogamy, I'm not. But I don't go and set up house with a dude then go off and have sex with other ones, yeah? Have you ever seen that work?"

"No," agreed Robbie, wondering where the espresso martinis were.

"Besides," said Evan. "Let's talk about you and Winston. What do you think?"

"He's nice," acknowledged Robbie. Seeing a bartender in the early process of making the espresso martinis, he realised, sadly, that they were at least a couple of minutes away. Robbie looked around Supermarket, a fairly large gay venue, situated in an eclectic shopping area in a highly developed, yet not exactly gentrified, part of Melbourne.

Supermarket, as far as Robbie could tell, was named for its close proximity to two supermarkets on the street, rather than any deeper association the establishment had with them. The place, set across two levels—with the bar and eating areas downstairs, and the dancefloor upstairs—had clearly never been used as a supermarket. And the pared-down, vaguely industrial, exposed brick fit-out—which looked more industrial cheap than industrial chic—owed no obvious inspiration to supermarkets.

"Nice?" scoffed Evan. "Is that all you have to say?"

"Hey, the evening is young," retorted Robbie. "We're going pretty well with the trivia."

Evan grinned. "Pretty well? You two are trivia fiends!"

"We do both seem to like it."

Evan grinned, again. "It's more than that, though, isn't it, Robbie? Win is clearly already fantasising about what you're going to do to him later tonight."

"If you say so," said Robbie, in a tone suggesting that this line of questioning was utterly distasteful.

"Oh please," insisted, Evan. "*You*," insisted Evan, "are doing exactly the same thing. I can tell. I reckon you're considering whether you should make him get on all fours, spank him until he screams—until he begs you to fuck him!"

"Evan!" said Robbie, trying not to rise to the bait. "We've known each other for almost fifteen years. Have you ever considered it's not necessary to try to be quite so shocking all the fucking time? I mean, I've heard it all."

"Robbie, have you ever considered that being so up-tight and respectable all the time does not actually mean you're any less gay than the rest of us?"

"Remind me why we're friends, again?" asked Robbie, not entirely joking.

"Because I'm the last one you have left," shot back Evan.

"Six espresso martinis," declared the bartender. "Do you need a tray, darlings?"

"Can't you just, I dunno, teleport these to the table, Robbie?" asked Evan, grinning sardonically.

"A tray would be great, thanks," said Robbie to the bartender, smiling sweetly. Then he looked to Evan. "So much for others being addicted to fucking *drama*!"

"You know you love it, babe."

"Here we go," said the bartender, handing Robbie the tray containing the espresso martinis.

Robbie liked to think Winston's face lit up at his return to the table. And it was a pretty face, with big eyes, a shy smile and very attractive bone structure. A bit like Alex, really. *You're comparing him to Alex? Seriously?* Robbie chided himself.

And Winston *was* very good at trivia. He also, as he whispered to Robbie at one stage, didn't like espresso martinis very much. Something with which Robbie agreed. As the trivia rounds progressed, he and Winston acted as a two-person team, with the others reduced to offering small-talk and filling in the comparatively rare queer pop-culture gaps.

They had even found themselves, on many occasions, realising the answer to particular questions at the same time, quietly mouthing the answers to each other at the same time.

"Who wrote *Brideshead Revisited*?" "Evelyn Waugh!"

"What French cooking sauce comprises egg yolks, butter, tarragon and a white wine reduction?" "Béarnaise!"

"What is the capital of Albania?" "Tirana!"

"What are the first ten elements on the periodic table?" "Hydrogen, helium, lithium, B, B … beryllium, boron, carbon, nitrogen, oxygen … something beginning with F? Fluorine!"

After making that list—which ultimately got them full points—Robbie and Winston embraced. The drag queen host noticed, asking the whole crowd, "Hey, hot trivia Asians? Do you guys fuck or just read Wikipedia together?" The crowd seemed to think her crack was funnier than it was, and—outrageously—not at all racist.

In the end, their team came second, pipped by one point. They had made up ground, but the 'sad old queens' had won based on a question—Robbie couldn't even remember what it was—to which the answer was Crosby, Stills, Nash and Young. Still, Robbie was feeling good. A second-place finish was pretty impressive and left them with a number of bar vouchers. Evan insisted they should go upstairs to spend the vouchers, in order to both "Hit the (dance) floor," and celebrate Winston's best month, by far, in real estate. "Keep this up, Win," he declared, "and you might be able to move out of your parents' place!"

Upstairs at *Supermarket*, Robbie noted a few more things. One of these was that shirtlessness was practically compulsory on the dancefloor. After some reluctance, Winston had pulled off his shirt and started dancing. He had a very, *very* nice little body, observed Robbie, who was ordering shots at the bar. Robbie had realised he was on the tipsy side of sober, but thought he was OK. He had to be careful, obviously, as a police officer. (Winding up arrested for public drunkenness, or worse, wasn't a good career move for a detective.)

"Here you are, hon, vodka shots!"

To be fair, at least Robbie was simply drinking a little too much. Drugs seemed to be, if not entirely compulsory, at least common in the club. There was a permanent, long line for the bathroom, presumably for those snorting cocaine. Those who preferred, for reasons of economy or otherwise, to get their fix in pill form seemed even less inhibited, their only concession to decency being to open their baggies and swallow their tablets just out of plain sight.

"Stop staring," chided Evan, also at the bar. "You're not on duty—and surely it hasn't been *so* long that you've forgotten that people take drugs in places like this."

"OK, I'll stop. I'm surprised you even noticed that I was looking."

"Oh, I always make a point of noticing things, Mr Detective," replied Evan. "You'd be surprised how useful that is in the real estate business."

Robbie nodded. "Actually, I can understand that."

Evan smiled. "I also noticed you looking at Winston. He has quite an impressive physique, doesn't he? You wouldn't pick it. I've seen it before, though."

"Wait, did you two—?" Robbie started asking.

"No, Robbie, we haven't had *sex*. We go to the gym near the office together sometimes and, you know, *change*."

"Oh," said Robbie, quietly.

"Anyway," said Evan, "given how well this is going with you and Win, are you going to forgive me for my, um, aggressive matchmaking?"

Robbie smiled at him. "So long as there is no more discussions of sexual techniques or positions, yes."

"Deal!" said Evan excitedly. He gave Robbie a hug and kiss on the cheek, then said, "Shall we?" pointing to the vodka shots.

"Shouldn't we call the others over, first?" suggested Robbie.

"Yes, let's," declared Evan, waving at the shirtless group on the dancefloor.

As the group crowded around the bar and downed their shots, Winston asked Robbie, "Are you going to come dance?"

"Yes, I will." He unbuttoned his shirt and tucked it into his pants. Winston grabbed his hand and led him to the dancefloor.

Evan whispered in Robbie's ear, pointing off to the side of the large space, "Do you know that hipster professor-looking guy over there? He's been looking at you for a while, when you were too busy ogling Winston and surveilling drug users."

Robbie looked where Evan had pointed. *Harry fucking Archer. That cannot possibly be a coincidence, can it?*

"Wait, is he someone you've investigated, or something?" wondered Evan, aloud.

"Is something wrong?" asked Winston, sounding concerned, as if he might have done something to offend Robbie.

"No, nothing's wrong, Win," replied Robbie, in the most reassuring tone he could muster. "Let's go dance."

And they did. Or, rather, they swayed a little as they enthusiastically made out. They kissed—full tongue, obviously—then Robbie started to kiss Winston's neck, even chew his ears, as Winston started to moan. *Maybe this is a bit much, in public?* thought Robbie, but not enough to stop.

Between moans, Winston managed to conduct a whispered conversation about magic. Given how close their ears—and lips and tongues, among other things—were, they could hear each other over the pumping dance music.

"I know you can do magic. What kind of magic?"

"Manipulation and Telekinesis. I can manipulate objects and teleport them, and myself."

"Cool. Do you use that in your work, for the police?"

Robbie thought of the ifrit. "Sometimes, but it's rare. I mostly investigate people using magic to do bad things. Sadly, there are a lot of people who—"

"Hi, Detective Chang."

Robbie recognised the voice. *Fucking Prince Harry!*

He extricated himself from Winston (no mean feat) with a muffled apology about "Needing to talk to this dickhead," and looked Harry Archer in the face. Harry looked much like he had last time they had spoken. Robbie doubted that Harry had been in the line for the bathrooms or had quietly pulled pills from his pockets.

"Yes, what is it?" he asked, sounding deliberately surly. "I'm off duty, and this is inappropriate," was the intended message.

"Look, I'm sorry to bother you, detective. I just found myself here with my cousin, Jamie—you would remember Jamie?"

Robbie just glared, making no attempt to search the room for anyone with long, blonde hair.

"You know, with your body, detective, I'm sure it makes sense not to wear a shirt to dance, or to do anything really."

One part of Robbie suspected that Harry was trying to throw him, make him uncomfortable—for reasons he would probably never fathom. The greater part, however, was feeling frustrated, sexually and in every other respect, and he just wanted Archer to go away. Immediately. "I'm sure you understand that we shouldn't be taking to each other in these circumstances. If you have any information relating to the case—"

"But I *do* have information. Or I might. Let me tell you quickly and you can get back to mauling your boyfriend."

He is not my boyfriend, and you are an epic asshole! "Like I said, there are appropriate channels to share information with us. There is a hotline," said Robbie.

"Oh please," said Harry. "You guys would be getting all sorts of nonsense coming in at the moment. I want to make sure that you and your partner—Alex, he's quite something, isn't he?—actually get the information."

Robbie couldn't help but note the reference to Alex, someone whom Harry had properly met once, days ago, and had almost nothing to do with when they were both at MMS. What was *the Prince* getting at with these references? Was he trying again to misdirect?

He sighed. "OK, Harry, what do you want to tell me?"

"Well," replied Harry, excitedly. "You know how you mentioned the word 'gatekeeper' to me, when we spoke?"

"Yes," said Robbie, curtly.

"Well, rumour has it that there was a card with that word on it at one of the crime scenes. And, I understand, there was another card with the word 'bibliophile' on it, in the necromancy book at MMS, which I hear was booby-trapped—"

"None of that information has been released," replied Robbie, crossly. "You know I cannot talk about it. And how do you even know about them?"

"You know I cannot tell you that, either, *Detective*. A journalist and his sources, and all that."

Robbie regarded Harry Archer with contempt. "You're not a journalist, Harry. More like a pest. And, anyway, I thought you wanted to tell *me* something."

"Yes, I know," said Harry, sounding absurdly earnest. "I'm trying to help. That combination of 'gatekeeper' and 'bibliophile', it reminds me of an obscure translation of an equally obscure prophecy from France, from the eighteenth century."

"A prophecy? Seriously?"

"Yes, I know, I know," replied Harry, remaining earnest. "I'm not saying it's real, but maybe the killer thinks it is, or is being inspired by it?"

That was annoyingly possible. "So, what is this prophecy, then?" asked Robbie.

"In English, it's called *Summoning the Ultimate Darkness*. Maybe get your Magic Squad experts to look into it, or … ask me?" he whined. (As if the answer would ever be anything but 'no'!)

"I'll get them to look into it, then. Good night," replied Robbie.

"Who was that?" asked Winston as Robbie turned his back on Harry.

"Nobody," said Robbie, loudly enough that he hoped Harry—who Robbie sensed was still lurking behind him on the dancefloor—might hear him even over the pulsing music. "Let's get out of here. Do you want to come to my place?"

"Yes!" Winston cried in response, realising almost immediately that he might have sounded too enthusiastic. Hesitating, not wanting to look more foolish, or ignorant, he finally asked, "Can we, like, teleport there?"

"No," responded Robbie smiling. "Way too far. But I can teleport us outside, if you'd like." When Winston nodded vigorously, Robbie put his hand around Winston's waist and told the younger man to put his hand on his shoulder, "Like we're doing a waltz."

Winston complied. "Should we tell the others we're going?"

"I'll send Evan a message," replied Robbie. And, with that, the pair vanished from the bustling dancefloor.

Robbie and Winston materialised on the street outside Supermarket. Robbie faced the road, which had an alley coming off it. The alley was dark, but Robbie was sure he saw something there: a huge, black, spectral dog, with glowing red eyes. These magic creatures were called barghests and lived in the spirit world. Common in folklore, they were often (wrongly, of course) seen as a bad omen, signalling impending death. For a moment, the beast just seemed to stare at him, balefully.

Then Robbie felt Winston's legs buckle. Clearly, the teleportation had not agreed with him.

"Sorry," said Robbie as he held up the sagging (thankfully smaller and lighter) man. "I should've warned you. Some people have a bit of a reaction to teleportation. Especially their first time."

Winston breathed deeply and regained his footing. "It's OK, I'm fine. I just felt, sort-of, seasick for a moment."

Robbie looked up, but the barghest was gone.

"That's quite a party trick!"

Robbie turned to see their drag trivia host standing beside the entrance to Supermarket, having a cigarette with the venue's bouncer at the door. She was still wearing her costume, including a massive red wig, shovelled-on green eye makeup and bunny ears. She also had a bizarre name, 'Myxie Matosis', which was a reference to a virus created (partially with magic) to control rabbit populations in the 1950s. While she had been typically loud, crude and over-the-top during the trivia session, her voice now sounded more natural, more masculine, less in-character.

"Thanks," said Robbie, simply, pulling out a cigarette of his own and lighting it with his finger.

"Show-off!" Myxie added.

"This may sound like a weird question," said Robbie, trying to sound casual. "But you didn't see a big dog across the road just now, did you?"

Myxie looked at him quizzically. "You haven't taken too much of something tonight, have you, honey?"

Robbie frowned. "I don't take drugs. I'm a police officer."

The quizzical look was deployed again, followed by laughter. "You sure don't look like a police officer."

"Well, I am," countered Robbie, "And I asked you a question."

"You know, honey, you might look more like a cop if you had a shirt on."

Robbie blushed, and clumsily put his shirt back on while keeping hold of his cigarette. "Happy now?" he said, defeated. Winston put his own t-shirt back on, much more elegantly, behind him.

"Not really. I think I preferred you with your shirt off, and you *still* don't look *anything* like a cop."

Robbie was lost for words.

"But," said Myxie, "I promise I didn't see any dog across the road."

"OK, thanks," said Robbie, butting his cigarette in the bin by the entrance to Supermarket.

"Car's here," said Winston.

As they both opened the door to their Uber, Myxie called to them. "Seriously, do come to trivia again. You guys came the closest ever to beating those humourless old nags—and I really want to see someone beat them."

"I'll think about it," Robbie called back as got in the car, enjoying what felt like a sudden reversal of power.

The car drove off, with Robbie and Winston in the back seat. "Sorry about that. I wasn't quite at my best," said Robbie, who had the (accurate) impression that Winston liked guys who were masterful, rather than ones who blushed when drag queens made a crack at their expense.

"Oh, don't worry," said Winston. "You were so sexy when you blushed." He paused for a moment. "But why were you asking about that dog? Was it something to do with that guy who was talking to you on the dancefloor?"

"Maybe," said, Robbie carefully. "But no need to think about that. Let's kiss instead."

"Hey," Winston called out to their driver. "Would you give me a bad score if we made out the whole way back?"

The Uber driver laughed. "So long as you keep your clothes on and let me choose the radio station, you can do whatever you want."

So, they did.

But even as Winston moaned and squirmed—clothes stayed resolutely on, of course, but they provided little barrier to Robbie's widely roving hands—Robbie was struggling to not think about the barghest he was *certain* he had seen. And Alex's theories about Harry Archer, and why he (and who else could it have been?) summoned it only to make a brief appearance outside a nightclub, after having cornered Robbie to tell him about some absurd French prophecy …

Stop thinking about Alex! He did his best to do so, as their car pulled out in front of Robbie's mother's house.

Through a sequence of surefootedness, and deft use of Robbie's telekinesis, the boys managed to make it out of the car, past the driveway, into the house, up the stairs and all the way to Robbie's bedroom without having to pull their lips and tongues apart.

Once in the room, Robbie pushed Winston onto the bed. Then Robbie grabbed Winston's ankles, pulling off his shoes and socks. While Robbie was doing this, Winston pulled off his t-shirt. Robbie leaned over, kissed Winston and pinned his arms to the bed—he thought roughly, but Winston did not—and in an impressive use of his fine telekinetic skills, held that position while magically removing Winston's belt, trousers and underwear, exposing his almost painfully hard-looking erection. Robbie stood up, looking hungrily at the younger man laying before him.

"Can I suck your cock, Robbie?" asked Winston.

"You sure can," said Robbie, dropping his pants.

He sat on the bed. Winston crouched on the floor and applied himself to Robbie's penis with almost extraordinary vigour. Robbie laid back on the bed, arms behind his head, and moaned in pleasure. "You're good at this, Win."

Winston did not reply, his throat being otherwise engaged.

Robbie was practically convulsing with pleasure as Winston enthusiastically sucked him. But he was conscious that, if this kept up much longer, he would climax. And that would, he suspected, not be entirely satisfactory to Winston.

"OK, OK, stop now, Win. You'll make me cum."

Winston stood up and joined Robbie on the bed. Robbie, with a combination of magic and economical movements, stripped fully naked and pulled Winston underneath him, pinning his arms to the bed again and licking his neck, then his armpits, as Winston moaned and moaned.

Then, suddenly—at least it seemed to Winston—Robbie sat up on the bed.

"What's up?" asked Winston, sounding a little alarmed. "Did I do something wrong?"

"No, no," replied Robbie, himself a bit agitated by Winston's question. "I just wanted—"

"Oh," said Winston, looking almost relieved. "You don't need to do the whole 'I'm not looking for a boyfriend, or whatever' thing. It's OK, I get it."

This sent Robbie's mind back to ten years before. The only difference was that Winston seemed to have even lower self-esteem than Alex had. He didn't even resist the idea that this might be a one-off or, at most, the start of some uncommitted series of hook-ups.

Robbie looked Winston in the eyes. "I wasn't going to say that. If it's not already eminently obvious, I'm super into you and want to be your boyfriend."

Winston's look of jubilation was almost pitiful in its intensity. "But wait, why did you stop, then?" he asked, now sounding matter-of-fact, rather than worried. "I figured you would've been inside me by now."

Deja-vu all over again. And, no, don't think about Alex, Robbie! "I just wanted to make sure we're both comfortable with what we're doing," said Robbie, hoping this sounded sensible and normal to Winston, rather than lame.

"You mean you fucking me?" he asked, in disbelief. "Surely you can assume enthusiastic consent?"

"I try not to," said Robbie. Then, he said, by way of explanation: "I'm a cop. I've done literally all the training: gender training, cultural awareness training, indigenous awareness training, LGBTQIA+ *plus* training, domestic violence training and, yes, multiple times—even back at uni—consent training. The basic premise of which is to assume nothing."

"Wow," said Winston cheekily. "You're like a walking, talking masculinity crisis."

"That's not fair. I'm just not into, you know, toxic masculinity. And besides, if I didn't adequately pick up on the signs that you were *enthusiastically consenting*, you managed to miss the abundant signals I was giving out that I was interested in more than just a one-night stand."

Winston replied, "I barely know what those signs are, Robbie. I've had literally one boyfriend in my life. Other guys thought it was a charitable act to fuck me, or expected a pat on the back for even replying to an Asian on the apps. The rest were, like, fifty and creepy."

They kissed. Then, Robbie pinned Winston on the bed again, licking him all over. Winston groaned.

"Can you please fuck me now? *Please?*" Winston asked.

"OK," said Robbie. "But you still need to tell me how you want me to do it."

"Robbie, some guys tell me what they're going to do to me. And they're the less dominant ones. None of them ever ask me what I want. Which I *like*."

"Sorry, Win," replied Robbie. "Clearly, I'm just not dominant enough for you. On the other hand, I'm not treating fucking you like a charitable act, asking for a pat on the back for replying to an Asian, or fifty and creepy. So, you'll just have to compromise, won't you?"

"OK," replied Winston. "How about you make me get on all fours, spank me, then fuck me? And rougher than you think you've been so far."

"You didn't say something to Evan about that, did you?" asked Robbie, remembering their earlier conversation.

"Of course not!" replied Winston. "He's my boss at the agency. Why do you ask?"

"No reason," replied Robbie, marvelling at Evan's prescience. "Now get on all fours. I'm going to spank you and fuck you."

Which he did. And it was amazing.

To be fair, there was yet another dominance fail when, after Robbie had cum explosively as he fucked Winston, the latter had asked for permission to cum, too.

"You're asking me whether you're, like, allowed to cum?"

"Yes!" cried Winston, in sexual desperation.

"Do you want me to say no?"

"No, I want you to say yes! You're so bad at this!"

"Yes, then," answered Robbie. "Do you want me to do it?"

"I want you to stop asking me what I want! Let me be submissive—I like it!"

"OK, then. I'll do it."

And he did. And, he was quite sure, it was also amazing. Winston's cries and contortions as he reached orgasm at Robbie's hand reminded Robbie of that scene in *The Exorcist*, when Linda Blair's possessed child character levitated above the bed.

But the boys now lay next to each other, panting and enjoying the afterglow of the sex.

"Let me get you a towel," said Robbie, in light of the quantity of ejaculate Winston had sprayed across his face and body. "I'll have to turn on the bedside light, so shut your eyes for a second."

Winston complied. Robbie switched on the bedside light telekinetically. He went to his cupboard and pulled out a towel, but also two pairs of tracksuit pants. He tossed the towel at Winston. "You should probably open your eyes now. It's not too bright."

"Thanks," Winston said, as he wiped himself down.

Robbie held up the two pairs of tracksuit pants. "Do you want one of these?" he asked. "I normally wear these to bed. One is black and one is grey, so they're not, like, matchy-matchy weird."

"Would that be weird?" wondered Winston, aloud. (Robbie genuinely managed not to be reminded of Alex and matching pyjamas.) "But, yes, sure."

Robbie handed over the grey tracksuit pants to Winston, who put them on. Robbie tossed the used towel towards the laundry basket. Without magical assistance, it did not land accurately.

"Is it OK if I pray, quickly?" asked Robbie. "I try to do it every day."

"Of course," said Winston. But he did sit up in bed, in Robbie's (for him) very oversized tracksuit pants. "You didn't mention you were religious."

"Christian. Catholic, actually. I normally wear a cross, but I didn't tonight, because it can just create a—a thing, in some circles. Is Jesus a dealbreaker?"

"No, no, not at all," said Winston, again showing some signs of alarm.

Robbie said nothing. He just kneeled and crossed himself. He pulled the cross necklace—the one he hadn't worn that evening and was sitting on a bedside table—to his lips and kissed it. He mumbled some phrases. Then he got back into bed. Winston shimmied over to him, and they lay together.

"You weren't, like, repenting for what we just did, were you?" asked Winston.

"No," said Robbie, putting his hand around Winston's head as the latter snuggled into his chest. "It's more about other people. Mainly people I've seen in my work. They need saving more than me."

"Oh, I see," said Winston, yawning.

"And it's not like I prayed for this to happen tonight, either. But it was amazing. Was it good for you—even though I know you probably don't want me to care?"

"It was great! Magnificent. I shouldn't have said all those things I said, you know, about you not being dominant."

"That's OK, Win. Let's just go to sleep."

Which they did, in each other's arms.

The next morning, late, they both woke up. They went downstairs to the kitchen, with Winston asking whether they should put on more clothes, beyond—in his case—hopelessly sagging tracksuit bottoms. "No," said Robbie.

"But your mum will be down there," protested Winston.

"I said no."

Robbie's mum, Michelle, was indeed downstairs, making coffee in a suspiciously timely way. "Hi, I'm Michelle," she said to Winston.

"Hi, um, Mrs, I mean, *hi Michelle*! I'm Winston," he replied.

"I was going to make scrambled eggs. Do you want some?"

"Mum, you don't have to do that."

"But, I wouldn't say no," said Winston, to Michelle's evident delight.

So, the two boys sat at the kitchen table, dressed just in their tracksuit pants, playing footsies furiously with their bare feet, and kissing rather often. After coffee and scrambled eggs, they retired to the couch, ostensibly to watch TV—*Squid Game*, as it happened—but mainly to make out. Robbie also padded outside for a cigarette many times, over several hours.

Then they went upstairs to shower. Winston sucked Robbie's cock while Robbie washed Winston's hair. Then they left the shower and dried each other off. Robbie pushed Winston onto the bed but, this time, he put him on his back.

"Spread your legs, Win," instructed Robbie. "I'm going to do you missionary, this time—so I can look in your eyes and hold you while I fuck you. Because that is what *I* like."

"Please do," said Winston, his eyes looking inflamed with desire.

Robbie did just that, applying lots of lube, starting slow, then going fast, kissing Winston all the while. Robbie managed to last longer than last night, he was sure, and Winston's physical reactions and ructions— and the noises he made—were possibly even more acute. Robbie came volcanically, again. This time, when Winston asked permission to cum, Robbie was more ready.

"I dunno," he said. "Why should I let you cum?"

"Because I'm so, *so* horny, Robbie. *And* because of what you just did to me. *Please* let me cum."

"Hmmm …" replied Robbie. "What would the creepy fifty-year-olds—and those mega-dominant guys you were unfavourably comparing me to, last night—do in this situation? Pull out and make you go downstairs and jerk off so my mother might hear you—or even see you? Make you go into the bathroom, maybe? Make you go into that courtyard downstairs? Or outside? Or just not let you cum at all?"

"Robbie, please. *Please* let me cum! I said I was sorry about what I said last night!"

"I get that you're sorry, Win. But that doesn't really answer my question."

"What question?"

"I guess the question of which is better: a guy who is good at being dominant, even if he's a dickhead, or me?"

"You, you, Robbie. *Please*."

"OK then," said Robbie, in his authority Robbie voice, again. With one hand, he started pumping Winston's cock, with the other he telekinetically summoned the towel from the washing basket. Winston's orgasm arrived just before the towel and created an even greater—if contained—mess than his one the night before. Robbie kissed Winston as he cleaned him up.

"See," said Winston. "You're pretty good at being dominant, in your own way."

"It seems I am," replied Robbie. "That was genuinely extraordinary."

"Sorry," said Winston, "but I do probably need to go home."

"I know," said Robbie. Winston dressed himself in his clothes from the night before, Robbie pulled on his tracksuit pants. Winston ordered an Uber.

"Do you want me to teleport you out front? It does generally get better. The sickness response, I mean."

"Sure," said Winston, enthusiastically. *He was hardly likely to do otherwise,* thought Robbie.

"Well then," said Robbie. "Remember the stance, like a waltz."

The two vanished from Robbie's room and materialised out front, by the driveway. Robbie kissed Winston goodbye, for as long as he could, until Winston's car pulled up. The latter showed no signs of sickness from teleporting this time. Robbie waved at Winston until he got into his Uber.

"Who was that?" asked a surprising, but familiar, voice. It was the neighbour, the one who was often—as now—gardening out the front of his house.

"My boyfriend, I guess," replied Robbie.

"I see," said the neighbour. "Good looking kid."

"Thanks," said Robbie, then vanished.

Back in the house, Michelle was now making dinner. "We're having pissaladière," she declared. This was a French pizza-style dish with a dough base, caramelised onions, olives and anchovies. It was pretty damn good.

"Thanks, Mum, I'm just having a cigarette," Robbie said as he magically pulled a whisky bottle from the pantry.

"I have some red," said Michelle, by way of command. "Have some of that, instead."

He did, taking the glass of wine outside with him. The night still warm, his bare feet felt cool against the tiles of the outside courtyard. A breeze blew across his chest as he smoked. Then he came back in and sat himself at the dining table. When Robbie was growing up, he and his parents had always eaten at the table—whenever they could—as a family. This tradition continued when Robbie moved in with his mother.

Robbie cut away and ate a piece of pissaladière. "This is great, Mum," he declared.

"I know," she said. "How was it with your new gentleman?"

"Great. I mean, really, great," replied Robbie. "Did you like him?"

"I'm sure I would have," she said, savouring a piece of pissaladière and a sip of wine, "had I had a chance to properly talk with him. If you hadn't spent so much time necking him, then—I assume—fucking him."

"Fair, Mum," said Robbie, feeling very, very good.

It was only after dinner that Robbie checked his phone, realising he had never actually messaged Evan about leaving Supermarket. He forgot about this again, though, when he saw how it had blown up with missed work calls and news alerts about yet another magical spectacle.

"Oh shit!" he whispered to himself.

24

Alex and Charlotte Attend
a Corporate Event

"The elite is a demographic, not a conspiracy," announced Simmo, sipping on a red wine as Alex looked around the room.

The same night Robbie went to Supermarket, Alex was at The Lake, a function centre in Albert Park, a large recreational area not far from Josh and Alex's home and dominated by a large, shallow lake. From its large outdoor terrace, The Lake also offered perhaps the best panoramic view of downtown Melbourne's skyline, especially at night, when the buildings glowed against the night sky. However, it was still early evening—the sun had not yet set.

Alex and Simmo were at The Lake for an important Bailey and Badenoch event, at which Josh was to be anointed a partner, and his big deal—which Alex already knew from Charlotte was the acquisition of Sourcery—would be announced. The event was only just beginning, but caterers were already swarming with trays of tasty (and tasteful) canapés and bottles of what Alex had decided was very good bubbles. This wasn't the sort of function where one had to hunt down a refill or nibble.

"We seem to be in the heart of it at this do. The elite, that is," replied Alex, rather dreading where this conversation might go. (Trump, Ukraine, the evils of progressives and 'globalism', whatever that is.)

"Exactly!" said Simmo. "I realise that I'm part of the elite. I basically gate-crashed it, didn't I?"

"Is this your working-class boy made good speech again?" asked Alex. (At least that was preferable to hearing about the many faults of Joe Biden.)

"I thought you might have some sympathy for class migration," replied Simmo. "Given you and Josh. He must have taken you to events that make this one look like a fundraiser for the lawn bowls club."

"Yeah, a few," Alex conceded. "Weirdly, I always get interrogated when people find out I'm a cop. They're so interested in what it's like."

"Of course. Being a cop seems so exotic when your job is buying and selling businesses or—with much of the Josh set—just being rich."

"I guess so, though none of them would admit their job was just being rich," said Alex, absently. He noticed Charlotte across the room, looking uncomfortable. "I think your fiancée is having trouble working out where she fits in in the crowd."

"You noticed that too?" replied Simmo. "Actually, I shouldn't be surprised. Isn't it interesting how people divide themselves?"

"Yeah, I guess," replied Alex, thinking maybe Simmo should rescue his fiancée rather than play amateur social anthropologist with him.

"You have the young go-getters—your boyfriend is their role model," said Simmo, gesturing at a group of well groomed, well dressed, generally tall twenty-somethings, mainly but not exclusively men.

"Yes," continued Alex, motioning subtly to a group of generally tanned, long-haired and high-heeled young women. "Then, you have their WAGs."

"While the boyfriends of the female go-getters tend to talk to the go-getters, rather than the WAGs," mused Simmo. "Which makes even the younger set very gendered, at least at parties like this."

"Even as gendered as the senior people's wives," agreed Alex, looking at the group of older, more modestly-dressed ladies, with shorter hair and heels and sporting elegant—yet obviously expensive—jewels.

"Then, of course, you have the senior bigwigs, practically all men—what the feminists would call male, pale and stale," Simmo concluded.

"Well, except for your biggest bigwig, Carolyn," countered Alex, seeing her talking to Josh animatedly.

"Yes, there is her," agreed Simmo, sounding like Carolyn was not quite his favourite person. "I guess she solved the problem of where she fits in with the crowd by being married to one of the other partners, and acting and sounding like a man."

"Wow," said Alex. "Not ladylike enough for you, I take it?"

At that moment, Carolyn and Josh started to approach Alex and Simmo. Before they could arrive, Simmo declared, "I think now might be the time to rescue my fiancée from Bailey and Badenoch clique confusion." He then vanished, as if he had teleported away, Robbie-style. *What an odd thought to have*, mused Alex to himself.

"Alex, hello!" Carolyn Fitzgerald, Asia–Pacific head of Bailey and Badenoch and rumoured (at least according to the *Financial Review*) anointed successor to Duncan Badenoch, the US-based founder and global chair and CEO. Carolyn was loud, agreed Alex, but she also had an endearingly cheeky smile and looked perfectly stylish in some loose-fitting silk trousers, coupled with a very expensive-looking fitted jacket and classic string of pearls.

Alex had only met Carolyn a handful of times, but she seemed perfectly nice. Simmo, he reasoned, obviously just resented the idea of a successful woman unafraid to speak her mind or crack a joke. But then, to be fair, how to explain Simmo's choice of Charlotte as a fiancée, rather than one of the more conventional WAGs with whom Charlotte visibly struggled to find any (non-magical) affinity?

"Good evening, Carolyn," Alex replied, as Carolyn reached in for an air-kiss. "It's great to see you again."

"And in such wonderful circumstances!" declared Carolyn, beaming. "Your partner here is the man of the hour!"

"I suppose he is," enthused Alex in reply. Josh looked mildly embarrassed by his boss' praise.

Carolyn went on. "He really hit it out of the park with the Sourcery deal—what a relief that we can talk about it now, Josh—and now he's our dashing young new partner. Not a bad day at the office!"

"Thanks, Carolyn," said Josh, quietly.

"You must be so proud of him, Alex!" declared Carolyn.

"I am," replied Alex, with what he thought was just the right amount of enthusiasm. (Which was possibly more than he would do otherwise, were he not in company with a woman who appeared to be speaking in exclamation marks.)

"Wait, you're a magician, too, aren't you, Alex?" Carolyn queried. Carolyn was, again per the *Financial Review*, a voracious networker, and Alex wondered whether remembering things about people was a learned behaviour. As against Alex's own, inherent, and not always welcome, tendency to do the same. "Maybe we should get you on the app!"

"Alex is not really a working magician," replied Josh. "He's a police detective, remember?"

"Of course I remember, Sachs—I mean, Josh. It was just one of my trademark bad jokes." A look of revelation suddenly crossed her face. "Wait, you aren't involved in that case with the revenant?"

Carolyn's question was cut off by the sound of metal hitting glass, the universal signal for guests to be quiet and, in this case, seat themselves.

"Looks like it's time for us to listen to the great man speak," said Carolyn, with an emphasis on 'great man' that suggested at least some degree of sarcasm. "Thankfully, we're all at the same table!"

As it turned out, the 'great man' was none other than Laurence Archer, who—standing at the podium about to share his wisdom with this crowd of financiers—looked to Alex almost exactly like what would enter his mind if someone said the words 'distinguished, middle-aged businessman'. He was also, as Carolyn explained, the new CEO of Sourcery. "The old man sort of came with the company, like a package deal," she said, again in a tone that suggested she wasn't sold on the merits of Laurence Archer.

Carolyn was able to tell him these things because, to Alex's bewilderment, they were not merely seated at the same table, but almost right next to each other, with Laurence and Josh between them. As Laurence was about to address the crowd, and Josh had been volunteered as MC (including explaining where the fire exits and bathrooms could be found) this left nobody between Alex and Carolyn.

The 'housekeeping matters' having been attended to, Josh returned to the table and Laurence commenced his speech. As Josh sat down, Alex heard Carolyn—trying but failing to be super-quiet—loudly 'whisper' to Josh. "You prepped him, right, Sachs?"

"Of course," replied Josh, more quietly, but still just audible to Alex. "He isn't going to say anything off-script."

And, indeed, he did not. Alex wondered whether it would be possible for a speech to be any more generic than the one given by Laurence Archer that evening. It seemed to check off every cliché: "sustainable growth", "partnerships", "diverse perspectives", "investment in people and technology", "new beginnings" and "working with the leading private equity firm in the Asia–Pacific". There was but the merest allusion to any legal problems, with "working through legacy challenges" serving as the acceptable euphemism. Aside from the more commercial elements of the speech, Laurence Archer could have been the Victoria Police Chief Commissioner at a staff 'town hall'.

The address was also, to be fair, mercifully brief.

Through polite clapping, Carolyn observed that starters were now being served. "I'm on after the entrées," she said. "If I get the beetroot salad, could one of you boys swap me for the smoked salmon? I think I need some protein before stepping on stage. I'm starving."

Alex didn't feel like he could say no.

Laurence Archer came to take a seat at the table. "How was the speech, Josh—good?" he asked, in a tone that suggested there could be only one correct answer.

Josh responded with compliant enthusiasm: "It was great, Laurence!"

"It's Laurie to you, Josh," replied Laurence, as Alex resolved he would do his level best to avoid that particular diminutive. Just as Alex had this thought, Laurence seemed to notice his existence. "Wait, Josh, is this Alex, the boyfriend?" Laurence stood up and proffered a hand. Alex, politely, did the same and shook it. "I know it's a cliché, but I've literally heard everything about you, the great detective! And you're even more handsome than I had expected!"

Alex wondered, uncharitably, why Laurence was now overdosing on the obsequiousness (and also speaking in exclamation marks). He decided that, given both Josh and Laurence needed each other to succeed, they had concluded that mutual flattery would help them on their way.

"Thank you," said Alex. "As you would understand, though, I've not heard so much about you." Though, since talking to Charlotte at the Lion, Alex had definitely done his research.

"Maybe we can remedy that tonight, Alex," replied Laurence, dripping with phoney charm.

Carolyn looked like she might be about to dry-retch.

Alex finished off his beetroot salad, having offered up his original smoked salmon to Carolyn, who had pretended to apologise for accepting his offering before devouring it with relish. As the others around him, including Simmo and Charlotte to his right, chatted politely, the conversation was peppered with her comments and weirdly endearing, cackling laugh.

She seemed especially interested in Alex. "I mean, I *know* you cannot tell us if you're on that horrible *revenant* case—but I'm just going to assume you are!" (Cackle.) "And that you also battled that fire sprite that was in the news. Oh, and that you captured those bikies with your magic!" (Cackle.) "OK, OK, I know, obviously that couldn't all be the same person." (No cackle; Alex said nothing.) "Actually, Alex, did I tell you that you remind me of my son, only in that I had hoped to marry him off to Josh, but I was too late, and you showed up!" (Cackle!)

"Carolyn!" cried Josh.

"OK, sorry," said Carolyn. "Anyway, I'm up."

As Josh and Carolyn returned to the podium, Laurence leaned towards Alex, smelling of beetroot, red wine and old man, and whispered, "I know you cannot tell me about the magic case. But could we have a chat later? I might have some information."

"OK," replied Alex, cautiously. "Let's talk in a bit."

As it turned out, Carolyn was quite good at providing a 'rally-the-troops' speech. It traversed some similar territory to Laurence's speech, but Carolyn, speaking without notes, managed to spice up her address with some calls to action, and even some jokes. "When we first started this Australian office, it was basically me, my future husband, a typist and half a receptionist. Now, we do deals all over Asia, and are bigger than the European office—take that, London!" The tables of young staff clapped; their WAGs tried to look vaguely interested. "The reality is, we make companies better. I'm no *financial engineer*—if I wanted to be an engineer, I would have built bridges. We build companies. I know we have at least three magicians at this event, but what we do is not magic. It's making businesses work better!" More claps from the young tables and, this time, also the old.

"And I hear," she continued, "about this great sense of resignation. People not liking their jobs, not getting ahead. *Well*," she gestured to Josh. "I think it's safe to say that we promote, we recognise. And nobody could be a better example of that than—sorry, I'm going to use the nickname—Sachs, here, whose contribution has been justly rewarded. And I introduce him as our newest and youngest partner at Bailey and Badenoch!"

Josh stood up at the podium. He looked amazing in his tailored suit and glitteringly polished shoes. His appearance was greeted with loud cheers from the tables of younger staff, and claps from the old guard. "Speech, speech, speech," they called, clapping rhythmically.

"Oh, I don't really have one prepared," called Josh from the podium.

"He's such a terrible liar," Carolyn said to Alex, loud enough for others to hear. "Of course, he has a fucking speech."

"Yeah," replied Alex, more quietly. "We workshopped it a couple of times."

"So, look," declared Josh from the lectern, "you all know I was born with a silver spoon poking out of my bum." Again, the junior tables cheered. "My boyfriend, Alex"—Josh pointed at him; Alex tried to disappear under the table—"thought maybe I should use the more conventional term. As I told him—babe, I know my audience!" More cheers.

"Now, I know I'm seen as something of a role model in this place, a paragon." (Cheers.) "So, I wanted to share my thoughts and tips on getting ahead, from Josh to you." (Muted cheers, more expectation.) "Tip one, find a mentor. I cannot imagine how Simmo and I could be any more different, but our partnership has been so successful." (Cheers.) "Tip two, interpret how you're going based on the actions of your superiors. Nobody is going to say: Hey, Josh, we kinda like having you around, but you're never getting ahead here. But, if they pass you up for promotion, that is what they're saying." (Cheers.) "Third tip, literally—and I know this might sound naff, but it's true—take every opportunity you can, even if it puts you outside your comfort zone." (Cheers.) "After all, who would have thought a conventional, by-the-book guy like me would have championed buying an app for magicians? But I did!" (Bigger cheers.)

Following Carolyn and Josh's speeches, the mains arrived. Alex quite liked his tender beef dish, but would probably have preferred the roast chicken breast, on-the-bone, with risotto. He ultimately decided not to suggest a reciprocal swap with Carolyn.

After the main courses, people started to mingle, either abandoning or swapping their allocated tables and moving through the whole function space. Initially, the line for the bathroom became suspiciously long. But, over time, both the younger staffers and their WAGs started to peel away, no doubt kicking on to other venues.

Carolyn stayed surprisingly close to Alex for much of the evening. She seemed interested in his life. "So, when is Josh popping the question?" she asked.

"We haven't really talked about that."

"Then maybe you need to give him a push. I did, with my husband. Sometimes, they need to know there are alternatives, like hot policemen, in your case."

You mean like Robbie? Alex thought to himself—to his great consternation.

Alex, come out here—there's a hellhound! And it's after Laurence Archer!

That voice in his head was immediately recognisable: Charlotte. *A hellhound? You're sure?*

Yes, I'm sure. Get out here or the thing is going to kill him!

On it. "Carolyn," said Alex mustering all of his inadequate reserve of authority. "We have a major magical hazard outside. I need you to seal the doors and make sure nobody leaves the venue. *Nobody.*"

Carolyn seemed unsure how to react. "But we were just talking. How do you—"

"I know," insisted Alex, speaking loudly and clearly. "I need you to do what I've told you to do."

"On it, *officer*," she replied, with what might have been the beginnings of a smirk. But then her booming voice silenced the crowd. "OK, we have an incident outside. A dangerous one. Nobody is to leave. I said, nobody!"

Alex spied Josh and Simmo on his way to the exit; no doubt they were mutually congratulating each other on their personal successes. Carolyn's calls to action had not quite pierced their discussion, as they sipped on red wine. "Babe, there is an incident outside. A *magic* one. I need you to call the police, *now*. Make it clear this is a magic threat, probably a hellhound."

Josh didn't answer back and pulled out his phone.

"Simmo, I need you to help Carolyn make sure nobody leaves. Check all the doors, tell the WAGs in the bathrooms. Nobody leaves, on pain of death or losing their stock options."

"Alex, this is private equity, we don't really do stock—"

Alex glared.

"OK, on it, mate!" he promised, and vanished towards the back of the venue as Carolyn continued to call out for people not to leave.

Alex, of course, had to leave, and fast. He bounded outside the events centre searching for Laurence, Charlotte and the hellhound, heading for the rear of the venue—which backed onto the flat, grassy, deserted expanse of Albert Park, before giving way to its huge, shallow lake. He caught a glimpse of Laurence Archer—looking desperate, even in the dark—and the hellhound.

The size of a bull and looking like a cross between a massive dog and wild boar, the hellhound appeared to be stalking Archer, breathing fire and smoke from its massive nostrils and pacing around its prey like a cat toying with a mouse. Archer, an illusionist—something anyone with access to Google could find out easily enough—was trying to delay the beast with conjured barriers and distractions. This included creating multiple duplicates of himself and letting them run off in different directions.

This didn't work. As Alex knew, and Laurence Archer presumably didn't—or he was just trying anything out of desperation—hellhounds were primarily smell-based hunters. Visual artifices, like most illusions, would not distract them from their prey. Which, reflected Alex, made them an entirely suitable summoned creature to assassinate an illusionist.

As Alex watched on, the hellhound pointed its snout at the 'real' Laurence Archer and charged at him as he fled. Laurence then became invisible. The hellhound continued to charge at the now hidden Archer. Alex, eyes glowing blue, shot a conical spray of ice and wind at the fiery monstrosity, throwing it off its stride and leaving it writhing on the ground.

"Get up a tree or something," Alex called to Laurence, as loudly as he could. "This thing isn't fooled by illusions! Remember your telekinesis training."

Laurence, with some difficulty, managed to levitate himself awkwardly into a nearby tree. Alex conjured a plume of solid ice to contain the hellhound. However, hellhounds, while not quite as strong and resistant to magic as revenants, were nonetheless very powerful spirit beings. This one started breaking the icy bonds with its struggles and fire breath, even as Alex tried to reinforce them.

As he struggled with the hellhound, he remembered Charlotte. *Where are you?* He called out in his head.

I'm fine, Alex. Don't worry about me. Worry about them!

It took a moment for Alex to understand Charlotte's reference to 'them'. Then he noticed: walking slowly towards him across the flat, grassy expanse was a figure whose appearance was obscured by flowing robes, a completely covered face, and a miasma of dark energy radiating coldness that even Alex could feel. The apparition reminded Alex of a Nazgul, the 'wraiths' in Tolkien's famous writings that were themselves inspired by folk ideas of necromancy. Coming just ahead of the obscured figure was another hellhound. But this one snorted freezing air and ice, rather than fire.

"You have got to be kidding me!" whispered Alex to himself.

Alex, said an unidentifiable, disembodied voice in his own mind. *I'm not here to hurt you. At least not yet, and if I can avoid it.*

This voice, no doubt, belonged to the shrouded, mystical figure—almost certainly the necromancer who had summoned the revenant. The frost-hound started pacing menacingly towards Alex, as he tried to contain the original hellhound in his spell of ice.

I'm a police officer—and you're under arrest! While trying to 'sound' as authoritative and confident as possible, even when communicating telepathically with this powerful sorcerer-assassin, Alex realised he was in a difficult position.

The 'Nazgul', meanwhile, couldn't hide their amusement. *You do play cop very well, Alex—despite not looking the part. And with your ex too. How cosy!*

Alex sent a wall of ice to check the advance of the frost-hound, while trying but ultimately failing to contain the hellhound. The latter broke free and started butting the tree in which Laurence Archer had taken refuge. "Help!" he cried, pitifully. Meanwhile, the hellhound appeared to realise that, if butting a tree was unlikely to bring it down, it could always burn it instead. Fire surged from its mouth and nose towards the trunk of the tree, as the frost-hound charged at Alex's wall of ice, which began to crack.

I don't play a cop, dickhead, I am one. And I'm fucking good at it. I'll work out who you are soon enough.

As his protective wall of ice started to shatter under the assaults of the frost-hound, Alex sent a cloud of super-cold, humid air at the hellhound, temporarily frustrating its ability to set Laurence Archer's sanctuary alight. It snarled in steamy impotence. But Alex realised this would be only a temporary setback.

And I look forward to you trying, Alex. But, to do so, you may just have to get out of my way. Retreat. You're outnumbered and overpowered. Though you're doing surprisingly well for someone who hasn't really done magic in ten years. A natural, aren't you?

Alex crouched like a sprinter about to start a race. His hands on the ground started to glow with blue energy and swirling, icy wind. *Do you seriously think I'm going to just watch on as you commit murder? No, I will not!*

Alex threw himself into the air and stayed suspended there, elevated on a platform of wind. He gathered together two balls of pulsating ice, water and air, then sent them hurtling at the two hounds. The beasts were thrown back and cried out in pain. But they got up again. He, by contrast, was now on the ground, panting with exhaustion.

Again, Alex could almost hear the necromancer's laugh. *You seem to be out of your depth again, Lexi—Alex.*

The frost-hound advanced on Alex. The hellhound recommenced its fiery assault on the tree. The prominent businessman, to Alex's unreasonable annoyance, continued to cry for help.

"Leave him alone, you *cunt*!"

"Carolyn?"

The voice was unmistakeable. Alex looked behind him, to the roof of the Lake event centre. It crackled and glowed with electricity. Carolyn, her elegant jacket and trousers barely visible beneath the lightning she had summoned around herself, lurched from the roof of the venue to a set of powerlines, sending arcs of energy all around. One of them struck the hellhound, sending it flying into the shallow Albert Park Lake, where it stayed—at least for now—still and coruscated with electrical power.

"Get back inside!" Alex shouted at her.

"No way. *Saruman* here can fuck right off. I'm not letting you get hurt if I can help it! And that is just a warning shot!"

"And so is this," declared the now vocal—rather than mental—disembodied and ambiguous voice. The necromancer raised a hand and sent a 'flock' of spectral, spirit-world bird-fish creatures, dripping with water, at Carolyn, water being elementally hostile to electricity. With multiple expletives, Carolyn fended off the spiritual assault, but it left her defeated, with her lightning bolts fizzling out with a noise like a short-circuit, and she retreated back to the roof of the event venue.

Alex picked himself up and moderated his breathing. He was very glad for the brief reprieve Carolyn's actions gave him. *I'm not done yet. It seems I'm still in your way.*

Javelin-like forms of solid ice started to form above his shoulders. Four in total. They stood, hovering in the air. Meanwhile, the frost-hound appeared prepared to strike at Alex.

I doubt your ice attacks will stop the frost-hound, Alex.

Nonetheless, he sent them screaming through the air at the abominable dog. It howled, paused, but hardly seemed deterred. This made sense. Whoever this Witch-King was, they'd chosen their tools well for this task. Particularly if that task had anticipated Alex's involvement. But, if it hadn't, why bring the frost-hound?

Meanwhile, the hellhound—maybe weakened, but clearly not destroyed—started to pad its way out of the shallow lake.

Oh my, Alex, what will you do now?

Alex struggled to stay standing. Yet he summoned four more javelins. But he was fighting a sense of despair. His only hope was that the police, preferably magical ones, would arrive soon.

The frost-hound, shaking off the ice javelins that had pierced its skin, also advanced towards Alex.

Then, a massive, shadowy figure appeared in the sky on the horizon, facing Alex but to the frost-hound's (and the necromancer's) rear. As the huge shadow rapidly approached, Alex realised that it was a giant bird—a *roc*—a mythical raptor with the wingspan of a whale, now found only in tiny numbers across its homelands in the Mediterranean and Middle East.

Hey, Alex, sorry I'm late. I had to catch the thermals—it took a while!

Charlotte?

Yes. Let's get rid of this ridiculous frost-hound, shall we?

In roc-form, Charlotte swept down at incredible speed. She grasped the monster in her talons and swept into the sky. Keeling back, now high in the air, she flew back over the event space and the warring mages. Over the lake, she let the frost-hound out of her grasp. Everyone—including the necromancer—looked on, transfixed. It hit the ground hard, clearly now dead.

Looks like the tables have turned, asshole! (That was Alex.)

Alex's ice javelins streaked through the air, ripping into the original hellhound's flesh and leaving it in a pile of blood and viscera, ebbing steam. At the same time, lightning crackled and sparked around the mysterious figure of the necromancer. Alex didn't look back, but it was clear that Carolyn had recovered. "Nice try, you dirtbag, but no fucking cigar!" she said.

Charlotte, in the form of the roc, landed next to Alex, sending the blades of grass on edge as her wings created wind. Her form stood several storeys high, and longer than a bus. Sirens became audible, and police car lights flashed in the distance.

Alex spoke out loud. "Time to give yourself up."

The figure itself also spoke in its impossible-to-place voice. "You've done well, Alex, but I always have an exit strategy." And, with that, the necromancer was consumed with an inky blackness and disappeared altogether.

Alex was reminded of the passage he had read so many years ago: "The summoner can create similar effects to any other school of magic". Then, he collapsed on the ground, utterly exhausted.

Almost immediately, at least it felt to Alex, Josh had taken him in his arms. "Are you OK, babe?"

"Yeah, I'm fine. Just tired."

"You were so good, babe," declared Josh, earnestly. "Both inside, giving those orders, and fighting those *things*."

"Thanks, babe," replied Alex, noticing that attendees at the function were now swarming out of the venue, including moving towards parts of the park that had been the site of the magic showdown. "Hey," he called out, weakly. "This is a crime scene. Stay away!"

"Yes!" shouted Carolyn, whose voice carried easily across the area. "Stay off the crime scene, idiots!" She looked at one of the WAGs, who was filming and walking on the grass. "That means you, dear. And stop filming. And get a dress that covers up your tits and bum while you're at it. This isn't fucking OnlyFans!"

The WAG stomped off in a huff, calling for 'Brendan', presumably her boyfriend.

"I never knew you were a magician," said Josh to Carolyn.

"Sachs, I'm a woman of many talents. But it's unusual I get to save the day!"

"Alex saved the day," declared Charlotte, who now appeared in her regular human form. "Or, at least, Alex with some help from the two of us."

"OK, then," conceded Carolyn. "*We* saved the day. Not bad for an old broad who buys companies and counts fucking money for a living, though, is it?"

"Mate, you were amazing," said Simmo, who had suddenly appeared with Charlotte. "You're a dead-set hero. Seriously."

The sirens were now louder and the lights visible, even to Alex in his exhaustion. Karen Park, head of the Magic Squad, appeared. "Alex," she said. "Are you alright?"

"I'm OK," replied Alex, unconvincingly.

"I want to take him home," announced Josh, authoritatively. "There are plenty of other witnesses here, and Alex can give a statement tomorrow."

Karen looked at Alex with genuine concern. "OK. We will talk to the others."

"You need to look for the card," said Alex. "But not tonight. I don't think it will be here yet."

Karen looked at him quizzically.

"I can explain tomorrow," he said quietly. "But you need to keep officers here. More than usual—to keep an eye out for someone."

"OK, we will," replied Karen. "Go home."

When Josh and Alex arrived home, much as he had the night after Alex's life had been turned upside down (the one when he cracked the Daylesford Distillery case, arrested the Teflon Bikie, outed himself as a magic-user and got pulled into this bizarre magic murder mystery all within about 10 hours) Josh undressed Alex like a small child, and put him in the pyjama bottoms Josh had worn the night before. (These ones were knee-length shorts, with a Scottish-style tartan pattern.)

Alex let Josh do this despite, unlike that night, feeling fine. He was tired, sure, but he wasn't in tears. He was, in fact, entirely lucid. Having said that, both he and Josh had remained silent on the ride home and ever since. But this was because, Alex was certain, Josh wanted to ask him something important. He thought his answer would not be the one Josh wanted.

"Babe," Josh finally said, as the two lay in bed, in each other's arms.

"Do you want me to take my pyjamas off?"

"No!" replied Josh, looking like the very idea that they might have sex in these circumstances was altogether indecent, vulgar and outrageous. "Babe, I want you to ask them to take you off this case."

That was, almost word for word, what he had expected Josh to ask him. And, as he had expected, Josh looked crestfallen at his firm, but tenderly delivered, answer: "Babe, I can't. I understand you're worried about me, but I need to solve this case."

"But *babe*," Josh said, begged, desperate, *almost* crying (Josh never cried; he was far too put-together for tears). "You've already been attacked twice. You've done enough—more than enough." Alex wanted to respond, but Josh wouldn't let him. "You have no idea how worried I've been the last few days, since that ifrit. When I'm at work, I cannot concentrate. I can't eat. *Please.*"

"I'm sorry," replied Alex. "I really am. I know how much you love me, and I understand how worried you are. But, like you said, this scumbag has attacked me, *twice*. And he's already killed once. I need to find him and stop him doing that ever again."

Alex paused to gauge Josh's reaction. He remained horribly disappointed and upset, clearly fighting back tears. It made Alex think of an immature teenage boy, struggling for dear life not to show any distress or weakness, even as his heart was breaking. It was pitiful. Pathetic. Ridiculous. And it was largely Alex's fault. Which made Alex feel genuinely awful. But he remained resolute. He had to. Otherwise, he would need to question his own overriding sense of duty—and pride—that was driving him to hurt and dismiss the person he loved.

A solitary tear trickled down Josh's cheek as he looked at his boyfriend with some combination of disappointment, concern and fear.

"Let's make a deal," said Alex. "I close this case, then that is it. No more magic cases again, ever. I'll tell them to forget any medal, any promotion. Just let me off the Magic Squad. And we can have a normal life again."

Josh sat up in the bed too, his mood entirely changed in an instant, as if by, well, magic. "OK, babe. Deal!" He kissed Alex deeply, and for what seemed like a long time.

It was only after Josh finally broke off their kiss that Alex had a realisation. "Wait, babe, was that, like, a negotiation for you? As if you're buying up a company or something? You knew I would never give up the case, but you asked me to in order to secure a promise that I wouldn't stay in the Magic Squad once it's over?"

Josh smiled in reply. "A little. But everything I said is true. I worry all the time, I cannot eat. Until I see you at home, I visualise all the ways this necromancer-thing could kill you. I can maybe do it for a month, babe. But I cannot do it *forever*. I just can't."

"OK," Alex conceded. "I guess that's fair. Just tell me this whole conversation wasn't planned in some spreadsheet."

Josh chuckled. "Of course not, babe. It's not like I rehearsed as some kind of act, either. And, anyway, what is it they say? Compromise is at the heart of any successful marriage."

Alex had noticed Josh had started referring to 'marriage', in the context of their relationship recently. "We aren't married, babe."

"Not yet."

"Is that a proposal?"

"Let's call it a promise," replied Josh. "A promise for a promise. And, as for the proposal, there definitely is a spreadsheet for *that*."

The pair kissed again, for even longer.

"Are you sure you don't want me to take off my pyjamas?" Alex asked, after they had finished kissing.

"Are you sure you're up for it?" replied Josh, sounding a bit concerned.

"I am," declared Alex, grinning. And, indeed, he was up for it. Something about the fear (and, in all honesty, the excitement) of the night's events, coupled with the impassioned talk they'd just had—including Josh's genuine, if calculated, show of emotional vulnerability—had made Alex very keen to have sex. Desperate, even. Alex moved Josh's hand to his crotch.

"Ah, I see," said Josh, looking satisfied. "You're up for it."

"I am *so* up for it! I want it bad. And rough. I know you're always so gentle and tender, which is great—*most* of the time. But tonight, I want you to make me get on all fours, spank me, then take me from behind. *Rough*!"

"Wow," said Josh, smiling hungrily at his lover. "You almost never talk like that!"

Josh took Alex into his arms and started kissing him all over. Alex moaned. Then he kept talking dirty.

"I want you to ask me whether I'm the most heroic slut ever, or the sluttiest hero."

"I want you to tell me that cops, real men, don't moan, whimper and yelp like bitches."

"I want you to tell me that nice boys don't beg their boyfriend to fuck them doggy."

"I want you to ask me what Pav would say if he saw me like this!" (Alex rather surprised himself by going there.)

"I want you to stop all this foreplay and do me now!"

Alex thought, as Josh fucked him rougher than he ever had, and managed to devise even more demeaning and creative insults than Alex had suggested for him, that this was their most passionate and genuinely pleasurable sexual encounter since the giddy, early stages of their relationship. And that, as much as Josh was being utterly and completely dominant—pinning Alex's hands to the mattress, using his greater weight to put Alex entirely under his control, like his toy, like his *property*—he was really just doing exactly what Alex had ordered him to do.

Which somehow made it all even sexier.

"Here, I made you some breakfast." said Josh, looking bright and smelling freshly washed. He was carrying a tray with a simple meal of toast, sliced apple and a cup of coffee.

After placing the tray on Alex's lap as Alex sat up in bed, and kissing him on the forehead, Josh continued. "Then, I guess you will need to have a shower, unless you want to show up at the station with all that dried cum on yourself."

"Thanks, babe," was all Alex said in response. Though he did take note that, even the morning after their wild session last night, Josh was still talking dirty to him. Which may be fair, given Alex was dirty. He did have his own dried cum on his face, neck, chest and stomach. (His orgasm has been explosive, and he hadn't permitted Josh to get a towel and clean him up.) Then, there was the colossal amount of Josh's cum that remained inside him. Not to mention the amount of sweat that must be caked onto him. There was even the hickey Josh had planted on his stomach in the throes of lust. (Alex had only just noticed it.) Alex was dirty. He was *filthy*, in a very good way.

Instead of saying anything more, Alex just looked up at his boyfriend, who was in his underwear, like a clean-shaven Hercules in white cotton boxer briefs. Josh looked like a puppy who had just been given a treat for good behaviour.

Josh noticed the way Alex was looking at him too. It turned him on. As did seeing Alex, eating his toast while covered in dried cum. Or, indeed, smelling Alex, who practically *reeked* of sex. Alex pretended not to see the tent growing tent in Josh's underpants, or to feel an entirely similar thing happening under his tartan pyjamas. As much as it was tempting to have a re-run of last night's festivities—leaving Alex *even dirtier*—duty was calling.

Or, at least, it was texting. Alex checked his phone as it pinged. It was from Karen Park.

When will you be at the station?

Give me an hour

OK. BTW, we caught him. He's waiting for you.

Alex scoffed down his toast and apple slices, and got up to go to the bathroom. "They want me down at the station."

"Now?" said Josh. "You would think they would give a hero a bit more time to rest!"

"A slutty hero?" said Alex, grinning sardonically.

"The sluttiest," replied Josh, also grinning. *Duty really is a bitch*, thought Alex. Josh continued. "But, to be fair, we weren't doing that much resting."

As Alex washed, shaved, applied his fancy face creams and dressed himself, he couldn't help but reflect that there was clearly nothing like a combination of mortal danger—and a conflict satisfactorily resolved— to restore the sexual spice to a maturing romantic relationship. He also couldn't help but notice he had not, through the whole course of last night, found the adjective 'comfortable' forming in his mind when he thought about him and Josh.

He also couldn't wait for Josh's foreshadowed marriage proposal.

"Babe," said Josh, brows furrowed. "What is the name for the symbol on that amulet the necromancer was wearing last night?"

"What?" replied Alex in bewilderment.

"I know it's a weird question babe," Josh said. "But I just started thinking about it when you were in the shower. And I can't Google it because I don't know the name of it."

"No, Josh," Alex clarified. "I hadn't noticed the dickhead was wearing an amulet." Then, in a self-critical tone, he continued. "And I'm supposed to notice *everything*."

"Babe," declared Josh, "I think you can be forgiven for missing a detail when you're fighting a necromancer and two hellhounds at once!"

Alex didn't respond to Josh's reassuring message, instead asking, "What did it look like?"

"It's hard to describe in words from the videos and pictures people were taking, babe," said Josh. "It's like ..." Josh made some gestures with his hands. He had intended to chart out a central leaf-like shape, running vertically, and two other, curved leaf-like shapes extending to its left and right.

All Alex saw was a squiggle. "Babe, that is so unhelpful," he said, a little cheerfully.

Josh wasn't to be deterred. "It's French, I think. From before the revolution. You must know what I mean. You're such a history buff."

"Trivia, really, babe. I'm a trivia buff," Alex replied, with the sort of implicit false modesty he carried from his MMS days. But then his eyes narrowed. "You don't mean a *fleur-de-lis*, do you?"

"I just told you I don't know what it's called!" replied Josh in frustration. But he did Google it. "That's it!" he announced in great triumph as he showed Alex his phone. "There were three of them, like in a row, on the amulet. You find that amulet, you find the killer!"

Alex looked at Josh in mild amusement. Josh may as well have said, "I'm helping you solve the case! Then, when you do, you can quit the magic squad—like you *promised*—and we can have a normal life. Then I can stop worrying! Then I can eat again!"

"Babe, this isn't some kind of trashy magical mystery novel. But, yes, you're right."

With that, Alex kissed his boyfriend. His boyfriend who was standing there, practically giggling with excitement at his detective work, in just a pair of tighty-whities. His boyfriend who looked like a mythological hero (not a slutty one). His boyfriend who was super rich and successful. His boyfriend who had bought him this amazing apartment, who had let him furnish it just how he wanted, while doing all the work himself. His boyfriend who did what he was told, who loved him, who was going to marry him and make him the luckiest man alive!

"I love you so much, babe."

As Alex, driving Josh's Tesla, waited for a chance to pull into the St Kilda Road traffic on his way to police headquarters, he noticed a raven perched on a dustbin in that somewhat regal and unsettling way so common to ravens. Previously, he wouldn't have noticed this at all. But ravens had always, and for typically spurious reasons, been associated with the spirit world in folklore. And they were looking for a summoner, after all.

Then, as he approached the entrance to Victoria Police headquarters after parking on the street, he saw yet another raven, again standing in that regal and unsettling raven way, on another dustbin. Was he being followed by spirit-ravens? In all the circumstances, this question didn't seem like paranoia.

Thoughts of ravens, spirit ones or otherwise, left his mind immediately as he saw Karen Park standing in her own rather regal (even, perhaps, ravenesque) way at the entrance to the building. "He's here," she said, emotionlessly. "He says he'll talk, but only to you."

"What a dick," declared Alex, as he walked up to the interview room.

25

Alex Describes a Meeting of the Melbourne Magic School Magic History Club

10 years ago

"I guess it was all pretty friendly. Normal, even," admitted Alex.

He was talking about a meeting of the MMS Magic History Club, but he could also have been describing where he and Yolanda were currently chatting over cocktails. Manhattans, to be precise, served perfectly between dry and sweet.

They were at Cathay Bar. Situated on the first floor of a nondescript building—up a wide, unremarkable flight of stairs, through an unremarkable, essentially unmarked door in a narrow alley in Melbourne's Chinatown—Cathay could scarcely have been more different to the Lion. For one, it had cocktails. Proper ones, excellent ones (to the extent that a nineteen-year-old could claim credible opinions on the matter). It was dark, with booths separated by curtains. And it had all sorts of oriental decorations hanging around. But the effect was classy, rather than twee or tacky.

Catherine had brought Alex and Ivan there a couple of months ago, and declared it the best cocktail bar in Melbourne. Alex figured she would know.

Before Yolanda could reply to his comment, he felt the need to add an addendum: "At least, it was, superficially."

"How so?" asked Yolanda, who was actually finding the Manhattan rather heavy going, given Manhattans are essentially jazzed-up straight rye whisky—and Yolanda did not have a Robbie to give her a taste, and tolerance, for straight spirits.

"Well, it was a trivia night. And I like trivia." He sipped his drink. "And, like, everyone was *nice*. Even Jamie, who had previously given off socially awkward vibes."

"Yeah, maybe being around his own people brought him out of his shell?" Yolanda offered.

"That's actually a really good way to put it, Yol," agreed Alex, to Yolanda's quiet satisfaction. "There was this sense of ... exclusivity, I guess you could call it. And, boy, were they *obsessed* with history. You know I like history."

"I do."

"But, these guys, *wow*. I've never heard so much passionate discussion of the fucking Byzantines, Greek fire, Justinian. But they never mentioned how Justinian actually *failed* to retake Italy but did manage to wreck it; and Greek fire hardly stopped the Turks, the Bulgars, even the crusaders— who utterly hated magic—from tearing the empire apart."

Yolanda smiled. "You really are into history."

Alex continued. "And then there's their *own* histories, their family histories. I've said it before, what *normal* people have any idea what their nineteenth century ancestors—or earlier—did with themselves? Those people *all* knew, tracing their origins back even to the Great Persecution. And they would ask me about *my* family, and I would have to admit that I was a *firstie*—they even have a fucking word for it!"

Alex drained the last of his glass. Yolanda had barely touched hers. She silently pushed her drink over to Alex, who took it and had another sip. Yolanda wondered whether Alex might not be drinking a little too much, but she was finding this largely one-sided conversation interesting, so said nothing.

"Then, they'd look at me with something like polite pity, you could call it. Like I wasn't quite as … *genuine*, maybe, as them. Then they'd change the subject and gush about me being on the magic team."

"Like you were lesser?" offered Yolanda, by way of clarification. "Someone to be tolerated. Or maybe, accepted, but not exactly embraced. Not quite one of us."

"Yes! That is exactly it!" Then, warming to that theme, Alex added an analogy. "It's like being an immigrant, I suppose, at least in the past. You have to be a couple of generations in before you can properly join the club."

"Or," suggested Yolanda, "You can be like my people and be hundreds of generations in and your application is still being considered by the membership committee."

"Yol—"

"Don't say it, Alex. I know you weren't trying to suggest the situations are the same." She paused in thought for a moment and added, "But, you know, Alex, these historians aren't normal or mainstream. There is a reason magic supremacy is not exactly *encouraged*."

"I *know* that, Yol. But the people at these meetings weren't, like, total weirdos or anything. I mean, none of our friends were there, but there were some faculty, even Nathan Beck was there."

"Who?"

"Nathan Beck, from the *Cockatrice*," Alex clarified. "And, be honest, it's not just the *historians*, really, is it? You're *all* like that, to some extent. The historians are just more overt and obnoxious about it."

"No, we aren't!"

"You kinda are, though," Alex insisted. "Take the family thing. The first thing Julius told me about were his ancestors. Robbie did the same. So did Assane. So did *you*. Or you practically did."

Yolanda was silent.

Alex looked apologetic. "Sorry, Yol. I didn't mean for this conversation to get so … heavy."

"That's OK, Ali," she said, soothingly. "But what are you trying to say? What does this all *mean*?"

"I genuinely don't know, Yol," Alex insisted in reply. "But—"

"But what?"

"You know, in that class—where Jamie put his foot in it a bit?"

"Yeah."

"And I was, like, isn't this all so great and stuff? Doing magic, learning about magic."

"Yes."

"Well, I think that the novelty may be wearing off and—"

"What?"

"I'll put it this way: perhaps this weird, wonderful, self-regarding magic world is a nicer place to visit—for me—than it is to live in."

26

Interviewing
Harry and Jamie Archer

Present day

Harry Archer sat in front of Alex and Karen in a special Magic Squad custody centre at Victoria Police headquarters. Designed to minimise a prisoner's ability to use magic, the walls were lined with sigils, patterns and ordinary words setting out warding incantations. These were rendered in silver, which tended to dampen magic use in general and spirit magic in particular.

On the table between the suspect and his interrogators sat a slightly blurred image of the necromancer wearing the fleur-de-lis amulet, as well as three business cards: the one from the original revenant summoning site, the one in the book in the MMS library that had been booby-trapped with the ifrit, and the one that Harry Archer had been caught trying to place, using a spirit form of teleportation, at the Albert Park Lake crime scene.

Karen had 'cautioned' Harry—the Victorian equivalent of reading him his rights. His expression was calm, almost inscrutable. This irritated Karen, who said, "You're in a lot of trouble, Harry. Tampering with crime scenes is not something taken lightly."

"I know," replied Harry, in a slightly pleading, yet still dignified tone. "But I promise I was trying to help. Please, let me explain."

"Then explain," ordered Karen. "Everything. From start to finish."

"OK," he commenced. "So that night Nerida was killed, I sensed something. I'm good at that, sensing spirit magic stuff. You would know, Alex, from my investigation of hauntings."

"Well, that's what you told me," replied Alex, coldly.

"It's true, though," insisted Harry, earnestly. "I could sense immediately that something was happening—spirit magic. So, I went there."

"How?" asked Karen.

"Through magic, of course. I used spirits to convey me to where I felt the spirit magic, the summoning, had taken place. And, of course, I immediately realised what it was."

"A necromantic summoning?" offered Karen.

"More than that," insisted Harry. "I knew, or at least had a strong sense, that this was something to do with '*Summoning the Ultimate Darkness*'. You know, the old French work."

"No, I don't," declared Karen, in her typically strict tone that made *authority Robbie* sound like a kindergarten teacher. "Explain it to me."

"Some people call it a prophecy," replied Harry, sounding inappropriately conspiratorial. "But a better way of thinking about it is as a ritual. People with certain characteristics are killed with—" Harry paused and put emphasis on the next word, "—*dark* spirit magic and that summons this mega-Lovecraftian horror into the world."

"And these people with certain *characteristics*," said Alex, motioning at the cards on the table. "This is a selection of those?"

"Yes," replied Harry, sounding almost excited. "The Gatekeeper—Nerida, who picked the students for MMS. The Bibliophile—Leon, who runs the library." Then, pointing at the final card, he said, "And the Merchant—Laurence Archer."

"Wait," said Karen. "How did you know, having sensed or whatever the summoning at Mewan's grave, that this had anything to do with that prophecy?"

"I didn't *know*, and I don't," admitted Harry. "I just, I guess, suspected it. A lot. And I wanted you guys to know."

"By planting fake evidence?"

"Yes, I suppose that's what I did," acknowledged Harry, looking ever so slightly ashamed of himself.

"But why did you suspect it *a lot*?" asked Alex. "I assume the spirits or whatever didn't just give you the intel."

"Good question," replied Harry, to Alex and Karen's visible irritation. "The main reason I suspected it was that there had been an obvious uptick at MMS in activity from … well, they call themselves *historians*."

"In what way?" inquired Karen, sceptically.

"It's hard to say," replied Harry, trying to sound reasonable. "But there is just more of it around MMS. The magic supremacy bullshit. Especially among that *cabal* I told you about, Alex. I guess they're getting grumpy and irritable in their old age."

"And we're just expected to believe this?" ventured Alex. "And, even then, is that really a reason to think your fellow faculty members want to summon the *Dark One*?"

"Do your research, Alex," countered Harry, sounding frustrated. "Many historians are obsessed with summoning the *Darkness*, if only to make themselves more relevant. You cannot fight an entity that creates endless night with tanks and drones alone, can you? And, as for whether historian activity is rising at MMS, just ask John Bishop."

"Why?" asked Karen.

"I saw him going into one of their events. A magic history trivia night, I suspect. He'd never been involved with them before. At least, not that I knew about."

John said that Nerida had been busy and less available recently, maybe because of a new man. (Alex)

But maybe he was the one who had become busy? (Karen)

Tammy Mazur said Nerida had not been seeing anyone for a while. (Alex)

"Finish telling us what happened, Harry," insisted Karen. "Like I said, beginning to end."

"As I was saying, I saw the summoning site, then I thought about how to make sure you would look into the ritual. I had the cards idea. So, I rocked up to one of those office supplies shops, which opened at 7 am, and had the cards printed."

"Wait, right there and then?" asked Karen.

"Yes," replied Harry. "I know it's not how it normally works, but I insisted. I actually behaved like a bit of a 'Karen' actually."

Karen Park glowered at him but said nothing.

"How did you know which card to leave, though?" asked Alex.

"Well, by about 8:00 to 8:30 am—I guess after Nerida's body was found—rumours started swirling on some WhatsApp groups that she was the victim. So, I took a punt and left the card there. I figured, even if it was the wrong card, it might still make you guys look into the ritual. But, as it happens, I left the *right* card, and you *still* didn't."

"Harry," said Alex. "Just because we're in the Magic Squad does not mean we jump down rabbit holes of investigating absurd prophecies."

"Rituals," corrected Harry, as if this was a very important distinction.

"Whatever," insisted Alex, "The point is, criminals who can use magic are the same as criminals who cannot. And we investigate crimes, not myths and legends."

"Should I keep going, *Officer Hicks?*"

"Yes," barked Karen.

"So, after that, I checked out that necromancy book at the library and put the bibliophile card in it. I knew you would want to look at that book because I recognised the ritual at the summoning site—which was initially in that book, even if it's also everywhere online."

"And, of course, you booby-trapped it with that ifrit summoning spell," Karen Park said, accusingly.

"No, I didn't!" cried Harry, in some desperation. "I promise I didn't do that. Why would I?"

"To be honest, Harry," replied Alex, coldly, "none of your actions here are making any sort of sense. Unless you're just trying to insert yourself into the action. An 'insider account' of a necromantic murder would probably be a more commercially promising book than one educating people about the reality of hauntings. Am I getting warm?"

Harry bowed his head. "OK, that is fair. The thought did occur to me. But not right away."

"Tell us about last night, Harry," ordered Karen.

Harry took a deep breath. "Again, I felt a big, hostile release of spirit energies. So, I conveyed myself to Albert Park just in time to see you, Alex, fighting those barghests."

"Hellhounds," corrected Alex.

"Oh shit," said Harry. "You would think I could tell the difference. Though my vantage point was pretty bad. I didn't want to be seen, obviously."

"Obviously," agreed Karen, sneering. "Then you came back in the morning, once the hubbub had died down a bit, and got caught planting the Merchant card?"

"Yes," said Harry. "But not before I tried to convince your colleague Rob—Detective Chang—to look into the summoning ritual first."

Karen and Alex looked at Harry, flabbergasted. "Wait, hold on," demanded the former. "When did you talk to my detective and how on earth did you know where to find him off-duty?"

"It was a coincidence. I was out with my cousin, Jamie. Do you remember him, Alex?"

Karen was plainly unconvinced—and unimpressed. "A coincidence? Really, Harry? In a city of almost five *million* people, you just so happened to bump into my detective on an innocent night out?"

Alex noted the familiar, *behind the eyes* expression dart across Harry's face. Karen pressed on. "We will get your cousin to make a statement, Harry. Do you think he is likely to confirm that this was *just* a coincidence?"

Harry sighed and his shoulders sagged. "Look, I—I've occasionally had some of my spirit friends follow detectives Hicks and Chang and, um, report on their, you know, comings and goings ..."

As Harry trailed off shamefacedly, Karen fixed him with a look of such severity that Alex felt mortified on his behalf. She spoke with quiet menace. "I don't need to tell you how inappropriate, *and illegal*, it is to place police officers under surveillance."

Harry appeared lost for words.

Alex said, "And you still haven't called off your ravens, Harry. Even *after* being caught."

"What are you talking about?" he sputtered. "I would never use spirit-ravens. How obvious and unoriginal."

Karen was looking at Alex quizzically. *Maybe it's just my imagination. But I've noticed ravens around me recently.*

Harry broke the silence. "But yes, of course, I'll never follow anyone like that ever again. I promise." Karen, still looking very severe, instructed him to keep going. "Detective Chang was at this gay bar, Supermarket. He was dancing, sort of dancing, mainly making out—"

"Harry!" snapped Karen. "We don't need to hear your observations about the off-duty, personal activities of our colleague whom you illegally placed under surveillance and whose privacy you violated."

"Of course," Harry said, feigning—at least, Alex thought he was feigning—contrition. Harry Archer was seemingly unable *not* to create some sort of drama. "I told Detective Chang that he needed to look into the summoning ritual. I told him I'd remembered the word gatekeeper."

"After initially lying to us," Alex reminded him.

"Yes, sorry, but I didn't want you to suspect what I was doing."

"Obviously," replied Karen, her voice laced with contempt.

"Anyway, he wasn't having any of it," continued Harry. "Then, he left, teleported outside. So, I summoned a barghest for a few seconds— thinking that barghests were what the necromancer had attacked you with, Detective Hicks. But, while I'm pretty sure Detective Chang saw it, nobody else did. And he was, well—without going into any detail— distracted. So, I realised I'd need to plant the card, despite the risk."

Karen tapped the blurry image of the fleur-de-lis amulet. "Does this look familiar to you, Harry?"

He answered quickly, but not quite with certainty. "I'm pretty sure that's in the MMS museum. Not on display, though—in the archives. If it's what I think it is, though, it's a summoning amulet."

"That may be the first piece of useful information you've given us, Harry," said Karen. "I think that's all we need from you for now. You will be taken back to the cells and charged."

"What will happen to me?" he whined.

"There are quite a few offences here, Harry. So, you'll just have to hope that the court takes into account your *eventual* cooperation and lack of prior offences."

With that, an officer led a dejected-looking Harry Archer back to a specialist magic holding cell.

"You know," said Karen to Alex, once Harry had been led from the room. "I've interviewed magic killers, a fire mage with a habit of disfiguring the faces of women who rejected his advances, and the ringleaders of a mind control sex trafficking ring—and I think I might dislike *The Prince* even more than any of them."

"He's congenitally, pathologically irritating," agreed Alex.

"Mind you, *Prince Harry* almost makes sense when you've met *Sir Laurence*," said Karen.

Alex smiled at this. "Did he have anything useful for us?"

"No. But he did have his own theory of the crimes. One which, *of course*, made them all about him and his Sourcery website."

"How?"

"No idea. I didn't say it was a *rational* theory of the case. Something about an unidentified, disgruntled investor killing Nerida Stein because she encouraged them to invest in the company—and him, obviously, because he ran it."

"To be honest, I don't hate that more than the crap about prophecies and Dark Ones," said Alex.

"He was going to share this theory with you at the dinner, until he went outside for a cigar—his *only vice* apparently—and was accosted by the hellhound."

"Sounds like I dodged a bullet, then. Hellhounds and a necromancer aside."

"Are you up to talk to Jamie Archer as well?" asked Karen. "He's agreed to come in to give a statement."

"Sure," Alex replied. "I did used to know him. A long time ago."

With his neat, short back-and-sides, Jamie no longer looked anything like a surfer. Alex could not help but observe quite how a man-bun—or its removal—shaped one's appearance. Which brought an uninvited image of Robbie into his mind.

"So, this is where you wound up, Al—can I call you Alex?"

"Of course you can, Jamie," said Alex, smiling warmly. (Karen had agreed, given their past history, that Alex should lead the interview.) "And yes, this is where I wound up." He added, for no particular reason, "But this is my first magic case. What about you, Jamie, what do you do now?"

Jamie smiled back, but he looked nervous. "Well, most recently, I've been working at Sourcery." His smile became a little rueful. "Which means I'll soon be working for my *dad*!"

"But I guess you're still working with magic, at least indirectly," offered Alex, trying to establish a rapport.

"True," agreed Jamie. "And I still do some magical sports. I keep in touch with things that way."

"Good," said Alex, not sure if he meant it. "Let's talk about Harry Archer. You were at the club with him last night?"

"Yes," said Jamie. Then he added, "As part of a group. He asked to tag along. It was a bit last minute."

"Was that normal?" asked Alex, eyebrows slightly raised.

"That he asked to come along?" asked Jamie. "I think it had been longer than usual since we'd seen each other. We generally meet up a lot. I'm close to Harry and my cousins. Closer than with my half siblings. They're older, obviously, and they always thought Dad doted on me more than them. And the divorce was nasty, apparently."

Alex cut in. "I'm surprised Supermarket was Harry's kind of scene."

Jamie grinned. "You mean, lots of gay dudes dancing shirtless? It was definitely *not* his scene! But, I think the word he used was 'an experience'. He's always prided himself on being open-minded and—like I said—it had been longer than usual between drinks."

There must have been something about Alex's nodding silence that made Jamie ask him a rhetorical question. "I guess it never came up back then. You know, that I was—"

"Gay?" Alex cut in.

"Yeah," said Jamie. Then, as his smile became almost cheeky, he added, "And we didn't all get the same level of attention as you!"

Karen Park, who had been silent throughout, supressed a smile at this. She also asked the next question. "Harry left at one stage, didn't he?"

Jamie's smile disappeared in the face of Karen's inherent authority. "Yes, for a little while. All he told me was that he thought 'something was up'. Then, when he got back, he went and talked to your ex, Alex. Who looked furious."

Seems to support Harry's eventual story. (Alex.)

Yes. Let's not mention what we know about Harry and his surveillance, at least for now. (Karen.)

Jamie looked nervous as the two detectives silently conversed. Alex decided to change the subject. "And your dad, Jamie, is there anyone who might want to harm him?"

Jamie turned from nervous to thoughtful. "*He* definitely thinks he has enemies," Jamie said, finally. "About all that PayNow stuff with the disgruntled investors. I thought he was being paranoid, but then last night happened."

"Anyone else?" asked Alex.

"Just, you know, I heard about some of that stuff about the MMS faculty but I really don't know much about it."

"OK," said Alex. "I think I have just one more question. You mentioned keeping up with the magic sports. Did you do the same with the Historians?"

The shadow of a very painful memory crossed Jamie's face. "No," he said, firmly. "Not at all."

"Given his relatives," declared Karen Park. "That kid seems amazingly normal."

"Yeah," agreed Alex, somewhat blankly.

"Why did you ask that last questions, about the Historians?"

"Just something I'm thinking about," replied Alex, cryptically.

Karen looked like that explanation was less than satisfactory, but then said, "You've probably earned yourself a day off tomorrow."

"That's OK. I'd rather come in. We need to interview the MMS museum staff. Or re-interview them—I assume some of the others already have."

"Yes, they did," replied Karen. "But I agree you and Robbie should have a go at them, what with this new information about the amulet. And I assume Robbie will be in tomorrow. I wondered if he might have been unwell, but—thanks to our Harry—it would seem we now know he was actually just too … distracted to answer my calls."

As she said the word 'distracted', the edges of Karen's lips raised ever-so-slightly. Alex imagined this was the Karen Park version of a naughty grin.

"I might see you tomorrow then," replied Alex.

"Though, first thing tomorrow, let's get you a proper magic pistol," Karen called, as he was leaving. "If you're going to be one of us, you'll need the proper kit."

Alex said nothing. *But I have no intention of becoming one of you. I made a promise to my soon-to-be-fiancé, and I'm going to keep it.*

27

On Wards, Barriers and Dampeners; Alex Has Coffee with His Dad

10 years ago

This class on wards, barriers and dampeners was technically a prac but, unusually, was being held in the familiar, cavernous MMS games room. Which meant the students—including Alex, Yolanda, Julius, Emma and Jack—had a chance to show off their taste in sport and athleisure wear.

Both Alex and Yolanda were wearing their MMS Magic Team hoodies, demonstrating their school spirit. (A spirit that, in Alex's case, was certainly starting to wane.) Julius was wearing head-to-toe black and white Adidas. Whether or not Yolanda loved her boyfriend's look, she clearly loved looking *at* him. For her part, Emma's sense of style didn't extend to anything athletic; she wore a baggy tracksuit and still managed to look uncomfortable.

Jack looked good. He was wearing a shiny white t-shirt with matching light jacket and shorts. It all fitted extremely well, enough to suggest a slim-but-muscular physique that Alex hadn't noticed before. And, as Alex was wont to notice—maybe given his uncomplimentary views on his own—Jack also had very nice legs and ankles.

He was also smiling, for no apparent reason. He was almost glowing. And, while he and Alex made eye contact only briefly, Alex was pretty sure Jack was no longer looking at Alex in *that* way. Which, on balance, was a relief. Alex wondered whether Jack had met someone else.

"OK, class, we've done the theory—now we're doing the practice." That was Tammy Mazur, Professor of Summoning. She was standing behind three classroom-style tables on which various objects were arrayed. On the table to the students' left, and on the central table, there was a variety of small trinkets of different shapes. On the right-hand table sat a range of silver hoops, large enough to step in and inscribed with runes. "But first, let's recap. While anything that reduces the effect of magic is often called a ward, we learnt that, more specifically, a *ward* does what?"

Unusually, Jack stuck his hand up.

"Yes, Jack?"

"A ward, which is usually specific to a particular type of magic, reduces the caster's ability to cast spells. They take more effort to cast, and their strength is reduced."

"Very good, spot on!"

Hey, do you think Jack seems a bit more … chipper than usual? (Emma)

Em, what if the Prof can hear us? (Alex)

I can! (Tammy) "Alex," said Tammy. "Why don't you recap us on barriers?"

"Sure," he replied, with a bit less self-assurance than Jack. "A barrier is like a ward in that it normally relates to a particular type of magic. But, instead of reducing the strength of the spell itself, it reduces the spell's impact on a particular affected object, space or person."

"Good answer, Alex," replied Tammy.

It was another student, one Alex did not really know, who explained the effects of dampeners. "Dampeners affect the use of magic in an area, again by making spells harder to cast, and less powerful when they are."

It was Yolanda who answered the final question, about how wards, barriers and dampeners interact. "It's just like with enchantments and rituals," she declared. "The effect is not linear, but exponential—the combination of two of them is greater than just adding them both together."

"Very good. I see at least some of you have been paying attention! Also, again, just like with enchantments and magnifiers, wards—in the broad sense—can come in all sorts of physical forms, but silver ones are most effective."

Tammy gestured to three tables. "OK, so, now we're going to experience how all of this works." She pointed at the table on the students' left. "This is table one. Here, there are wards, in the specific sense. There is one for each of you, according to your affinity. If it's not obvious which ones reflect your affinity, based on the shape and imagery of the object, it's fine to ask me." She pointed at table two, in the centre. "This table has barrier objects. Again, same drill as the wards." Finally, she pointed to the table on the students' right. "Table three. This one has dampeners, in the form of hollow discs that you put on the floor and stand inside. These are all the same: one size fits all." Making a come-forward motion with her hands, Tammy commanded: "So, come on, form an orderly line."

The students obeyed, lining up and passing each table, as if taking food from a hotel buffet.

Tammy continued to offer instructions. "And, just to be clear, as there is always one or two who do it. This, I stress, is not an opportunity to show off. It's not about trying to impress your friends, nor me—though, trust me, you will not impress *me* anyway—with elaborate demonstrations of your abilities. Nor is it about trying to push through and *beat* the wards. Is that clear?

"Ah, Emma, Alex," Tammy said, in a tone that was hard to place. "You're our only mentalist, Emma. Unlike the others, you can hardly cast spells on your own mind."

"Yes," replied Emma, in a voice that suggested she had no idea where this discussion was going to go.

"Which means you need a partner," added Tammy. "And why not your friend, Alex, here?" As if in response to the uncomfortable silence of the two students, she added, "After all, it's a better use of your mutual talents than just passing mental notes in class, isn't it?"

Both Emma and Alex nodded sheepishly, collected the remainders of their needed objects, and went back to their positions.

"OK, now, first step," ordered Tammy. "Keep your wards on the floor, not too close to you. Manifest some magic based on your affinity—but no show-offs!"

Yolanda evoked a grapevine around herself. Alex conjured a small, contained storm of wind and rain. Julius made himself look like Psy, the K-pop artist who had recently gone viral with his song, 'Gangnam style'. Jack expanded his right hand to triple its original size. Emma, as instructed, started communicating with Alex.

Did you watch Fast and Furious—Six, Alex? (Emma)

Yes, and I liked it too. So there. (Alex)

So did my kids. (Tammy) "OK," declared Tammy. "Now, it's time to put on the ward."

The students all complied. Yolanda's grapevine was noticeably more threadbare. Alex found it harder to create his contained storm. Julius still looked like Psy—at least, his top half, while his legs remained in his black Adidas pants. Jack struggled to make his hand double in size, let alone triple. Emma was clearly trying to communicate:

You ... H—wood ... 'rap ... populis—t—'astes.

As much as Emma's communications sounded like they had been jammed, her film snobbery shone through. "You [something] Hollywood crap, populist tastes."

Now, it was time to try things with the barriers, which the students put on after ditching the wards.

Yolanda's grapevine and Alex's contained storm were similar to their pre-ward scale, but they hung away from their casters, refusing to come closer. Julius' Psy impersonation was essentially the same as when restricted by the ward: his face looked right, his bottom half did not. Jack seemed equally to struggle to grow his hand more than double in size. Emma's communications were also equally jammed.

I ... 'ought, 'ou, 'ould, 've 'etter ... 'andards.

Again, Alex could decode the message: "I thought you would have better standards."

"Now, for the dampeners," declared Tammy Mazur. The students dutifully dropped the dampeners onto the floor, placed the hoops onto the ground and stepped inside them.

Given their more broad and general effect, the dampeners placed less of a restriction on the students' magic use than the other wards. Yolanda's grapevine, and Alex's contained storm, were smaller than pre-wards, but larger and more stable than with the others. Julius was Psy again, if with the odd flicker. And Jack's hand was almost as big as the initial control run—but he did look like he was making more effort. All the discs glowed with light of varying hues, as the students sought to affect their magic despite them.

Emma was similar: *You 'ink you know a 'erson ...* she 'said'.

Finally, it was time to try everything at once, with the wards, barriers and dampeners altogether. It was impossible not to feel the effects. Yolanda's grapevine looked like a dead seat of twigs. Alex's storm, as much as he tried not to push things, looked more like steam coming from a kettle. Julius looked like Julius, with an intermittent hologram of Psy overlayed on himself. Jack's thumb expanded, the rest of his hand did not. And Emma could barely start communicating: *'ex ... I ... 'nt ... 'ay ... 'thing.*

"Lastly, the effect of wards can be magnified significantly by being 'activated' by a magic user." Tammy waved her hand and the wards, barriers and dampeners glowed with a soft light. Yolanda's grapevine ceased to exist; Alex's storm vanished; Julius was entirely himself; Jack's whole hand was Jack's and Emma frowned in complete, mental radio silence: ...

In the end, there were no dramatic show-offs. Everyone lined up neatly again to leave their wards on the relevant tables.

Alex, next time we get the chance, I'm going to teach you do this via private channel. (Emma)

Cool.

As the students filed out of the games room, the group came together. "Hey, Jack," declared Yolanda. "I have to say, you look pretty good in sports gear."

"Thanks," replied Jack, without a hint of awkwardness.

"I reckon Ali has leg envy," Yolanda added, *of course.*

"Very droll, Yol," replied Alex, as Jack simply smiled.

"Should we catch up for coffee?" suggested Emma.

"You guys go ahead," replied Alex. "I'm meeting my dad."

"You guys are close." That was Julius.

"Yeah, we are."

Max and Alex Hicks sat in Baba Beans, a trendy café close to MMS. Behind a navy façade, the café boasted concrete floors, a bare brick wall, and exposed timber beams, in a converted warehouse setting. In other words, it was practically the archetypal Melbourne coffee shop, with merchandise in the corner, an all-day breakfast menu, and baristas with tattoos.

"How is it all going, Ali? Well?" Max's expression changed as he saw his son's. "Is something wrong?"

"No, no, Dad," Alex insisted in reply. "I guess I've just been thinking about things."

"What does that mean, my darling?" replied Max, nursing an old-school cappuccino with cocoa sprinkled on the top. (Very uncool.) Alex was sipping a strong latte.

"It's hard to explain," argued Alex, in an attempt to delay an admission.

"I'm all ears." Max, looking at the counter, waved over a waiter and ordered a caramel slice. "I haven't really eaten all day," he added, by way of justification.

"Well, Dad, I guess it's just …" Alex trailed off.

"What? You know you can tell me anything."

"OK," Alex took a gulp of coffee. "Just to start, I don't want any *I told you so* stuff."

"Why would there be any of that?"

"Seriously, Dad! You cannot say you were *thrilled* that I decided to study magic. Anyway, you know that one of the reasons I wanted to study magic was—"

"Aside from not having a clue what you wanted to do with your life, you mean?" Max smiled back at his son with genuine affection. Not that Alex acknowledged it.

"Yes, Dad, *aside* from that." His dad remaining quiet, Alex continued. "I guess I wanted to … find my people. You know, I was never—"

"Cool in high school?" Max finished Alex's sentence.

"Yes."

"But who was cool in high school?" replied Max. "I mean, I wasn't. I know your siblings were. Your mother was too, but *normal* people—"

"Can I *please* finish, Dad?"

"Of course, sorry."

"And, on one level, it's all great. I'm doing well—"

"—Very well, your mother and I are so pleased!"

"And socially, too, it's all great. I've made all these friends, and then there's Robbie. And the magic team stuff, the nationals in Canberra coming up …" Alex, again, trailed off.

"But?" his father prompted. Of course, there must be a 'but'.

"*But*," agreed Alex, "The thing is, magic people are like this weird little club who feel like they're better than others—even the ones that try not to—but they also feel, sort of, persecuted. And they're all *obsessed* with their ancestors. Their magic ones, anyway—and I don't have any of those."

"So what you're saying is maybe they're not quite *your* people?"

"Yes. And there is the practical side, too."

"How so?"

"I'm finally thinking about what I want to do with my life."

"Don't take my earlier comment too seriously, Ali," said Max, finishing off the last of his caramel slice. "Some people know exactly what they want to do with their lives. Most of us don't. We just fall into things and hope we find something we enjoy, or at least see as interesting or worthwhile."

"Don't worry, Dad," said Alex. Then, putting on a cheeky grin, added, "I have no intention of taking you seriously."

Max just smiled back at his son.

Alex continued. "But, even if I don't know what I want to do with my life, I have to do *something*. And I'm pretty sure I don't want that to involve magic."

"Are you thinking of anything in particular?" asked Max.

"Well, I'm tossing up transferring to commerce next year. You know I'm interested in business stuff."

"I do. I remember your mother used to have to go hunting for the business section of the paper," his father replied, with a smile of recollection.

"Or, maybe, even the police?"

"Really?" Max looked surprised.

"Yes, really. I don't know what you told Robbie, but he's super excited about it. I guess it's rubbing off! He even started the recruitment process already."

"Hey, I can be convincing," declared Max. "Just not, it seems, with my *own* children. And, you know, you could do both. We need more educated police. Robbie would be great, I know it. Speaking of which, have you talked to him about any of this?"

"Not yet," confessed Alex. Then, by way of self-justification. "I mean, Robbie graduates at the end of this year, anyway. And it's not like I've actually *decided* anything yet."

"I don't know, Ali," replied his father. "You sound like you have."

28

Alex and Robbie Interview the MMS Museum Curators

Present day

On Monday, mid-morning, Alex sat in a chair at the Victoria Police headquarters across a table from Robbie, who looked in good spirits. Alex, on the other hand, was looking down at the holster of his new magic pistol. Rather than being just inert metal, the enchanted firearm seemed to squirm with something almost life-like. He found that unusual, novel, and unsettling. It would be overkill to say it felt like having a mouse in his pocket, but not by all that much.

"The coverage is getting insane," said Robbie, looking up from his tablet.

"I know," said Alex, sounding bored. Almost all night yesterday, Josh had been reading various articles about the case, linking it to all manner of magical incidents around the world. Which annoyed Alex because he had hoped that, rather than stare into a screen all evening, Josh might instead have flung Alex onto the bed (or maybe the couch, or even the floor) and repeated what he had done on Saturday night. Mind you, Alex could hardly begrudge Josh his obsessive news consumption, given it was likely some kind of counter-intuitive coping mechanism.

His own coping mechanism, by contrast, leaned more towards ignoring any media coverage of the case as much as he could. It would be nice if Robbie could oblige that.

"This dumb rag is asking: 'Are we looking at the magic-pocalypse?' How ridiculous!"

"Can we talk about something else?"

"At least they're keeping your name out of it," Robbie said. "Though there are rumours swirling on social media."

Alex decided that was quite enough. "How was your weekend, Robbie? Karen said you went totally off the grid."

Robbie actually blushed. "Yeah," he stammered, sheepishly. "I was. I went out and—"

"Met someone?"

Robbie remained sheepish. He was clearly reluctant to talk about his likely escapades. But then, Alex reasoned, they needed to talk about something. And Robbie's suspected hot hook-up was a better topic of conversation than anything that happened between them a decade ago, or hysterical media coverage of their case. "Yes," Robbie finally conceded, monosyllabically.

"Come on, Robbie," encouraged Alex. "Tell me what happened."

Robbie hesitated but, implicitly admitting defeat, he explained, "We met at Supermarket—Karen told me what fucking Harry Archer said, by the way—and we hit it off. It was actually a set-up by a friend but, well, it was terrific."

"The sex you mean?" teased Alex, with a gleefully wicked grin.

"Yeah," acknowledged Robbie. "But not just that. I mean, everything was terrific. We're seeing each other again. Like, as boyfriends."

"I'm glad to hear that," said Alex, genuinely. "What's his name?"

"Winston," replied Robbie. Then, with a conclusive air, he determinedly moved the conversation on. "Let's talk about the case, Alex."

Alex and Robbie spent the time between the terminated conversation and their arrival at MMS discussing the earlier interview notes of the two curators of MMS Museum.

"It seems like a pretty shoestring operation," declared Robbie. "There's the full-time curator, Theo Georgiou, older guy, fire affinity. Then there is the assistant curator, Naomi Trinh, younger. That seems to be a part-time gig. Her main job is as a lecturer in magic history."

"And her affinity?" asked Alex, not sounding especially interested, looking at the road as he drove.

"Summoner, actually," said Robbie. "Which means we should probably look into her a bit further. Assuming Harry Archer is right, she would've had easy access to the amulet."

"True," said Alex. "But remember what John Bishop said: 'With practice, it's possible to master any magic discipline'." Then, he asked: "Alibis?"

"Not really," replied Robbie. "Georgiou claims to have been at home. But his non-magic wife was out most of the night, got home late and couldn't confirm his whereabouts."

"And Naomi?"

"She supposedly had a drink with a friend earlier in the evening. Her neighbour in her apartment building saw her a bit later, but she claims to have been home alone at the key times."

"It would be nice if some MMS faculty did have alibis," said Alex, wistfully. "We could then start ruling people out." Changing tack, he asked, "What did they have to say about the MMS generation wars?"

"Theo does obliquely mention having something to do with the Bishop–Mazur–Stein clique. So, actually, maybe the generation wars did come up. But Naomi is apparently friends with Harry Archer."

"We're desperate, aren't we?" said Alex. "You know what we say about motives, that they're for novels and juries, but here we are scrambling around for a motive in the most stupid of places. I cannot believe we're indulging this millennials versus boomers bullshit, in a murder investigation of all things!"

"It's not all nonsense, Alex."

"Yes, it is, Robbie," insisted Alex, with the sort of corrective certainty he might've used if Robbie had claimed the earth was flat. "It's a complete creation of the media. My parents go out for avocado toast, I bet your mum uses social media, doesn't she?"

"Yes, she does," agreed Robbie, as if Alex was missing an important distinction. "She's basically our church's social media coordinator. But—"

"See?" cried Alex, triumphantly. "And workplace rivalries between the ambitious young go-getters and the established senior people is older than Aristotle. Bullshit." He said it again, just to confirm, "Bullshit."

"But you're missing the real key grievance," replied Robbie, insistent on contesting the point. "Generational wealth inequality, and younger people having fewer opportunities *is* real. I mean, it's obviously less acute for you—"

"What are you talking about?" raged Alex, struggling to maintain his concentration on watching the road.

"Well, it's just … your boyfriend."

"Who told you about my boyfriend?" Alex thundered. "My *rich* boyfriend, you mean, obviously."

Robbie looked down at the floor in front of his seat and said nothing.

"Fucking Pav!" fumed Alex. Then, moments later, he calmed down. "Let's just talk about the case, Robbie."

"Here we go," said Theo Georgiou as he pressed his (ordinary) access card against an (ordinary) card reader to admit Alex, Robbie and himself to the backrooms of the MMS museum, where the items in its collection were kept when not on display. Theo was built on similar dimensions to Tammy Mazur, but with thinning black hair, rather than a bob.

"Who has access to this area?" asked Robbie.

"Faculty has access," said Theo. "Students can get access too, for their research, but that needs to be approved and is time-limited."

"But students can access the main museum any time?" asked Alex, remembering his night-time visits with Robbie (and Assare).

"During the day, when it's open, yes," clarified Theo. "But we have cameras and alarms in there now. Things have changed a bit since you two were here."

Another one who remembers us.

"You used to use student volunteers for the public open days," said Robbie. "Do they get access too?"

"No," said Theo. "Just the main museum."

"Hello, detectives." This was Naomi Trinh, an attractive young woman with a black bob hairstyle and vividly painted nails.

"Hello," replied Robbie. "I'm Detective Chang, and this is Detective Hicks. We're from the Victoria Police Magic Squad."

"They're asking about the *Jacques* amulet," said Theo.

Robbie held up his tablet, which had the blurred image of the fleur-de-lis amulet on it. As he did so, he turned his head sideways, as if—for some reason Alex couldn't fathom—he was trying not to look at it himself, much like Alex, being arachnophobic, might avoid looking at an image of a spider.

"Oh, why are you asking about that?" asked Naomi, in what seemed like surprise.

"We think it might have been stolen and used in connection with a murder case," replied Robbie.

Naomi (and Theo) clearly took the hint. "We can check that now, then," declared Naomi.

The pair of curators led Alex and Robbie down a passageway that made Alex think of the adjectives 'musty' and 'fusty', without him being entirely sure quite what either word meant. Then, as a storage drawer was opened, revealing the stark absence of any fleur-de-lis *Jacques* amulet, both curators adopted a suitable air of shock. (Again, Alex noticed Robbie looking away, as if he did not want to see the amulet had it been there.)

"It's gone!" announced Theo in a glaring statement of the obvious.

"When did you last see it?" Robbie asked.

"We catalogued this part of the collection about six months ago," replied Theo.

Six months! thought Robbie and Alex at once, realising it would be almost impossible to identify who might have stolen the amulet from entry records.

Theo seemed to read the implicit disappointment and reproach on Robbie and Alex's faces. "The thing is," he stammered, "not that many people have access to this part of the museum, and—unlike the exhibits on display—very little of these pieces are worth anything."

"Because of that, we thought the risk of theft was low," added Naomi, gamely trying to support her senior colleague.

"What can you tell us about the amulet?" asked Robbie, his air of headmasterly disappointment coupled with pragmatic urgency almost making Alex smile.

It was, to Alex's mild surprise, Naomi who answered. "It was made in the 1950s for a travelling performer. He styled himself *Jacques Le Merveilleux*, supposedly descended from a court sorcerer of Louis XIV— his name was actually Jack Hegarty, an Irish Catholic at a time when that *mattered*."

"Hence the fleur-de-lis design," offered Alex. "Part of the exotic, faux-French shtick."

"Yes, it was," agreed Naomi. "Jack would go around the country, mainly towns and small cities, doing summoning tricks as part of travelling circuses, carnivals, even itinerant boxing shows, which used to be a thing. He had all sorts of French-style props and sets, *Ancien Régime*-type stuff, pre-revolution style."

"What was the amulet *for*?" asked Robbie, clearly trying to force the discussion back towards matters beyond merely academic interest. "What sort of powers did it have?"

Naomi answered Robbie's question eventually, but was struggling to stick to the point when discussing something she found visibly fascinating. "Jack would do multiple shows across the afternoon and at night," she explained. "It was gruelling. Using the amulet meant he could do all those performances one-after-the-other without completely exhausting himself. It was a difficult way of life, one which people today have largely forgotten about."

Alex's (evidentiary) interest was piqued. "Hold on, to confirm, the amulet was about magic endurance, rather than intensity—keeping on for longer rather than enabling, say, more spectacular individual summons?" He silently added: "Like keeping a summoned revenant in line while travelling significant distances, or managing summoned hellhounds, while being able to conjure even more malignant spirits?"

"Yes, one hundred percent," Naomi replied, with total confidence. "Like I said, it was hard work. Pretty exploitative, too. The promoters tended to trouser a large part of the proceeds. Jack needed to do all those shows just to keep his head above water. It didn't help that Jack was an Irish Catholic either. *Or* that he was a magic user."

"You seem to know a lot about this off the top of your head," observed Robbie, to Alex's disappointment. (He would have preferred to keep Naomi going on this point.)

"It was my PhD thesis," explained Naomi. "Well, not Jack Hegarty specifically, though I researched him a lot. It was about mid-20th century travelling magic shows. It's like a lost world—by the 1970s, with TV and changing tastes, travelling magic shows were daggy and dying. But they have always fascinated me."

Alex, to Robbie's evident consternation—despite his family's own history as travelling magicians, he wasn't interested in this particular history lesson—asked, "What was the focus of the thesis, in particular?"

Naomi was more than prepared to answer. "Like I said, the exploitation of magic users as part of these shows. And the tensions, even discrimination, between the fake carnival attractions—tarot card readers, bearded ladies, card trick spivs, that sort of thing—and the genuine magic ones. Obviously, the phoney ones felt threatened, so magic users could be isolated and lack support, hence the frequent exploitation."

Naomi is a historian! declared Alex, triumphantly, to himself. He, of course, knew the type, and had heard that sort of rhetoric before. He said, mildly, "That's fascinating."

Drawing the conversation to a close, Robbie announced, "We will need to take statements from both of you. Can you come down to the station with us?"

"Yes, of course."

As the end of the day approached, Alex and Robbie sat around a table at Victoria Police Headquarters, having taken statements from Theo and Naomi. Naomi had admitted to attending "maybe a few meetings" of the MMS Magic History Club. She claimed this was "natural, given I'm a historian," which she seemed to be using in the literal, rather than figurative and euphemistic, sense.

She also said that she may have seen John Bishop at one or more of those meetings but she "couldn't really be sure" as they hadn't spoken. "We're not exactly friends," she'd said, by way of explanation. She confirmed that, unlike with John Bishop, she was friends with Harry Archer. She also confirmed that Harry could, indeed, sense spiritual energies, much more so than she could. "He's like the spirit-whisperer," she gushed. "He's truly gifted like that. And his work with bereaved families is really remarkable. Noble." (Following this comment, she insisted, when pressed, that, no, her and Harry had never been romantically involved.)

Conversely, she seemed to downplay any generation wars at MMS in general, and between Harry Archer and the Bishop–Mazur–Stein *baby-boomer cabal*, in particular. But that was all they got from her by way of new information.

They got even less from Theo who, much like Leon Mazur, expressed some sympathy for Harry Archer, but found him generally insufferable. That, and that both Theo and Naomi may have heard of Harry Archer's ridiculous Dark One summoning-prophecy-ritual, but neither was at all into necromancy as it "gave them the creeps."

"At this point," declared Alex, disappointed, "All we really know for sure is that the killer really *has* to be faculty. I mean, we can chase down that list of students with access to the museum, but the working assumption has to be that only a faculty member is likely to be familiar enough with the museum's— I don't know—catacombs, to surreptitiously swipe the amulet *and* not arouse any interest or suspicion while doing so."

"Agree," said Robbie. "But we have no way of narrowing it down beyond that, do we?"

"Nope. Which is frustrating, given our necromancer literally showed himself for all to see a couple of nights ago—yet we're still so far from identifying him."

"Are we still so sure it's a 'him'?"

"You mean Naomi Trinh?" Alex asked back, rhetorically. "Definitely, for means and opportunity, she has to be the most likely culprit, given what we know now."

"I'll ask Karen to get some of the guys on the taskforce to find out more about her," said Robbie.

"Hey PB, hey Robbie!" That was Pav, with Isabella in tow, both carrying print-outs of documents.

"Hey Pav, hey Isabella," replied Robbie, sounding friendly.

Alex wanted to say, "Why did you tell Robbie about my fucking boyfriend, Pav?" but chickened out and instead grunted by way of greeting.

"While the superhero squad was out skylarking," Pav said, "Izzy and I were reading up online about this prophecy-thing of Harry Archer's. You know, the Dark One."

"Yeah," continued Isabella. "I have to say, necromancy discussion boards make *Twitter* look normal. Seriously."

"You've got your curious magic types, your death-obsessed weirdos, incels—lots of incels—and even more conspiracy theorists of various shades," said Pav.

"There's even a conspiracy theory that the ritual itself is a conspiracy theory," observed Isabella.

"How does that work?" asked Robbie.

"It doesn't," replied Isabella. "But when has that stopped people believing things on the internet?"

"Fascinating as all this is," said Alex. "I cannot see how it's relevant to the case. And when did we start using words like incel unironically?"

"Haven't you done the training?" asked Pav, all too innocently, as if he was trying to irritate Alex.

"We all do the same training, Pav."

"And I have young granddaughters," declared Pav, as if this was self-evidently relevant to the issue. "I have photos. Robbie, would you like to see photos?"

Before Robbie could respond, or Pav could pull his phone from his pocket, Alex implored, "Can we talk about the case, Pav? Even if that means you explaining this ridiculous ritual."

"Alright," said Pav. "So, there are a few versions of it going around, with some fairly small differences."

"There isn't exactly a single source of truth on the original wording," clarified Isabella. "Which, let me tell you, causes some *passionate* debates on the boards."

"But, overall," explained Pav, "The idea is that, if this sequence of people with particular characteristics are killed using dark magic, it will summon this big demonic beastie, who will turn the sky black, ruin crops, and make dogs and teenagers go even crazier. All the typical bad stuff."

"But," insisted Isabella, "there is some debate—again, passionate— about quite how much the sequence itself matters, or even if it matters at all."

"That's right," agreed Pav. "And, in fact, some of the sequences are slightly different."

"As are the specific names of the … what, targets, sacrifices?" said Isabella.

"Can we get to what the sequence of targets actually is?" Alex practically begged.

"Sure thing, PB," said Pav, affably. "So, the first, in practically all versions, is the Gatekeeper."

"Which, in some tellings, is replaced by Guardsman," clarified Isabella (again).

"Then there is Bibliophile—which is actually more often rendered 'Librarian'," said Pav. "Following that, there is Merchant—these are the ones we know about already."

"Indeed, we do," Alex mused, already bored.

Pav continued. "The next one is Monk, then Soldier." ("Or 'Man-at-Arms'," clarified Isabella.) "Then Exile," said Pav, "which is the weird one, not being a job."

"And that's always worded the same," said Isabella.

"Bishop and Duke—"

"Or, in some cases, Count," clarified Isabella, mercifully for the last time as the list of ritual victims ended.

"Oh, sometimes the Monk comes after the Soldier," Pav noted, as if such a trivial detail of something so outrageously silly could ever be relevant to *anything*.

"You know," Robbie said, "that list of people, they almost sound like what you might find in a medieval city, in a broadly ascending order of status."

"Yes, exactly," replied Isabella, as if Robbie was her student and had just offered a correct answer in class. "That is the prevailing theory online. You despatch representatives of the different social classes in a medieval city and, bang, Big Bad manifests itself."

"Exile is a bit more confusing," argued Robbie, continuing to take this all rather too seriously. "What would that represent?"

"Excellent question!" declared Pav, now himself playing the role of happy teacher. "Remember, in the middle ages, aristocrats who had done something naughty—or whose existence was inconvenient to the person right above them in the line of succession—would be sent, or flee, into exile, often to the court of a relative. So, the exile would be a noble too, hence why they're just below the Duke."

"That explanation is one of the rare things the necromancy web seems to agree on," confirmed Isabella.

"Can I make an observation?" Alex asked, mildly.

"Sure," replied Pav, as if he were a teacher indulging a dumb question.

"The problem with all this, leaving aside that 'dark' magic doesn't really mean anything outside of tabloids, folklore and fantasy novels—it all depends on the intentions of the caster."

Isabella interrupted, "That may be true, sort of, but I think most of us would argue that revenants and hellhounds count as pretty 'dark', at least in a general sense."

"OK," conceded Alex. "Fine. But the *other* problem is that, without that context of a medieval European city, these archetypes or whatever are broad to the point of meaninglessness." He motioned around the room. "Any one of us could be the Guardsman or Gatekeeper, being cops. We could probably even qualify as Men-at-Arms, at a pinch." He started getting a bit of a head of steam. "Robbie, you're a devout Catholic, you could be the Monk too."

Suddenly, subtly, the mood in the room shifted. Then the penny dropped.

"Oh, sorry," Alex said. "I figured people would already know."

"It's not a thing. Don't worry, Alex," said Robbie, reassuringly.

"Someone has forgotten the training, clearly," said Pav, with a cheeky smile. "Also, you could be the Duke, I reckon, PB." Then, a similar penny seemed to drop for him. "Oh, wait."

"Don't worry, I told Robbie about Josh," Isabella said.

"*You* told him?" Alex asked, sounding both surprised and betrayed.

"Yeah, sorry, it just came up. Robbie didn't ask me or anything."

Cutting short an awkward silence, Pav declared, "Well, I reckon it's time for Izzy and me to head off. Don't stay too much longer, boys."

With that, Pav and Isabella left the room, leaving Alex and Robbie alone.

"You know," said Robbie, cautiously. "You could also qualify as the Exile, Alex."

"How do you mean?" asked Alex, eyes narrowed in thought.

Robbie looked hesitant. "Well, you know, how you ..." He trailed off.

But Alex knew what he meant. After all, he had fled. Run away from MMS, from the magic world, seeking exile in normality. He had only now, unwillingly, been sucked back into it. "It's OK," he said. "I get it." Then, he rallied somewhat. "But that just goes to show that, if this stupid ritual-prophecy-fantasy-whatever-it-is has anything to do with our case, we're looking for a rolled-gold, first class, loony-toon of the first order as our killer."

"You really shouldn't talk like that, Alex."

"What?"

"Words like loony-toon," Robbie explained. "They stigmatise the mentally ill."

"For fuck's sake, Robbie!" Alex cried. "This is a *private conversation*. When did you and *Pav* start letting diversity training language intrude on your conversations with *friends*?"

Robbie smiled. Alex wondered if that was because he'd described Robbie and him as friends. Which, Alex thought, they were at least becoming. After all, they were getting along fine, as much as boundaries were sometimes being tested.

"You sound like Winston," Robbie said, his affection for his new boyfriend clear from his tone. "He accused me of taking all the training far too seriously."

"I like him already," grinned Alex.

"*Actually*," continued Robbie, "He accused me of being a walking crisis of masculinity—but I think that is what he meant."

Alex thought, really, he shouldn't pry. He should just leave it. But he couldn't help but think about that time, which felt so long ago—but also fresh in his mind—when Robbie, while Alex desperately hoped he would throw him on the bed and ravish him, had instead paused for the 'consent talk'. Had that happened with Winston? Winston who, given his name, must be some worshipful Chinese bottom. (Alex did not consider that, despite having *definitely done* the training, and *taking it seriously*, he was indulging in classic—if in this case accurate—gay ethnic stereotyping.)

In the end, Alex couldn't resist. He grinned and asked, "Was that when you were in bed, with Winston almost crying in anticipation of an epic fucking, and you gave him *the talk?*"

Alex could tell from Robbie's reaction that he was right, but also that Robbie didn't want to talk about it. "OK, Alex, safe word," said Robbie, firm but calm. He wasn't quite *authority Robbie*, but he was getting there.

"What do you mean?"

"You know what a safe word is, don't you?"

"Yes!" insisted Alex. In truth, Alex had never really used 'safe words' himself. "But are you saying we need a safe word for our *conversations?*"

"Yes. At least if we're going to have any banter in this partnership, which I want. You, despite implicitly raising it just now, don't want to talk about the past. I'm reluctant to go into too much detail about my brand-new boyfriend and our sex life. So, we need a safe word."

"Oh, OK," said a blindsided Alex.

"And," Robbie declared, as if such a thing was entirely obvious, "why have a safe word other than just saying *safe word?*"

Alex could not fault that logic. "OK, it's a deal," he agreed. Then, standing up, he said, "Now I'm going to go home to my rich boyfriend."

He walked home, as he did often when the weather was good. (The journey being a bit more than half an hour.) As he walked through the inner Melbourne streets, he was sure he saw a raven. This one was in the sky, flying, but was seemingly crossing his path more than was reasonable.

If you keep thinking about these ravens, you'll do your own head in and become a word that stigmatises the mentally ill, he thought to himself.

INTERLUDE
– The next six months

Present day

29

Dinner with the Hicks Family;
Shabbat with the Goldmans

Around the time Josh and Alex moved in together, Alex's parents had decided to completely renovate their family home of decades. It was the alternative to downsizing, which ultimately didn't appeal to them. So, out came the carpets and in came polished floorboards. Exposed brick walls were plastered over and painted in tasteful neutrals. Dated arched entrances to rooms were demolished, establishing a pure open plan. The kitchen and bathrooms, last renovated in the 1990s (with terracotta tiles, no less—how mortifying!) were totally redone with understated marble and white tiles.

In the end, the whole thing took longer than expected, and left Alex's parents feeling dissatisfied, even adrift in their own abode. It turned out that floorboards were actually dull, and noisy to walk on. Tasteful neutrals were "beige and boring". Open plan layouts were "very display home—and expensive to heat and cool". The kitchen felt "cold and cavernous". Terracotta tiles felt less mortifying and more "interesting" once they'd been torn out and replaced with white. Even the newly-refreshed bathrooms felt "like a hotel room's".

Max and Yvonne, being pragmatic and sensible people, shared their feelings with each other—and their adult children—then moved on. The 'Great Renovation' would not be spoken of again. (Even if, as both Alex and Catherine insisted at the time: "This is actually a big improvement. You just need to get used to it!")

All of which meant that the dining table at which Alex and Josh sat—alongside Alex's parents, Ivan, Catherine (who was pregnant) and their partners—was a very different table, in very different surroundings, to the one that he and Robbie had sat at all those years ago. Not that Alex was thinking about this. He was too aware of the oppressive sense of disapproval his parents and siblings had been broadcasting since his and Josh's arrival, coupled with the growing discomfort of their partners, who could sense the unspoken awkwardness in the air.

In the end, it was Yvonne, as family matriarch, who gave voice to the family's discontent. "When were you going to tell us, Alex?"

"I dunno, Mum. Tonight, I guess. I mean, it wasn't something I thought would be suitable for the family WhatsApp."

"It would have been nice to hear about it from you, though, Ali, rather than my old police contacts," said his father. "We had no idea you were even working for the Magic Squad."

"I'm not … not really," insisted Alex, rather missing the point. "I just got pulled into this case. I didn't, like, volunteer or anything."

"And you got attacked by that fire thing *and* those—what, *hellhounds?*" continued his mother, waving her hands around dramatically. "And you thought you could wait for our regular family dinner to mention *anything?*"

It was a very Josh move to both snap and maintain his composure at the same time. He cast an angry gaze across the table to the frowning Yvonne, Max, Ivan and Catherine—and their partners, who seemed to be studiously examining their empty plates. Then, adopting a tone that could best be described as one of calm fury, he said, "Sorry, Yvonne and Max, but your son did not ask to be shot at, did not ask to be attacked by an ifrit, nor by hellhounds and a necromancer. And neither did he, nor I, ask to have you spit the dummy because Alex was insufficiently timely in updating you all on how many times his life was threatened last week."

Alex could feel the retreat among his family members, even though an awkward silence hung in the air for a moment afterwards.

In the end, the silence was broken by a beaming Catherine. She pointed at Alex and Josh and declared, "You two are *so* going to get married! I'm calling it!" She got up. "I'm going to make sidecars to celebrate—even though I can't have one myself!" She left the room, her partner scurrying after her.

Suddenly, everyone seemed more relaxed. His father spoke again. "Shot at? You mean it was you who collared Rodney Church? Nobody even mentioned that."

"Yes, that was me," replied Alex. "That was what set all the events in motion."

From then on, all went well for the evening.

Despite the length of their relationship, Alex was still not entirely sure he understood Josh's (or his family's) attitude to their religion. Did Josh genuinely believe in God, or were his (limited) concessions to Judaism more about tradition than genuine faith?

Alex realised that one of the reasons he was unsure of the answer to that question was that he had, in fact, never asked. He'd never asked himself either, having grown up in an entirely agnostic household and gone to a school which was Christian largely in name only. There were always so many other things to talk and think about, matters like salvation and the divine had never commanded much of his own attention.

Until, that is, he'd found out Robbie had become an observant, if liberal, Catholic.

One concession the Goldman family made to their religion was a monthly observance of Shabbat, at the home of Josh's parents, Ben and Dara, and with Josh's sister, Anna. This was where Alex found himself, in a palatial Victorian residence overlooking St Vincent's Gardens, a London-style garden square surrounded by magnificent 19th-century mansions. This was Josh's childhood home.

Ben Goldman, who had been described by the financial press as "a *dashing* corporate raider" in the late 1980s, and who still looked rather dashing in spite of his advancing age, was performing a Kiddush—reciting a blessing over a silver goblet of wine. After completing the recitation, he drank from the goblet. Then, the others drank from small cups of wine that had been poured before the ritual began. (An alternative would be to pass around the goblet, but Dara thought individual portioning of wine was more "hygienic".) After this, the braided Challah bread was uncovered and a leisurely meal of roast chicken and vegetables was prepared by the Goldmans' housekeeper, Hamia, who had been with the family since Josh was a toddler. Hamia joined them to eat following the Kiddush.

Conversation and wine flowed freely in an atmosphere of comfortable conviviality. Alex's case came up just once.

"Laurence Archer says you saved his life," declared Ben to Alex as the two sat down in plush armchairs in the equally plush formal lounge. The others sat on the (also plush) sofa, except Anna, who disappeared to the bathroom. Ben poured himself some port, not offering Alex any because he knew Alex didn't like port.

"Dad, I don't know that Alex wants to talk about his case tonight," countered Josh. "Besides, talking shop is forbidden on Shabbat."

"Saving lives is hardly talking shop, Josh," declared Ben. "I would say it's more like giving thanks, which is totally kosher on Shabbat."

"It's alright, babe," said Alex, sinking further into the armchair, full and tipsy. "I guess I did save his life. Lucky there were some others around to save mine, though." Alex suddenly thought of the necromancer's claim that he didn't want to hurt Alex—at least, *not yet*. This made him think of that ridiculous prophecy-ritual. So, he asked a question instead. "How do you know Laurence Archer? Through Josh?"

Dara rolled her eyes. "No. I used to sit on a board with him, for my sins."

"I've known him for decades," added Ben. "Corporate Australia can be a bit … incestuous, and not always great at identifying merit."

Ouch, thought Alex. Clearly, Carolyn Fitzgerald wasn't the only person who didn't quite rate Laurence Archer.

"He's not *that* bad," insisted Josh.

"Honey," retorted Dara. "You're only saying that because you needed him to do a deal that made you partner."

"Shop talk!" cried Josh in reply.

With that, Anna returned and placed a ten dollar note on a coffee table.

"The bathroom?" Dara asked her daughter.

"Yeah," she said simply, sitting down and taking a sip of wine.

Turning on lights was forbidden, as a form of work, on Shabbat, so, by extension, switching *off* lights was also a no-no. While the Goldmans were not so adherent as to leave rooms in the dark, they, as many Jewish families did, created a bit of a game of it. In their case, if you switched off a light, you had to pay a 'fine' of ten dollars. At the end of the year, the money was donated to a charity. In fact, the eventual annual sum wasn't a trivial amount: not switching off lights, especially in the bathroom, was a hard habit to break. Alex had himself paid several such fines, once his 'gentile grace period' had ended.

"Dad, can I speak with you in private?" asked Josh—rather suddenly, Alex thought.

"Sure," he replied, and the two disappeared.

They didn't return until Alex was in bed, wearing Josh's pyjamas from the night before (shorts, this time, with stylised cow faces) and finding himself—again—contemplating religion and the existence of God. More specifically, and slightly uncomfortably, he found himself wondering what had driven Robbie to 'find' Him. He speculated it was probably not some great good fortune he had enjoyed; after all, adversity seemed to be a greater driver of piety than prosperity or comfort. He could just ask, of course, but suspected that might earn him the 'safe word' treatment.

"Sorry, babe," said Josh as he entered the room and started undressing. "Dad and I were talking for longer than I expected."

Alex waited until Josh had come into bed before asking, "Were you talking about—"

"Marrying you?" Josh finished his sentence.

"Yeah," replied Alex, reflecting that their conversation following Alex's encounter with the necromancer had left their relationship in an uncomfortable position. They weren't engaged, but there was now a mutual expectation—which others, like Catherine, were picking up on—that an official engagement was a mere formality.

"We were just talking about some practical stuff," Josh explained, vaguely. "Not, like, asking permission—not that he doesn't approve anyway."

"Do you mean, like, a pre-nup or whatever we call it?" asked Alex, assuming that 'practical stuff' was most likely a euphemism for that. (There was family money to protect, after all.)

"No!" exclaimed Josh in reply, as if the mere mention of a pre-nup was scandalous. "Of course not, babe. But there are just some things with, you know, trusts and stuff that need to be sorted out. I wasn't trying to be all Secret Squirrel about it or anything."

"OK," said Alex, not really wanting to push the matter.

"I know it's all a bit weird, babe, but I promise the proposal is not *that* far away. I just need to sort some things out—and find a time when it will be special."

Again, Josh had seemingly been able to read Alex's mind.

Alex thought of a trip they had planned to a fancy eco resort in the Blue Mountains in New South Wales in a couple of months' time. That would be an opportunity for a 'special' proposal. And it wasn't *that* long to wait. *And* it was sweet that Josh realised that he had created a rather awkward state of affairs by so clearly foreshadowing things.

Alex smiled at him, by way of reassurance that he was happy, and all was well.

Josh picked up on this, asking simply, "Are you going to top me tonight, babe?"

This was Josh and Alex's own Shabbat ritual. The first time Alex had come for Shabbat with the Goldmans—having met Josh's parents a couple of times before—Josh had taken Alex up to his former childhood bedroom (which was unrecognisable from his younger years, having been denuded of any teenaged posters) and became immediately amorous.

"Wait, Josh," Alex had said at the time. "Should we be doing this here? Now?"

"Sure, babe," he had said, smiling. "Sex is fine on Shabbat. It's a Mitzvah, like a commandment."

"Between married straight couples, though."

"Babe, if we're going to be that old-fashioned about it, we could never have sex at all!"

"I know," Alex replied, feebly resisting as Josh started disrobing him. "But I just, I—I don't want to upset your parents."

"Babe, I don't want to be crude, but you're not the first dude who's fucked me on Shabbat. I actually lost my anal virginity on Shabbat, in this room."

"Wait, you want me to top you?" asked Alex, in mild surprise. As it happened, Alex had always considered himself rather versatile—or 'vers', in the lingo—meaning he enjoyed both giving and receiving anal sex. When he was younger (the 'borderline sexual predator' stage) the challenge had been finding any guys who would ever let him top (or gave a shit about what he wanted in general). Later, post-Robbie (who had let Alex top, on occasion) when Alex had been hooking up on the apps, he actually got more attention from guys who wanted him to fuck them.

The problem then, aside from the whole app thing being utterly hellish, was that those guys were often not the sort of tall, athletic, cocky-jock-Robbie-Josh-type guys Alex saw as proper boyfriend material. And the guys who *were* proper boyfriend material (in Alex's narrow mind) generally saw bottoming as inconsistent with their (toxic) masculinity. Or maybe Alex just suspected they did.

Anyway, Josh had replied in the affirmative. "Yes, babe, I want you to fuck me tonight. And every time we do Shabbat. It only seems fair." Then pausing a moment, he continued. "I can tell you've been wanting to ask me about it for a while."

"I have," Alex conceded. "I thought you might say no."

"Well, babe," said Josh, now disrobing himself. "This is your chance. I should warn you, though, I can make quite a bit of noise when a guy is fucking me—particularly when I'm in love with him."

That was actually the first time Josh had said the 'L'-word to Alex. Alex thought the circumstances were a bit weird, but he was happy to take it, nonetheless. "I love you too, babe," he replied. Then, he said, "Now get on your back. I want to see your face when I put myself inside you."

"Now you're talking!" Josh got on his back and, true to his word—from that first Shabbat to this one—he did make quite a lot of noise.

Years later, as the couple snuggled post-coitally in the same bed, Alex found himself thinking again about God and religion.

"Babe," he said, quietly. "Do you believe in God?"

"Of course," Josh replied, as if stating the obvious. "I know I don't talk about it much but, yeah, I do." Then, after a pause, he asked, "Do you?"

Alex thought for a moment, then replied, with total honesty, "I don't know. I just realised I've never really asked myself the question."

30

Re-interviewing the MMS Faculty

"**D**id you find anything on Naomi Trinh?" asked Alex. He, along with the unofficial Taskforce Revenant subcommittee (comprising Alex, Robbie, Isabella and Pav), was sitting in the (unofficial) taskforce subcommittee headquarters—a windowless, if fairly large, meeting room at Victoria Police HQ. They were looking at an image of MMS Museum's Deputy Curator on the whiteboard.

"Nah, not really," conceded Isabella. "No priors beyond a single speeding ticket. No magic history, interestingly. She was the first in her family to have the *gift*."

"I guess it's a bit interesting," said Alex, sounding less than interested. "In my experience, *historians* are usually from the multi-generational magic families. I think it makes them more likely to think they're special."

In retrospect, Alex was surprised that neither Pav nor Isabella asked what 'experience' Alex had had with historians.

Robbie spoke next. "Then there's the John Bishop thing. When Alex and I re-interviewed him, he copped to going to *a couple of meetings* of the historians."

"Which is pretty similar language to what Naomi Trinh used, isn't it?" added Isabella, in the form of a rhetorical question.

"Yeah," agreed Robbie. "And he also said that maybe he saw Naomi at those meetings, but he wasn't sure because *they didn't have that much to do with each other.*"

"Also very similar language," declared Isabella. "But not exactly the same."

"Like they rehearsed?" That was Pav.

"Maybe," replied Alex. "Or maybe not. Maybe they were just telling the truth."

"But, Alex," countered Robbie, "John Bishop *did* lie to us, initially, when he implied it was Nerida who was vanishing off to secret meetings and stuff."

"Exactly," replied Pav. "And his explanation for lying seemed pretty odd, too."

"Remind me what it was," asked Isabella.

"Oh, something about being afraid of being identified as a historian, given their—he argued *erroneous*—association with necromancy, in light of Nerida's cause of death."

"And he claimed he was in shock and all that," added Robbie.

"All a bit sus, don't you think?" declared Pav. Then, looking at Alex. "I said sus, don't you think, PB? Are you going quiet on us, again?"

"No," replied Alex, sounding irritable. "And, yes, sure, it's sus. But they're *all* sus! Not a decent alibi among them, plus means, opportunity— how do we separate any of them?"

"You sound a bit frustrated, PB," said Pav, grinning a little.

"I *am* frustrated, Pav!"

Suddenly, Karen Park appeared among them, with what, for her, might have qualified as a smile. "There have been some developments," she declared. "First, this." She placed a printed photograph on the table. A candid crowd shot from a small party, it showed Harry with Naomi in his arms, whispering in her ear or, perhaps, kissing her on the cheek. "They look rather more intimate than *just friends*, wouldn't you agree?"

"Where is this from?" asked Alex.

"One of the officers trawling through social media found it on a friend of Naomi's Instagram account. It's from a party a year ago."

"Interesting," said Alex.

"Naomi is nowhere to be seen in any of Harry's very extensive social media posts," said Karen. "But there is no shortage of him posing with other attractive young women."

"Sus," declared Pav.

"There's more," said Karen, placing some more sheets of paper on the table. These were print-outs of text message exchanges between Leon Mazur and Nerida Stein, taken from her phone. They constituted a sequence of emojis: smiley faces, phone booths, teddy bears, crosses, houses and cars—repeated throughout with no clear pattern.

"A game?" suggested Isabella.

"Or a code," replied Alex.

"Either way," said Karen. "It's hardly typical for middle-aged professors who are friends to send messages like this to each other."

"Sus," declared Pav.

"I agree," said Karen. "And we also discovered today that Leon and Tammy Mazur are no longer cohabiting."

"That *is* interesting," said Robbie.

"My last one is even better," said Karen. "I got some officers to cross-reference the application files in Nerida's house with MMS enrolment records." She paused, for dramatic effect. "Some of them are missing."

"Sus!" declared Pav.

"I want you boys to re-interview our MMS faculty friends. They have all been fucking *lying* to us."

Tammy Mazur Interview

If Tammy had looked flustered when they first spoke with her at MMS, she now looked utterly terrified as she sat in an interview room at Victoria Police HQ.

Alex spoke first this time. "The files on your desk, Tammy, when we spoke to you at MMS. They were Nerida's files, weren't they? The students she admitted in exchange for cash."

Shock replaced terror, at least for a moment, on Tammy's face. "How did you …?" Composing herself with what looked like a herculean act of will, she said. "I don't think I should answer that question."

"Oh, come on, Tammy," said Robbie. "We know who the students are. We cross-referenced the data. If we started contacting them and their parents, how long do you think it would take before one of them decided to cooperate and dump you in it?"

"But I had nothing to do with it!" exclaimed Tammy. Realising that she misspoke, panic crossed her face. It was followed by the appearance of that tell-tale look—the one 'behind the eyes'—that suggested Tammy had decided that her best path forward was the truth or, at least, part of it. "Not at first. I had nothing to do with it at first," she said, shoulders sagging in defeat. "I only found out when I became dean. I mean, I had suspicions. She confessed. I knew she was always sympathetic to students from established gifted families, but *that*?"

"What did you do?" asked Robbie.

"Well, I …" Tammy threw her hands in the air. "I guess I let it go. Nerida promised to stop. Laurie—Laurence Archer, the outgoing chair— he said—"

"You both decided to cover it up?" suggested Robbie.

"Yes, I suppose we did. Not that *he* really needs to care, now that he's moving on to run Sourcery. He doesn't need his little consolation prize anymore. Besides," she added bitterly, "There's nothing even tying him to it. Nothing written down." Tammy paused. It seemed coming clean had become something of a relief. She almost smiled, but her face retained an edge of disgruntlement. "The thing is, one of the reasons Neri started accepting cash for enrolments was to make up her finances after investing in Laurence's company. Wait, you do know about Sourcery, don't you?"

"Yes, we do." That was Robbie, a little disappointed Tammy's revealing monologue had come to an end.

"At one point, you know," she said, "it looked like we would all get nothing."

Robbie sought to redirect. "Did John Bishop know about the bribes?"

Tammy Mazur smiled. "Nerida insisted he didn't. *Insisted.*"

"You didn't believe her?" suggested Robbie.

"No," Tammy scoffed, the bitter tone returning to her voice. Then she leaned forward, almost sounding conspiratorial. "Isn't it just so *typical*, detectives, that all the men here have plausible deniability, thanks to the women trying to protect them?"

Alex also leaned forward. "Does that apply to your husband too, Tammy?"

Tammy threw herself back in her seat and actually laughed—a loud, bitter one. "Nothing gets past you two, does it?"

"He was having an affair with Nerida Stein," said Robbie, not as a question.

"Not exactly," said Tammy. "We had, ah, agreed to, ahem, open up our relationship." Seeing the raised eyebrows of the detectives, she continued, "I was working a lot—which is what you *do* if you want to be appointed dean. Leon never really understood that. He was never very ambitious, but we had *agreed*."

"Was he feeling neglected?" offered Alex, sounding sympathetic.

"Yes!" said Tammy. At this point it was almost like she was enjoying herself—being able to take petty revenge on at least one of the people in her life who had let her down. "Apparently, we used to have *fun*!" She paused, then continued. "Of course, it was supposed to be one-offs—just sex—on the apps and the like. But Leon hated, *hated* the apps."

Robbie (and Alex) had to suppress a feeling of sympathy for Leon Mazur on that score.

Tammy went on. "Then, Nerida happened. I'm not even sure how it started. He was *supposed* to be doing random hook-ups, not dating old friends! You must have seen their silly coded texts, like they were playing a game. Ridiculous!"

"But you tolerated it?" asked Alex, again sounding sympathetic.

"I did, at least until I found out about the bribes. I was furious with Nerida. I told Leon he had to break it off with her."

"Did he?" Alex again.

"At first, he refused." Tammy shook her head in scornful disbelief. "Eventually, I gave him an ultimatum and he agreed to tell her it was done."

"And the next morning, she's dead and her files are on your desk," said Alex, again not as a question.

Tammy just nodded.

Robbie cut in, "Just to confirm, then, you and your husband were not at home watching *Squid Game*?"

"No. He was out—supposedly ending it with Nerida. I was at home."

"When did he get back?"

"I have no idea. I was having a heart-to-heart with a bottle of gin and fell asleep."

"Which meant," said Alex, "you both had incentives to give each other phoney alibis."

Tammy nodded again.

"Say yes for the recording, please," Robbie ordered.

"Yes, we decided to give each other false alibis. And to lie about Nerida not seeing anyone recently."

"Why admit this now?" asked Alex with sympathy. "And why stop living together?"

"Detective, do you have any idea what it's like living with someone you suspect may be a killer, *and* who may have tried to frame you for it?"

Leon Mazur Interview

Leon Mazur sat down in the interview room. Robbie was brutally direct. "It would seem, Leon, that you're at least someone's idea of a sexy librarian. Someone other than your wife's."

Alex could tell that Leon's mental cogs had reached a setting—he was going to (at least selectively) spill. "You've talked to my wife."

"You were sleeping with Nerida Stein."

"Not just sleeping, detective, dating. That was the problem."

"Can you explain that?"

"When we opened up our relationship, it was supposed to be just sex, one-offs. We actually came up with a set of rules, which is common. In retrospect, they were the sorts of rules ..." Leon trailed off, as if searching for the right words.

"Rules that were inevitably going to be broken?" Alex offered.

Leon nodded. "Like a smoker limiting themselves to ten a day, or an alcoholic not drinking before 5 pm. Except when they don't." He added a snide aside: "You could ask my wife about that second one."

"But it was you who broke the rules?"

"I shattered them, really," said Leon. Alex wasn't sure from his tone whether he was contrite about this, or possibly even proud. He could even have been some mix of the two. "I had never seen Nerida that way before. We had just been friends. But when we got together, it was just amazing."

If Leon Mazur was faking his admiration for Nerida, thought Alex, he had missed his calling as an actor.

"Did John Bishop know?" Robbie asked.

Leon paused. "Yes, I think so. Nerida told John everything. They were best friends. John and Nerida were like a two-for-one deal. They came as a pair."

"Did he care?"

"What, that Nerida and I were seeing each other? Why would he?"

"Word is that he had been keen on him and Nerida becoming more than friends for ages. Then she starts something up with a *married man* who was also a mutual friend. He could have been jealous."

Leon smiled indulgently at Robbie, as if he was a student who had just said something foolish. "I think, after over a decade, even John Bishop got the hint that nothing was going to happen."

"You said it was amazing," said Alex. "But you did break it off, *eventually*. Why?"

"Duty. Loyalty. I *was* very cross with her when I found out about the bribes. But, ah, I found Nerida a hard habit to break. And she had been in a bad way at the time. She'd lost money—I assume you know about it—and she was also angry at the school, at the *system*, over John Bishop being passed over for dean."

"Your wife said there was an ultimatum," said Robbie.

"I would have said a massive guilt trip, but it was close enough to an ultimatum."

"So, you ended it, that night. At her house. Where she was murdered."

"I know how it looks, detective. But I did not kill her. I mean, I—"

"Was in love with her?"

The expression behind the eyes appeared again. Finally, Leon said, "Yes—and I never *did* actually break it off with her."

This latest revelation almost cracked Robbie's usually bullet-proof inscrutability.

Leon continued. "I went for a long walk. For hours. I had told my wife that I was going to end it, but I wasn't sure. I mean, why sacrifice what I have—had—with Nerida for a marriage that felt terminal? When I finally got to her house, it was so late and Nerida was dead. It was …" He trailed off, eyes tearing up.

"What did you do then?"

"Panicked, I suppose. Raced home. Tammy was passed out—no great shock there. I tried to go to sleep. Then, in the morning, I told Tammy what had happened."

"That was when you decided to give each other alibis?"

Leon grinned sardonically. "No, that only happened when my beloved got to the office and found Nerida's files all over her desk."

"Did you put them there?"

"No! Why would I?"

"To frame her, after you killed Nerida Stein."

"No! I told you—"

"You told us a nice story, Leon. But that is all it is. There is no evidence to support any of it. For all we know, Nerida had already ditched you and, rather than going for a walk, you took a visit to the cemetery and summoned a revenant."

"Well, I didn't."

"And John Bishop did say that Nerida tended to enjoy the early bits of a relationship before losing interest."

"That's what John told himself to protect his own ego." He paused, looking daggers at an emotionless Robbie. "Are you going to arrest me, detective?"

"No," replied Robbie, impassive.

"Then I think I'm done. I have nothing more to say to you."

Alex asked, "Leon, just one thing, before you go: do you know why your wife made you leave the house?"

"Made *me* leave? Detective, I can assure you, the decision was all mine. I just couldn't stay in that house anymore—not with *her.*"

"And why was that?"

"Do you have any idea what it's like to try to live with someone who you think may be a murderer—*and* who had tried to murder you?"

John Bishop Interview

"Even I got the hint after ten years," said an unruffled John Bishop. "I moved on."

"But Leon Mazur," said Robbie. "A mutual friend, a *married* one. That must have cut you, at least a little, as a man."

John laughed. "Detective, not every straight man suffers from toxic masculinity. I cannot say I *approved* of what they were doing, but it wasn't my business."

"Do you know whether they were still together when Nerida was killed? You told us before that she tended to get sick of her men fairly quickly."

John nodded. "I did say that. And it was true. But, as far as I know, they were still seeing each other. But, the other thing I said—about us not seeing as much of each other before she died—is also true. So, I may have been less in the loop by the end."

"Speaking of being in the loop, what did you know about the bribes and when?"

"I found out about them just before Tammy Mazur did. Nerida admitted it when I confronted her."

"What made you suspicious?"

"She let in one too many real stinkers. I'm talking neither talented *nor* smart—not even one or the other! But they were from old magic families. With money. I guess I finally stopped being able to deny it to myself." John sighed. "I mean, nobody likes to think their best friend is dodgy, detective."

Robbie ignored the bait. "You have to admit, John, that it's quite convenient that Nerida is not around to contradict any of this. How do we know you weren't in on the scam from the start?"

"You don't, and I can hardly prove a negative, can I?" He added, with some feeling. "But I didn't kill Nerida."

Harry Archer Interview

"Did she?" said Harry Archer, looking like he was enjoying himself immensely. "I shouldn't be surprised. It's not like she had any real *principles*—take my grant application, for example. Utterly malicious. But taking cash for enrolments?" He was grinning ridiculously now.

Robbie was finding Harry's glee especially distasteful. He put the picture of Harry and Naomi at the party on the table. Harry's glee evaporated. In the end, Robbie didn't even need to ask a question.

"Ah, detective, you see. There was a brief, a brief *flirtation* between us."

"You will need to be a bit more specific, Harry," Robbie said, unimpressed.

"We banged a couple of times, detective. Literally, twice. Is that specific enough for you?"

"But nothing beyond that?"

"No. I mean, I thought at the time that she might have wanted more than was on offer, but that happens, doesn't it? And it was a while ago. I didn't think it was at all relevant, and it *isn't.*"

Naomi Trinh Interview

"We had sex twice. That was it," insisted Naomi Trinh. "I knew he wanted more. They normally do. But it was ages ago."

"Why lie to us about it, then?" asked Robbie.

"I didn't exactly *lie*, detective," she replied, sounding sincere. "I guess I just couldn't see how it was *relevant*."

The Debrief

"The extraordinary thing about this case," declared Karen Park, managing to be both fascinated and frustrated at the same time, "Is that, after a mini-series worth of melodramatic revelations, we've been unable to eliminate any of our main suspects!"

There was general nodding around the room—except Alex who, rather than nodding, looked apparently listlessly out of a window.

"Are you with us, Alex?" asked Karen Park.

"What? Sorry, yes. I am," replied Alex.

"Any big deductions, PB?" asked Pav.

"No—and, yes, I'm still frustrated, Pav." Alex touched his hair. "The thing is, we're still getting a curated version of the truth. And it's *super sus*, Pav, that all our suspects seem to be using such similar language, like they rehearsed. Tammy and Leon, Leon and John, John and Naomi, Naomi and Harry Archer. Then there are the relationships. We've unpeeled the onion on the baby-boomer cabal's middle-aged virtual swingers' party. But there is another dimension that we haven't."

"What dimension?" asked Pav.

"The *historians*, Pav. And, as much as my sensible, cognitive mind dismisses it out of hand, I can't help but think that the stupid prophecy might be involved somehow, beyond Harry's ludicrous card game. Anyway, I think there are two questions we need to answer, and one fact we need to establish—and I have no idea how to do any of them."

"What are they?" asked Isabella.

"One," replied Alex. "How many people are involved in the killings? I think we've assumed a lone wolf, but that seems increasingly unlikely.

Two, how do John, Naomi and Harry fit together? And three, whether Nerida herself was a historian."

Shocked silence hung in the room. Then, it was Pav who said: "Wait, Nerida was a historian?"

"Of course, she was, Pav. Think about it. Her best friend has basically admitted to being one, and she was obsessed by lineage, by the *established* magic families—they all are. It's basically their thing. Nerida was a historian. I know it."

31

Alex and Charlotte Meet for Drinks; Robbie meets the Li Family

"You know, Lottie,"—that was Alex's new pet name for Charlotte—"If we're going to be BFFs, we need to find a new venue for our catch-ups."

Alex and Charlotte were in the smoking area of The Lion Hotel. They had met up here a few times in the last month-and-a-half, as Charlotte seemed to be cultivating him as a friend. Maybe to be her 'support animal' at any future Bailey and Badenoch events, having not quite hit it off with the WAGs. Or, to be fair, maybe fighting hellhounds together creates something of a personal bond.

"I quite like it," insisted Charlotte, sipping some rosé and smoking. "It's close to you, not far from me and the Courts. And it's quaint, old school."

"Old school?" sneered Alex. "Firstly, Lottie, nobody has used that expression non-ironically since I was at MMS. Secondly, this place is a dump."

"I've heard some cops say it's going posh," Charlotte retorted.

"Serving re-heated frozen croquettes does not make a place *posh*, Lottie. Besides, I may bump into Pav here. I've told you about Pav?"

"Many times," said Charlotte, rolling her eyes. "He's the old colleague of yours you will not admit to being friends with."

"Charlotte!"

"Alright, I will agree to locate a suitably fancy venue for our catch-ups in future. But you need to do me a favour in exchange."

"What sort of favour?"

"MC the wedding?" Charlotte gauged Alex's immediate reaction, then added, "*Please?*"

"Seriously?" Alex whined. "Why me? Surely there's some old friend or relative you could prevail upon to do it instead?"

"Maybe," said Charlotte. "But being MC would mean you'll be in the groom's party, with Josh. And, besides, so many people are so funny about public speaking, but Si tells me you captained your high school debating team."

"Did he just?" replied Alex, accusingly. Then he paused, remembering he and Josh had received a 'save the date' for mid-September recently, but had otherwise heard nothing about the wedding. "Have you got a venue and everything yet?"

"Yes, we have!" declared Charlotte, excitedly. "It's at a winery in the Yarra Valley, Chateau Vincent. Have you heard of it?"

"Yes, I have." He had actually been there a few years ago, pre-Josh. Not for the first time, he reflected that Charlotte and Simmo—well, at least, Charlotte—had quite good taste.

"We will be sending out the invites soon. Si has been super-organised with the whole thing. Josh helped him set up a spreadsheet, apparently."

Alex laughed. "Of course, he did!"

"So, will you do it?" Charlotte pleaded.

"OK, I will," replied Alex, defeated.

"Great! I'm going to get us some bubbles to celebrate."

"I'm not sure I would trust the sparkling wines here, Lottie."

"Don't be silly," she shot back, before disappearing into the pub.

She quickly returned, carrying a bottle rather than just two glasses. This seemed like rather a bit for a 'school night', but Alex was hardly one to complain about that, or judge. Instead, he said, "I think we might need a safe word for this growing friendship of ours."

"What?"

"You know, a safe word. Like, you know, in bed, when someone is—"

"I know what a safe word is," insisted Charlotte. "But I don't understand—"

"Like, when one of us—but, let's face it, probably you—is trying to push things too far, too fast, the other can say 'safe word,' and we both agree to move on."

"That sounds utterly ridiculous."

"It works surprisingly well, though," insisted Alex. "My partner on the case, Robbie, came up with the idea."

"Oh, wait," said Charlotte, grinning. "Is that the one you have history with?"

"Safe word!"

"Seriously?" groused Charlotte. "At least tell me how the case is going."

"That is practically safe word territory too," replied Alex, morosely.

"That bad, huh?"

"Yeah," he sighed. "All the leads are exhausted. Which leaves us trawling through reams and reams of mostly useless information, hoping to find something that was missed originally."

"Sounds a bit dull."

"It is. And the taskforce is winding down, so there are fewer and fewer of us to do all the grinding. Half of the officers on the case have been moved to that Stonington Snatcher case."

"Those home burglaries around Toorak?" asked Charlotte, referring to the leafiest of Melbourne's leafy neighbourhoods.

"The very same. It's ridiculous, really. After all, none of the victims were hurt, none of them were even *home* at the time. But when you have some minor celebrity footy WAG-slash-influencer-slash-natural-skincare-entrepreneur tweeting the Premier about it, you get a police taskforce."

"Cherie Holt is hardly a *minor* celebrity WAG. She's the most famous of the lot!"

"Are you a fan, follow her on the 'Gram?"

"No!" replied Charlotte, in semi-outrage. "I just obviously follow the football more than you."

"I think everybody in this town does," conceded Alex. "Anyway, my colleague, Cecile—she's on the case—she says they're the most glamorous crime scenes she has ever seen." Then he paused, then asked, "What about *your* case?"

"The Sourcery one? I think it should settle soon. That's what the system encourages, with these *dollars* cases. It's kind of disappointing that it hasn't been relevant to your matter. I mean, as much as commercial and corporate litigation is itself *fascinating* ..." Charlotte trailed off, noticing that Alex appeared deep in thought. "What is it?"

"Oh, sorry," replied Alex. "You made me think about the case."

"What about it?" asked Charlotte, looking intrigued.

"Connections," replied Alex, cryptically. Wondering how much he could safely tell Charlotte, he went on. "Connections between our suspects on the MMS faculty."

"One of which is Sourcery?"

"Yes, that is one of them. One of three."

"What are the other two?" Charlotte was leaning forward. Alex regretted saying anything.

"Well, the second one, believe it or not, is a sort of middle-aged, academic love polygon."

Charlotte's eyes lit up with excitement. "My God, how dramatic!"

"Yeah."

"What is the third?"

Alex hesitated, as Charlotte stared at him expectantly. He worried he was digging a deeper hole for himself. But he caved in, answering her question with a question. "What do you know about *historians*?"

Charlotte's eyes widened. "You mean, like, magic supremacist *historians*?"

"Yes."

"I guess I know a few of them. The Melbourne Magical History Society is *full* of them. And some of the more serious ones are ... out there." She paused. "But wait, what does that have to do with your case. Are some of the suspects—"

"*Historians*? Yes, and I think the victim was. But I have no way of knowing."

"Wouldn't it be obvious from stuff on her computer?" said Charlotte, reasonably.

"Not necessarily," countered Alex. "Nerida had a computer and an iPad, but she seemed pretty analogue in many ways. She still used paper files. Also, *historians* can be rather secretive."

"That's true," agreed Charlotte.

"Which means," continued Alex, "it's not like Robbie and I can just front up to a meeting of that historical society of yours and start asking questions about Nerida Stein."

Charlotte looked disturbingly conspiratorial. "*You* can't," she exclaimed. "But *I* could!"

"We met through a mutual friend," said Robbie. He was having dinner with Winston's parents at their home, which was really very similar to the one he shared with his mother. It was, in fact, in the next postcode along from theirs.

This was a high stakes event, by all accounts. Or, at least, by Winston's. Over the last couple of months, Robbie had been fed a regular diet of the many ways in which Winston's parents were disappointed (seriously, *disappointed*) in their son. Whether it be his sexuality, his relative lack of academic success, his real estate career, or even the fact he had given up the violin. "Seriously?" Robbie had asked.

"They insisted I had potential."

"Did you?"

"No!"

The whole thing felt like something from an unoriginal sitcom about Asian people, but Winston was very insistent about it all.

Robbie had even been convinced to cut off the man-bun and replace it with a centrally parted 'do which left his hair slightly long, dancing around behind his ears. He didn't love it, but he'd been assured it would more likely meet with Li family approval. And it *was* about time for a change, Robbie had reasoned. However, he had put off getting the chop until the day before, so had not yet gotten used to the sensation of having shorter hair, worn loose.

This exacerbated his nervousness in the presence of the two stern-looking middle-aged people opposite. Everything about them screamed distrust and scepticism. Robbie found himself wondering whether it was obvious that he was ten years older than the elder Lis' only child (something he'd barely thought about until this evening); whether they would ever accept their son being with a man; whether they knew Robbie was a magic user. (And, if so, whether that would be a problem too.) What about the fact he smoked?

Most important was the nature of Robbie and Winston's relationship itself. Clearly, they *were* boyfriends. Robbie had conceded as much, and more. They were exclusive. They spent time together—they'd even won the latest round of drag trivia at Supermarket. He enjoyed spending time with Winston. And their physical chemistry was great. Winston had been staying over with Robbie (at his mum's place) most nights. And, most of those nights, they fucked like rabbits. But, on the other hand, relationship youth was a phase, not a characteristic. And, Robbie reasoned, how much of the emotional side of their connection was simply driven by his own fear of being alone?

"And then there is fucking *Alex*," he mused to himself. The one that got away. The one with his bizarre, brilliant mind; his frustratingly endearing mannerisms; his absurdly cute face, hair, body. The one with the horribly inconvenient, rich, hot, apparently adoring boyfriend. The one he now, for his sins—and Robbie wasn't a believer in Catholic guilt—was seeing *every*, *single*, fucking *day*.

Back to the present, Winston had said that his parents might take a little while to 'warm up' to him. Which turned out to be very true. The conversation at the table felt like an interrogation. Robbie was far more used to being the interrogator than having to answer the questions.

"Winston tells us you're a police officer?"

"Yes, a detective."

"How did you get into that?"

I had no fucking idea what else to do! "I wanted to help people, I suppose."

"Where do you live?"

"Oh, with my mother. Just over in Glen Waverley."

"What do your parents do?"

"My mother is retired. My dad still works as a tax accountant. They are, um—"

"Not together anymore?"

"Yes."

"Oh, that is a shame."

Robbie needed more wine. But Winston's parents seemed so abstemious—they were still on their first glass and the main course was almost eaten—that he felt he shouldn't. He also *really* needed a cigarette. But that seemed even more out of the question. Things continued in a similar vein as dessert was served, which was Mr Li's signature home-made vanilla ice-cream with his equally signature chocolate sauce. Robbie barely registered that the dessert, while simple, was delicious.

"Winston told us you're an only child as well."

"Yes, that's right."

Awkward silence.

"Do you have any hobbies?"

"Not really. Um, I guess I like trivia."

"Winston likes trivia too. He's good at it."

"I know, we met at trivia."

Then the ice-cream was finished. Mrs Li and Winston got up and started clearing away dishes.

"Would you like some whisky, Robbie?" asked Mr Li.

Yes! "If you're having some, of course."

"Let's take it outside," he continued, with something almost like a smile. "I expect you will want a cigarette."

Robbie sat down in the courtyard. Mr Li poured Robbie and himself some whisky. Robbie politely sipped it; Mr Li downed his in one. Seeing that, Robbie did the same and accepted a refill. He pulled out a cigarette. In a panic, he realised that he didn't have a lighter. (After all, why would he?)

Sensing Robbie's alarm, Mr Li said, "It's OK. We know about the magic thing."

Robbie lit his cigarette, as he always did, with his finger.

"Sorry if that all felt like an ordeal," Mr Li continued.

"Oh, it wasn't too bad," Robbie lied.

Mr Li actually laughed. "Yes, it was! You probably felt like one of your suspects!"

"A little," Robbie conceded. He and Mr Li were now on nip number three.

"My wife and I, well, especially my wife, we can find it a bit difficult to deal with Winston and his … his men." Mr Li paused. "It's not so much about him being gay—though that was difficult at first. His ex was just bad news—and he was the one Winston was actually prepared to tell us about. We knew there were others, too, no doubt even worse news. It's not what we had expected or hoped for him."

"I understand," said Robbie. He couldn't think of anything else to say.

"You seem different, though," said Mr Li. Then, he stood up and said, "At least, I hope you are."

Robbie woke up, sweating and panting. They were back. The anguished screams. The pitiful cries, the tears of relief—which were worst of all. The grinning faces of the scumbags who did it. The news of suicides. The squalid conditions behind the opulent façade. The mind-control charms. The fleurs-de-lis.

Robbie took a moment to realise that Winston was shaking his shoulder. That must have been what woke him up.

"Robbie, are you OK?" Winston said, his concern so evident in his voice that Robbie could imagine it on his face through the darkness of the room. "What is it?"

"Nothing, Win, just a nightmare," Robbie replied, shocked at how convincing he sounded. "Go back to sleep."

The Case Update – Part 2

"You look *even better* with the new hair!" gushed Pav. "Don't you think so, PB?"

Fuck off, Pav! "I do like it," Alex replied, neutrally.

"So do I," said Isabella, with greater enthusiasm.

"Thanks," said Robbie, sounding mildly embarrassed. "I thought it was time for a change."

"I think that means Winston didn't love the man-bun," Isabella teased.

"Can we talk about the case?" replied Robbie.

"I was looking at the statement from Charini Dissanayake—Mewan's wife," said Alex. "My friend is the barrister representing the investors in Sourcery, so I thought I'd revisit that angle." He didn't say it, but he'd also remembered his earlier exhortation to Robbie that "they needed to investigate the murder weapon", which he felt had been taken over by subsequent events, notably ifrits and hellhounds.

"The Laurence Archer theory?" said Isabella, sceptically. "Really?"

"Anything significant?" asked Pav, sounding genuinely interested.

"I don't know," replied Alex, honestly. "Two things stuck out. Firstly, Charini thought that the hostility between the Mazur–Stein–Bishop faction and Harry Archer was actually less about him getting promoted too soon because of favouritism, and more about him supposedly getting Mewan to convince the Mazurs, Stein and Bishop to invest in Sourcery."

"It's weird how the MMS staff barely mentioned Sourcery," added Robbie. "But, then, it isn't as if they lost their life savings or anything, did they?"

"Still, I reckon Hot Rod had plenty more stashed away than he invested in the Daylesford Distillery scam," said Isabella. "And he was still utterly filthy about losing the cash—and his cronies losing cash too."

"That's also true," agreed Alex.

Pav looked to Robbie and explained, "That was the case where Alex—"

"It's alright Pav," said Robbie, politely cutting Pav off. "Alex has told me about that case—more than once!"

"Oh, *of course* he has," said Pav, grinning cheekily.

"The other thing, which struck me a bit," continued Alex. "Mewan spent the last year of his life with terminal cancer. And the last few months, he refused treatment, no more chemo and stuff."

"So?" said Pav. "That is not so unusual, is it?"

"It's a bit unusual, in some ways," replied Robbie. "Magic users are significantly less likely than other people to die of cancer. It's one reason we live longer, on average."

There was a pause.

"I also have some news," declared Isabella. "The curators, Theo and Naomi, *finally* completed a full stocktake of the MMS artefacts that are not on display."

"And something's missing?" asked Alex.

"Yes. This one is a sort of talisman-thing. A protective one—they call them wards."

Isabella showed the others an image of the object on her tablet. It looked like it was made of metal, possibly silver, and comprised three circles in a broadly triangular design. The circles contained, respectively, a stylised drop of water, which itself contained stylised waves—Alex concluded this represented wind—a stylised flame and what looked like mountain peaks.

Isabella went on. "It dates from the First World War, when wards like this were issued to soldiers in the magic brigades. Because of that, there were quite a lot of them produced, hence—like with the fleur-de-lis amulet—this one isn't worth much and wasn't on display in the MMS Museum."

"Why are there only the three?" asked Pav, in a voice that suggested he was proud of 'doing his research'. "What about the electrical affinity?"

"We often call that a sub-affinity," replied Robbie. "It's rare today and was even rarer then. Interestingly, magic users only started manifesting electrical affinities after electricity started to be used in industry, but especially used in households, which was in its infancy then."

"That *is* interesting!" replied Pav, in a voice that suggested he was shamelessly (still) trying to ingratiate himself with Robbie.

"But did any eyewitnesses actually see the necromancer wearing it?" asked Alex, in a voice that suggested they should talk about the case.

"No," conceded Isabella. "But he could have been wearing it underneath his clothes."

He could have done the same with the fleur-de-lis, thought Alex. Which rather begged the question why he hadn't.

Isabella continued. "I mean, I get that it could have nothing to do with the case. But—"

"But what?" asked Alex.

"But the fleur-de-lis amulet and this one are the only items to be stolen from the archives of MMS Museum in decades, so it would be a weird coincidence if the two weren't connected. And—"

"And what?" asked Alex.

"Your statement! I read it. We all did. The necromancer knows you or, at least, knows about you. So, he must have known you would be at The Lake that night. I mean, do I have to spell it out? The amulet would protect him from your—"

"No," replied Alex, quietly, cutting Isabella off. "You don't have to spell it out. I'd rather not think about it." Which, Alex reasoned, was entirely justified. After all, would you like to think about possibly being the intended target of a murderous maniac?

32

Charlotte Attends a Historian Party

Alex knew, of course, that this was a shockingly, outrageously, extravagantly terrible idea.

He'd told Charlotte as much back at the Lion, when she suggested that she could covertly attend a gathering of historians and discreetly inquire as to Nerida Stein's historian status (or lack thereof). Something which would obviously not seem at all suspicious, nor interfere with their actual police investigation, nor put Charlotte in any sort of danger. When it would, of course, do *all of those things*.

"No, you can't, Charlotte. You *definitely* can't."

"Why not?"

"Because this is a *murder investigation*, Lottie. It would be dangerous. Besides, someone would recognise you—"

"I won't be going as *me*, silly."

Suddenly, Charlotte was replaced with a taller, more buxom, more bronzed, more blonde woman, wearing a dress that remained just shy of escort-chic and whose excessively full lips fell just short of trout-pout. The best Alex could say for the transformation was that it looked absolutely nothing like the real Charlotte.

"You look ridiculous. What is this, your 1990s Pamela Anderson impersonation?"

"I'm Candy, from the Sunny Coast," replied Charlotte. "I've just moved down to Melbourne to get a job."

"Oh *really*," replied Alex. "Whereabouts in the Sunny Coast are you from?"

"Um, oh, you wouldn't have heard of it."

"How convincing!"

"I can work on the backstory."

"This is a fucking awful idea, Charlotte."

'Candy' grinned at him. "Do you want to find out if Nerida was a historian, or not?"

Alex had to admit that, in the end, the answer was yes. And it was yes in spite of the obvious, abundant risks. The risk of getting caught for professional misconduct for letting a nosy civilian into a police investigation. A fucking *murder* investigation. The risk that a killer might realise that 'Candy', improved backstory notwithstanding, wasn't who she said she was. And the risk that the killer might do something about it. And the risk that Alex, sitting in Josh's Tesla a couple of blocks from the party—right next to the Melbourne General Cemetery, of all places— couldn't intervene in time to stop them.

If anything happened to Charlotte …

"It won't," he insisted to himself. As his sweaty hands gripped the steering wheel, he tried, unsuccessfully, to stop his heart beating so fast.

Charlotte was doing so well as 'Candy' that she'd even stopped having to remind herself that she was 'in character'. She'd been able to enter the party, which was a private affair being hosted by the deputy chair of the Melbourne Magic History Society's Tourism Committee, with ease. After all, as she had *patiently* explained to Alex, nobody kicks a beautiful young woman out of a party, even if she's not invited. And while she hadn't been able to confirm Nerida's status as a historian, she'd already made separate sightings of Naomi Trinh and John Bishop. And the night was young.

Everything was going swimmingly.

Charlotte had known Alex would come around, if grudgingly, in the end. The whole idea—while bold and not 'by the book'—clearly made sense. And, as she had argued—as a barrister, it was her job to be convincing—she would do better if Alex shared some information about his case and the MMS suspects. That was how she had recognised both John Bishop and Naomi Trinh.

Charlotte—no, *Candy*—surveyed the room. She reflected that a belief in magic supremacy brought all sorts of magic users together. The crowd filled the spacious townhouse in which the party was being held, and seemed to represent all ages. The only skew, concluded Candy, was that attendees probably hewed posh. This variety of guests, and the fact they all mingled unusually well across ages, meant the affair felt somewhere between an elegant drinks party and an impromptu student share-house piss-up.

The large clump of people—mainly men—settled around a television probably tacked more to the piss-up demographic, as they chugged beers and cheered at a TV screen. Charlotte saw that the TV was playing a fight between a cockatrice and a chimaera.

The cockatrice, a mix between a huge, horse-sized cockerel and a serpent, stalked around a massive indoor fighting ring. Its opponent, a lion with a snake for a tail and with a goat's head rising from its back, intermittently lunged at it, the goat head breathing fire and the snake-tail snapping. Candy stood momentarily transfixed as the cockatrice, waving its bat-like wings, launched itself into the air.

The chimaera, showing a degree of intelligence, cowered back. It stalked one corner of the arena as the cockatrice flew around it. Then, the cockatrice swooped. The chimaera's goat head spat fire but, meeting the cockatrice's gaze, the head slumped—either unconscious or dead. The rest of the chimaera was still active. The cockatrice's rooster head expelled a cloud of visibly noxious gas at the chimaera, but not before the latter was able to rear itself on its hind legs and deal a nasty blow to the cockatrice's serpentine form. At the same time, the chimaera's snake-tail struck at the cockatrice's left wing, tearing the flesh and, presumably, injecting some poison into the arteries of the beast.

"From here, it's a waiting game."

"Sorry, what?"

"They're both injured. It becomes a question of which one will die first. Pretty shocking, I reckon, the whole thing."

'Candy' finally looked away from the now-wounded creatures on the screen, circling each other with wary suspicion, and looked at the owner of this new voice. She supressed both a gasp and a smile. Standing before her was a young man, no more than mid-twenties. He had a luxuriant mop of dark, curly hair that danced just above his large green eyes. He smiled a big, white, toothy grin, just as she turned around. His jaw was like an ironing board. His muscular chest and biceps were obvious underneath a very fitted t-shirt. Overall, he looked like someone who might be cast as the hot boy-next-door in a soap opera, with the writers instructed to find as many opportunities as possible for him to take off his shirt.

Or, wondered Candy, he may be someone purpose-designed to appeal to a girl like her. She was immediately suspicious.

"I'm Matt," said the young man, pointing at that muscular chest and continuing to grin that toothy smile.

"I'm Candy."

"You look like you're new here," said 'Matt', perhaps a little cautiously.

"What makes you think that?" replied Candy, a note of challenge in her otherwise very friendly voice.

"Uh, nothing, really," replied Matt, who had clearly picked up on her tone. "Just, I guess, maybe it takes one to know one? I'm new in town too."

Candy, still smiling, nodded her head. "Well you *are* right about me being new to Melbourne, Matt." She added, very intentionally, "Where are you from?"

"Tassie."

"Whereabouts?"

"Oh, um," Matt hesitated. "Northwest, you've probably never heard of it."

"Try me."

"Um, Scottsdale."

Ah-ha! Candy thought to herself, triumphantly. She had no idea whether or not Scottsdale was in north-western Tasmania (it certainly was not) but his obvious hesitation confirmed to Candy that Matt was clearly someone else in magical disguise.

It did, however, occur to Charlotte—Candy—that, fabulous magical disguise and awesome backstory notwithstanding, someone had clearly also suspected that *Candy* was also not whom she claimed to be. Quickly scanning the room, she saw no sign of Naomi Trinh, nor John Bishop, though they could be downstairs. She was reminded of two things she had also read at magic school. *A summoner can have the same effect as any other school of magic*, including changing one's own shape. And, *with practice, anyone with any affinity can master any other discipline.*

Could Naomi Trinh have summoned a spiritual disguise? Could John Bishop have taught himself transformation?

She really needed to reply to Matt. "Fair enough," she smiled even more brightly at him. "I haven't heard of it." She continued. "I'm from the Goldie—the Gold Coast. Broadbeach, actually, one of the places with the canals."

"Canals?" replied Matt, who also seemed to be struggling for something to say.

"Yeah, canals," said Candy, brightly. "Of course, you get the sharks in them, too."

"Sharks?" replied Matt, sounding confused.

Clearly, Candy would need to change the subject if she wanted this conversation to be less monosyllabic—and to convince whoever Matt really was that Candy was, indeed, Candy. "Yes, sharks. Bull sharks. But anyway, Matt, what brought you to this party? How do you know the host?"

Matt hesitated. "Um, I don't, really. I guess I just wanted to meet people."

"You mean you gate-crashed the party, Matt?"

He blushed, sheepishly. "Yeah, I guess I did."

She leaned in and whispered in his ear, quietly, huskily, *sexily.* "So did I. Lucky we're both so good-looking. Nobody would turn either of *us* away from a party."

Matt continued to blush and look sheepish. Maybe talk was no longer the best way to throw Matt off the scent. After all, just as nobody ever kicked a beautiful young women out of a party, men were in the habit of thinking the best of beautiful young women who were into them. And, even if Matt wasn't really a man, that was the thing about transformation—you did, at least in many ways, become what you transformed yourself into.

Deciding she was committed, she reached around Matt's back and pulled him into her. They were close enough that she could feel his chest against her breasts, she could smell the musky cologne on his neck (a nice touch) and feel what was certainly becoming his erection.

She whispered, even more huskily. "You know, Matt from Tassie. If we're both alone in Melbourne, maybe we should keep each other company?"

Matt seemed lost for words. Clearly, man or woman, Matt had not expected this, and was struggling to know how to react.

"Just for fun," she continued. "Then, we can see where things g— Oh!"

"What?" said Matt, as he felt Candy pulling away.

Candy had just spied Laurence Archer across the room. Neither Charlotte nor Alex had expected him to be at a party like this. And he appeared to be by himself, walking towards a row of ice buckets on a bench to get a drink. As much as Candy wanted to convince Matt that she was a real human being, and not a snooper in disguise, she couldn't pass up the opportunity to talk to the former MMS board chair, new CEO of Sourcery, almost victim of their necromancer and possible closet historian. *He must know something, even if he doesn't know he does!*

Now, she just had to dispose of Matt.

"I'm really sorry, Matt," she said with total sincerity. "I just saw the only person I know at the party over there and I *really* need to speak with them."

"Uh, OK," Matt half-grunted in response. Candy wondered whether he might have sounded genuinely disappointed.

"I'll explain later, OK?" she insisted. "But I really want to see you again."

Matt just nodded.

"I'll try to find you after," she promised. "Otherwise, DM me. I'm on Insta. Just Google Candy Krush—with a K—Carter." With that, she blew him a kiss and said, "By the way, I agree. The fights *are* shocking."

As she approached Laurence Archer, Candy took a quick look back, hoping to gauge Matt's expression at her departure. But he was gone.

Candy greeted the distinguished businessman. "Hi, sorry. I know this sounds cheesy, but have we met before?" She looked at him as coquettishly as she could and added. "You seem very familiar."

Laurence Archer was clearly trying, with limited success, not to look at Candy's ample cleavage. "Ah," he grunted. "Maybe you've seen me in the news. I'm a, um, should I say, *prominent* CEO. My name is Laurence, Laurence Archer." He said this with a "surely you know me?" type of tone.

Candy wasn't sure how to respond to this. How likely was a Gold Coast airhead, even a magical one, likely to know about prominent CEOs, even of magic-related businesses? More generally, how could she get Laurence Archer to spill on anything related to the necromancer, MMS admissions scandals (which had just become public—Laurence Archer denied any knowledge) or the magic supremacist proclivities of the murdered instigator of that scandal? He would almost certainly not want to talk about *any* of those things.

She had an idea.

"I'm not really into business," declared Candy. "But, wait, Archer, is that like Harry Archer, from the TV?"

"Yes," Laurence replied, possibly put out that Candy had heard of his relative but not *him*. "He is my nephew."

"Oh, that's amazing," enthused Candy. "I learnt more about magic from him talking on TV than in the classes and camps." She added airily. "He's not here tonight, is he?"

"No," replied Laurence, firmly. Then, softening, "He doesn't come to functions like this, at least not any—"

Candy had to cut in. "Sorry, um, Laurence, I see some people I know over there." Indeed, across the room, she saw none other than Naomi and John, walking together up some stairs to the third floor of the house. "It was nice to meet you," said Candy.

"Uh, yes," was all Laurence could manage, before disappearing into the crowd.

Candy followed Naomi and John up the stairs, trying to be surreptitious—which was one situation where being a beautiful young woman was far from ideal. The landing at the top of the stairs was deserted. The landing had two doors. One, at the far end, seemed likely to be a bedroom. The nearer one would lead on to the front of the townhouse, which she reasoned was more likely to be a living room— and more likely to be where Naomi and John had gone, presumably to talk.

As she entered the elegant sitting room, it was clear her reasoning was correct. On the balcony onto which the sitting room opened, John and Naomi were clearly in the midst of a blazing row. "People who *don't know each other well* would never have that kind of argument," she concluded to herself. "They're *lovers!*"

Unfortunately, due to a combination of the party noise downstairs, and what looked like new, double-glazed French doors onto the balcony, Candy couldn't hear a word of what was being said. Nor were there many clues in the body language. Each of them seemed equally angry, gesticulating and pointing fingers. Candy approached the doors leading to the balcony, reaching into her handbag for a cigarette, by way of explanation for her intrusion.

The couple—as she was now thinking of them—saw her before she even got her hand to the doorhandle.

As she opened the door and came onto the balcony, both John and Naomi stared at her—silent, stony-faced, entirely composed. "Sorry," said Candy lightly. "I didn't see you there. I was just hoping to have a cheeky cigarette up here." She waved the cigarette in the air.

"We were just leaving," said Naomi, coldly.

With that, the pair vanished back downstairs.

Candy couldn't follow them immediately. Instead, she lit her cigarette and looked down from the balcony, which was above the only entrance to the house. It seemed unlikely that Naomi and John would be staying much longer at the party after an altercation like that. And, sure enough, before she had time to finish her cigarette, she saw Naomi Trinh exit the house and walk away, quickly.

Charlotte, who suspected that the usefulness of her 'Candy' persona was now at an end, was struck by indecision. Should she follow Naomi? Should she wait for John Bishop? Or should she simply quit while she was ahead and return to Alex, who had no doubt spent the last few hours wracked with anxiety? After all, following an individual magic user, who may well be a necromancer *and* a killer, was hardly the same as going incognito at a party full of people. The latter *was* clearly more dangerous, she had to concede. But then, she *was* committed.

She made a decision. And, with that, Candy vanished and an owl flew into the night, following Naomi Trinh.

Alex! Ghouls—I can't transform!

On hearing Charlotte's mental voice, Alex leapt from the Tesla. *Where are you?*

Near the cemetery—fuck!

Alex bent his knees, put his hands to the ground and launched himself into the air on a cyclonic rush of air, rain and ice.

I see you.

And he did. With his bird's eye view in the sky, he saw Charlotte running away from the cemetery. She was being chased by a host of ghouls, or lesser revenants—undead creatures created from corpses. Much less powerful than true revenants, they nonetheless tended to impede transformation, were resistant to magic—especially his own cold-based magic—and could swarm. And they could move faster than most fictional portrayals led people to believe.

And they were gaining on Charlotte, with murderous intent.

As he approached the small army of twisted former human beings, with fanged teeth and vicious claws, he sent a massive blast of wind with spears of ice at the group. This scattered the minor horrors and stopped their advance, at least for now.

Get the fuck out of here, Charlotte!

Charlotte, now far enough away, became a powerful owl again, and vanished into the night.

Alex reached the ground and froze it, which would at least slow down the zombies as they sought to right themselves and pursue their new target: him. There must have been at least a dozen of them. Most were just gnarled, corrupted bone, but a handful had the remains of flesh, in various stages of decomposition. A couple of the necrotic monsters, impaled on Alex's ice javelins, seemed to be finished. Others were scratching and scrambling themselves upright.

Alex was tired. The night had already been exhausting with stress, and his period of flight, huge elemental attack and freezing the ground had sapped his reserves of energy. Panting, he pulled out his magic pistol, which felt even more alive in its holster than before and started shooting at the creatures before they could get up.

His first shot shattered the chest of one ghoul. Its body convulsed with magical energy, leaving it nothing more than a pile of bones. The next did the same to one of the still-fleshy monsters, causing its ichor and viscera to spill on the ground.

He pointed at a third skeletal attacker. But, before he could pull the trigger, he became aware of something behind him. Spinning around, he just had time to create a shield of ice around his left arm to block the claws and fangs of another animated corpse, with the remains of eyes, teeth and long hair on its disfigured skull. With his right hand, he shot the monster in the side of its head, leaving his own face covered in its disgusting remains.

As he stepped back, he realised that he had been flanked by a smaller group of lesser revenants who had snuck up behind him. He was surrounded.

Realising escape was his only option, he sought again, despite his growing exhaustion, to raise himself into the air. But one of the original set of ghouls, now recovered if not quite fully upright, grasped his ankle and pulled him to the ground before he could do so.

Shouting in pain as the creature's claws bit into his skin, he tried to remain upright as he blasted the head of his most recent assailant into oblivion. But there were more, too many, and all around him. He sent a pulse of supercharged wind out from his body, slowing the advance of his attackers—but barely. He shot another one. And another. How many more magic bullets were even left in the clip?

Claws gripped his shoulders and spun him around. The claws were sharp, and painful. The arms attached to them were super-humanly strong. Alex couldn't even struggle, let alone extricate himself. The face of the thing that held him so inescapably gazed for a moment at Alex. Entirely skeletal, it had even more exaggerated fangs and horns than the others.

Then, its head exploded. It released Alex and dropped to the ground, still writhing.

Behind him, another skeletal abomination collapsed, as if the spirit animating it had been banished altogether. It now lay as just a pile of bones on the ground.

It was only then that Alex saw them. John Bishop and Naomi Trinh advanced towards him, from opposite directions. John was bursting ghoul chests, or ripping their limbs away. Naomi Trinh was simply de-animating them with little more than a stare and gesture.

Soon enough, all Alex's undead assailants were neutralised: gone altogether, or in pieces, twitching uselessly on the ground.

As Alex heard the police sirens approach, John and Naomi stood staring at each other in cold silence.

John Bishop's Fourth Interview

"Why did you lie to us—again?" asked Karen Park, with her customary severity.

John Bishop sighed. "Because Naomi insisted."

"And why did she *insist?*" pressed Robbie. Alex was sitting out this interview because he was in hospital—and in the metaphorical doghouse.

"Why don't you ask *her* that?" John snapped back. Then, seemingly thinking better of it, he said, "She always wanted to keep us a secret.

Something about the fact we worked together, maybe? Then, after Nerida was killed, she—I don't know—she seemed paranoid about becoming a suspect via me. Which is ridiculous, obviously."

"Why did you go along with it?" asked Robbie.

John smiled that bitter smile that was becoming synonymous in Robbie's mind with the complicated love lives of MMS's seemingly otherwise staid academics. "Detective, when you're in my situation and a young, attractive woman shows that kind of interest, you make … accommodations."

"Like lying to the police?" That was Karen.

"Yes, like lying to the police. Not that it made any difference, in the end."

"What do you mean?" Karen again.

"The fight your undercover officer saw—the one disguised as an AI-generated swimsuit model—"

"She wasn't one of us. But go on."

"Wait, then, who? Well, anyway, Naomi spoke with her, in her own ridiculous, unconvincing disguise. Your … I mean, the person in disguise … I don't think she said anything to Naomi in particular. But just her being there made Naomi blow up at me completely. She insisted I must have said something about us to the police. She just wouldn't believe me when I promised that I hadn't."

"Is that why you were shouting back at her?" asked Robbie. "The witness, the AI swimsuit model, she thought it looked like a two-sided row."

John Bishop sighed again. "Partially. There was also—in the interest of full disclosure—the matter of her essentially accusing me of being the killer."

Robbie reflected that there was nothing like a murderer mixing in an insular community to destroy relationships with doubt and suspicion. But he said: "So, John, again in the interest of full disclosure, was Nerida a historian?"

John Bishop smiled. "Do you even need to ask? *Of course* Nerida was a historian!"

Naomi Trinh's Third Interview

Naomi Trinh chuckled, scornfully. "Sure, I wanted to keep John and me a secret—for *a number of* reasons. But that wasn't what our fight was about."

"What *was* it about, then?" asked Robbie, wearily.

"The fucking admissions scam!" she practically shouted in response. "John told me about it *minutes* before it went public. I was furious."

"Because he hadn't told you earlier, when he first found out?" asked Karen Park.

"Yes, that," Naomi said. "But more importantly, I wasn't sure I believed him when he said he knew nothing about it and wasn't involved." She leaned forward. "He knew—he *knew*—how much I hated this fetish in the magic world for established, old families. Like some kind of fucking aristocracy."

"You assumed a magic disguise," said Robbie. "You spoke with another disguised—"

"—Who wasn't one of ours," insisted Karen Park.

Naomi sounded cautious. "Yeah, I did. It was pretty obvious she, or maybe even he, I guess, was poking around the party."

"That freaked you out? Why?" asked Robbie.

"Because I never wanted to get caught up in this *murder*," insisted Naomi. "Then, more importantly, there was, was ..." Naomi trailed off.

"What?" asked Karen, severely.

"The fact I couldn't help but think John may well be the killer."

The Aftermath: Charlotte and Simmo

"Hun, you could have ruined Alex's career," Simmo declared to his fiancée.

"His *career?*" replied Charlotte. "Si, I almost got him *killed*. I almost got *myself* killed!"

"I know that, hun." He sighed. "That just doesn't bear thinking about."

"I'm sorry, Simon," said Charlotte, sincerely. "It just seemed so, so … exciting. And I have to admit, it *was* exciting."

"I understand that too, hun. But next time you decide to involve yourself in a police investigation, try to do it in a way that doesn't put anyone's career, *or life*, in danger."

"Next time?"

"Yes," said Simmo. "I have a sinking feeling there may be a next time. You seem to have your heart set on helping Alex solve this case, one way or the other."

Charlotte leaned in and kissed her husband-to-be. "You're amazing!"

"Don't think flattery will get you off the hook, hun."

"It sounds like I'm already off the hook, Si." She pressed herself onto her fiancé, kissing him again, more deeply, with more tongue. She started unbuttoning his shirt.

"If you weren't such a good kisser …" said Simmo, as he let his shirt drop to the floor. He picked Charlotte up in his arms and took her to the bedroom. There, with a series of economical movements, he pulled her dress off over her head and pulled down her panties, which she kicked off as she removed her bra.

Then, she laid herself on the bed, legs spread wide. She motioned at Simmo. "And, my love, if you didn't give such extraordinary head."

Needing no further invitation, Simmo leaned into Charlotte's spread legs. As always, she started to moan, then scream with pleasure. But it was only when she was convulsing with orgasm that Simmo lifted his head, gently climbed on top, and penetrated her.

Afterwards, cigarette in hand—this was the only form of occasion where Charlotte was permitted to smoke inside—she said, "Alex will be furious at me, won't he?"

"Oh, I dunno," replied Simmo. "I suspect that depends on how much whatever you found out helps with his case."

The Aftermath: Alex and Josh

"Please, babe, say something," Alex begged Josh as they sat at opposite ends of their huge brown leather sofa. *"Please."*

Josh had said nothing, had barely looked at Alex, since he arrived at the hospital where Alex was under observation: his cuts were healed at the scene, but any injuries from undead meant a risk of sepsis. Josh remained silent as Alex was discharged, as they drove home and, now, as they sat in their living room.

Needless to say, Alex had never seen Josh this angry at him.

"I know it was wrong, babe. I do. And I'm *sorry.*"

Josh looked at the floor. He sighed and—finally—spoke. "That's just it, babe," he said. "Are you *really* sorry? Or are you just sorry it went wrong and you got caught?"

Alex didn't know what to say to that. Josh was right, of course.

"And will you even be sorry about *that*, if Charlotte managed to find something out that will help close your case?" He sneered bitterly. "Your precious case!"

Alex didn't know what to say to that either.

Josh looked at Alex, with a disgruntled smile. "Now who is the one who isn't talking?"

"Josh, please—"

"No, Alex. Here is what is not going to happen. I'm not going to get angry. You're not going to turn on the waterworks. I'm not going to forgive you, on cue, and we're not going to have wild make-up sex." Josh rose. "I'm going to bed. You should too. I expect it will be a rough day at the office tomorrow."

Josh was right.

The Aftermath: Alex and Robbie

"Robbie, Karen has already torn strips off me. So—"

"*Alex*," Robbie fumed in reply, across a table at Victoria Police HQ, with coffee in hand and printed materials—including images of woodcuts—in front of him. "You're lucky she didn't sack you altogether. I mean, what were you thinking?"

"You know what I was thinking," replied Alex, defensively. "I was trying to find out how the historians fit into this. I should've told you."

Robbie scoffed. "If you'd told me that you were conspiring with your friend to run an unauthorised undercover operation, I would have stopped you. Which is precisely why you *didn't* tell me."

Alex just looked at the floor, as he had with Josh. Robbie was right, Josh was right and Karen had been right when she practically eviscerated him.

Robbie's expression changed as he looked at his partner with something that might have been sympathy. "Just don't do it again. OK?"

Alex nodded. "OK."

"Besides," said Robbie, smiling. "You can make it up to me by listening to what I've found out about the ritual."

"Wait, seriously?"

"Yes, seriously. If you're investigating a magic case, Alex, you have to accept that magic might have something to do with the motives." Robbie started to look at some of his notes. "Besides, you yourself acknowledge that there may be a historian angle to this case and, like we all agree, at least a small number of hardcore historians are interested in the ritual."

Alex sighed in defeat. "Fine. But is it really a *ritual* in the proper sense?"

"That is what its proponents think, anyway," said Robbie, clearly still more fascinated by this subject than Alex thought was warranted. "I mean, we know that organic matter—particularly flesh and blood—can be powerful reagents. Just look at our necromancer and their antics with corpses."

"That is true," said Alex, begrudgingly.

"Not only that," continued Robbie. "But there has been at least one case where there was an attempt to complete the ritual."

"Really?" said Alex, sceptically. "When was that?"

"Rouen, in France. Around the 17ᵗʰ century." Seeing the expression on Alex's face, Robbie said, "I know it's not exactly *recent*."

"No, it isn't."

"*But*," Robbie insisted. "There are some contemporary records of that suggest there might be something to it. It caused a sensation at the time."

"The time when—and I don't need to tell you this—the Great Persecution was still in full swing and there had been religious conflicts in France, a war with England, probably other stuff that doesn't spring to mind."

"I *know*," replied Robbie. "And, yes, a lot of the accounts are cast as part of the Catholic–Protestant wars. But still."

"OK," said Alex. "Tell me the story."

Robbie did. First, a town guardsman had been found dead, with "his eyes missing, entrails removed, replaced by vermin." Then, a monastic archivist was assassinated by "a fell beast of sorcerous origin." Later, a prominent textile merchant was found quartered "by hooked chains, pulled by phantom horrors."

"Very evocative," said Alex, drily. "It doesn't lose much in the translation, does it?"

Robbie looked frustrated. "Very funny. But the thing is, even with just the first three killings in the sequence, apparently, the ritual started to have an effect."

"Let me guess, crops failed, there was an outbreak of disease, the milk soured. All the usual clichés they used to say about us."

"Yes, true. There is quite a bit about that. But the reports also cite things like the dead rising from their graves, an increase in hauntings and a reasonably credible description of an unseasonal shortening of the period of sunlight each day."

Alex remained visibly unimpressed.

"Lex—Alex, all I'm saying is that someone may see something plausible here and try to test the theory in practice."

"I don't necessarily disagree with that," said Alex, trying to sound conciliatory. "But, think about it. Why go the effort of targeting magic users? I mean, like I said before, there are thousands of people who would potentially qualify as guardsmen, librarians or merchants who have nothing to do with magic or MMS."

Robbie suddenly looked rather self-satisfied. "That's just it. While it doesn't get much attention, the guardsman who was killed had been accused of witchcraft, but the court didn't buy it—they were trying to limit the hysteria around magic by that point. *And* it was discovered that the archivist had so-called Satanic books in his room. There's nothing similar about the merchant. But—"

"*But* these 17th century possible murder victims may have been closet magic users?"

"Yes!" declared Robbie, excitedly. "It makes sense, doesn't it? We know, scientifically, that the most powerful necromantic spells are cast using the corpses of magic users. Why would this ritual be any different?"

"Summoning a revenant with a magician's corpse is not quite the same as this idea, Robbie."

"Sure, but it's not that *different*, either."

Alex didn't say anything because, perhaps against his better judgement, he had to agree that it really didn't seem *that* different.

33

Josh Proposes (Properly)

The evening after Karen tore strips off Alex over his and Charlotte's rogue undercover operation, Josh had still been quiet. The day after that, he seemed almost normal. On the fourth day, he declared that he had forgiven Alex, but there still wouldn't be any 'wild makeup sex'. That happened on the fifth day.

Since then, Josh had been especially chirpy and cheerful. Alex suspected (correctly) that this was because the time Josh had chosen for his carefully planned marriage proposal was drawing near.

Alex was very excited at this prospect. He genuinely loved Josh and wanted to marry him, and everyone in Alex's life asked him constantly about the subject. "Is Josh going to propose?" "Why hasn't he proposed yet?" "Why don't you propose to him? You're both men, you can do whatever you want!" He'd momentarily contemplated doing the latter but figured gazumping his soon-to-be-fiancé with an insufficiently grand or special proposal wouldn't go down especially well.

The thought of marriage was also a pleasant distraction from the frustration that he felt at how his murdering necromancer quarry felt so close, yet so far away. Despite the continuing crimes of the necromancer, the taskforce was practically disbanded now; Alex, Robbie, Pav and

Isabella were almost all that was left. It also didn't help that, as Josh had cheerily announced one morning, the Stonington Snatcher—or, as it turns out Snatchers—had been nabbed.

In an act of foolishness, the burglars had tried to sell some of the more unique items taken from their victims to undercover cops posing as specialist fencers of fancy antiques. While this wasn't included in the media coverage, Alex knew that one of the fake fencers was none other than Cecile Nguyen. She had mesmerised the police crowd in the Lion with her stories about it the previous evening.

Why couldn't *he* have a perp that stupid?

Josh was even more animated this particular morning because he and Alex were going for a long-planned romantic extended long weekend away at a luxurious, all-inclusive eco resort and rewilding project in the Blue Mountains region, west of Sydney.

"You all packed and ready to go, babe?" Josh called out from downstairs, just as Alex had finished packing. "The car's about to arrive."

"I am, babe," Alex called back. Alex always had the impression that Josh thought he was always too last-minute and insufficiently deliberate with his own packing. Josh was, of course, meticulous.

"You've packed some nice stuff, yeah?" Josh called back.

"Yes!" Alex shouted in reply.

The 'car' was no regular taxi, but a big black saloon, whose driver wore a suit. The car whisked them to the airport, at which they breezed through the first class check-in and were shown to seats at the very front of the plane.

After landing in Sydney an hour-and-a-half later, they were directed to a helipad, where a chopper sat, ready to take off.

I think we can safely agree tonight is the night, thought Alex as the helicopter swung across Sydney Harbour, offering one of the most amazing views he had ever seen.

About 45 minutes later, the helicopter landed at Wombat Valley. (Alex would soon come to understand quite how apt that name was.) From the helipad, they were driven—in a black, old-fashioned-looking Land Rover—towards a huge main building, largely made of wood.

"I thought there might be snow at this time of year," said Josh, a little disappointed.

"We don't get snow here much," said the driver. "We're too low-altitude."

The interior of the main building was tastefully opulent, as well as wooden and—for reasons Alex couldn't quite put his finger on—very Australian. After checking in, while enjoying the resort's signature drink, they were given brochures for the many rustic and ecologically-aligned activities available to guests. They realised that, after they took their luggage (or rather, arranged for their luggage to be taken) to their 'villa', they'd have enough time to eat a quick lunch, change into boots and do a tour of the 'Riparian Zone' of the property, which was being rewilded.

As they walked from their 'villa'—a wooden mini-chalet, with a huge bed, an equally huge 'rainforest shower', covered and heated patio, and private mini-pool—towards the start-off point for the Riparian Zone tour, Alex thought he saw a familiar face. But the familiar face had obviously registered him first.

"Alex!" It was Yolanda, looking not so different from when Alex had known her ten years ago. "It's great to see you!"

"Likewise!" replied Alex, as the two embraced. He motioned at a bemused Josh. "This is Yolanda. We knew each other in my magic school days."

"Knew you—we were friends, and teammates!"

Alex didn't reply to this directly. Instead, he said, "And this is Josh. He's my partner. And he's …"

"Normal?" Yolanda offered, as Alex paused.

Yes! Josh is blissfully normal! Alex just nodded. Josh politely introduced himself.

"What are you doing here?" asked Alex.

"I work here," she replied, as if such a thing should have been obvious. "I'm your tour guide—and I work on the reforestation of the place. You know, speed it up with a little Yolanda magic." Other guests were arriving for the tour. "Duty calls, Alex. Maybe we can catch up later?"

And the tour commenced, involving a light hike along the side of the river. Yolanda offered regular fun facts and explanations. And, in quite the flourish, the activity concluded with Yolanda using her magic to turn a recently planted native sapling into a mature tree in moments. The small crowd was duly enraptured.

"You are ever the showman, Yolanda," whispered Alex, to nobody in particular.

✿

Alex refused to pay extra for the special steak at dinner that night, dismissing it as 'too extravagant'. Josh looked unreasonably crestfallen at Alex's insistence. But, as he reminded Josh, he *had* agreed to pay extra for Dom to celebrate and of course, "Compromise is important to a successful marriage." Josh had taken the hint.

And the dinner, including the standard, included steak, had been terrific. Alex felt bloated as he and Josh walked from the restaurant—housed in the main building—to their villa along an illuminated gravel path.

"It's cold, babe," said Josh.

"I know. But we're almost there."

More so than the cold, Alex noticed the wombats. Both the burrows, which seemed to be everywhere, and also the animals themselves. Indeed, there was one standing (do wombats *stand?*) right at the entrance to their villa. Clearly used to humans, it simply stared at the pair as they approached.

"Look, a wombat out the front of our villa!"

"Yeah, cool," said Josh, not at all excitedly.

Cut him some slack, Alex thought to himself. *He's about to ask you to marry him—he's nervous.*

Josh opened the door and the pair entered the open-plan lounge-bedroom of their villa.

Alex screamed. "Eeeek!"

A large spider had taken up residence on the glass sliding door that led out to the covered patio. Worse, the configuration of the external lighting caused shadows of the spider to project themselves across the interior of the room, making it look as if massive, dark, hairy spidery legs were surrounding the room.

"It's just a spider, babe," Josh said. Josh was, infuriatingly, not afraid of *anything*. Well, except Alex getting killed by a necromancer. "And it's *outside*."

"Do something!" cried Alex in reply, his legs shaking, his heart racing.

"Babe, it's so cold outside," replied Josh. And, he added reasonably, "What would I use to get rid of it? Can't you use your—what is it— telekinesis?"

"Wait, you want *me* to kill it?" Alex practically sobbed at the thought.

"Do you even need to kill it, babe?" Josh queried, in spite of Alex's evident agitation. "Can't you just like, magically throw it into the grass, or something? We're in the country, there are going to be creepy-crawlies as well as wombats."

Alex was aghast, but Josh just looked at him. And *somebody* needed to do *something*. Alex couldn't bear the giant ghost-spider shadows any longer. "Fine," he declared simply, and indignantly. He couldn't reach through glass, so he'd have to do it from outside.

As he exited the villa via the front door—he was definitely not going anywhere near the glass sliding door—Josh called out to him, "You're amazing, babe!"

Alex wasn't going to dignify *that* with a response. Instead, he walked around the side of the villa to the patio. Holding his right hand before him and trying to look at the spider only as much as was absolutely necessary, he carefully pulled it off the glass. Suspended in mid-air, it frenetically writhed its legs in evident distress. This was possibly even more unpleasant to see than the massive spider shadow. But, swallowing his pulsing, if irrational, fear, he conveyed the spider as far away from the villa as his telekinesis skills would allow, and dumped it onto the grass.

When he returned to the villa, Josh was kneeling on the floor, holding a small box.

"Alex Peter Hicks," he said, solemnly, slowly, "will you marry me?"

Alex looked at his boyfriend for a moment. His eyes were so wide, and beautiful; his expression was so sincere, and his lips so kissable; even his stance and position seemed to radiate love and commitment, and his physique really was amazing. It was all enough—just enough—to make Alex forget (or, at least, forgive) Josh's arachnid-related husbandly failure.

"Of course, I'll marry you, my love," he said. Then, "So, are you going to put a ring on it?"

Josh, as he generally did, complied with Alex's command. Then, Alex slid a matching ring onto Josh's finger. Then they embraced, kissed, and went to bed. Or, rather, they *eventually* made it to the bed, via the couch, the floor and the 'rainforest shower'.

The morning after, Alex woke early and forced Josh out of bed. Josh expressed reluctance: "Can't we just stay in bed this morning, babe? Or maybe hit the shower together again?"

"No! Get up, fiancé!" Alex led Josh outside the villa. There, he saw Alex's handiwork.

Pure white snow covered the area around the villas and pathway, which were dotted with snowmen. As Josh looked around in delighted awe, snow started to fall, very gently, around the area. People were gawking, but Alex (and Josh) didn't notice.

"Do you like it?"

"It's extraordinary, babe. I'm the luckiest man alive."

Case Update – Part 3

Pav was the first to notice Alex's (very elegant, Josh really did have good taste) engagement ring. *Of course* he was. "Ah, so Josh proposed, did he, PB? You really are a lucky bugger, all-round."

"O-M-G!" cried Isabella. "Congratulations! Let me look at the ring. Oh, it's lovely!"

Robbie's reaction was much more muted. "Congratulations," he said, with a rather mediocre smile.

"Yes, yes, he proposed," confirmed Alex. "Now can we talk about the case?"

"No," replied Isabella. "There's nothing to talk about with the case. That is why it's so shit. Tell us about the proposal!"

Alex did. And, given he was feeling so chirpy and cheerful himself—despite the case definitely being shit—he even omitted the bit about the spider from the tale. That, and Pav really didn't need yet another thing about Alex to make fun of.

34

Another Necromantic Attack; Dinner with Charlotte and Simmo

Alex and Robbie's phones rang, simultaneously.

"A what?" said Robbie, bewildered.

"Holy shit!" added Alex.

"It's just close enough that I could teleport us there. It will take a few jumps, but—"

"Let's do it."

"Do you remember the position?"

Alex was already ready to waltz.

Alex was momentarily queasy as he and Robbie finally arrived, on their sixth 'port, at the scene of the disturbance: a small, closed dog park, otherwise deserted in the advancing darkness of early evening.

"He's reanimated the fucking morgue at the animal hospital!" shouted Robbie, as Alex got to his feet.

Robbie raced towards a scene equally horrific and bizarre. At one end of the small park, a group of twisted, hybridised, undead domestic animal corpses were clustered together—almost looking like a combined unit—and apparently attacking a victim, who was obscured by their own hideous presence.

As Robbie approached the malignant herd, some of them saw him and charged. The first to reach him was a huge, bloated, hairless cat with red eyes and exaggerated claws and teeth. It let out a pitiful, distorted meow as Robbie sent it flying through the air and into the boundary fence of the park.

Next was an extraordinary combination of a rabbit and a large dog, with huge ears and pointed rabbit-teeth. With disproportionately large hind legs, it half-ran half-hopped towards Robbie, making oddly menacing, otherwise indescribable, noises. With an obvious effort of concentration, he raised the beast into the air and ripped its limbs from its body, letting it fall to the ground, individual legs and abdomen still twitching.

Alex barely noticed this altercation. As soon as he had retained his faculties after the jump, he had seen it, at the other side of the park. The necromancer itself.

Meanwhile, Robbie was barely able to dodge his third assailant, a cat-parrot with outsized wings, cat eyes and dangling, undersized cat legs, which dive-bombed him from the air. Only noticing it seconds before impact, Robbie was able to duck in time for the creature to sweep over his head. As it did so, he managed to take control of it with his magic and throw it back towards its companions.

This group now, as a whole, turned away from their victim towards Robbie. There were about a half-dozen remaining animal-revenants, mainly dogs or what appeared to be dog–cat combinations. However, they were joined by a large undead horse, with blotchy hair, glowing eyes and crocodilian teeth.

As Robbie had been fending off necromantic attackers, Alex was pointing his sorcerous gun at the necromancer. *Call off your stupid zombie zoo and surrender—or I'll shoot.*

The figure, swathed in darkness and unidentifiable, laughed. *If you shoot me, my little creations will run rampant. And we're right next to lots of apartments, and a hospital.*

Alex just glared at what he could only think of as his nemesis, with their concealed face, black cloak and surrounding fog of dark energy. *You're under arrest.*

No, I'm not, Alex. Besides, you're too late—and shouldn't you be helping your partner?

"Alex!"

Alex turned to see Robbie fending off the dark menagerie, look balefully in his direction. "Fuck!" Alex whispered to himself as he ran towards the group of corpse-pets, eight ice javelins forming around his shoulders. These, he shot towards the undead horse, which fell to the ground mid-gallop, making noises that were nothing like a neigh.

Meanwhile, Robbie eviscerated a dog-cat, with a flat-whiskered face and the tail of a fox. He also sent two dead dogs—one a decaying Alsatian, the other a fanged, clawed poodle with what remained of a ridiculous pom-pom groom—flying across the park.

By then, the sirens were audible. Shots rang out, killing most of the remaining murder-pets. The remaining ones were engulfed in magical flames.

The two detectives were first to see the remains of the re-animated animals' victim. Even more damaged than Nerida Stein, her body was largely reduced to bone and pulp. Her head was almost completely detached from her body. Half her face had been ripped off by one of her sorcerous assailants. But what remained of it was recognisable enough. The necromancer's second successful murder victim was Naomi Trinh.

"What the fuck was that all about, Alex?" Robbie fumed, having finally gotten Alex by himself back in a small room at Victoria Police HQ, hours after the confrontation with the necromancer and its pets.

"I was trying to arrest our suspect, Robbie," Alex replied, coldly.

"Yeah, while their undead fucking *pet store* was trying to kill *me*!"

"After you basically charged at them, Robbie, *by yourself*—which nobody asked you to do."

"They were *killing her*, Alex!"

"She was already dead. We were too late."

"Is that what the necromancer told you, in your head?"

"Yes, and it was true. And you *knew* it."

"I—"

"Yes, you fucking did, Robbie. But you just couldn't help but ride in like a knight in shining armour."

"Oh, that's rich, Alex, coming from you."

"What is that supposed to mean?"

"You know what it means. You're so obsessed with solving this case, you—"

"I *what?*"

"What is this, a lover's tiff?" That was Karen Park, who had managed to sneak up on them unnoticed.

"Fuck off, Karen!" said Robbie.

Karen's eyes widened. It was clear Robbie had never said anything remotely like that to her before. Still, instead of chastising him, she put something on the table in a clear plastic bag. It was the elemental warding charm, with its stylised representation of the three elements.

"It was found in Naomi Trinh's apartment," said Karen Park. "It has a serial number. Theo Georgiou confirmed it as the one stolen from MMS."

"*Where* was it found in her apartment?" asked Alex.

"Back of a junk drawer in her spare room," replied Karen.

"So, was it hidden *by* her or *from* her?" mused Alex.

"Prints?" asked Robbie.

"We will get those tomorrow," said Karen. "Thankfully, one of her hands survived intact. DNA will take longer. But."

The two detectives nodded together, but it was Alex who spoke. "But, most likely, our necromancer—our remaining necromancer—has assassinated their accomplice."

"Looks like you were right about there being two of them, Alex," said Robbie.

"Yeah, but who is the other one?" replied Alex in frustration.

"It's late," said Karen. "I want you two to get some rest and cool off. And," she added, "I'm deliberately not going to ask what you were arguing about, but I suspect *neither* of you exactly followed standard procedure tonight."

"OK, boss," said Robbie.

Josh was worried, but not angry, when Alex returned home that night. After all, this time Alex had just been doing his job. And, as he re-iterated to Josh: "After this is over, never again."

"You're the first people we've had over since we moved in together," declared Charlotte as they arrived at Charlotte and Simmo's (previously just Simmo's) house.

Simmo had described this as the "reconciliation dinner" but, in truth, Alex had struggled to remain angry at Charlotte. She had also endured a horrible dressing down from Karen Park, which had "made her cry." (Alex and Simmo had agreed that this was well deserved.) Also, as she insisted, her actions had exposed the relationship of Naomi Trinh and John Bishop. And, would John Bishop have outed Nerida as a historian if Charlotte hadn't helped catch him out in (another) lie?

Ultimately, Alex had to concede both that Charlotte had advanced his case—without, annoyingly, quite blowing it open—and that there was something about her that made her very, very convincing. This was another sentiment endorsed by Simmo.

Alex had been to the house once before. It was a small, single-storey Victorian-era home that had been renovated—though not extended—by the previous owner. It looked much as it had when he'd visited last. If Charlotte had plans to put her own stamp on the place, she hadn't started doing so.

Alex had been impressed—and it didn't go unnoticed by Alex how often Simmo surprised him—by Simmo's surprisingly good eye for attractive old furniture and decorations. To Alex's taste, there was probably too little of the new, leaving the home looking a bit like an antique shop. Still, it could have been much worse.

"How are you finding living together?" asked Josh, as Simmo appeared with a bottle of Dom and glasses.

"Oh, it's bloody great, isn't it, hun?" said Simmo as he handed glasses around. "Cheers—to engagement, cohabitation and, ultimately, marriage!"

"Cheers!" agreed the group, in unison.

As they sat down, Charlotte said, "Yes, it's been going really well. But Simmo has a bit of an obsession with switching the lights off."

"I'm all about saving energy," retorted Simmo, looking at his fiancée with his customary adoration. "And money—what with all this inflation and rising interest rates."

"I figured you would have views on those, Simmo," teased Alex.

"As if you don't," countered Charlotte. Then, pointing to a platter with crispbreads, baguette slices, various cheeses and olives, she asked, "Nibbles?"

"Don't mind if I do," replied Josh, using a cheese knife to cut a chunk of what looked like Manchego and place it on a crispbread.

Charlotte, continuing on her theme, asked, "Or are we still doing our"—she adopted a high-pitched and camp tone of voice—"'I'm just a cop, babe' thing?"

Josh and Simmo laughed, as Alex glared at his fiancé. Alex downed his Dom, Simmo provided a refill and Charlotte served herself some soft cheese from the platter. After swallowing it, and maybe to fill the silence, she asked, "Seriously, though, what do higher interest rates mean for private equity?"

Alex jumped at his chance to even the score. "Worried you might have to make some cut-backs, Lottie?" he asked. "Veuve rather than Dom?"

Josh and Simmo both laughed. Alex smiled in satisfaction.

"Veuve is for the doomsday bunker, Alex," replied Simmo. "And you be nice to my fiancée if you want to reserve a place."

Josh brought the conversation back to Charlotte's question, having eaten another piece of Manchego. "Rising rates make funding deals with debt more expensive," he told Charlotte. "But private equity survived the global financial crisis, and so much money has come in over recent years, it's just waiting to be invested—"

"So, you will be able to afford to leave the lights on," said Alex, cutting across Josh.

"No, she won't," asserted Simmo. "I would have thought you and—" he looked at Josh, "—*Tesla* here would be all about saving energy and reducing carbon emissions." He stood. "Now, I'm going to finish up the main. You'll have to entertain these meanies for a bit, hun."

"I'm sure I'll manage," replied Charlotte, smiling, as Simmo disappeared into the kitchen.

The main was a rich meat ragù, served with tagliatelle. It was delicious. They had moved from the Dom to a very nice red. Alex had about five glasses in total. Possibly six—certainly no more than seven. The company was good; conviviality hung in the air as Alex finished up the last of the sauce with some bread.

"We will probably move out of here," announced Simmo. "It's too small, really. But you need to sequence, don't you? We have the wedding soon, then we can move house, then babies." Simmo had also cleaned his plate. He took a gulp of wine and continued. "After all, *Sachs*—Josh— you can only have too many personal spreadsheets on the go at once."

"I contest that notion," replied Josh, grinning. He was doing his thing of leaving a small amount of food left on his plate. He saw it as a form of ritual restraint—as much as he was definitely at least six glasses of wine in, Alex had observed.

"Speaking of kids," added Charlotte, innocently. "Noting the *engagement*, have you two thought about children?"

"Yes," declared Josh—too definitively, thought Alex. "I think we want them, eventually."

"You would make great dads," said Simmo, airily.

Maybe with some, in retrospect misguided, idea of correcting the record, Alex countered, "Though it's not straightforward for us, obviously. It's not like we can, just, you know, *have* children."

"You're talking about surrogacy?" asked Charlotte, rhetorically.

"Yes," agreed Alex. "Which is illegal in Victoria. I mean, unless you can get someone to have your baby for you *altruistically*, without getting paid."

"Sounds like a *paleo-feminist* stance," added Simmo, sounding disapproving. "Very Victorian Labor Party."

"Would you go overseas?" asked Charlotte, ignoring her fiancés contribution.

Alex was finding this conversation uncomfortable. "No," he said firmly. "Procuring commercial surrogacy overseas is also illegal in Victoria and—even if I'm not *just* a cop—I'm *a* cop."

"So it's extra-territorial?" asked Charlotte in reply, sounding like she was talking about something esoteric, of merely academic interest.

"Yes, it is," replied Alex.

Simmo shook his head in bewildered disapproval. Josh looked nervous, like he was worried where the conversation was going. Alex continued. "You're the lawyer, Charlotte."

"Well, I cannot be expected to know about every law on the Victorian statute books, can I?" she countered, reasonably.

"What about adoption?" added Simmo. Josh opened his mouth, as if to interrupt, but it was too late. Oblivious to this, Simmo added, "I mean, I guess it's not exactly the same, but—"

Alex interrupted him. "Shit, Simmo, adoption is even *harder*. How is it people don't know this?" Alex started waving his arms. "What, do you think you just go down to the baby showroom, like buying a car? Ooo, that one is cute—wait, that one is even cuter! Do you have that one, but in a girl?"

"Alex!" Josh said, in despair.

Charlotte looked mildly shocked at Alex's intensity.

Simmo just smiled and said, "That was funny. But maybe we should talk about something less controversial, like Ukraine? Or the Nazis?"

"I'll get dessert," said Charlotte, getting up. "I made lemon pudding."

In the Uber on their way back home, Josh didn't mention Alex's comments about babies, surrogacy or adoption. Instead, he just mouthed platitudes about how great a couple Charlotte and Simmo were; how well they get along; how wonderful their wedding will be. And how Simmo's ragù was really nice, wasn't it?

Alex gave the minimum level of responses to Josh's comments: just enough so that Josh didn't think anything was amiss. Meanwhile, he looked down at his engagement ring. He couldn't help but think it strange—wrong, maybe—that, after several years together and impending nuptials, Alex had only recently established his life partner's views about God. Which, despite Alex's own historical indifference, was a pretty fundamental thing. On top of that, he wasn't sure they had reached a meeting of the minds on something as definitively, uncontestably fundamental as whether they wanted—or, to be more specific, how far they would go to obtain—children.

So, frustrating as it had become, he forced himself to think about the case instead.

✦

Case Update – Part 4

"A guy using telekinesis to rob a jewellery store? Really?" groused Alex at Karen Park. He was sitting opposite her desk, with Robbie beside him. "That is the case you're giving us?"

At least Alex and Robbie had patched things up since the 'Zombie Zoo Incident', as one tabloid had dubbed it. Much like Josh had done, Alex had felt Robbie's silent treatment—*why am I likening Robbie to Josh?*—for several days. But, just as Josh had done, Robbie had warmed up steadily.

On the fourth day, Robbie had said, "You were right, Alex. I shouldn't have charged at those undead animals." Alex had actually been doing some reflections of his own and immediately regretted not being first to broach the issue.

"Maybe you shouldn't have, but how was that any different to what I did on the night Laurence Archer was attacked?"

"Like you said," Robbie had replied, "Laurence Archer wasn't already dead."

"That's still no reason for me not to charge in with you, rather than fantasise about arresting our suspect while you're fighting necrotic parrots."

"True," agreed Robbie. "Are we good?"

"Yes, we are." Then, they'd hugged. Alex couldn't help but feel the muscles under Robbie's shirt, the warmth of his flesh, and his smell. It was all so very familiar, even after all this time.

"Yes, it's the case I'm giving you," replied Karen, in the here and now—and in her most authoritative voice yet. "You need something to do aside from going over the revenant case files again and again, hoping to magically find some lead that you've somehow missed the last several times. You need a *distraction*."

This assertion made sense. After all, leads had been chased down, witness statements pored over, theories debated, dismissed, debunked. And, while the necromancer had claimed their second victim, now confirmed as Naomi Trinh, the team seemed no closer to identifying their perpetrator.

If anything, with the death of their co-conspirator in Naomi, caching the killer seemed further away than ever, especially if they chose to stop murdering people. Not that serial killers tended to stop, Alex reasoned to himself. Wait—was he hoping that there would be another murder, or even attempted murder, because that might flush out the identity of their suspect? What would Robbie make of that?

Why are you worried about what Robbie would think?

In the moment, however, Karen's suggestion felt like an accusation of failure and a dismissal of his ability. "Wait, if I'm not going to be on the revenant case, why can't I just go back to regular CID?"

Karen replied as if she had fully anticipated his reaction and had a response ready. "I'm not taking you off the revenant case, Alex. You boys can keep working on that case alongside this one, so long as you take the theft seriously and get a result." She added, in a statement of the obvious: "That is the quid pro quo, OK?"

"Alright," agreed Alex, resentfully.

35

Wedding Stuff

Somehow, Alex had managed to be invited to both Simmo's buck's night—arranged with meticulous spreadsheet precision by Josh—*and* Charlotte's hen's do. Both were all-day, and practically all-night, affairs. (When did these sorts of events get so elaborate, anyway?) The buck's was in a week, the hen's the following week. Today was final suit fittings for the groomsmen (and the MC, apparently) at Simmo and Josh's (and, by extension, Alex's) favourite tailor in Prahran. When was Alex supposed to plan all his witty remarks for the wedding?

"You two look great all dressed up together," declared Simmo.

"Yes, you and your partner *do* look great," agreed Simmo's brother, Mick.

"He's my fiancé," Josh corrected. Mick did not seem to understand the distinction.

Simmo's buck's had started off well enough, with a visit to a horserace meeting at Caulfield Racecourse, in Melbourne's south-east. Mick and Brad—Simmo's childhood best friend who was, in just about every respect, seemingly identical to Mick—were self-declared 'punters', devouring the form guide and almost immediately making a beeline to the bookmakers. Alex never placed bets on the horses normally, except during Melbourne's flagship Spring Racing Carnival. However, he found being at the track quite fun and himself placed a few bets, half of which were winners.

"Your partner is a lucky punter," Brad declared to Josh.

"I'm his fiancé," insisted Alex, in reply. Again, Brad did not seem to notice the distinction.

The next stage of the festivities was a whisky tasting, which suited Alex well enough. The only problem was that, while he was successfully managing to pace himself, the others didn't seem to be showing the same level of discipline.

Mick and Brad seemed particularly unsteady on their feet as the group, inevitably, wound up at a strip club. This progression had had all been meticulously planned by Josh. *Of course.* Everyone seemed to be enjoying themselves. Simmo relished the special lap-dance, performed while the groom-to-be's mates sat around gawking, something which apparently formed part of the obligatory bucks' night strip club package.

Alex spent the rest of the evening sipping on ridiculously overpriced gin-and-tonics, remaining abstemious as the rest of the party got ever looser and wobblier. He busied himself by looking daggers at the many young women, in tacky lingerie and tackier heels, who roamed the premises, zeroing in on the often depressingly young male crowd that filled out the venue.

"Why are all these young dudes hanging out at this awful place?" he asked, out loud, to himself. "Why aren't they going out on a date with a woman who actually likes them?"

"She wants me to go to the Capitol with her," Mick slurred to Alex, as he part-slumped, part-fell on a chair next to him, pointing to a negligée-clad, bored-looking woman. "What is Capitol?"

"It's obviously a brothel, Mick," declared Alex wearily. "Google it." Mick did, and it was. Though he still seemed to be weighing up a visit.

Mercifully, he, Simmo, Brad, Josh, and the nameless other ones were too drunk to kick on to a brothel or anywhere else. Alex managed to get them all into cabs, sighing with relief. It was finally over! Indeed, as he put Brad, the last of them, into an Uber, Brad declared to Josh, as if Alex wasn't even there, "Your partner, he's alright. I like him."

Josh was too drunk to contest the terminology this time. Alex was too tired and desperate to get home to do the same. Instead, he just slammed the door and motioned for the driver to leave.

Charlotte's hen's do, attended by what seemed like her small army of gal-pals—Alex was one of two men at the event—also started off convivially enough, with a champagne and mimosa brunch in South Yarra. Well, at least it became convivial, once the group got over sharing vapid or backhanded—or both—compliments with each other on their clothes, accessories, hair, etc. (That gobbled up the first hour.)

Through the course of the brunch conversations, Alex concluded that about half of Charlotte's friends were lawyers. A smaller group had children and had become stay-at-home mums. A bizarre proportion of these were wearing floaty linen or overtly retro-style floral dresses. A smaller-again group seemed to be bulging with fillers and Botox, which left them looking anywhere between thirty and fifty years old. It was impossible to tell them apart—they all looked the same. With (alleged) job titles ranging from 'influencer' to 'model' to 'entrepreneur', Alex decided the only sane thing was to steer clear of that particular cohort.

But, by then, they were at the spa, and someone was slathering expensive creams on Alex's face. He didn't love the feeling—he was quite capable of slathering expensive creams on his own face. But he preferred that to the massage, both the standard one and the hot rocks one.

It was during the latter, when he was lying next to Charlotte, that she announced: "Hey, Alex, I meant to tell you—the Sourcery case has settled."

He tried to nod on the massage table, but his head was too constrained. He reflected that at least nobody had described Josh as his 'partner' at this event. Mind you, there had been altogether too much fuss for his liking about his ring, and his fiancé's appearance (Alex had shown pictures) and wealth. Alex suspected that Josh's practically non-existent Instagram following would at least double following Charlotte's hen's.

Then, it was off to a downstairs private room in a city cocktail bar. Sadly, the cocktails were intentionally novel—dirty martini with rosemary and preserved lemon, asked no-one ever. And, of course, of *course*, there was a stripper. In a police uniform, no less. "This is an affront to my profession," declared Alex, now drunkenly, to one of the lawyers.

"Maybe, but my main thought is, hot body, shame about the face," the lawyer declared in reply. (Alex was a little regretful that he did not get that one's number.)

The 'show', including a 'Full Monty' and some grinding of fake police groin into lawyer, mum, and influencer faces, was mercifully short. And Alex's hostile expression—or, perhaps, the performer's preference not to include men in the audience participation component of the show— meant he was spared a face-full.

When it was over, Charlotte was smoking outside the venue, looking very unsteady on her feet.

"Night, Lottie," said Alex, tipsy and cheery. "I had loads of fun," he added, not at all dishonestly.

"Wait," said Charlotte, suddenly draping herself over Alex. "I need you to take me to the hotel. I have a room at the Hyatt."

"That's just a block-and-a-half away," countered Alex. "You just go up there and turn left."

"Alex, I can barely walk five metres unaided. Can you come with me? *Please?*"

"OK. But do I have to stay with you in the room?"

"That would be so cool!" cried Charlotte, like a child. "Tanya was supposed to stay with me, but she had too much booze—and coke—and had to go home."

Alex hitched Charlotte's arm over his shoulder and started leading her to the hotel. "Wait, which one was Tanya? One of the lawyers, the mums, or the influencers?"

"She calls herself an *entrepreneur*," replied Charlotte, sounding doubtful about the term. "She was the one who looked like a middle-aged alien."

"There were a few of those, Lottie," said Alex, as they crossed the road into the lobby of the hotel. "Do you have your keycard for your room?"

Thankfully, Charlotte did. And, as they entered the room, Alex observed that it was quite large and generally very nice. Charlotte decamped to the bathroom. Despite her turning on the fan, and some kind of running water, Alex could hear that she was vomiting.

Alex texted Josh: *Turns out I'm staying with Charlotte tonight. Love you.*

No hanky-panky, yeah? ☺ came the reply.

Charlotte emerged from the bathroom and flopped on the bed.

"I thought some of your friends would be magic users," said Alex, absently, as he pulled off his shoes and socks.

"Practically half of them are," replied Charlotte, sounding half-asleep.

"None of them said anything," said Alex, now working to take off his belt and making heavy weather of it in his state.

"Oh, I just think they were being polite. I never mentioned …" Charlotte was now asleep.

Alex lay on the bed and also fell asleep immediately.

Obviously, there was no 'hanky-panky'. But there was a buffet breakfast the next morning. And some shopping. And lunch, with more champagne and conversation. It was definitely fun. Alex and Charlotte had, it would seem, definitely become BFFs.

Then, at the end of the month, it was time for the wedding itself.

Chateau Vincent was a glorious, Victorian-era mansion, just as Alex had remembered it from his pre-Josh visit. With white walls and grey roof, it sprawled across acres of verdant—yet meticulously manicured—grounds.

It was a perfect venue for Simmo and Charlotte. Lavish, but elegant; full of old-world charm, but also bright and fun. As was the event. Simmo had told Alex that he'd invited only the bare minimum of work people, "Otherwise, it might turn into a fucking networking function."

"But you like networking functions, Simmo."

"I know, but I'm abnormal. I want people, the *normal* people to have *fun*! We want our guests to let their hair down!"

And they did. The ceremony was short, but heartfelt and avowedly secular. (Alex was surprised at himself for even noticing that.) Charlotte looked beautiful and Simmo looked like, well, Simmo, if a more polished version. As predicted by Mick, Josh looked great in his suit. Mick and Brad, meanwhile, looked like people unused to wearing suits.

Following the ceremony, Charlotte walked up to Alex, embraced him and handed him her bouquet. "Don't you normally throw it?" he had asked.

"Nobody does that anymore," Charlotte replied. "Besides, you *are* the next one getting married, anyway." Alex struggled to contest that logic.

Then, there was what seemed like an eternity of obligatory photos. Once eternity ended, it was time for the reception, and show time for Alex as MC.

He started by performing his "sacred duty" as MC: "Bathrooms are down the back and to the left." That line got a few polite laughs. He then declared, "With Charlotte, it was love at first sight. And I think it was the same for Simon, too." That got more laughs. "And, on Simmo, I think it's fair to say that we see eye-to-eye on absolutely nothing, except Charlotte, and maybe Josh, my fiancé. Speaking of my fiancé, and of being engaged, I've been thinking about marriage and why we get married."

With that, Alex announced he was going to list his own top five reasons to get married. "Number five, you can stop worrying about when you can start calling your partner your partner, rather than boyfriend or girlfriend."

Polite laughs.

"Is it when they leave a toothbrush at your place, or start insisting on having some space in your closet, or—for you heterosexuals—she demands basically the whole closet?"

More laughs, but some a little nervous, with 'can he say that?' vibes.

"Is it when you stop calling going out to dinner or the movies together a date? Is it when you have to start asking permission to go out with the boys, or girls, on Saturday night, instead of spending the evening watching Netflix in your pyjamas with your boyfriend or girlfriend or partner?"

Genuine laughs.

"Anyway, marriage solves that problem! Number four reason to get married: people *stop asking* 'when are you and so-and-so getting married?'"

That one actually scored some whoops.

"Reason number three, people stop calling your fiancé your partner. Nobody seems to say fiancé anymore!"

Some chuckles, except for Brad and Mick, who were in hysterics.

"Reason number two: you can finally, finally just *let yourself go*! He's finally put a ring on it so, yes, I *will* have that second slice of cheesecake! I'm off the shelf now, so I can *finally* ditch that cardio and do some day-drinking instead! Bring on the dad-bod!"

Claps as well as laughs.

"Which brings me to reason number one." Alex's tone became more serious. "Because, when it's special, you know it. When someone makes you feel like you've never felt before, you know it. When it all—*everything*—comes so easy, you know it. When you cannot imagine not being with them, not waking up next to them, not coming home to them—you *know* it." He raised a glass of bubbles. "With Simon and Charlotte, we know it, too. And it's such a great privilege to be able to share this day with them."

Alex was fairly certain there wasn't a dry eye in the house. Even Josh's weren't, as Alex gazed at him sitting at the head table.

"Now," Alex continued, "Please welcome Charles Bonnet, father of the bride, who will be saying a few words."

Alex couldn't deny he really quite loved the applause that followed. He liked it even more when Charles Bonnet—a distinguished-looking man, approaching old age, with quite a resemblance to Charlotte—declared, "Well, that is a hard act to follow."

Alex downed his sparkling wine and decided he would, having got the more difficult part of his official duties out of the way, properly let his own hair down.

Case Update – Part 5

Alex stared at a large, fuzzy, blown-up image of the necromancer's fleur-de-lis amulet on the virtual whiteboard. Pav would have disdained his use of it as unnecessary technology-for-its-own-sake, but Pav wasn't there.

Alex and Robbie had caught the telekinetic jewel thief the day before. It even got some press attention, particularly after a certain WAG—yes, Cherie Holt again, who happened to be a brand ambassador for the target of the heist—tweeted about the result. To top it off, Karen Park had also smiled at them.

In the end, it wasn't a complicated case. Its solution, like most investigations, required little in the way of magnificent feats of deduction. Instead, it had been a matter of interviewing people, gathering information and unpeeling the onion.

Like many such crimes, Alex and Robbie had started from an assumption that someone 'on the inside' was involved. (After all, even when you can use magic, it's helpful to have someone to tell you where the loot is kept, and the most opportune time to pull off the theft without getting caught.) After much digging around, they had established a connection: a store staff member, Rachel, was besties with Sophie, whose boyfriend, Tommy, was a magic user with a manipulation and telekinesis affinity, and a set of petty priors.

So, there was a pair of prime suspects. However, in the absence of any direct evidence of conspiracy, there was no basis for an arrest, or even a search warrant. It was Robbie who, observing that Tommy was a handsome bad-boy type, queried whether Rachel and he might have paired intimate liaisons with their criminal enterprise. It was Rachel's sister, Stacey—who was terrified of the police—who confirmed that yes, the pair had been mixing (illegal) business with pleasure.

On being confronted with this, Sophie spilled the beans, stating that Tommy had admitted the theft to her. She coupled this allegation with passionate lamentations about how stupid she had been to date a man who was both a criminal *and* a cheat—rather begging the question as to whether one or the other would have been acceptable on their own. Warrants followed and searches of both Rachel and Tommy's homes revealed enough stolen jewellery to make any confessions academic.

Rachel claimed she had been manipulated and influenced by an infatuation with the *wrong man*. She was a *good girl*, really. The wrong man, Tommy, scolded himself for letting that *dumb, ugly scrag* seduce him (multiple times) and *ruin everything*. Alex and Robbie closed the case, received a pat on the back, and decamped to the Lion.

There, it was Pav who put into words exactly how Alex felt. "If only our bloody necromancer made those sorts of dumb mistakes."

If only.

Now, Alex stared at the image of the amulet, as if it would lead to some miraculous lightbulb moment. It was getting late. Maybe he should just go home? But, given Josh was away at some big private equity convention in New Orleans, there wasn't much drawing him there, either. Would two visits to the Lion in as many nights be too many? And where was Robbie?

As if reading his mind, Alex heard his partner behind him as he said, "Hey, Alex, do you want to go—"

Alex turned around to see why Robbie had stopped talking. He was on the floor, hyperventilating.

Alex immediately kneeled down next to Robbie, placing a hand on his shoulder. Speaking soothingly, he said, "You're having a panic attack. It's OK, I'm right here." Robbie continued to hyperventilate. Alex continued, even more soothingly, "These tend to pass fairly quickly. Just breathe. Do you get panic attacks?"

Robbie nodded. Alex noticed that Robbie was looking away from the image of the fleur-de-lis. "Is this image a problem?" he asked. Robbie nodded again. Alex said, "OK, look, it's just a picture. I can switch it off." Which he did, and the virtual whiteboard screen went blank.

After this, it took Robbie a few minutes to settle. "Sorry about that."

"Don't be ridiculous, Robbie," declared Alex, in reply. "Now let's get you home."

Instead of the Lion, Robbie and Alex found themselves at Robbie's mother's home. Michelle was away—leading some kind of Catholic Bible camp, apparently—so Alex and Robbie sat outside in the courtyard, drinking whisky and—in Robbie's case—smoking.

"Do you want to tell me what happened, partner?" asked Alex, quietly.

Robbie, who was lucid but still shaking, hesitated but ultimately explained. "I worked a case. A sex-trafficking one. They used mind control charms. You couldn't imagine what it was like when we cracked the case and took off the charms."

"I think I can at least imagine—" replied Alex.

"No, Lexi—Alex, you can't," declared Robbie, cutting Alex off. "I can still see the expressions: grief, relief, shame. I can still hear the cries of joy, of anguish, of rage, of futility. There were suicides."

"And the charms you're talking about, they used the fleur-de-lis pattern?" asked Alex—coldly forensic, as it seemed to Robbie.

"Yes. The mastermind, who wasn't a magic user himself, got his offsider to craft these charms with a fleur-de-lis. They were all different: some were necklaces, others were bangles, bracelets, rings, all sorts of things. But they all used the fleur-de-lis pattern. The punters paying for sex wouldn't notice, but the cunt ringleader knew. He said, *I run a class establishment*. Like a fucking little in-joke."

"I'm sorry," said Alex. "And the fleur-de-lis became a trigger?"

"Yeah."

"Let's get you to bed. Should we call Winston?"

"I don't want him to see me like this, Lex—Alex."

Alex didn't contest this, at the time. Instead, the pair went to Robbie's room. Robbie sat on the bed. On reflection, Alex wondered why he insisted on undressing Robbie, as Josh had recently done to him, twice. After all, Robbie was lucid, calm, if still clearly distressed. He could unbutton his own shirt. He could draw the shirt off his own shoulders. He could undo his own belt and pants. Take off his own socks, pull down his own pants. Put on his own tracksuit bottoms.

Indeed, he could have done all these things without even physically using his hands.

Yet Alex did all of this for him. And, again on reflection, he didn't need to let his hands linger on Robbie's shoulders, arms, thighs and calves as he undressed him, then as he pushed Robbie's legs into some black tracksuit pants. He didn't need to do the same to Robbie's big, bare feet after he pulled off his socks. He didn't need to spend the whole time looking into Robbie's deep, dark, troubled eyes, still swollen from tears. He didn't need to keep smelling Robbie's distinctive scent as he did so. Yet he did. He did it all.

At least, when Robbie gingerly begun to suggest, "Alex, maybe you could—" Alex had been firm.

"I can stay here," Alex finished Robbie's sentence. "But not in the same bed, or even the same room."

"Maybe sleep in my mother's, then," suggested Robbie, sounding pitiful but also … something else. "I have some tracksuit bottoms in the drawer there." He motioned to his bedside table. "Mine are too big, but Winston's would be too small." Alex selected a grey pair; they were Robbie sized, and smelled like him.

It was hard to hear Robbie from his mother's room, which smelled not at all like Robbie and more like soap. But, after Alex thought he heard Robbie's breathing go from irregular waking to regular sleeping, he decided to let himself go to sleep too.

And, on reflection, he did not need to masturbate first. But he did.

Then, in the morning, he awoke to a picture of Josh in New Orleans on his phone. It was a full-body image, with Josh, in swim trunks, lying by the pool looking altogether magnificent.

The text read: *Missing you, babe, but duty calls* ☺. *PS, Simmo took the picture.*

Two Conclusions

Part 1 – 10 years ago

36

Alex and Robbie Arrive in Canberra for the Nationals

Alex had discovered, at the airport, that Assane had finally gotten himself, if not a harem, at least a girlfriend. She was entirely suitable: statuesque and gorgeous, with long dark hair, big eyes and glowing olive skin. Assane had introduced her as Maria, a fellow grad student at MMS. She even shared Assane's fire affinity, and—of course—she could track her ancestry back to "witches persecuted in the Spanish Inquisition". So, Alex reasoned, she was a *far* more suitable match for Assane than Alex would have ever been.

Alex had also discovered, to his surprise, that Jack was coming up to Canberra: "To support the team. You know, school spirit. I even got some merch." (Yolanda had quipped the day before that there would be more MMS people on their flight than in class on any given day.) The 'merch' Jack was referring to was an MMS Magic Team hoodie, which he was wearing alongside shorts and trainers, with those hidden anklet socks. Alex admitted to himself that he did have leg envy.

He also observed both that Jack's outfit was essentially the same as Robbie's and that Robbie was looking at Jack warily when they bumped into each other. A wariness, Alex thought, that couldn't reasonably be explained by unintended matchy-matchy dressing. Especially because just about half the gate lounge—except Alex and Emma, who was also coming along, and obviously did not *do* hoodies—was wearing an MMS hoodie.

"I was just surprised to see him. That's all," Robbie had said later, when Alex mentioned Robbie's expression during the flight.

Before that, though, Yolanda and Julius had appeared, again in matching MMS hoodies, with his-and-hers black Adidas leggings and trainers. They also expressed some surprise at seeing Jack but seemed delighted. "Hey, Jack!" declared Julius. "The whole gang will be together!"

"Yeah," agreed Yolanda, enthusiastically. "It'll be great to have you cheering us on. Sadly, I think we're going to need it."

"Why's that?" said Alex, in surprise.

"I do my research, Alex. And it would appear that the Queenslanders, of all people, have a great routine this year." She paused for effect. "And a *time* mage!"

The others fell silent, in evident shock. "When was the last time anyone fielded one of *them*?" asked Assane, quietly.

"Anywhere?" replied Yolanda. "Germany, five years ago. It's been decades since any time mage competed in the Australian nationals."

Assane smiled. "So maybe Jamie is not as *special* as he thought."

"Where is Jamie, anyway?" asked Alex to the group.

"Dunno. He probably just took the earlier flight," suggested Yolanda.

"I need to speak with him," replied Alex.

"Your flight to Canberra is now boarding," announced the PA system.

Having arrived at AMS (Australian Magic School—affiliated with the Australian National University), Alex discovered both that the magic athletes' accommodations were Spartan to the point of requiring room-sharing, and that Jamie had indeed taken the earlier flight.

Alex discovered this when Jamie, breathless and distressed, ran up to him as Robbie, Alex, Assane, Yolanda and Nora (Robbie's Manipulation and Telekinesis partner) were discussing room allocations. "Alex! Alex, I need to talk to you!"

"OK, Jamie. What's up?"

"I mean, can we talk privately?" insisted Jamie.

He really is agitated, thought Alex. "Sure, have you got a room yet?"

"Yeah," replied Jamie. Wordlessly the pair walked a short way down the hall and into one of the plastic-looking cells, with two small beds and two small writing desks, that they would be staying in for two nights. Jamie sat—slumped, really—onto one of the beds, and Alex sat down on the other one. (As expected, it was uncomfortable, even as a seat.)

"Is this something to do with the *Cockatrice*?" asked Alex immediately.

"How did you know?" Disbelief replaced anxiety on Jamie's face.

"I didn't *know*," admitted Alex. "I guess I just suspected it, like, the penny dropped. It was just too much to believe that Nathan Beck was genuinely interested in becoming a member of the historians. I figured he was actually after an article. You know: *Inside MMS's Secret Magic Supremacist Club*, or something."

Jamie just nodded, in silence.

"It was very gutsy of him," added Alex, probably unhelpfully, "to just hide in plain sight like that."

Jamie just nodded again, with a bleak expression.

"How did *you* find out?" asked Alex. "Did Nathan call you or something?"

"Yeah, he did. I'm not even sure why. But he did."

It was Alex's turn to nod. Then he asked, "Can you remember what you said to him? At the party, I mean?"

"Not really. But *he* remembers," replied Jamie, bitterly.

"So, he's quoting you?" Alex asked, in response. "What did you say?"

"Something like: I just think magic users should be given the recognition they deserve," replied Jamie, bleakly.

"Well, that isn't too bad, is it?"

"It's not great though, either. And when put into the context of some kind of hit-job article ..." He trailed off, then rallied a little. "He did also mention you."

"And what did he say?"

"That he thought you were, I think he said, more historian-curious, or historian-tourist. He's waiting to see what happens tomorrow to decide whether to mention you at all."

Alex nodded again. That made sense. If their team won at the nationals, an *MMS Magic Team Stars Attended a Secret Magic Supremacy Meeting* would be an appealing angle.

"I'm glad you're so calm," said Jamie, still looking much less than calm himself.

And Alex *was* calm. Almost so calm he surprised himself. Obviously, he had begun to expect to be featured in a *Cockatrice* exposé. But even now that his growing expectation had been confirmed, he felt little anxiety or stress. It actually felt like another notch in the 'pro' column in his mind for shifting from Theory and Practice of Magic to Introductory Microeconomics and Accounting 1A next year. But that wasn't a decision for now.

"You will calm down too, Jamie. In time," Alex said. "Here's the plan: we go to eat; we don't mention this to anyone else, *yet*; I stay here tonight, and we win the nationals tomorrow. Then we can deal with any lame, largely-unread school newspaper article when it appears."

Jamie looked unconvinced but stood up. "OK," he said, weakly.

Alex could tell Jamie was trying to keep a brave face on through the 'opening' dinner—the 'gala' dinner was tomorrow, after all the athletes had actually competed. (Which made sense, as that meant the competitors could actually relax and cut loose.) Jamie, never exactly a social butterfly or enthusiastic conversationalist, was stone-faced and almost silent throughout. The closest thing to a smile to cross his face was when he batted away a concerned inquiry about whether he was 'feeling alright'. It wasn't at all convincing.

After dinner, and kissing Robbie goodnight in the room he had ordered him to share with Assane, Alex returned to his and Jamie's room. Jamie was already in—or, rather, on—the bed. Fully dressed, but for his removed shoes, he was staring blankly at the ceiling.

"I take it you aren't feeling much better, then?"

"No."

"You need to sleep. Things will feel better in the morning."

They didn't.

345

37

The Nationals

"Did you sleep?" Alex asked Jamie, as he sat up in the small, uncomfortable AMS bed. He had, to his surprise, slept well and felt surprisingly refreshed—and not even especially nervous about the competition to come. This made him think of his father's suggestion that he had "already made up his mind" about leaving MMS.

Jamie, by contrast, looked exhausted and stressed—almost haunted. "Not very much," he replied, with tired, red-eyed honesty.

"Are you going to be OK to compete?" Alex asked, concerned for Jamie's wellbeing rather than the prospect of having to forfeit the competition.

"Of course," said Jamie, no doubt trying to sound more certain than he did. "I would never let the others down."

Alex got up and sat on Jamie's bed, which wasn't such an easy thing to do without sitting on Jamie himself—there really wasn't much spare real estate. "I just want you to know, there is no pressure from my end. If you're not up to competing today—or not up to doing the *showstopper*—I understand." Jamie didn't immediately respond, so Alex decided to reiterate his sentiment more starkly. "After all, Jamie, we're not Usain Bolt and this isn't the London Olympics, it's just some silly school magic show."

As soon as he saw Jamie's body stiffen at the word 'silly', Alex realised he had compounded his folly with a terrible choice of words. Jamie sat up, quickly—almost dislodging Alex from the bed.

"It's not silly to *me*, Alex," he snapped. "Neither is it *silly* to Yolanda and Assane. I'm going to compete today, and we're going to do the showstopper." He stood up and grabbed his towel and toiletries out of his suitcase. "I mean, shit, Alex, I get that you don't *get it*. It's fine if this is all a bit of a *jolly* for you and you're, like, above it all. But that doesn't make you, like, the font of all fucking wisdom!"

With that, Jamie flounced out of the room towards the showers.

Jamie's words, "You don't get it," marinated in Alex's mind as he rose and opened his suitcase to retrieve his towel and toiletries. Jamie was right. He didn't get it. This whole exercise did, indeed, feel more like a jolly than a matter of great import. A bit of fun before 'real' life started. In commerce, that is. Alex realised that, if he had not done so already, he had now made his decision.

So, as he wrapped his towel around his waist and walked towards the showers, he began to workshop in his mind how he would break the news to Robbie and wonder, in the circumstances, whether Robbie would even really care.

"I met your time mage last night, Lexi. At dinner."

This was Robbie. He, and the MMS magic team were eating lunch in the misnamed, plastic 'dining room' at AMS—it felt like more of a mess hall. That morning, Robbie had finished second in the Manipulation and Telekinesis individual event. Despite the loss, Robbie's routine had clearly been a personal best. There had been more balls in the air, more teleportations, and a quicker run across the obstacle course. And he seemed happy—very happy. As he had observed, "The teams' event is our main game. Nora is amazing, she has improved so much."

"What was the time mage like?" Alex asked, uninterestedly picking at his grilled chicken, green salad and bread roll. He was still struggling not to think about Jamie, who clearly remained devastated and horribly sleep-deprived.

"His name is Jacobus," said Robbie, which he pronounced as 'Yaco-boose'. "His family is South African. Everyone calls him Jack."

Alex was unresponsive. He was struggling to eat, struggling to concentrate.

"He's over there." Robbie pointed his fork at a young man who looked, coincidentally, much like their own Jack. He was a bit taller; his hair was longer and a dirtier blonde. Still, they looked very similar. And as Robbie and Alex looked over at him, Jacobus caught the eye of the two young men. He even waved, in a low-key fashion. Alex liked to think he was sure Jacobus wasn't looking at Robbie *that* way.

"He's a nice guy," insisted Robbie. "Funny, self-deprecating, but also a bit cocky. A bit like you, actually. He even wished you luck this afternoon."

"As in, because we will need it?" proposed Alex.

"As in, he hopes your routine is as good as it possibly can be," replied Robbie. "Because, as he said, he likes other teams to do well—and likes a hard-won victory." Robbie paused. "Like I said, Lexi, he's very much like you."

"If you say so, Robbie."

Is, what's his name, Jamie alright? (Emma, on their new 'private channel'.) *He looks terrible.*

No, he isn't alright, but he doesn't want to admit it—nor does anybody else, apparently.

What is the matter?

I'll tell you later.

In the end, he never did.

Around the AMS games room, which was almost identical to the MMS one, the atmosphere, as the cliché goes, was electric. The stands were packed. Jack boasted he'd managed to nab one of the very last tickets available. "Maybe because of the time mage?" he had speculated.

The home team, the Australian Capital Territory, was the largest contingent of spectators, creating a sea of Australian National University gold in the stand. But all the other states were represented; even Tasmania—Australia's least populous state—boasted a fair contingent in black and red.

Indeed, the Tasmanians would be up first in the elements competition. They would be followed by the Queenslanders, whose large group of supporters sported purple. Then, it was Alex, Assane, Jamie and Yolanda for Victoria, followed by Western Australia, South Australia and, finally, New South Wales.

"Are we going to smash it?!" shouted Assane, as he, Alex, Yolanda and Jamie joined in a huddle, as they had done at the state competition.

"Yes!" cried Alex, Yolanda and Jamie in unison.

"Are we going to the APAC finals in Osaka?" shouted Assane, even louder.

"Yes!" the other three yelled in response.

"Are we going to lose to—" Assane adopted an even more exaggerated sneer than he had for Monash. "*Queensland?!*"

"No!" they all shouted, louder than ever.

To an uninformed observer, they would have sounded entirely convincing. However, for both Alex and Jamie, the enthusiasm was forced.

The Tasmanians fielded two earth mages and two water ones. Their routine was another arty affair, somewhat along the lines of the Hopetoun performance. It seemed to be a commentary on the land, but a more specifically Tasmanian one, which was greener, wetter and more temperate than much of the rest of the country. The earth mages created a large expanse of grass and rock, with the water mages conjuring gentle rain that became more intense as the rock and grass formed itself into a hill with a large depression. As the rain sluiced down into the central depression, it created something like a dam.

"Is their team sponsored by Hydro Tasmania?" Yolanda snarked.

"I dunno, Yol, I don't mind it," countered Assane. "It's another clever one."

The 'dam' opened at four places, sending flowing torrents of water in the four cardinal directions. They ran in a magical torrent almost right up to the stands, until they stopped suddenly and receded. In the meantime, the 'dam' had transformed into a more pointed, conical hill, with a small hole at the top.

"Still, I don't think they're going to be beating us," said Jamie, vacantly.

The finale of the routine saw the returned water surging up and out of the hole in the top of the hill, as a geyser.

There was whooping from the Tasmanian spectators, in their black and red, and rather polite cheering and clapping from other quarters.

"No, I don't think they will," smiled Yolanda.

Alex said nothing. Instead, he was trying to convince himself that everything would be fine. After all, they had performed their routine over twenty times now. It had become intuitive, instinctive, mechanical. Even if Jamie was distracted, the showstopper would work out. And, in any event, Jack was overreacting. Most magic users seemed to be closet 'historians' when you scratched the surface. Or, at least, they were sympathetic to the cause, whatever that cause even was. And who even cared what some wannabe journo writes in a silly school rag—it was basically one rung up from actual toilet paper.

Besides, it should be Jamie's call whether he wants to do the showstopper, and he obviously did.

But wasn't this shit supposed to be *fun?*

The Queenslanders were up. Anticipation was in the air. The audience went silent as Jack-obus (that was what Alex was calling the time mage in his mind) took his position at the centre of the arena. He really did look like Jack. To his right and left a water mage hovered in the air atop eddies of wind and water. Behind Jack-obus, a fire mage towered above him atop a pillar of gentle flame.

"That is their little gimmick in the black shorts, yeah?" said Assane, dismissively.

The routine commenced, with the fire mage projecting huge jets of flame towards the water mages, and the others responding with equally large spears of ice. Then, as the elemental projectiles were just about to collide, time stopped. Or, at least, it did in the centre of the arena, as the crowd gasped.

The time mage rose into the air. He moved to his left, touching the stationary, yet somehow also dynamic, stream of ice. He raised himself higher and to the right, and did the same with the living, burning arc of fire. Then, time started again, but incredibly slowly, like a live time-lapse video. The audience was in awe as the fire and ice made contact with each other. Eagle eyed audience members could see as ice became water, water became steam and the fire hissed and disappeared.

"A bit of a novelty," opined Assane.

"But it's sort of … impressive," replied Yolanda, sounding uncharacteristically worried.

Jamie and Alex said nothing.

Time moved from incredibly slow to blindingly fast in the centre of the arena. Arcs of flame and sheets of ice danced at light speed around the performers, creating a storm of red flame, shattering ice and steam. Then, for another moment, the storm of hostile elements stood still, entirely obscuring the magic athletes. A moment later, it was all gone, and the Queenslanders stood next to each other at the centre of the games room and bowed in expectant triumph as the audience went wild with whoops, claps and whistles.

"They didn't even use any of the apparatuses," groused Yolanda, lamely.

Then it was their turn. Assane and Yolanda looked steely, rather than confident. Jamie looked like he was daring Alex to say something. Alex didn't.

Their routine was much like before, but on an ever grander scale. Yolanda expanded the earth apparatus to cover almost the whole performing space of the games room. Her huge tree was even larger; the dense, leafless branches reached even higher into the air. Next, as they had done so many times now, Alex, Assane and Jamie levitated themselves, on a pillar of wind, fire and electricity, respectively. They each carried even larger spherical concentrations of their affinity elements. Jamie raised the contained storm apparatus, which crackled and flashed intensely with lightning.

So far, so good.

The three spheres, again, hovered above the tree, looking like a crown: fire on the left, water in the middle and solid lightning on the right. Then, the spheres came together. The fire and water ones created masses of steam, forming a dense cloud around the top of the tree. Alex remained in the air. Assane dropped to the ground and created a moat of intense, towering fire around the base of the tree.

Jamie launched himself towards the system of wires in the games room, which were just like those at MMS. The resulting mosaic of electricity on the wall was even more dazzling than before.

Now, it was time for the showstopper. Alex couldn't help but grimace.

Jamie launched himself at the head of a huge arc of electricity and flew right into the centre of the massive cloud atop the tree. There was a sound something like a short circuit as Jamie's lightning fizzled. Something had gone wrong.

Alex immediately dismissed the huge tree-cloud into nothingness, revealing a limp Jamie falling to the ground, in slow motion. Slow enough that someone had time to telekinetically 'catch' him before he hit the ground. As Jamie fell gently towards the floor, Alex saw Robbie, arms stretched in front of him, and with a look of concentration on his face. The 'someone' had been him.

And, standing next to Robbie in the athlete's stand was none other than Jack-obus.

Everyone, it had seemingly been agreed, was certain Jamie would be "absolutely fine". He was, of course, "just a bit shaken". There were no broken bones and Jamie "had not been shocked by the electricity, nor burned by steam or ice". Therefore, insisted the medics who swarmed the centre of the games room before carrying Jamie away, there was "no need" for Alex to come to the hospital. "He'll be alright. Just enjoy the rest of the championships."

Alex was disgusted at that suggestion. And that the competition recommenced almost immediately, as if nothing had happened. "The show must go on, I guess," Robbie had said. "You're alright, aren't you?"

Alex had just nodded.

He was equally disgusted at Assane and Yolanda's griping about how "this just *had* to be the time for something to go wrong". *Go wrong*! The fact is, had it not been for the incredibly fortuitous presence of Jack-obus—and Robbie's quick thinking—Jack would certainly have not been 'fine'. There would, at the very least, have been "broken bones".

Despite his deep indignation, Alex said nothing to Yolanda or Assane. He didn't want to talk to them. He didn't want to talk to anyone. He wanted to tell Robbie he was quitting magic, then get the absolute fuck out of there. Out of AMS, out of Canberra and back home. (By which he did not mean MMS.)

Unfortunately, telling Robbie meant sitting through the rest of the afternoon's events, which included both the rest of the elements competitions, and the Manipulation and Telekinesis teams championships.

It did bother Alex that he couldn't bring himself to concentrate even on his boyfriend's routine with Nora. The pair flew around the arena like sparrows, charging each other in the air before teleporting away just before impact. They hurled battalions of balls around, before making them vanish. They surged, in a blur, across opposite end of the aerial obstacle course, before again teleporting past each other.

It was a great performance. They were clearly the best of the group, being last on the bill. But all Alex could manage was some performative clapping and cheering—obscuring a burning desire for it all just to be over.

At least, when the routine was finally done and Robbie took Alex into his arms, he could greet his boyfriend with a genuine smile. One of relief rather than pride, joy or excitement; but genuine, nonetheless. "That was amazing, Robbie!" he declared.

"Thanks, Lexi, I'm so happy!"

"Hey, babe," said Alex, trying to sound nonchalant. "I do need to talk to you about something."

Robbie's face nonetheless flashed with concern. "Oh sorry," he replied. "I need to go do something first."

"What, now?" Alex replied in disbelief.

"Yeah, sorry," said Robbie, now smiling. "But we will talk before dinner, OK?"

With that, he was gone.

38

Alex Breaks up with Robbie

Alex spent the first hour or so after Robbie disappeared rehearsing what he was going to say:

"This doesn't mean anything for our relationship."

"I'm leaving MMS, not leaving you."

"I love you, my darling." (A word he had never used to address Robbie before, but seemed somehow appropriate, in the circumstances.)

But then, as the events of the day concluded, and spectators and athletes alike started departing the AMS games room—and with Robbie still nowhere to be seen—something else started to occupy Alex's mind. A theory, and one for which he could identify an unsettling body of evidence. Why had Robbie kept teaching Jack manipulation and telekinesis even after he had supposedly made good progress? Why had Jack shown up to this event, buying a last-minute ticket—not having shown any interest in magic competition before? Why had Robbie looked so warily at Jack at the airport? Why had Robbie vanished right after his moment of triumph?

Had Robbie cheated on Alex with Jack?

After satisfying himself that Robbie was definitely not in the games room as it cleared out, Alex checked out the 'dining room'. No Robbie.

Then, his search took him to the accommodation area. He was interrupted by Jack. Or, rather, he was simply brushed aside by Jack, as he—with his attractive legs and floppy hair—bounded past Alex on the way to somewhere else. His eyes were red. His expression was pained. Until, that is, he realised whom he was running past, and his expression morphed into something like bitter hatred, or maybe scorn. Jealousy, at the very least.

What more confirmation could you want, Alex?

Alex found Robbie slumped in the corner of the room he and Assane were sharing. (No doubt Assane was out having fun somewhere, probably with Maria.) Robbie was dressed in his competition gear. His long legs and big, bare feet spread out from the corner. His eyes were red too, and he tried to project some kind of normality, without any sort of success.

"Hey, Lexi," he said, pathetically. "What did you want to talk about?"

"Don't give me that shit, Robbie. What the fuck happened with you and Jack?"

Alex could see Robbie crumble. Physically. It was like a wall had fallen on him and Robbie was trying, desperately, futilely, to somehow climb out of the rubble. "Baby, Lexi," he said to Alex's rising disgust. "I made a mistake. Something happened, it was wrong. I just, I just ..."

"How about I just lay it out, Robbie?" Alex snapped. "And you can nod your head if I'm right."

Alex paused, momentarily, then continued. "You and Jack—for whatever fucking reason—hooked up. Fucked, I guess, maybe a couple—a few—times. You ultimately thought better of it, he followed you here and you had some ridiculous *Fatal Attraction* bust-up about it, and I almost interrupted. Is that just about it?"

Robbie nodded, weakly. "Lexi, I mean, I know it was wrong. It was a mistake. I chose you."

"You chose me?" Alex sneered. Then, he added, "Robbie, when I'm your ride, you don't get to fucking test drive other models."

"Could you, maybe, like ... forgive me?" asked Robbie, still sprawled on the floor. He couldn't look Alex in the eyes. "I know I hurt you. It was wrong. *Please.*"

"No," replied Alex, firmly. He continued, as Robbie started to openly sob. "You know, Robbie, the nicest thing I can say about you is that—

before I met you—I would have forgiven you. I would have stayed with you, because at least you aren't one of those fucking *cunts* I used to date. And you aren't. You really *aren't*, Robbie. You have, at least, given me some degree of self-respect."

Robbie was now practically in the foetal position. He was crying, pulling his legs and feet, those feet, close into his body. He did not say anything.

Alex pressed on. "Also—and, I promise, this is not about you—I'm leaving MMS. I'm switching to Commerce next year."

Strangely, that caused Robbie to rally in shock. "But why?" he said. "Leave me, but why leave MMS? You're so good at this. At magic."

"Because you were just about the only thing keeping me here," admitted Alex. "And, you know, I need to work out what I ultimately want to do. And I do like business, more so than magic. It's just, just *normal.*"

"Is this about what happened today, with Jamie?"

"Partially, but I had made my decision last night."

Robbie just stayed in the corner, silently, for what felt like a long time. When he did speak, he was calmer, his voice more measured. He even sat up properly, if still on the floor. "Maybe you do like business more. The number of times you've told me what's going on in the stock market, or whatever." Then, with some effort, Robbie stood. He walked over to Alex and embraced him, then kissed him on the forehead. "Am I allowed to say," he asked, "that I will miss you? Miss you horribly."

"Yes, you are," replied Alex, who also kissed Robbie on the forehead. "But I need to go now."

It was only when Alex was sitting on the bed in his room that he realised he was still wearing the blue shorts—and nothing else—for the championships. He hadn't thought about his legs or the rest of his body at all. Until now. He dressed, then he called his father. "Hey, Dad, it's Ali."

"I know, my dear, what's up?"

"I'll need to use the emergency credit card. For flights and stuff. Something has happened."

"What happened?"

"I'll tell you when I get back."

"Wait, won't you miss day two of the nationals?"

"Yes, but it's basically just a recovery brunch and the medal ceremonies."

Alex paused, then asked, "Anyway, how do you even know—"

"I'll be here waiting for you, son."

"Thanks, Dad. See you soon."

"I love you, Ali."

39

Alex and Max Have
a Heart-to-Heart

In the taxi from Melbourne Airport, Alex's driver seemed intent on educating Alex about the ins and outs of contemporary Pakistani politics. Apparently, Imran Khan, the former cricket star and press-anointed 'sex symbol', was running for office to shake up the status quo in Islamabad—and the driver was obviously in favour of just such a thing.

Alex had no great interest in, nor really any knowledge of, Pakistani politics. But his interest in history meant he had more than a passing interest in current politics and world affairs. So he was, compared to most youths in a taxi of an evening, less bored stiff of the one-sided conversation. In any event, talking about political goings-on on the other side of the Indian Ocean felt vastly superior to thinking about his failed relationship, failed magic performance at the nationals and failed tilt at magical study.

"He's not anti-Western, you see," insisted the diver. "He's pro-Pakistan!"

Alex didn't say anything.

"It's really the military's fault. They're always meddling …" The driver paused as they turned into Alex's parents' street. "We need someone who will stand up to them."

"Yes," replied Alex.

"Real democracy," concluded the driver. "Ah, your house is here?"

"Yeah," said Alex, undoing his seatbelt and paying the fare. "Thanks for the ride."

"I will get your bags," declared the driver.

"Oh, you don't have to." replied Alex, but the driver was already out of the car.

"Goodnight," he said, smiling cheerily. "I hope I didn't talk too much."

"Not at all," said Alex. "I had some things on my mind, so I was happy to listen."

"I hope everything is all right," said the driver, sounding sincere as he got back into his cab and drove off into the night.

Max Hicks was already standing in the doorway as Alex approached. Alex reasoned he must have been sitting at a window, waiting for him. The elder Hicks was smiling in the light of an outdoor lamp, holding a bottle of whisky and two glasses. Alex embraced his father.

"Hi, Dad."

"Hi, Ali. Why don't you join me at the back? You can leave your suitcase in the hallway."

Alex did as he was instructed. He and his father sat on the back veranda, lit by an insect-repelling lamp. Max poured two measures of whisky. "Now," he said, "I wouldn't normally advocate drinking when you're feeling down. But." He downed the nip. Alex did the same. Then, Max pulled out a cigarette, even offering Alex one. "I know you've been smoking," he said, by way of clarification. "But, if you're going to be moving back here, you'll have to at least *try* to quit. Otherwise, your mother will be upset." (In the end, it would only be with Josh—who had never smoked—that Alex would kick the habit altogether.)

"Wait," said Alex, surprised. "How did you know I'm moving back? That I'm—"

"Quitting magic?" said Max, finishing his son's sentence. "The conversation we had before, of course. Like I said, you sounded like you had made up your mind. And there was your tone of voice on the phone. And the fact you were blowing off the second day of the nationals. *And …*" he paused for effect. "Ali, I have a confession to make."

"That you're secretly a magic user?"

Max sputtered. It was his turn to be surprised. Rallying, he lit his cigarette with a tap of his finger. "How on earth did *you* know *that?*"

Alex smiled. "Of course, I didn't *know*, Dad. But I came to suspect it."

"How?"

"Firstly, magic is generally inheritable—as much as we don't quite know the mechanics of it—and I take after you in almost every respect. Then, there's the fact that I was accepted into MMS at all. Mages are obsessed with ancestry: I can only conclude some kind of Hicks name recognition got me over the line. Even though it doesn't seem to be a prominent magic name." Alex paused. "And how else would you know that the national championships were over two days? I never told you, and you have—at least, pretended to have—absolutely no interest in magic. What other explanation could there be?"

"I'm impressed," said Max, smiling. "You're quite the detective. Maybe you *should* join the police?"

This was, no doubt, an attempt at humour. But Alex wasn't willing to let his father off quite so easily. On one level, he was surprised he wasn't reeling with rage and sorrow at his father's betrayal. But a feeling of satisfaction at his recent, serial feats of deduction couldn't make up altogether for years of secrecy and lies, even if they were lies of omission.

On the other hand, he had never been able to remain angry at his father.

Finally, he said calmly, "Dad, you're really starting to form a habit of telling me things I should know only *after* I should have known them."

Max seemed momentarily confused. Then, he asked, "You mean the sex stuff?"

"Yes, Dad. That."

"I guess I was in denial about it. Just like I was in denial about the magic stuff. And you only told me you were applying for magic school after you had done it already, and—"

"That was no reason not to say anything before now!" Alex protested. "You could have said something when I first manifested, or any time after that! Why on earth didn't you?"

Max sighed. "I know it was wrong, Alex. I do. I'm sorry. But, like I said, I was in denial. And Ali—"

"What?"

"Would it really, in either case—sex or magic—have made any difference?"

Not for the first time, Alex was struck by how much insight his father seemed to have, instinctively, into Alex's mind. It might not make it right, or fair, that his father kept things from him. But, Alex had to acknowledge, his father was correct. Max telling him about sex—and, realistically, what would his father have told him that he didn't already know?—wouldn't have stopped him hooking up with random douchebags (and from keeping this from his parents). And finding out his father was a mage would almost certainly have made Alex *more* likely to study magic and wind up exactly where he was now.

"OK, Dad. No, it wouldn't. That's true." Then, Alex added, with emphasis, "But that's no reason not to tell me things. From now on, you need to promise not to keep any secrets from me."

His father nodded. "I promise, if you do the same."

Part of Alex wanted to say, *But I never kept secrets from you! At least, not except the douchebag hook-ups.* Instead, he just said, "Deal."

His father smiled, clearly relieved at how well Alex had taken his great revelation. He poured some more whisky and lit another cigarette. "Now, do you want to tell me what happened?"

Alex lit another cigarette himself and took another sip of whisky. (Robbie had never quite got him used to downing a shot in one.) "No, you first," he insisted. "I want to know what happened to you, Dad. Why *you* quit magic."

Max exhaled a deep, long sigh. "OK, Ali. I'll tell you. But that will make for a long night."

"So be it," replied Alex, smiling. He was now genuinely intrigued. And, besides, he still needed to build himself up to reliving the events of the last 24 hours.

Max recounted his story. "So, at some stage—generations ago—a Hicks married a mage and, since then, *gifteds*—" Max said the word in a way that made clear he thought magic was anything but a gift—"have popped up every so often in the wider family. I guess I'm one of them. But nobody in my immediate family was a magician and it didn't help that my affinity—I manifested about the same age as you—was fire."

Alex nodded. "Keep going."

"Obviously, fire is dangerous. Especially when a thirteen-year-old is in charge of it. I think my family became wary of me, understandably. They tried to hide it, but I could tell, even as a kid." Max lit another cigarette. (So much for keeping it to five a day; he was tracking at five an hour.) "I wanted to study magic for the same reason as you: to find *my people*. But, and I don't want to dismiss your experience, Ali, I think it was even more urgent for me."

"I think you're right."

"I guess I wanted to escape. So, I went to magic school. And I was *so* desperate to fit in and succeed at magic. To find my, sort of, magic family." He shook his head slightly. "I ultimately reached the same conclusions you did, Ali. It just took me longer because I so wanted to buy into it all and belong."

"So, you made it through to the end?"

Max nodded. "Yes, but by then I was just really going through the motions and knew magic wasn't for me as a lifestyle or career. Or, I suppose, identity." There was more whisky. "At least, when I came back home afterwards, I was a proper adult, and professionally trained in using magic. So, my own family was *way* less wary of me."

"That's good."

"But then I needed to work out what to do with myself. Having resolved to leave magic behind, I decided to join the police. *But—*" Max said this with evident regret—"The easiest pathway in was through the Magic Squad."

"Wait," said Alex, leaning forward. "*You* joined the Magic Squad?"

Max nodded. "I thought I would hang around there a couple of years and get out. Which I did. Eventually." He sighed. "But, before that, there was your crazy uncle. Not crazy, evil."

"You mean that story about the uncle is actually true?"

"Only in the most sanitised of ways, Ali. First, he wasn't really your uncle, he was some kind of distant relative. I had never met, never even heard of him before." Max lit another cigarette. "He was a mentalist, and … a rapist. My partner and I were put on the case. It was a big one. We were lucky it was the early nineties. No internet. And there was a recession happening, the Soviet Union had collapsed, and there was a child killer called Mr Cruel stalking Melbourne. So, they managed to keep it largely out of the news."

"What happened, Dad?" Alex pressed, realising his father was stalling.

"It was my partner and I who tracked him down in the end. Now, normally, it's not like TV. Most suspects surrender. At worst, they run. This scumbag didn't. He wanted to fight. God knows why. I could tell he was … starting to control my partner. And the thing with a mentalist like that is, you can't wait. You need to strike fast."

"Which you did?"

"Yes. I didn't mean to kill him but, like I said, fire is dangerous. And I needed to incapacitate him. There was no suggestion of excessive force."

"Then what happened?"

"It took years to extricate myself from the Magic Squad," replied Max. "But I did, then I just left magic behind altogether. Oddly, even people in the force seemed to forget I ever used magic. To an extent, even *I* did."

"Until I came along and manifested, at least."

Max nodded. "And now we come full circle."

"Thanks for telling me all this, Dad. *Eventually.*"

"You're welcome, Ali. Now tell me what happened to *you.*"

Alex did.

After what felt like a very long story, concluding with Robbie sitting in tears on the floor, Max sighed, again. "I'm disappointed in Robbie," he said. "I have to say, Ali, you're taking it all very well."

"I know. I've actually surprised myself. But, while part of me thought Robbie and I would be together forever, another—less naïve—part realised that it was never likely my first boyfriend at uni would be the one I would grow old with. And, on MMS, I probably made my mind up a while ago. It just took the last day or so to realise it."

It had, indeed, been a long night, with too much whisky and too many cigarettes for both father and son. Max sat back in his chair. "What will you do now, Ali?"

"What you did, Dad," replied Alex, with a tone of finality. "I will get through final exams, transfer to commerce, move on from this magic stuff and lead a nice, *normal* life."

Which he did, at least for the next ten years.

Two Conclusions

Part 2 – Present day

40

The Fleur-de-Lis Amulet is Found

The death toll of Hamas' assault on southern Israel has risen to 1400 killed, with potentially hundreds of hostages taken back to Gaza. Reports have also surfaced of torture, rape and banned magic being used by Hamas fighters in the attack.

Alex put his phone down on the table in the meeting room of Victoria Police HQ.

"How's Josh?" That was Pav.

"How do you think?" retorted Alex. Then, seeing the look of consternation on his colleague's faces—and belatedly recognising the genuine concern on Pav's—he softened. "Sorry, Pav. Not well. Thanks for asking."

"Does he have many Israeli connections?" asked Isabella.

"Not really," replied Alex. "But let's just say it ruined the weekend." Indeed, the other event that had taken place that weekend, or actually the Friday, was that Laurence Archer, mainstay of Melbourne's business and magic communities and (as described by the *Financial Review*) "Late career CEO of private equity owned magical services booking app Sourcery" died suddenly of a heart attack. Alex couldn't help but detect some note of relief in Josh's otherwise sincere tone of regret when he told Alex of the news. Alex wondered how Carolyn Fitzgerald would have reacted.

Robbie suddenly appeared in the room, looking excited. "They found the amulet, the fleur-de-lis one," he said. Then, addressing Alex specifically, he added, "At the Billabong."

Pav and Isabella looked bemused at the reference to the Billabong, being entirely unfamiliar with MMS. But neither Robbie nor Alex offered an explanation. Instead, with a flash of concern, Alex asked, "Are you sure you want to come, Robbie? One of the others—"

"I'm sure, Alex," he replied, firmly. "I'll be fine."

Pav and Isabella continued to look bemused, being also entirely unfamiliar with Robbie's past experiences with fleurs-de-lis amulets.

"It's still magnificent," Alex observed, soaking in the scene of the MMS Billabong, which was no less impressive by day as it had been at night. Or, rather more specifically, *that night*, when Alex had first met Robbie.

"Who found it?" asked Robbie of Tammy Mazur, in his full *authority Robbie* voice. She looked, Alex thought, like a dead woman walking. It was hard to believe that she wouldn't be forced to resign, given MMS had ordered an external inquiry into the handling of the admissions scandal. She was still in place as dean, for now.

"Just a student," she replied. "A first year. First years love the Billabong. Mostly just to hang out, or, um ..."

"Hook up?" said Alex.

Tammy Mazur just nodded.

"I take it just about anyone has access to the Billabong, even at night?" asked Robbie, rhetorically. He also couldn't help but be reminded of *that night*.

"Yes," admitted Tammy. "We're actually planning to restrict access—you know, mainly for safety reasons. But that's all still in the works."

"We will need to take a statement from the student who found the amulet," Robbie said, looking at the open area of waterfront where crime scene officers had marked the spot where the amulet was found.

"Of course," replied Tammy. Then, pausing, she said, hopefully, "I wonder if this might mean it's over."

"Obviously, we cannot know that one way or the other," replied Robbie, with a severity that was cold even for authority Robbie.

"No," agreed Tammy, sadly.

"It's definitely not over," declared Alex to Robbie in the car on the way back to Victoria Police HQ. "Our necromancer fully expected us to find it. They're fucking taunting us!"

"I'm just here for old times' sake," announced Cecile.

The informal Taskforce Revenant Committee, comprising Alex, Robbie, Isabella and Pav—joined by Karen Park—had convened a few days later. Its members sat around the same space that had been used earlier to workshop the Daylesford Distillery case. And, just as in that case, there was an entirely analogue 'map' of the clues and suspects. This had been prepared by Pav, who took not a little pride in it, and seemed to have anointed himself to lead the discussion. Alex, sat on a desk, dangling his legs and touching his hair.

"So, first thing's first," Pav said. "Did our first-year magic student see anything?"

"No," said Robbie. "He'd actually been there with a ... companion the night before and they had slept there all through the night. Neither of them saw or heard a thing."

"Geez, these kids today. But can we rule *them* out as suspects, at least?" asked Pav.

"Definitely," Robbie confirmed. "Thankfully, they're quite the party pair. Solid alibis a-go-go for most of the crime dates."

"OK. Still on alibis, do any of our suspects have a decent alibi—for once—on the night before the amulet was discovered?"

"No," said Isabella.

"Well, except for Theo Georgiou," clarified Robbie. "But that doesn't mean much. We never really rated him as a suspect."

"OK, then," Pav announced, pointing at his elaborate whiteboard. "First, Naomi Trinh. Now, we can be effectively certain that she was one of our necromancers."

Everyone nodded, except Alex, who just absently stared at the whiteboard.

Pav went on. "But who was her accomplice?" He pointed at the whiteboard again. "Let's start with John Bishop."

"I'd say he's our number one suspect," said Isabella. "He had motive—Nerida had spurned his advances for years, started seeing his *married* friend instead, *and* potentially implicated him in an admissions scandal. He has motive to spare."

"And he's powerful and smart enough to learn necromancy on the side," Robbie added. "Not to mention, him and Naomi were both there after the, um, party, when our necromancer—or necromancers—decided to reanimate half the Melbourne General Cemetery."

"But why kill Naomi?" asked Cecile. The others looked her way. "Hey, I'm just providing some sense of challenge here."

Karen Park looked at her younger colleague with what could almost—almost—be professional approval. "Whoever our other killer is, I suspect they killed Naomi because they thought she was getting too paranoid and making mistakes. One of the few things I'm certain of in this case is Naomi raised the corpses at the cemetery. The other killer thought that was a big mistake and decided to get rid of her."

"That stands to reason," agreed Isabella. "Also, she did leave the party before John Bishop, giving her more time to do it."

"Why was that?" asked Cecile, again with her challenge hat on. "What was he doing?"

"Picking a fight with Laurence Archer," proposed Robbie, off the top of his head. "Apparently, he told the great man that he was a coward and a disgrace for not owning up to being involved in the admissions cover-up. Archer admitted, before he died, that the argument happened but, *obviously*, denied that he actually knew anything."

"Interesting," said Cecile. "But, on the admissions stuff, why would Bishop leave the files on Tammy's desk? Or Naomi, for that matter—who claimed not to have known about the bribes at the time of the murder?"

"To be fair, Naomi Trinh was a killer who lied to us," said Robbie. "But, more importantly, *if* John Bishop is our other perp, everything about that night at the party could have been staged, right? The row with each other, the row with Archer, the leaving separately, the supposed ending of their relationship afterwards."

"But then, if Bishop was in on raising the dead, why kill Naomi?" Cecile challenged. Karen Park nodded. "There is also the question, then: why go after Leon Mazur and Laurence Archer? I suppose that could have been because of Sourcery?"

"Or," said Robbie, "and I know this is not a universally popular theory of motive, but could Naomi and our other killer really have been trying to complete the dark summoning ritual? Hence attacking Leon Mazur and then Laurence Archer—before their plans started going off the rails?"

"That sounds like a segue into our next suspect, Harry Archer," said Pav.

"Do we still see him as a suspect?" asked Cecile. "I mean, why leave those cards at crime scenes if you're really the killer?"

"To make us *think* this was about the ritual," argued Isabella. "Harry Archer hardly lacked conventional motives for wanting to harm Nerida Stein or the Mazurs. He was, by all accounts, very upset about missing out on that grant. And he and Naomi were closer than they wanted us to believe."

"But close enough to plan murders together?" asked Karen, sceptically. "Unless Naomi was conducting another secret affair, this time with Harry Archer, it's hard to see why she would have helped him. I mean, it's *possible*, obviously."

"And, again, there is the Laurence Archer factor," said Cecile. "From what I can tell from the files, Harry was reasonably fond of his uncle— even if he thought he was a silly old man. *And* old man Archer seemed almost at pains to insist Harry wasn't involved."

"All true," said Karen.

"Which leaves us with the Mazurs," said Pav.

"To me, given their actions post-killing," said Isabella, "they seem unlikely to have been in cahoots with each other. But I guess it's not impossible."

"A murder threesome?" said Robbie. "What a thought!"

"The thing is," said Karen. "Each of them have a strong motive for *parts* of this. For example, Tammy must have been furious at Nerida over the admissions stuff—which is likely to kill her career one way or the other. And she was equally furious with her husband for effectively running off with another woman. She also had plenty of motive to wish harm to Laurence Archer."

"And she had opportunity," added Cecile, attracting another look of approval. "She had means too, being a summoner."

"The same goes for her husband," added Isabella. "For all we know, Nerida could have already dumped him. He kills her out of jealousy, puts the admissions files on his wife's desk to throw us off the scent, booby-traps the book in his own library to do the same and—once he has a taste for the killing—goes after Laurence Archer for his Sourcery losses. Or maybe he blames Archer for tipping Nerida into corruption."

"But the missing link here is Naomi," argued Cecile. "The Mazurs were not historians, not especially close with Naomi. How would either of them have got involved with her?"

"Unless," countered Isabella. "She *did* know about the admissions and was so outraged she somehow made common cause with either one of them?"

"Maybe," said Karen Park, doubtfully.

Pav looked towards Alex. "This is about the time I might expect you to have something to say."

Alex touched his hair. "I guess what I have to say is, as much as this discussion is fascinating, why aren't we talking about what we know for sure?"

"And what is that, *exalted* one?" replied Pav sarcastically.

"First, that we have a magic user—a possibly mediocre one, but nonetheless—who is known to all our suspects, who has just very conveniently died. Second, that we know the optimal time for summoning a revenant is seven to nine days after death, with embalming. Third, we know our perp left the fleur-de-lis amulet somewhere where it was bound to be found almost immediately." Alex paused.

"And?" pressed Pav, starting to show his familiar frustration at Alex's periods of silence and long-winded explanations.

"*And* that gives us a clear window for when our necromancer will strike again. We need to be there. I mean, I know the timing is terrible—"

"Terrible?" That was Karen Park looking at Alex with the opposite of professional approval. "You're talking about this Friday and Saturday night. There are big protests planned, *and* we are working on credible threats of political violence, *including* magic ones. We will be swamped."

"I *did* say the timing is terrible," agreed Alex. "But this is our only chance to nab the killer before they strike again. We have to do *something*."

"Based on your hunch that the killer left the amulet where they did as some kind of signal? This isn't like putting a business under surveillance, Alex, like you did with your distillery case. This would be a big operation. And in circumstances where we really have no idea who the killer even is."

Alex looked at his frowning superior with a smile that would have been familiar to many of his police colleagues.

"Here it comes," said Pav, grinning. (Cecile and Isabella grinned along too.)

"That's just it," said Alex, innocently. "I'm almost certain I *do* know who it is. I just cannot prove it, yet."

"Then who is it?" demanded Karen in exasperation.

Alex told her.

After he had done so, Karen said, "I'll have to see what I can do." Then, looking around the group and noting their looks of anticipation, added, "That is not a yes."

Pav looked pleadingly at Karen, while pointing to Alex. "Come on, how can you say no to that face?"

41

The Showdown

"No," Alex insisted, as firmly as he could. "That is utterly out of the question. Impossible."

It was Thursday and Alex was talking to Karen Park. Robbie, Isabella, Pav and Cecile were also in the room. Karen had just explained that the latter three would form part of the sting operation at the cemetery where the body of Laurence Archer, now seven days dead, was buried.

"They insisted," replied Karen, speaking on behalf of Alex's non-magical colleagues. "I know it's not ideal, but we can ward them up, give them some silver bullets—"

"Silver bullets?" sputtered Alex in reply. Then, intentionally calming his tone of voice, he said to Karen, "Can I talk to you alone, please?"

Karen sighed. "OK," and motioned for the others to leave the room.

As soon as they had left, Alex practically hissed at her. "You know it's going to be hard to stop our perp from summoning the revenant. You *know* that. We can do wards around the grave, we can try to intercept the necromancer. But these summoners can do just about anything to evade us." He stopped for breath, then continued. "And what happens if they succeed, and you have non-magic police there, with just silver-plated pea-shooters to protect them?"

"Of course, I know that," replied Karen, tersely. "But *you* know that these next two nights are among the busiest for Victoria Police in a *decade*. And *you* insisted that this operation go ahead."

"I didn't insist *they* have any part of this."

"Well, *they* insisted. Bottom line, Alex, *you* can have your operation with your willing, professional colleagues—who have been told the risks and still want to help *you*—or you cannot have your operation at all." Karen did not need to say "professional, unlike your friend, Charlotte," but it seemed implicit.

Alex frowned. "You're acting as if this is my decision."

"It isn't," replied Karen. "It's theirs, and it's mine. And it has been made."

"Fine. Call them back in," Alex huffed.

Karen magically opened the meeting room door with a wave of her hand and the others filed in. Alex glowered at Isabella, Cecile and Pav, in turn. He said, with quiet force, "It seems you've all made your decision. To be clear, I don't agree, and *I* don't want you anywhere near any of this. But if you insist, I'm telling you—whatever you think the plan is, whatever *she* tells you," Alex motioned at Karen, "if you see anything like a revenant, you *run*. And you *keep* running."

With that, he left the room, slamming the door for good measure. As he walked away, he heard Karen say, with infuriating cheer. "OK, let's get you kitted up and briefed."

Friday had been a bust. Their perp was a no-show. But Alex had calmed down about the presence of his colleagues. This was despite him not even being able to vent to Josh about their presence. Indeed, he had told Josh the bare minimum about what he was doing, both for secrecy and to contain Josh's inevitable horror. Having failed at the latter, it hardly seemed a good idea to highlight quite how dangerous this mission would be for Isabella, Pav and Cecile.

The cemetery was dark on this Saturday. Darkness would make it easier for the necromancer to get close enough to Laurence Archer's unmarked grave to use his remains to summon a revenant, but the presence of light—magic or otherwise—would likely alert the killer to *their* presence. Of course, magic lights had been prepared to illuminate themselves when—not *if*, Alex was certain—their suspect did show up.

Thankfully, the modern suburban cemetery where Laurence Archer was buried contained lots of trees, offering hiding places for the police officers in fairly close proximity to the grave site. Wards had been placed around the grave, which may slow the necromancer from summoning a revenant, but would be unlikely to stop them altogether. As well as the trees, there was a high retaining wall about twenty metres to Alex's left. Beyond that, more magic police—those whom they had managed to scrimp together, plus Karen Park herself—lay in wait. So, all Alex and Robbie would have to do is contain any necrotic horror until the cavalry could arrive. Alex didn't kid himself, though—any revenant could do a lot of damage in seconds, let alone minutes.

Then Alex noticed the ravens. They had arrived silently, quickly, in large numbers. Ravens were generally not, in spite of popular belief, nocturnal. Nor, indeed, did ravens usually collect in large flocks, known— particularly aptly, in this case—as an *unkindness*.

"It's show time," declared Alex quietly into his headset. "They're coming."

"How do you know?" Alex heard Karen reply. "Have you sighted the perp?"

"No. I know because of the ravens. It's just a matter of when."

Karen Park seemed unaccountably satisfied with this response and the comms went silent again.

Alex checked his watch. It was a little after eleven.

He and his colleagues, arrayed around Laurence Archer's grave based on the pattern of the trees in this conveniently verdant home of the dead, would wait almost another hour for the arrival of their quarry. It felt like longer: the appearance of the ravens, and Alex's message to the group, had put everyone into a state of heightened alert.

Then, a few minutes to midnight, he heard through his earpiece: "We've sighted a hellhound. Will neutralise."

The voice belonged to one of the Magic Squad officers on the other side of the retaining wall, someone barely known to Alex. Alex spoke to the group. "Contain it with minimum resources. It's a diversion."

"Agree," came another voice, that of Karen Park.

In spite of this, Alex knew that, as much as a diversion had been contemplated in the planning for this operation, a hellhound was still a hellhound. Alex imagined the beast running away from the site of Laurence Archer's grave, probably towards a residential area. And how could police not give chase to ensure the monster did not hurt anyone? The cavalry would, thus, necessarily take longer to arrive—or arrive in fewer numbers.

Alex only barely made it out in the darkness. There was a shape, small and obscure, burrowing through the dirt towards the grave. It moved fast, leaving little furrows in the earth. Whatever it was, it was clearly a spirit summon of some sort, conjured by the necromancer.

And it reached the grave before Alex, or anyone, had time to react. It ripped up the wards around the site. Then, almost immediately, the ground erupted and a *thing*—Alex could think of it as nothing else at the time, or since—emerged in its utter, immense hideousness.

What appeared under the magical lights that activated and spread its awful shadows everywhere was some combination of spider and corpse. It hung, suspended, hovering in the air. It had six legs that were a mix of human arms, legs, hands, feet and arachnid. It had a body that was part distended, bloated, giant human belly, and hairy spider. It had another two massive, extended legs at the front, which coupled human-looking shoulders and forearms, black chitinous joints and pointy ends that looked almost like fangs.

Alex made sure not to look at the thing's face, or whatever passed for it.

At least Pav, Isabella and Cecile ran. Indeed, at least one, or more, of them—he couldn't tell—screamed. But they disappeared, away from the light.

Alex conjured more ice than he ever had before, encasing the abomination in it, dragging it to the ground. He kept the mantra in mind: contain the beast, wait for the cavalry, then kill it. But he was duelling a foe that was resistant to magic, especially his own affinity. As the horror flailed against his attempt to contain it, he couldn't help but notice how its foul appendages swept aside his icy manacles as quickly as he could cast them into existence.

Then, he noticed Robbie. His eyes were buggy and vacant. His expression was robotically emotionless. He was staring at the face of their enemy. Alex realised, with a fear that was wrenching in his gut, that Robbie's mind was now under the control of the monster. And Robbie was motioning towards Alex, presumably intending a (forced, unintended) sorcerous attack.

Alex created a wall of ice, water and wind between the two men, but this was brittle, unsubstantial, insufficient. It also meant the cocoon of ice he was trying to maintain around the revenant became even more inadequate. The monstrosity swept it aside with apparent ease. Then there were the ravens, whose potential as a weapon had not yet been realised—but stood there in malign reserve. Alex, for the first time, began to genuinely fear for his own mortality.

Pav appeared from behind a tree. Alex had just enough time to see him look at Robbie, then look at Alex's expression of terror. Pav fired. It was probably at least three times. The horror responded, clearly with something like pain. But then it rose, shaking off the last vestiges of Alex's ice spell, and vanished momentarily in a cloud of darkness, stench and evil.

Just as soon as it had done that, it materialised behind Pav. It raised its disgusting human-spider leg-fang forearms in the air then, like a pincer, swung them downwards and carved Pav almost in two. There was no doubt, no hope: Pav was dead. His corpse, spewing blood and dropping organs, fell to the ground.

The necromancer appeared, in a plume of deeply black smoke. *You're in a bit of a bind, aren't you, Alex?*

Fuck off!

Do you like my little creation? I know how much you like spiders.

Alex whispered into his radio to his colleagues: "Where the fuck are you?!" He was shaking, struggling to move, to think. And, in an experience he had never had before, he felt utterly cold. Frozen, even.

The *thing* materialised right in front of him. And, in the moment, he couldn't avoid looking at its face. Its mouth was flanked by spider fangs, but had lips—bloated ones leaking dark ichor, but lips all the same—and shockingly white human teeth. Its 'cheeks' were pure arachnid, hairy and awful. And it had more eyes than Alex could count. But they were all, unmistakably, horrifyingly human.

Alex froze altogether. Even as the thing lifted its foul forelegs into the air—just as it had with Pav—he remained motionless, rooted to the spot. His brain was telling him to move. His body would not, even as the thing went to slice him to pieces.

But the pincer move was stopped in mid-flight, as if hitting an invisible wall.

"Alex! Snap out of it!"

That was Robbie, who was clearly protecting Alex with his magic. Pav's sacrifice had freed Robbie from the control of the fiend, and he was back on Alex's side. Which, Alex realised, meant Pav had saved his life. He resolved that his death would not be in vain.

Hot fury neutralised the cold terror. Alex adopted a sprinter's starting stance—as he had a decade ago—and launched himself within a huge, pointed arc of ice. He slammed into the thing and drove it into the retaining wall, using the weight and force of the ice to pin it down. Its forelegs snapped at him, until Robbie held them back with telekinetic force.

At that point, the ravens moved. But, instead of flying at Alex or Robbie, they attacked the necromancer in a swarm, leaving the former flailing.

I cannot go near that thing, Alex: it'll interrupt my transformation. You take it on—I'll deal with this dickhead.

Charlotte?

Yeah. Sorry I couldn't say anything earlier. The necromancer could have heard it. Get out of here at once!

Seriously? You need all the help you can get!

Unfortunately, this was true.

The necromancer flailed in shock and frustration as Charlotte's *unkindness* pecked and scratched, neutralising any further intervention by the killer.

As Alex continued to conjure more and more ice around the spider-revenant, its forelegs were being pushed further back by Robbie's magic until they snapped and fell apart. Even as Alex pulled out his enchanted pistol, the forelegs had already begun to regenerate. It was a loathsome detail Alex would stubbornly remember years later.

Robbie fired first. Alex counted eight shots—the whole clip. The thing's face had almost ceased to exist. However, Alex stood in place several second longer, looking at the mess of shattered bone, splintered chitin and burst eyes, until he was convinced it was genuinely, completely 'dead'.

Karen Park materialised among them. With a wave of her hand, she illuminated a set of wards that surrounded the necromancer in a broadly pentagram shape. Isabella and Cecile emerged from the shadows. Alex realised that, rather than running—which he had explicitly told them to do—they must have placed the wards as the necromancer was distracted by Charlotte, whom Alex had also explicitly instructed not to intervene.

Later, he would have to acknowledge that he was rather fortunate that, in this case, most people (Josh aside) indulged their habit of not doing what he told them to do.

He also saw that Robbie had passed out after killing the spider-revenant and lay on the ground. No doubt the experience of having his own mind controlled had brought back very traumatic memories. At least he had waited until the thing had been killed before allowing them to overwhelm him.

Alex felt himself start to wobble on his feet. Something like relief was flooding his mind, coursing through his body, making him dizzy. It was over.

But those legs, that face, those *eyes.*

Alex buckled at the knees and joined his partner on the ground, unconscious.

Which meant he missed Isabella snapping handcuffs on the wrists of the necromancer, as the wards she had helped put in place prevented him from making a sorcerous escape. He also missed Karen Park saying, "Harry Archer, you are under arrest for murder."

383

42

Alex Talks to Harry, Reluctantly

"That is an absolutely terrible idea," Alex declared to Karen Park. It was now a little over a week since Alex had woken up in hospital. The first thing he had seen was Josh's face. His eyes were red from crying, but he was otherwise calm. Before he could say anything, Alex had placed a hand on his forearm and said, "It's over, babe. Never again. I promise." It was the most sincere and heartfelt thing he had ever said.

He had been given the next week off. Or, rather, Karen had insisted he take it. He spent his time reading mystery novels, the *Brandstetter* series in particular, and drinking too much. He had met Charlotte at The Lion, who brushed off his scolding.

He went to the tailor and ordered some shirts. He made beef Wellington, just for him and Josh. (His version didn't quite reach the heights of Josh's, but Alex's fiancé appreciated the gesture.) He went to the National Gallery of Victoria, where he was surprised to see some works by Assane as part of an exhibition of young contemporary Australian artists.

It was all so very normal. After all, it was over. He had promised as much.

Then, there was Pav's funeral. It was held at Springvale Botanical Ceremony, in the Macedonian Orthodox tradition with a cast of mourners, as they say, of thousands. More than half of them seemed to be police officers. Alex stood stone-faced through the scripture readings and prayers, trying to hold himself together.

He held even as he paid his final respects to Pav as he lay in state. At least, thought Alex, the horror, Harry *fucking* Archer's horror, had spared Pav's face, which looked remarkably peaceful. He held it together even as he watched Pav's family members—including the granddaughters he had tried to show Robbie pictures of—do the same. He broke at the graveside service, as his colleague, his friend, was finally put into the ground.

He couldn't really stop crying after that. He moved quietly among mourners at the wake, holding Josh's hand. He met the children, the grandchildren. He managed to say, inadequately, that their father and grandfather had saved his life. That he had done so willingly, knowing the risk. He had sacrificed himself. They should be so very proud. He received polite smiles in response from the adult children, and blank stares from the young granddaughters.

That is all he deserved, really. After all, what comfort is it if your loved one died for the sake of a stranger's life? The abstract, almost constructed idea of heroism is nothing against the deep, basic, essential feeling of grief. And Pav should never have been there. Were it not for Alex's obsession, his arrogance, his hubris, his pathetic *desperation*, Pav would still be alive.

Alex's stomach churned with a whole ecosystem of guilt and shame. Many would argue that he should have tried to calm the churn, kill the whole ecosystem. Forgive himself. He wasn't sure he wanted to. At least, not yet. Not today.

When Alex saw Robbie duck out, presumably for a cigarette, he followed with Josh's permission. Josh was happy to say hello to Isabella and Cecile ("They saved your life too, babe") and, after all, Robbie and Alex hadn't seen each other since that night.

Alex hadn't known what to expect when he interrupted Robbie as he was about to light a cigarette with his finger. As it happened, Robbie immediately embraced Alex, holding him tight. Alex could feel Robbie squeezing the muscles on his back. He could also smell Robbie: that ultimately familiar scent from a decade ago mingled with a hint of tobacco smoke. He also found himself squeezing Robbie's back muscles too.

Alex concluded, after the fact, that it was he who had ended the tight, intense hug. He simply asked Robbie, "Are you OK?"

"I've been better."

"Winston isn't here?" Alex knew he wasn't.

"No."

"You didn't want him to see you like this?" Another rhetorical question. Alex could see Robbie's red eyes.

Robbie lit his cigarette and took a long puff. Alex had never felt a greater desire to have a smoke than now, but ultimately thought better of asking Robbie for one.

"You didn't come out here to ask me about Winston, did you, Lexi?" Unlike other times he had almost used his old pet-name for Alex, Robbie made no effort to correct himself, letting the violation hang in the air.

"I have a favour to ask, Robbie. Could you, will you, pray for Pav? Like, for me?"

"You could do that yourself."

"But why would he listen to me?" protested Alex, starting to tear up again.

"He will listen, Lexi, if you talk to him." Robbie sounded warm, tender even. Then, he passed his thumb under Alex's eyes, wiping away the latter's tears. He continued. "And, of course, I will pray for Pav. I already am." He kissed Alex on the forehead. "And, I will pray for you."

But now, Alex stood in Victoria Police HQ, having yet another disagreement with Assistant Commissioner Karen Park, who must have stood about five ranks above him in the police hierarchy.

"He insists," replied Karen, as if that would settle the matter.

"He *insists*?" replied Alex, scornfully. "And how is he in a position to *insist* on anything?"

"You know why," replied Karen, wearily. "Think about it. We only really have him for Pav's killing, which he could spin as manslaughter."

"That's ridiculous."

"No, it isn't," replied Karen, as if talking to a child. (Which made Alex even more irritated.) "He will argue that the thing he summoned killed Pav of its own volition, not at his direction. Sure, there will be additional penalties for necromancy, but Harry could be out in ten years. Unless, as he has promised—"

"Promised? Are you for real?" Alex thundered at his superior. "The fuckwit is a serial killer, he's not about to honour some gentleman's agreement for the sake of it."

"But *if* he does," continued Karen, "he has promised to confess to everything, if you will talk to him. He will go down for life for two premeditated murders, attempted murder, plus other crimes, irrespective of what he will claim is his cooperation."

Alex seethed. "I just want you to know that you're asking me to talk to someone who murdered my friend. Someone who is obsessed with me, who *knows* about me. He even knew I hate spiders! And you want me to indulge him in some fucking repartée?"

Karen's expression softened, just a little. She conceded, "I know it isn't fair, Alex. I'm sorry."

Alex said, very quietly and not really to Karen, but more to himself, "It so fucking isn't *fair*. None of it is."

Alex entered the unique remand cell that had been specially customised, with layers of runes, wards and silver plating, for Harry Archer. Incongruously, compared to the rest of the room, the man—the killer— sat at an ordinary, plastic table on an ordinary plastic chair. He wore drab, dark green prison clothes, but his hands—which sat in front of him on the table—were shackled with elaborately inscribed handcuffs, also covered in silver.

Healing magic, applied just after his arrest, meant Harry bore no scratches or cuts from the claws and beaks of Charlotte's ravens. Part of Alex wished, perhaps unprofessionally, that Harry would at least have borne some scars from his rampage. Harry had also lost the hipster stubble-beard, and his hair was now cut short. Were he not so thoroughly revolting, Alex had to acknowledge he may be considered good-looking. More unsettlingly, he also wondered whether the *Prince* had acquired one or more of those prison pen-pals who fixate on notorious, handsome killers.

Harry put on a terrible, psychotic grin as Alex sat down opposite him. Alex placed his phone on the table. He said, "I'm starting our session now. As agreed, you have an hour." He glared at the serial murderer opposite him and clarified. "As much as I don't want to be here for even a minute."

Harry continued to grin. Alex continued to glare.

Finding the silence unbearable, Alex challenged Harry. "So, what do you want to tell me?"

"Lexi," replied Harry, as Alex stiffened at his use of that name. "I don't want to tell you anything. At least, not yet. First, I want *you* to tell *me* how you figured it all out."

Alex rallied internally. If Harry wanted mind-games, he would get them. And, if Harry was going to indulge himself, Alex would do the same. He smiled, with deliberate, exaggerated smarm. "Well, Harry, you were just too clever, too theatrical, for your own good."

Harry was unresponsive; the psychotic grin did not flinch, twitch, or move at all.

Alex shouldn't have filled the silence, but he did. (Round one to Harry?) He continued. "You were so keen on misdirection, you loaded us up to the point that your narrative fell apart under its own contradictions."

"How did you untangle them?" asked Harry. "Please, I insist on the whole story."

"Fine," said Alex. "It all started to fall into place when you admitted that you'd been able to follow Robbie and me around with your spirit helpers without us ever noticing. If you could keep police under surveillance, you could easily have done the same for the MMS faculty. Which meant I was pretty sure you were lying when you said you didn't know about the admission scandal. *Of course*, you knew about it."

Alex paused. Harry just continued to look at him with an impassive, *keep going* expression. So, he did.

"This was your first misdirection: the dodgy admission files. Obviously, there was no point trying to hide your motive for killing Nerida, so you didn't. If anything, you tried to exaggerate it to the point of parody. To put us off the scent, you—or Naomi—took the files, knowing that would eventually expose the scandal. Putting them on Tammy's own desk was a particularly theatrical flourish. But you must have been thrilled at quite how disruptive it was, and destructive to the Mazurs' marriage.

"The cards were less successful, really. A bit too clever, by half." Alex thought he detected the slightest bristle from Harry at this comment, but it could've been his imagination. "But the riskiness of that strategy only became clear later, once you failed to kill Leon Mazur. The next step was your third piece of misdirection: attacking Laurence Archer to make us think Sourcery, and the faculty members' losses, might be involved somehow. On top of that, it was a chance to give yourself an alibi. Maybe you even wanted to send Laurence Archer some sort of warning? It seemed significant that you were with his son the night he was attacked."

Harry remained unresponsive.

"Of course, at that point, I really had no idea that the person leaving the cards and the killer were not the same person. I think *you* had the same idea. To bolster your alibi, you decided to *deliberately* get caught placing the cards at the site of the attack on Laurence Archer. You thought it would put you in the clear. Obviously, I eventually realised that it was Naomi who was there on the night. After all, the summoner who wouldn't have needed reagents or rituals to conjure a revenant would *hardly* need a summoning amulet to manage a couple of hellhounds, nor an elements ward to protect them from little old me. That, and an expert like yourself could easily tell your barghest from your hellhound, no matter how far away you were. But it took me a while for that penny to drop. Any questions so far?"

Harry now frowned, but didn't say anything.

"I assume that it was after you decided to get caught placing the cards—your first *big* mistake—that Naomi started to get agitated. She'd made mistakes herself, of course, ones you were no doubt more attuned to than your own. She had visibly worn the fleur-de-lis amulet, which we started asking questions about. That probably made her even more erratic. Your approach, almost from the beginning, was to focus attention on John Bishop. Hence the admission files, implicating him as well as Tammy, and your very strategic comment, with the fake reluctance, about Leon Mazur and Nerida having got together.

"When Naomi realised there was a disguised spy at the *historian* party—and I'm sure you and her were in communication—you told her to have that highly visible, unlikely fight with John Bishop. Clearly, it was a fake relationship altogether. In reality, it was you who was in a relationship with Naomi. After all, and I find this mystifying, you seem to be particularly good at getting certain people to do what you want. I mean, you got Mewan wrapped around your little finger, and I can only assume you weren't fucking *him*."

Harry definitely bristled at this suggestion. He whispered: "Naomi and I were not fucking, Lexi."

Alex ignored him. "What you didn't expect her to do was attack my friend with the reanimated corpses. That was genuinely stupid and unnecessary. It also broke the camel's back, didn't it? You decided she was now surplus to requirements. You killed her because of it, after luring her to somewhere I'm sure you two had met many times before. You hoped this would put Bishop in the frame, thinking we would get a search warrant for his house, where you had no doubt found a way to hide the fleur-de-lis amulet from him, in plain sight. When that didn't happen, you instead placed it in the Billabong, knowing it would be found. Your arrogance and theatricality have been a standout element of this case, Harry."

Harry was now glaring at Alex. But he said nothing, so Alex went on. "But it was that mistake, putting the Bibliophile card in the necromancy book, which got you in the end. Obviously, you thought Leon Mazur would go straight to the book and get fried by the ifrit. It was a problem that he wasn't, but was an *even bigger* problem that I *eventually* realised that whoever had placed the card in the book probably had to do it at the same time as booby-trapping it. I mean, it wasn't impossible that the card had been put in earlier and the killer didn't notice it—or just didn't see its significance—but that wasn't especially plausible, given the time-frames.

Which meant, in my mind, it *had* to be you. It didn't help you that, in your third *big* mistake—killing Naomi—you had practically ruled out either of the Mazurs as suspects. That was a dumber move than anything your accomplice ever did."

"But by then, of course, you'd been successful. Nerida Stein, whom you hated—who had denied you your academic prize—was dead. Tammy Mazur's career, one way or other, was over. As was her marriage. John Bishop may not have been successfully framed for murder, but he had lost his best friend, his honey-pot lover, and—one way or the other— his professional reputation. That was probably enough punishment for them, in your eyes.

"But Leon Mazur was another matter. If anything, you blamed him more than you did Nerida. He was supposed to be your friend, to the extent a psychopath like you has friends. But he didn't, at least in your own head, do anything—or, at least, do enough—to help you get your grant application over the line. So, after Laurence Archer suddenly died, you saw an opportunity to finally give him what you thought he deserved. You had probably hoped there would be enough left of Naomi to re- animate her, but—again—that was another plan of yours that didn't quite pan out. And, of course, by this point you were enjoying yourself far too much to stop the killings."

Alex paused for breath. Harry's glare had taken on an element of bewilderment. Once Alex had settled himself, he said: "And that is it, Harry. That is the whole story."

Harry banged his fists on the table. "Lexi, you are the most brilliant, most frustrating person ever!"

Alex took a moment to recover from Harry's comment, then simply stared back at the agitated murderer. It was his turn to remain silent.

Harry eventually filled the air. "Who else could get everything so right but *everything* so fucking *wrong?*"

Alex wanted to say nothing but couldn't help but take the bait. "What did I get *fucking* wrong then, Harry?"

"First, like I said, Naomi and I were not lovers—not everything revolves around sex! Also, I did not have some kind of hold on Mewan. He, Naomi and I simply had a common purpose." Alex was tempted to ask Harry to explain this "common purpose", but Harry went on. "And you were right that Leon Mazur was going to be the next victim but for utterly wrong reasons!"

Alex, again, couldn't resist. "And what was the real reason, Harry?"

"Because he was the Bibliophile, the Librarian, the next stage of the *ritual*."

Alex actually laughed in disbelief. (Or was it really nervousness?) "Come on, Harry, don't embarrass yourself. Do you have any idea how few insanity defences ever succeed?"

"It's not ridiculous, Alex. It's a ritual like any other. And it will be completed, by me or by the others."

Alex snorted. "*The others?* How long have you been workshopping this crap in your own head?"

"Haven't they told you about what they found in my online history and correspondence, Lexi? There are hundreds of us, all around the world. Others will take my place."

"Incel mages talking shit online is not the same as actually summoning revenants and killing people in real life, Harry. If you're trying to make me think you're actually delusional, it isn't working."

"Lexi, I'm not trying to convince you that I'm delusional," insisted Harry, sounding sincere, although Alex thought it wasn't good enough. Harry obviously thought he was a more talented actor than he was. "I'm simply telling you—warning you—what is coming." Harry grinned. It was an arrogant, swaggering, nasty expression. "And I'll tell you why you should know this is true, *Lexi*. But first, how much longer do we have to talk?"

Alex checked his phone. "You have twenty-five more minutes to keep spouting shit at me, Harry," he replied.

"Oh good. Then we have time to talk about a few other things."

"Like what?"

"Like, Lexi, whether you appreciated my little gesture, leaving the fleur-de-lis amulet at that place that was so special to you and Detective Chang, all those years ago."

How the absolute fuck did he know that?

Harry paused. "Can I touch your face?"

"What?"

"Your skin looks so smooth," Harry continued. "Did you shave today?"

"Yes. But, Harry—"

Harry reached his cuffed hands across the table and touched Alex's cheek. Alex was outraged. How could Karen have made him do this? But Harry spoke first. "Was it for me, Lexi?"

"No," Alex responded, firmly. "I usually shave every second day. You just happened to be on one of those days."

Alex wanted to look at his phone, to see how much longer this ordeal would last. But he didn't want to give Harry the satisfaction of seeing him so uncomfortable. Clearly, that was what this monster was going for, and Alex had indulged him enough.

"Would you like to know how I found out about your arachnophobia, Lexi?"

"I cannot say I'm dying to find out that information, Harry."

"Well, that is just the thing about a captive audience, Lexi. I can tell you whatever I want."

"Why don't you go ahead, then?"

"It was when you were at that posh eco-resort in the Blue Mountains. I had my little wombat spirit-spy at your cabin. I saw how freaked out you were by that spider on the window." Alex was impassive, hoping this would shut Harry's (disturbing) little anecdote down. It had the opposite effect. "*Then*," continued Harry, "I saw how that hot, rich boyfriend of yours made *you* deal with the spider. But that didn't stop you accepting his marriage proposal, did it?"

Alex said nothing. So, Harry pressed on. "*Then*, I saw how he fucked you. He fucked you on the couch, on the floor, in the shower, on the bed. It really was quite something, seeing you squirming and moaning, begging him for it. I've always thought of myself as a bit sexually fluid but, wow, that turned me on more than I might have thought."

Harry just let his comment hang in the air. Alex did his level best to hide his rising sense of disgust, of unease, of fear. This was the first time in this hellish, absurd conversation that Alex had contemplated leaving, running out to safety, to Josh's arms. But he did not. Harry would likely use any excuse to renege on his deal to confess, if he had any intention of honouring it at all. And, besides, the hour was almost over.

"Cat got your tongue, Lexi?" Harry asked, with a sweetness that made the whole thing feel even more disturbing. "Let me guess. You're wondering how I managed to follow you—with my little spirit helpers—a thousand kilometres away. But, more importantly, you're wondering whether all these wards, all this silver, will stop me from doing the same in the future?"

Yes, of course I'm fucking wondering that! Alex settled himself and smiled, he hoped even more (faux) sweetly than Harry. "I'm wondering, Harry, why you haven't answered my question about how you're not lying, or crazy."

"Well played. I remember that artist friend of yours loved your fake bravado, Lexi. When, of course, what you really like the most is to be dominated by another man. A taller, more confident and—in your fiancé's case, richer—man."

Alex managed to force himself—he was surprised that he managed it—to ignore the fact that this was probably the most intimate, most historical detail of Alex's life that Harry had yet revealed that he knew about.

Harry pushed on. "Which makes me wonder, Alex, whether you are secretly enjoying our little chat."

"We're running out of time, Harry," Alex shot back. "Unless you're happy for me to think you're simply a bad liar with a flair for the theatrical, rather than some visionary who plans to summon the dark one."

"OK, Alex," replied Harry, "it's not at all complicated, really. You must know about Mewan, that he refused treatment. He was in on the plan to murder Nerida. Again, there was no weird hypnotic influence or whatever. It was a common *purpose.*"

Alex was impassive.

"Didn't you ever wonder *why* Nerida hated me?" asked Harry, now starting to sound grotesquely earnest. "*Why* she snubbed by grant application? I mean, I assume you were too smart to buy the whole baby-boomer cabal, generation wars bullshit."

Alex was reminded he had also previously described generational antagonism to Robbie in precisely the same terms. But he simply replied: "People fall out, Harry. Or never get along in the first place." Alex's tone sounded unconvincing, even to himself.

Harry grinned again. "Except, in this case, there was a reason for the falling out. By now you know that quite a few of the MMS faculty were *historians*. I was too, along with Nerida and Bishop. Except we disagreed, and so I had to leave."

"Disagreed? About what?"

"Purpose," said Harry, simply. Then, seeing Alex's sceptical face, he realised he would need to elaborate. "The thing about most historians is that they are really phonies. Mewan, Naomi and I called them *courtiers*, because they were happy to just be a little minority on the fringe, rather than taking control, putting us back in charge."

"By summoning the beast?" said Alex, unimpressed.

"Yes!" insisted Harry. "If we summoned it, and controlled it, they would be reliant on us to protect them. We could dictate terms, change the world—and not just for magic users."

"You're going to tell me Nerida disagreed and that's why you hated each other?"

"I am."

"Personally, I think the baby-boomer cabal explanation is more credible."

Harry was undeterred. "And why do you think I waited to try to kill Leon again? I know the first attempt was sloppy. Budget. But, think about it: if I was trying to complete a *ritual*, rather than just a murder, wouldn't it stand to reason that—just like the most powerful revenants are created from newly-dead magic users—using a revenant to further the ritual would enhance its effects?"

Alex affected an air of nonchalance. "Cool story, Harry."

Harry chuckled. "Again, with the bravado, Lexi," Harry gloated. "You have to admit you now have doubts, don't you?"

"I don't admit anything, Harry."

Harry sat back in his chair and said, "Of course, in spite of my efforts, you did get me in the end. I've said it before, you really are special, Alex the *Exile*, in so many ways. Your sacrifice will be a great loss, but you will be remembered as a martyr to the cause—an unwilling one, bit still."

Alex's phone alarm went off.

"Time's up, Harry," he declared, sounding more relieved, and less triumphant, than he would have liked. "I'm going to go have a drink, and a shower."

"They're coming, Alex," Harry called to Alex's retreating back.

Alex didn't turn around, he didn't stop, he didn't even slow down. "They, and you, aren't my problem anymore, Harry. Enjoy life behind bars."

And, as he exited the room, he added in a whisper to himself, "Never again."

43

Alex Quits the Force

Jamie cradled a cup of coffee in his slim, delicate hands. They matched his attractive face. Alex wondered why he had never noticed that before.

"It's a relief, in a way," said Alex, as the two men sat outside at a Melbourne city café, near Sourcery's offices.

"What, that my psycho cousin pressed me for information about you?" said Jamie, with something like bewilderment.

"Yes," insisted Alex. "It's better than the alternative."

Jamie nodded, now understanding. "You mean that he hadn't somehow been stalking you for a decade?"

"To be honest, I'm surprised you remembered so much after ten years."

Jamie smiled back at him. "You were *glamorous*, Alex Yolanda was practically obsessed with you—she told me about the Billabong. And I didn't need to be a detective to tell that Assane had it bad for you. Or even that Jack kid."

"Wait, you didn't—"

"Have a crush on you too?" Jamie did not quite chuckle. "No, Alex, there was at least one non-heterosexual student at MMS who was not into you." He added. "I was still going through my hooking-up-with-dickheads phase then."

Alex almost chuckled himself. "Don't worry, I had one of those too."

Jamie's expression became more serious. "But I did value your friendship—even if you might not have seen it that way. You were *nice* to me. You were the only one who saw me as a human being beyond the showstopper. I was pretty devastated when you just vanished." Alex was uncharacteristically lost for words. Jamie went on. "I'm sorry I didn't think to say anything about it when you interviewed me. You might have caught him earlier."

"We didn't ask," replied Alex.

"True," said Jamie. "And to be honest, he was pretty good at just working it into conversation. It didn't actually feel like he was pressing me, at least not at the time."

"Harry was good at getting people to do things," said Alex. "One of his many talents."

Jamie nodded. "And he started asking me about you months before anyone turned up dead."

He what? Alex said nothing.

Jamie looked even more serious. "Do—do you have any idea *why* he did it, Alex?"

Alex tried to look sympathetic, because he was. "Jamie, there are some things I cannot tell you, yet. But, to be honest, I'm not really sure myself. I am not convinced *he* is even sure."

"It wasn't something to do with the historians was it?" asked Jamie.

Alex hadn't really been expecting this. "It … let's say it came up in the case," he replied, carefully.

Jamie sounded rueful. "That historian thing is like a genetic defect in my family. It was like"—he paused for a moment—"I mean, Harry and Dad were successful, you know, but it was never enough. Maybe that had something to do with it."

Not really knowing what to say to this, Alex explored a tangent. "Hey, did that wannabe journo ever publish that article? About the historian meeting?"

Jamie smiled. "Yeah, but it pretty much got overtaken by the coverage of us crashing out of the competition. And the headline didn't focus on me—I wasn't the big drawcard anymore."

Alex smiled back. "I'm glad it wasn't so bad in the end." He rose from his seat. "Thanks for meeting me, Jamie. I am so sorry about your father, again. And … your cousin."

"You're welcome. And thanks. It hasn't exactly been an easy couple of weeks." As Alex got up to leave, Jamie added: "And, thanks for meeting me here, rather than making me go to the police station. That place is intimidating."

"It is supposed to be, I think," said Alex. "But no problem, I'm not going to be a cop too much longer anyway."

"I'm very … disappointed to see you go." Alex got the distinct impression that Karen Park was trying to contain herself, and that this was something she rarely had to do and found unpleasant.

"I've made up my mind."

"Clearly," said Karen, in a voice that betrayed (unreasonable) anger. "But why, Alex? You're a hero. You solved the case! And it worked, didn't it? I know it was unpleasant, but Harry copped to everything after speaking with you. He'll never be able to hurt anyone again."

"I did, and he won't," replied Alex. "And now, it's time to do something else."

"Are you sure you won't regret it?" said Karen, pretending (at least, Alex thought she was pretending) to be interested in him and his career and needs, rather than the inconvenience he was causing her by quitting— an entirely normal and *common* thing people did every day. "Maybe you could stay on the force but leave the Magic Squad?"

I never even properly joined the Magic Squad, Karen! On one level, Alex wanted to explain that this wasn't realistic. That, if he stayed on the force—any part of the force—he would inevitably get dragged into any major magic case. He was reminded of his father's comments, all those years ago, about how hard it had been to extricate himself from the Magic Squad.

After all, how long would it be before a rogue fire mage burnt down a building, or a transformation mage impersonated bank customers to steal their savings, or (remembering Robbie's past history) some sick mentalist made sex-slaves of mind-controlled women? Indeed, it was this very inevitability that no doubt made Karen so keen for him to stay on the force.

For that reason, it was also a necessary step to make sure he kept his promise to Josh.

But Alex didn't say any of this, however reasonable it was. He refused to argue the point. Instead, glancing for a moment at his elegant, simple engagement ring, he just said, "Karen, I'm sure I won't regret it. I've made my decision."

Karen sighed. "I'm sure this won't help, but it's true. Like I said, it was *my* call to make, and I made it. And I knew it wasn't fair, to you. But it *did* work."

Again, Alex decided there was nothing to be gained by arguing the point. He turned to leave the room.

"Alex," Karen beckoned. Alex turned back around to face her. (Even having given one's notice, one struggled not to obey Karen Park.) "Keep going to the sessions. They help, and we will provide them for as long as you need them. Robbie is wrong, you cannot just ignore, suppress and pray your trauma away. But you can treat it. You can try. I know."

"I will," replied Alex. Then, taking himself as having been dismissed, he again turned to leave.

"Wait, have you told Robbie yet?"

"He's up next."

"What?" Robbie shouted, in evident disbelief.

Robbie and Alex were standing in a remote, windowless meeting room at Police HQ. Alex had chosen the venue in anticipation of this kind of reaction. He had considered, but rejected somewhere public, like a café. It would be better to have any scene play out where nobody else could see and hear it.

"I'm leaving the force. It's the only way to get out of—"

"Get out of what?"

"This!" Alex replied, loudly. "Everything. The whole fucking magic shitshow. I'm done with it. I never even wanted back in. And I promised Josh."

"But quitting the force altogether, Lexi? Why?"

In the circumstances, Alex let the 'Lexi' go (again). He tried to sound reasonable. "Because it's the only way to get out. If I stay in the force, I'll inevitably get drawn back into some ridiculous magic case, again. Karen Park will make sure of it."

Robbie wasn't convinced. "But what will you do?"

"I've applied for a job as a senior investigator at ASIC."

"ASIC?" Robbie responded, with scornful disbelief. "What, are you going to investigate crypto scams or something?"

"Crypto and scams are in ASIC's corporate plan, so maybe," Alex replied, calmly.

"Are you fucking serious, Lexi?"

"Yes, Robbie, I am. And it's Alex now, remember?" He forced a smile. "And, if that doesn't work out, Josh seems to quite like the idea of making me a house-husband."

Alex's attempt at levity went down less like a lead balloon and more like an extinction-level meteorite.

"You're running away again," whispered Robbie, bitterly, close to tears.

"No, I'm not. Ten years ago, I *was* running away. From magic, from you—and your betrayal—from a world I just didn't, and don't, belong in. I'm not doing that today. I'm running towards something: a normal life, a future, the regular world that I belong in. We've talked about starting a family, Robbie." (Alex would wonder in the future why he added that last bit. It felt unnecessary and was practically a half-truth anyway.)

Robbie looked defeated, bereft, pathetic. The tears came, as much he was hopelessly, ridiculously trying to stop them. "Alex, but I—"

"No, you don't," Alex interrupted him. "And, if you do, it's not me. It's a ten-year-old fantasy of me. Before life got hard, before you—you and I both—got … damaged."

Robbie shot back, in a tone that was part accusatory, part imploration. "Alex, even you cannot deny that there *is* something there. What about the night you stayed with me? The funeral?"

"*Of course*, I know there is something there," replied Alex, trying not to sound too frustrated. "But you have a boyfriend, I have a fiancé. That is why we need to, to …" Alex paused, struggling to actually articulate the words in the moment, suddenly reluctant to make his decision real: "… not see each other again."

That was the blow that finally knocked Robbie down completely. His knees buckled. He had to grab the table in the room to stabilise himself. The tears that were once quiet and reluctant became loud, uncontrolled. They were also contagious. Alex felt the heat of a tear run down his cheek. Then another.

Ultimately, all Alex could do, in a gesture magnificent in its utter inadequacy, was to hand Robbie a tissue. In time, he continued. "I do care about you, Robbie. I will never speak badly of you. You saved my life, more than once. You will always be special to me. I'm doing this for you, as much as for me."

Robbie calmed down just enough to reply, in angry despair: "You know that isn't true, Alex. Not that last bit."

Alex ignored this. Instead, he said, "Stay with Winston, and don't treat him as a consolation prize. And go to the counselling sessions. Karen Park is right: things won't go away if you're just strong enough for long enough—or pious enough. Please, for my sake, go to the sessions."

"That's all a bit rich, given what you've just said to me, Alex." As much as his words were harsh, his tone was not. He was now calm, maybe resigned.

"That's fair, Robbie," he said. "But I hope you believe me that I wish you all the best." He paused again, looking at Robbie for what he assumed would be the last time. "But this is goodbye."

With that, he turned to leave.

"Wait," said Robbie, now composed. Alex turned back around. "I meant what I said, at the funeral. If you talk to Him, He will listen."

✻

Alex sat in bed that evening, touching his hair, wearing pyjama bottoms with images of teddy bears, when Josh arrived home.

"Hey babe," Alex said as his fiancé went over to their cavernous walk-in robe, taking off his suit jacket.

"How did it go?" Josh called from the closet.

"Oh, fine," replied Alex, airily. "And I have an interview for that ASIC job."

"I *meant*, how did they take it?" asked Josh. "The cops. You quitting the force."

Alex paused. "I guess you could say Karen Park was not happy."

"And Robbie?" Josh came back into the bedroom proper, now wearing blue-and-white-striped shorts, and sat next to Alex on the bed.

"What about Robbie?" asked Alex.

"*Babe.*" Josh took Alex's hands into his own. "It's not like I don't know that you two have a history."

Alex leaned his face towards Josh's, looking him right in the eye. "OK, yes, he was devastated. But that doesn't matter." He kissed his perfect fiancé on the forehead. "It's like I said, it's over. Never again."

Josh just smiled for a moment. Then, he gestured towards Alex's pyjama bottoms. "How about you take those off?"

Alex did.

About the Author

Adam is a first-time writer and long-time reader.

His particular loves are classic mystery novels and speculative fiction, which he has sought to combine in his debut novel.

A born and raised Melburnian, his writing also serves as a love letter to Australia's coolest capital.

Adam has worked at the Australian Securities and Investment Commission for eighteen years and holds a Bachelor of Commerce and Masters of Business Administration from the University of Melbourne.

He accepts that these are unusual qualifications for a fiction author.